The Fascinating Stranger
And Other Stories

Booth Tarkington

The Fascinating Stranger and Other Stories

ISBN: 978-1-64799-884-4

To
S. K. T.

CONTENTS

THE FASCINATING STRANGER

MR. GEORGE TUTTLE, reclining at ease in his limousine, opened one eye just enough to perceive that daylight had reached his part of the world, then closed that eye, and murmured languidly. What he said, however, was not, "Home, Parker," or "To the club, Eugene;" this murmur of his was not only languid but plaintive. A tear appeared upon the lower lid of the eye that had opened, for it was a weak and drowsy eye, and after hours of solid darkness the light fretted it. Moreover, the tear, as a greeting to the new day, harmonized perfectly with Mr. Tuttle's murmur, which was so little more than a husky breathing that only an acute ear close by could have caught it: "Oh, Gosh!" Then he turned partly over, shifting his body so as to lie upon his left side among the shavings that made his limousine such a comfortable bedroom.

After thousands of years of wrangling, economists still murder one another to emphasize varying ideas of what constitutes the ownership of anything; and some people (the most emphatic of all) maintain that everybody owns everything, which is obviously the same as saying that nobody owns anything, especially his own right hand. So it may be a little hasty to speak of this limousine, in which Mr. Tuttle lay finishing his night's sleep, as belonging to him in particular; but he was certainly the only person who had the use of it, and no other person in the world believed himself to be its owner. A doubt better founded may rest upon a definition of the word "limousine;" for Mr. Tuttle's limousine was not an automobile; it had no engine, no wheels, no steering-gear; neither had it cushions nor glass; yet Mr. Tuttle thought of it and spoke of it as his limousine, and took some pleasure in such thinking and speaking.

Definitely, it was what is known as a "limousine body" in an extreme but permanent state of incompletion. That is to say, the wooden parts of a "limousine body" had been set up, put together on a "buck," or trestle, and then abandoned with apparently the same abruptness and finality that marked the departure of the Pompeiian baker who hurried out of his bakery and left his bread two thousand years in the oven. So sharply the "post-war industrial depression" had struck the factory, that the workmen seemed to have run for their lives from the place, leaving everything behind them just as it happened to be at the moment of panic. And then, one cold evening, eighteen months afterward, the excavator, Tuttle, having dug within the neighbouring city dump-heap to no profitable result, went to explore the desert spaces where once had been the

1

bustling industries, and found this body of a limousine, just as it had been abandoned by the workmen fleeing from ruin. He furnished it plainly with simple shavings and thus made a home.

His shelter was double, for this little house of his itself stood indoors, under a roof that covered acres. When the watery eye of Mr. Tuttle opened, it beheld a room vaster than any palace hall, and so littered with unaccountable other automobile bodies in embryo that their shapes grew vague and small in the distance. But nothing living was here except himself; what leather had been in the great place was long since devoured, and the rats had departed. A night-watchman, paid by the receiver-in-bankruptcy, walked through the long shops once or twice a night, swinging a flashlight; but he was unaware of the tenant, and usually Mr. Tuttle, in slumber, was unaware of him.

The watery eye, having partly opened and then wholly closed, remained closed for another hour. All round about, inside and outside the great room, there was silence; for beyond these shops there were only other shops and others and others, covering square miles, and all as still as a village midnight. They were as quiet as that every day in the week; but on weekdays the cautious Tuttle usually went out rather early, because sometimes a clerk from the receiver's office dawdled about the place with a notebook. To-day was Sunday; no one would come; so he slept as long as he could.

His reasons were excellent as reasons, though immoral at the source;—that is to say, he should not have had such reasons. He was not well, and sleep is healing; his reasons for sleeping were therefore good: but he should not have been unwell; his indisposition was produced by sin; he had broken the laws of his country and had drunk of illegal liquor, atrocious in quality; his reasons for sleeping were therefore bad. His sleep was not a good sleep.

From time to time little manifestations proved its gross character; he lay among the shavings like a fat grampus basking in sea-foam, and he breathed like one; but sometimes his mouth would be pushed upward in misdirected expansions; his cheeks would distend, and then suddenly collapse, after explosion. Lamentable sounds came from within his corrugated throat, and from deeper tubes; a shoulder now and then jumped suddenly; and his upper ear, long and soiled, frequently twitched enough to move the curl of shaving that lay upon it. For a time one of his legs trembled violently; then of its own free will and without waking him, it bent and straightened repeatedly, using the motions of a leg that is walking and confident that it is going somewhere. Having arrived at its destination, it rested; whereupon its owner shivered,

2

and, thinking he pulled a blanket higher about his shoulders, raked a few more shavings upon him. Finally, he woke, and, still keeping his eyes closed, stroked his beard.

It was about six weeks old and no uncommon ornament with Mr. Tuttle; for usually he wore either a beard or something on the way to become one; he was indifferent which, though he might have taken pride in so much originality in an over-razored age. His round and somewhat oily head, decorated with this beard upon a face a little blurred by puffiness, was a relic; the last survival of a type of head long ago gloriously portrayed and set before a happy public by that adept in the most perishable of the arts, William Hoey. Mr. Tuttle was heavier in body than the blithe comedian's creation, it is true; he was incomparably slower in wit and lower in spirits, yet he might well enough have sat for the portrait of an older brother of Mr. Hoey's masterpiece, "Old Hoss."

Having stroked his beard with a fat and dingy hand, he uttered detached guttural complaints in Elizabethan monosyllables, followed these with sighing noises; then, at the instigation of some abdominal feeling of horror, shuddered excessively, opened his eyes to a startled wideness and abruptly sat up in his bed. To the interior of his bosky ear, just then, was borne the faint religious sound of church bells chiming in a steeple miles away in the centre of the city, and he was not pleased. An expression of disfavour slightly altered the contours of his face; he muttered defiantly, and decided to rise and go forth.

Nothing could have been simpler. The April night had been chilly, and he had worn his shoes; no nightgear had to be exchanged for other garments;—in fact no more was to be done than to step out of the limousine. He did so, taking his greenish and too plastic "Derby" hat with him; and immediately he stood forth upon the factory floor as well equipped to face the public as ever. Thus, except for several safety-pins, glinting too brightly where they might least have been expected, he was a most excellent specimen of the protective coloration exhibited by man; for man has this instinct, undoubtedly. On the bright beaches by the sea, how gaily he conforms is to be noted by the dullest observer; in the autumnal woods man goes dull green and dead leaf brown; and in the smoky city all men, inside and out, are the colour of smoke. Mr. Tuttle stood forth, the colour of the grimy asphalt streets on which he lived; and if at any time he had chosen to rest in a gutter, no extraneous tint would have hinted of his presence.

Not far from him was a faucet over a sink; and he went to it, but not for the purpose of altering his appearance. Lacking more stimulating liquid, it was the inner man that wanted water; and he set his mouth to the faucet, drinking long, but not joyously. Then he went out to the sunshine of that spring morning, with the whole world before him, and his the choice of what to do with it.

He chose to walk toward the middle part of the city, the centre of banking and trade; but he went slowly, his eye wandering over the pavement; and so, before long, he decided to smoke. He was near the great building of the railway station at the time, and, lighting what was now his cigarette (for he had a match of his own) he leaned back against a stone pilaster, smoked and gazed unfavourably upon the taxicabs in the open square before the station.

As he stood thus, easing his weight against the stone and musing, he was hailed by an acquaintance, a tall negro, unusually limber at the knees and naïvely shabby in dress, but of amiable expression and soothing manners.

"How do, Mist' Tuttle," he said genially, in a light tenor voice. "How the worl' treatin' you vese days, Mist' Tuttle? I hope evathing movin' the ri' way to please you nicely."

Mr. Tuttle shook his head. "Yeh!" he returned sarcastically. "Seems like it, don't it! Look at 'em, I jest ast you! Look at 'em!"

"Look at who?"

"At them taxicabs," Mr. Tuttle replied, with sudden heat. "That's a nice sight fer decent people to haf to look at!" And he added, with rancour: "On a Sunday, too!"

"Well, you take them taxicabs now," the negro said, mildly argumentative, "an' what hurt they doin' to nobody to jes' look at 'em, Mist' Tuttle? I fine myse'f in some difficulty to git the point of what you was a-settin' you'se'f to point out, Mist' Tuttle. What make you so industrious 'gains' them taxicabs?"

"I'll tell you soon enough," Mr. Tuttle said ominously. "I reckon if they's a man alive in this here world to-day, I'm the one 't can tell you jest exackly what I got against them taxicabs. In the first place, take and look where the United States stood twenty years ago, when they wasn't any o' them things, and then take and look where the United States stands to-day, when it's full of 'em! I don't ast you to take my word fer it; I only ast you to use your own eyes and take and look around you and see where the United States stands to-day and what it's comin' to!"

But the coloured man's perplexity was not dispelled; he pushed back his ancient soft hat in order to assist his brain, but found the organ still unstimulated after adjacent friction, and said plaintively: "I cain' seem to grasp jes' whur you aiminin' at. What you say the United States comin' to?"

"Why, nowhere at all!" Mr. Tuttle replied grimly. "This

4

country's be'n all ruined up. You take and look at what's left of it, and what's the use of it? I jest ast you the one simple question: What's the use of it? Just tell me that, Bojus."

"You got me, Cap'n!" Bojus admitted. "I doe' know what you aiminin' to say 't all! What do all them taxicabs do?"

"Do?" his friend repeated hotly. "Wha'd they do? You take and look at this city. You know how many people it's got in it?"

"No, I don't, Mist' Tuttle. Heap of 'em, though!"

"Heap? I sh'd say they was! They's hunderds and hunderds and hunderds o' thousands o' men, women and chuldern in this city; you know that as well as I do, Bojus. Well, with all the hunderds o' thousands o' men, women and chuldern in this city, I ast you, how many livery-stables has this city got in it?"

"Livvy-stables, Mist' Tuttle? Lemme see. I ain't made the observation of no livvy-stable fer long time."

Tuttle shook a soiled forefinger at him severely. "You ain't answered my question. Didn't you hear me? I ast you the simple question: How many livery-stables is they?"

"Well, I ain't see none lately; I guess I doe' know, Cap'n."

"Then I'll tell you," said Tuttle fiercely. "They ain't any! What's more, I'll bet twenty thousand dollars they ain't five livery-stables left in the whole United States! That's a nice thing, ain't it!"

Bojus looked at him inquiringly, still rather puzzled. "You interust you'se'f in livvy-stables, Mist' Tuttle?"

At this Mr. Tuttle looked deeply annoyed; then he thought better of it and smiled tolerantly. "Listen here," he said. "You listen, my friend, and I'll tell you something 't's worth any man's while to try and understand the this-and-that of it. I grew up in the livery-stable business, and I guess if they's a man alive to-day, why, I know more about the livery-stable business than all the rest the men, women and chuldern in this city put together."

"Yes, suh. You own a livvy-stable one time, Mist' Tuttle?"

"I didn't exackly own one," said the truthful Tuttle, "but that's the business I grew up in. I'm a horse man, and I like to sleep around a horse. I drove a hack for the old B. P. Thomas Livery and Feed Company more than twenty years, off and on;—off and on, I did. I was a horse man all my life and I was in the horse business. I could go anywhere in the United States and I didn't haf to carry no money with me when I travelled; I could go into any town on the map and make all the money I'd care to handle. I'd never go to a boarding-house. What's the use of a hired room and all the useless fixin's in it they stick you fer? No man that's got the gumption of a man wants to waste his money like that when they's a whole nice livery-stable to sleep in. You take some people—women, most

5

likely!—and they git finicky and say it makes you kind of smell. 'Oh, don't come near me!' they'll say. Now, what kind of talk is that? You take me, why, I like to smell like a horse."

"Yes, suh," said Bojus. "Hoss smell ri' pleasan' smell."

"Well, I should say it is!" Mr. Tuttle agreed emphatically. "But you take a taxicab, all you ever git a chance to smell, it's burnt grease and gasoline. Yes, sir, that's what you got to smell of if you run one o' them things. Nice fer a man to carry around on him, ain't it?" He laughed briefly, in bitterness; and continued: "No, sir; the first time I ever laid eyes on one, I hollered, 'Git a horse!' but if you was to holler that at one of 'em to-day, the feller'd prob'ly answer, 'Where'm I goin' to git one?' I ain't seen a horse I'd be willin' to call a horse, not fer I don't know how long!"

"No, suh," Bojus assented. "I guess so. Man go look fer good hoss he fine mighty fewness of 'em. I guess automobile put hoss out o' business—an' hoss man, too, Mist' Tuttle."

"Yes, sir, I guess it did! First four five years, when them things come in, why, us men in the livery-stable business, we jest laughed at 'em. Then, by and by, one or two stables begun keepin' a few of 'em to hire. Perty soon after that they all wanted 'em, and a man had to learn to run one of 'em or he was liable to lose his livin'. They kep' gittin' worse and worse—and then, my goodness! didn't even the undertakers go and git 'em? 'Well,' I says, 'I give up! I give up!' I says. 'Men in this business that's young enough and ornery enough,' I says, 'why, they can go ahead and learn to run them things. I can git along nice with a horse,' I says. 'A horse knows what you say to him, but I ain't goin' to try and talk to no engine!' "

He paused, frowning, and applied the flame of a match to the half-inch of cigarette that still remained to him. "Them things ought to be throwed in the ocean," he said. "That's what I'd do with 'em!"

"You doe' like no automobile?" Bojus inquired. "You take you' enjoyment some way else, I guess, Mist' Tuttle."

"There's jest one simple question I want to ast you," Mr. Tuttle said. "S'pose a man's been drinkin' a little; well, he can git along with a horse all right—like as not a horse'll take him right on back home to the stable—but where's one o' them things liable to take him?"

"Jail," Bojus suggested.

"Yes, sir, or right over the bank into some creek, maybe. I don't want nothin' to do with 'em, and that's what I says from the first. I don't want nothin' to do with 'em, I says, and I've stuck to it." Here he was interrupted by a demand upon his attention, for his cigarette had become too short to be held with the fingers; he

6

inhaled a final breath of smoke and tossed the tiny fragment away. "I own one of 'em, though," he said lightly.

At this the eyes of Bojus widened. "You own automobile, Mist' Tuttle?"

"Yes, I got a limousine."

"What!" Bojus cried, and stared the more incredulously. "You got a limousine? Whur you got it?"

"I got it," Mr. Tuttle replied coldly. "That's enough fer me. I got it, but I don't go around in it none."

"What you do do with it?"

"I use it," said Tuttle, with an air of reticence. "I got my own use fer it. I don't go showin' off like some men."

Bojus was doubtful, yet somewhat impressed, and his incredulous expression lapsed to a vagueness. "No," he said. "Mighty nice to ride roun' in, though. I doe' know where evabody git all the money. Money ain't come knockin' on Bojus' do' beggin' 'Lemme in, honey!' No, suh; the way money act with me, it act like it think I ain' goin' use it right. Money act like I ain' its lovin' frien'!"

He laughed, and Mr. Tuttle smiled condescendingly. "Money don't amount to so much, Bojus," he said. "Anybody can make money!"

"They kin?"

"Why, you take a thousand dollars," said Tuttle; "and you take and put it out at compound interest; jest leave it lay and go on about your business—why, it'll pile up and pile up, you can't stop it. You know how much it'd amount to in twenty-five years? More than a million dollars."

"Whur all that million dolluhs come from?"

"It comes from the poor," said Mr. Tuttle solemnly. "That's the way all them rich men git their money, gougin' the poor."

"Well, suh," Bojus inquired reasonably, "what about me? I like git rich, too. Whur's some poor I kin go gouge? I'm willin' to do the gougin' if I kin git the money."

"Money ain't everything," his friend reminded him. "Some day the people o' this country's goin' to raise and take all that money away from them rich robbers. What right they got to it? That's what I want to know. We're goin' to take it and divide it among the people that need it."

Bojus laughed cheerfully. "Tell Bojus when you goin' begin dividin'! He be on han'!"

"Why, anybody could have all the money he wants, any time," Tuttle continued, rather inconsistently. "Anybody could."

"How anybody goin' git it?"

"I didn't say anybody was goin' to; I said anybody could."

7

"How could?"

"Well, you take me," said Tuttle. "John Rockafeller could drive right up here now, if he wanted to. S'pose he did; s'pose he was to drive right up to that curbstone there and s'pose he was to lean out and say, 'Howdy do, Mr. Tuttle. Git right in and set down, and let's take a drive. Now, how much money would you like me to hand you, Mr. Tuttle?'"

"Hoo-oo!" cried Bojus in high pleasure, for the sketch seemed beautiful to him; so he amplified it. "'How much money you be so kine as to invite me to p'litely han' ovuh to you?' Hoo! Jom B. Rockfelluh take an' ast me, I tell 'im, 'Well, jes han' me out six, sevvum, eight, nine hunnud dolluhs; that'll do fer this week, but you come 'roun' nex' Sunday an' ast me same. Don't let me ketch you not comin' roun' every Sunday, now!' Hoo! I go Mist' Rockfelluh's house to dinnuh; he say, 'What dish I serve you p'litely, Mist' Bojus?' I say, 'Please pass me that big gol' dish o' money an' a scoop, so's I kin fill my soup-plate!' Hoo-oo!" He laughed joyously; and then, with some abruptness descended from these roseate heights and looked upon the actual earth. "I reckon Jom B. Rockfelluh ain' stedyin' about how much money you and me like to use, Mist' Tuttle," he concluded. "He ain' comin' roun' this Sunday, nohow!"

"No, and I didn't say he was," Mr. Tuttle protested. "I says he could, and you certainly know enough to know he could, don't you, Bojus?"

"Well," said Bojus, "whyn't he go on ahead an' do it, then? If he kin do it as well as not, what make him all time decide fer not? Res' of us willin'!"

"That's jest the trouble," Tuttle complained, with an air of reproof. "You're willin' but you don't use your brains."

"Brains?" said Bojus, and laughed. "Brains ain' goin' make Bojus no money. What I need is a good lawn-mo'. If I could take an' buy me a nice good lawn-mo', I could make all the money I'm a-goin' a need the live-long summuh."

"Lawn-mower?" his friend inquired. "You ain't got no house and lot, have you? What you want of a lawn-mower?"

"I awready got a rake," Bojus explained. "If I had a lawn-mo' I could make th'ee, fo', fi' dolluhs a day. See that spring sun settin' up there a-gittin' ready to shine so hot? She's goin' to bring up the grass knee-high, honey, 'less somebody take a lawn-mo' an' cut it down. I kin take a lawn-mo' an' walk 'long all vese resident'al streets; git a dozen jobs a day if I kin do 'em. I truly would like to git me a nice good lawn-mo', but I ain' got no money. I got a diamon' ring, though. I give a diamon' ring fer a good lawn-mo'."

"Diamon' ring?" Mr. Tuttle inquired with some interest. "Le'ss see it."

"Gran' big diamon' ring," Bojus said, and held forth his right hand for inspection. Upon the little finger appeared a gem of notable dimensions, for it was a full quarter of an inch in width, but no one could have called it lustrous; it sparkled not at all. Yet its dimness might have been a temporary condition that cleaning would relieve, and what struck Mr. Tuttle most unfavourably was the fact that it was set in a metal of light colour.

"Why, it ain't even gold," he said. "That's a perty pore sample of a diamon' ring I expect, Bojus. Nobody'd want to wear a diamon' ring with the ring part made o' silver. Truth is, I never see no diamon' ring jest made o' silver, before. Where'd you git it?"

"Al Joles."

"Wha'd you give Al Joles fer it?"

"Nothin'," said Bojus, and laughed. "Al Joles, he come to where my cousin Mamie live, las' Feb'uary an 'bo'de with 'er week or so, 'cause he tryin' keep 'way f'm jail. One day he say this city too hot; he got to leave, an' Mamie tuck an' clean up after him an' she foun' this ring in a crack behine the washstan'. Al Joles drop it an' fergit it, I reckon. He had plenty rings!"

"I reckon!"

"Al Joles show Mamie fo' watches an' a whole big han'ful o' diamon' pins and rings an' chains. Say he got 'em in Chicago an' he tuck 'em all with him when he lit out. Mamie she say this ring worf fi', six thousan' dolluhs."

"Then what fer'd she take and give it to you, Bojus?"

"She di'n'," said Bojus. "She tuck an' try to sell it to Hillum's secon' han' joolry sto' an' Hillum say he won' bargain fer it 'count its bein' silvuh. So she trade it to me fer a nice watch chain. I like silvuh ring well as gol' ring. 'S the diamon' counts: diamon' worf fi', six thousan' dolluhs, I ain' carin' what jes' the ring part is."

"Well, it's right perty," Tuttle observed, glancing at it with some favour. "I don't hardly expect you could trade it fer no lawn-mower, though. I expect—" But at this moment a symptom of his indisposition interrupted his remarks. A slight internal convulsion caused him to shudder heavily; he fanned his suddenly bedewed forehead with his hat, and seemed to eat an impalpable but distasteful food.

"You feel sick, Mist' Tuttle?" Bojus inquired sympathetically, for his companion's appearance was a little disquieting. "You feel bad?"

"Well, I do," Tuttle admitted feebly. "I eat a hambone yestiddy that up and disagreed on me. I ain't be'n feelin' none too well all morning, if the truth must be told. The fact is, what I need right now—and I need it right bad," he added—"it's a little liquor."

"Yes, suh; I guess so," his friend agreed. "That's somep'n ain' goin' hurt nobody. I be willin' use a little myse'f."

"You know where any is?"

"Don't I!" the negro exclaimed. "I know whur plenty is, but the trouble is: How you an' me goin' git it?"

"Where is it?"

"Ri' dow' my cousin Mamie' celluh. My cousin Mamie' celluh plum full o' Whi' Mule. Man say he goin' buy it off her but ain' show up with no money. Early 's mawn' I say, 'Mamie, gi' me little nice smell o' you' nice whisky?' No, suh! Take an' fretten me with a brade-knife! Mad 'cause man ain' paid 'er, I reckon."

"Le'ss go on up there and ast her again," Tuttle suggested. "She might be feelin' in a nicer temper by this time. Me bein' sick, and it's Sunday and all, why, she ought to show some decency about it. Anyways, it wouldn't hurt anything to jest try."

"No, suh, tha's so, Mist' Tuttle," the negro agreed with ready hopefulness. "If she say no, she say no; but if she say yes, we all fix fine! Le'ss go!"

They went up the street, walking rather slowly, as Mr. Tuttle, though eager, found his indisposition increased with any rapidity of movement; then they turned down an alley, followed it to another alley, and at the intersection of that with another, entered a smoke-coloured cottage of small pretensions, though it still displayed in a front window the card of a Red Cross subscriber to the "drive" of 1918.

"Mamie!" Bojus called, when they had closed the door behind them. "Mamie!"

Then, as they heard the response to this call, both of them had the warming sense of sunshine rushing over them: the world grew light and bright and they perceived that luck did not always run against worthy people. Mamie's answer was not in words, yet it was a vocal sound and human: somewhere within her something quickened to the call and endeavoured to speak. Silently they opened the door of her bedroom and looked upon her where she reposed.

She had consoled herself for her disappointment; she was peaceful indeed; and the callers at once understood that for several hours, at least, she could deny them nothing they would ask. They paused but a moment to gaze, and then, without a word of comment upon their incredible good fortune, they exchanged a single hurried glance, and forthwith descended to the cellar.

An hour later they were singing there, in that cool dimness.

10

They sang of romantic love, of maternal sacrifices, of friendship; and this last theme held them longest, for Tuttle prevailed upon his companion to join him many, many times in a nineteenth century tribute to brotherly affection. With their hands resting fondly upon each other's shoulders, they sang over and over:

> *Comrades, comrades, ev-er since we was boys,*
> *Sharing each other's sorrows, sharing each other's joys,*
> *Comrades when manhood was daw-ning—*

Our own, our native land, somewhat generally lawless in mood of late, has produced few illegal commodities more effective than the ferocious liquid rich in fusel oil and known as White Mule. Given out of the imaginative heart of a race that has a genius for naming things, this perfect name tells everything of the pale liquor it so precisely labels. The silence of the mule is there, the sinister inertia of his apparent complete placidity as he stands in an interval of seeming patience;—for this is the liquor as it rests in the bottle. And the mule's sudden utter violence is there, with a hospital cot as a never-remote contingency for those who misunderstand.

Over-confidence in himself was not a failing of the experienced Tuttle; and he well knew the potencies of the volcanic stuff with which he dealt. His sincere desire was but to rid himself of the indisposition and nervousness that depressed him, and he indulged himself to-day with a lighter hand than usual. He wished to be at ease in body and mind, to be happy and to remain happy; therefore he stopped at the convivial, checking himself firmly, and took a little water. Not so the less calculating Bojus who had nothing of the epicure about him. Half an hour after the two friends had begun to sing "Comrades," Bojus became unmusical in execution, though his impression was that he still sang; and a little later Mr. Tuttle found himself alone, so far as song, conversation and companionship were concerned. Bojus still lived, but had no animation.

His more cautious friend, on the contrary, felt life freshening within him; his physical uncertainties had disappeared from his active consciousness; he was a new man, and said so. "Hah!" he said with great satisfaction and in a much stronger voice than he had dared to use earlier in the day. "I'm a new man!" And he slapped himself on the chest, repeatedly. Optimism came to him; he began to believe that he was at the end of all his troubles, and he decided to return to the fresh air, the sunshine and an interesting world. "Le'ss git outdoors and see what all's goin' on!" he said heartily.

But first he took some precautions for the sake of friendship.

Fearing that all might not go well with Bojus if Mamie were the first to be stirring and happened to look into her cellar, he went to the top of the stairs and locked the door there upon the inside. Then he came down again and once more proved his moderation by placing only one flask of Mamie's distillation in his pocket. He could have taken much more if he wished, but he sometimes knew when to say no. In fact, he now said it aloud and praised himself a little. "No! No, sir!" he said to some applicant within him. "I know what's good fer you and what ain't. If you take any more you're liable to go make a hog of yourself again. Why, jest look how you felt when you woke up this morning! I'm the man that knows and I'm perty smart, too, if you ever happen to notice! You take and let well enough alone."

He gave a last glance at Bojus, a glance that lingered with some interest upon the peculiar diamond ring; but he decided not to carry it away with him, because Bojus might be overwhelmingly suspicious later. "No, sir," he said. "You come along now and let well enough alone. We want to git out and see what's goin' on all over town!"

The inward pleader consented, he placed a box against the wall, mounted it and showed a fine persistence in overcoming what appeared to be impossibilities as he contrived to wriggle himself through a window narrower than he was. Then, emerging worm-like upon a dirty brick path beside the cottage, he arose brightly and went forth from that quarter of the city.

It suited his new mood to associate himself now with all that was most brilliant and prosperous; and so, at a briskish saunter he walked those streets where stood fine houses in brave lawns. It was now an hour and more after noon, the air was lively yet temperate in the sunshine, and the wealth he saw in calm display about him invigorated him. Shining cars passed by, proud ladies at ease within them; rich little children played about neat nursemaids as they strolled the cement pavements; haughty young men strode along, flashing their walking-sticks; noble big dogs with sparkling collars galloped over the bright grass under tall trees; and with all of this, Tuttle now felt himself congenial, and even intimate. Moreover, he had the conviction that some charming and dramatic adventure was about to befall him; it seemed to be just ahead.

The precise nature of this adventure remained indefinite in his imagination for a time, but gradually the thought of eating (abhorrent to him earlier in the day) again became pleasant, and he sketched some little scenes climaxing in banquets. "One these here millionaires could do it easy as not," he said, speaking only in fancy and not vocally. "One of 'em might jest as well as not look out his big window, see me, and come down his walk and say, 'Step right in,

12

Mr. Tuttle. We got quite a dinner-party to-day, but they's always room fer you, Mr. Tuttle. Now what'd you like to have to eat? Liver and chili and baked beans and ham and eggs and a couple of ice-cold muskmelons? We can open three or four cans o' sardines fer you, too, if you'd like to have 'em. You only got to say the word, Mr. Tuttle.'"

He began to regret Bojus's diamond ring a little; perhaps he could have traded it for a can of sardines at a negro restaurant he knew; but the regret was a slight one; he worried himself little about obtaining food, for people will always give it. However, he did not ask for it among the millionaires, whose servants are sometimes cold-hearted; but turned into an unpretentious cross-street and walked a little more slowly, estimating the houses. He had not gone far when he began to smell his dinner.

The odour came from the open front door of a neat white frame house in a yard of fair size; and here, near the steps of the small veranda, a man of sixty and his wife were discussing the progress of a row of tulips about to bloom. Their clothes new-looking, decorous and worn with a little unfamiliarity, told everybody that this man and his wife had been to church; that they dined at two o'clock on Sunday, owned their house, owned a burial lot in the cemetery, paid their bills, and had something comfortable in a safety deposit box. Tuttle immediately walked into the yard, took off his hat and addressed the wife.

"Lady," he said, in a voice hoarser from too much singing than he would have liked to make it, "Lady, I be'n out o' work fer some time back. I took sick, too, and I be'n in the hospital. What I reely wish to ast fer is work, but the state of unemployment in this city is awful bad. I don't ast fer no money; all I want is a chance to work."

"On Sunday?" she said reprovingly. "Of course there isn't any work on Sunday."

Tuttle stepped a little closer to her—a mistake—and looked appealing. "Then how'm I a-goin' to git no nourishment?" he asked. "If you can't give me no work, I ain't eat nothin' at all since day before yestiddy and I'd be truly thankful if you felt you could spare me a little nourishment."

But she moved back from him, her nostrils dilating slightly and her expression unfavourable. "I'd be glad to give you all you want to eat," she said coldly, "but I think you'd better sign the pledge first."

"Ma'am?" said Tuttle in plaintive astonishment.

"I think you've been drinking."

"No, lady! No!"

13

"I'm sure you have. I don't believe in doing anything for people that drink; it doesn't do them any good."

"Lady—" Tuttle began, and he was about to continue his protest to her, when her husband interfered.

"Run along!" he said, and tossed the applicant for nourishment a dime.

Tuttle looked sadly at the little round disk of silver as it lay shining in his asphalt coloured palm; then he looked at the donor and murmured: "I ast fer bread—and they give me a stone!"

"Go along!" said the man.

Tuttle went slowly, seeming to be bowed in thoughtful melancholy; he went the more reluctantly because there was a hint of fried chicken on the air; and before he reached the pavement a buxom fair woman, readily guessed to be of Scandinavian descent, appeared in the doorway. "Dinner's served, Mrs. Pinney," she called briskly.

Tuttle turned and looked at Mrs. Pinney with eloquence, but she shook her head disapprovingly. "You ought to sign the pledge!" she said.

"Yes, lady," he said, and abruptly turned away. He walked out into the street, where a trolley car at that moment happened to stop for another passenger, jumped on the step, waved his hand cordially, and continued to wave it as the car went down the street.

"Well of all!" Mrs. Pinney exclaimed, dumfounded, but her husband laughed aloud.

"That's a good one!" he said. "Begged for 'nourishment' and when I gave him a dime went off for a street-car ride! Come on in to dinner, ma; I guess he's passed out of our lives!"

Nothing was further from Mr. Tuttle's purpose, however; and Mr. and Mrs. Pinney had not finished their dinner, half an hour later, when he pushed the bell-button in their small vestibule, and the buxom woman opened the door, but not invitingly, for she made the aperture a narrow one when she saw who stood before her.

"Howdydo," he said affably. "Ole lady still here, isn't she?"

"What you want?" the woman inquired.

"Jest ast her to look this over," he said, and proffered a small paper-bound Bible, open, with a card between the leaves. "I'll wait here," he added serenely, as she closed the door.

She took the Bible to the dining-room, and handed it to Mrs. Pinney, remarking, "That tramp's back. He says to give you this. He's waitin'."

The Bible was marked with a rubber stamp: "Presented by Door of Hope Rescue Mission 337 South Maryland Street," and the card was a solemn oath and pledge to refrain from intoxicants,

14

thenceforth and forever. It was dated that day, and signed, in ink still almost wet, "Arthur T. De Morris."

Mrs. Pinney stared at the pledge, at first frowningly, then with a tendency toward a slight emotion; and without speaking she passed it to her husband for inspection, whereupon he became incredulous enough to laugh.

"That's about the suddenest conversion on record, I guess!" he said. "Used the dime to get down to the Door of Hope and back before our dinner was over. It beats all!"

"You don't think it could be genuine, Henry?"

"Well, no; not in twenty minutes."

"It could be—just possibly," she said gently. "We never know when the right word may touch some poor fellow's heart."

"Now, ma," he remonstrated, "don't you go and get one of your spells of religious vanity. That was about as tough an old soak as I ever saw, and I'm afraid it'll take more than one of your 'right words' to convert him."

"Still—" she said, and a gentle pride showed in her expression. "We can't tell. It seems a little quick, of course, but he may have been just at the spiritual point for the right word to reach him. Anyhow, he did go right away and get a pledge and sign it—and got a Bible, too. It might be—I don't say it probably is, but it just might be the beginning of a new life for him, and it wouldn't be right to discourage him. Besides he must really be hungry: he's proved that, anyhow." She turned to the woman in waiting. "Give him back the Bible and his card, Tilly," she said, "and take him out in the kitchen and let him have all he wants to eat. Tell him to wait when he gets through; and you let me know; I'll come and talk to him. His name's Mr. De Morris, Tilly, when you speak to him."

Tilly's expression was not enthusiastic, but she obeyed the order, conducted the convert to the kitchen and set excellent food before him in great plenty; whereupon Mr. Tuttle, being not without gallantry, put his hat on the floor beside his chair, and thanked her warmly before he sat down. His appetite was now vigorous, and at first he gave all his attention to the fried chicken, but before long he began to glance appreciatively, now and then, at the handmaiden who had served him. She was a well-shaped blonde person of thirty-five or so, tall, comely, reliable looking, visibly energetic, and, like her kitchen, incredibly clean. His glances failed to interest her, if she took note of them; and presently she made evident her sense of a social gulf. She prepared a plate for herself, placed it upon a table across the room from him and sat there, with her profile toward him, apparently unconscious of his presence.

15

"Plenty room at my table," he suggested hospitably. "I jest as soon you eat over here."

"No," she said discouragingly.

Not abashed, but diplomatic, he was silent for a time, then he inquired casually, "Do all the work here?"

"Yep."

"Well, well," he said. "You look too young fer sech a rough job. Don't they have nobody 'tend the furnace and cut the grass?"

"Did," said Tilly. "Died last week."

"Well, ain't that too bad! Nice pleasant feller was he?"

"Coloured man," said Tilly.

"You Swedish?" Tuttle inquired.

"No. My folks was."

"Well sir, that's funny," Tuttle said genially, "I knowed they was somep'n Swedish about you, because I always did like Swedish people. I don't know why, but I always did taken a kind o' likin' to Swedish people, and Swedish people always taken kind of a likin' to me. My ways always seem to suit Swedish people—after we git well acquainted I mean. The better Swedish people git acquainted with me the more they always seem to taken a likin' to me. I ast a Swedish man oncet why it was he taken sech a likin' to me and he says it was my ways. 'It's jest your ways, George,' he says. 'It's because Swedish people like them ways you got, George,' he says." Here Tuttle laughed deprecatingly and added, "I guess he must 'a' be'n right, though."

Tilly made no response; she did not even glance at him, but continued gravely to eat her dinner. Then, presently, she said, without any emphasis: "I thought your name was Arthur."

"What?"

"That pledge you signed," Tilly said, still not looking at him, but going on with her dinner;—"ain't it signed Arthur T. De Morris?"

For the moment Mr. Tuttle was a little demoralized, but he recovered himself, coughed, and explained. "Yes, that's my name," he said. "But you take the name George, now, it's more kind of a nickname I have when anybody gits real well acquainted with me like this Swedish man I was tellin' you about; and besides that, it was up in Dee-troit. Most everybody I knowed up in Dee-troit, they most always called me George fer a nickname like. You know anybody in Dee-troit?"

"No."

"Married?" Tuttle inquired.

"No."

"Never be'n?" he said.

16

"No."

"Well, now, that's too bad," he said sympathetically. "It ain't the right way to live. I'm a widower myself, and I ain't never be'n the same man since I lost my first wife. She was an Irish lady from Chicago." He sighed; finished the slice of lemon pie Tilly had given him, and drank what was left of his large cup of coffee, holding the protruding spoon between two fingers to keep it out of his eye. He set the cup down, gazed upon it with melancholy, then looked again at the unresponsive Tilly.

She had charm for him; and his expression, not wholly lacking a kind of wistfulness, left no doubt of it. No doubt, too, there fluttered a wing of fancy somewhere in his head: some picture of what might-have-been trembled across his mind's-eye's field of vision. For an instant he may have imagined a fireside, with such a competent fair creature upon one side of it, himself on the other, and merry children on the hearth-rug between. Certainly he had a moment of sentiment and sweet longing.

"You ever think about gittin' married again?" he said, rather unfortunately.

"I told you I ain't been married."

"Excuse me!" he hastened to say. "I was thinkin' about myself. I mean when I says 'again' I was thinkin' about myself. I mean I was astin' you: You think about gittin' married at all?"

"No."

"I s'pose not," he assented regretfully; and added in a gentle tone: "Well, you're a mighty fine-lookin' woman; I never see no better build than what you got on you."

Tilly went out and came back with Mrs. Pinney, who mystified him with her first words. "Well, De Morris?" she said.

"What?" he returned blankly, then luckily remembered, and said, "Oh, yes, ma'am?"

"I hope you meant it when you signed that pledge, De Morris."

"Why, lady, of course I did," he assured her warmly. "If the truth must be told, I don't never drink hardly at all, anyways. Now we got prohibition you take a poor man out o' work, why where's he goin' to git any liquor, lady? It's only rich people that's usually able to git any reel good stew on, these days, if I'm allowable to used the expression, so to speak. But that's the unfairness of it, and it makes poor people ready to break out most anytime. Not that it concerns me, because I put all that behind me when I signed the pledge like you told me to. If the truth must be told, I was goin' to sign the pledge some time back, but I kep' kind o' puttin' it off. Well, lady, it's done now, and I'm thankful fer it."

"I do hope so, I'm sure," Mrs. Pinney said earnestly. "And I want to help you; I'll be glad to. You said you wanted some work."

"Yes'm," he said promptly, and if apprehension rose within him he kept it from appearing upon the surface. Behind Mrs. Pinney stood Tilly, looking straight at him with a frigid skepticism of which he was fully conscious. "Yes'm. Any honest work I can turn my hand to, that's all I ast of anybody. I'd be glad to help wash the dishes if it's what you had in your mind, lady."

"No. But if you'll come back to-morrow morning about nine or ten o'clock, I'll give you two dollars for cutting the grass. It isn't a very large yard, and you can get through by evening."

"I ain't got no lawn-mower, lady."

"We have one in the cellar," said Mrs. Pinney. "If you come back, Tilly'll have it on the back porch for you. That's all to-day, De Morris."

"All right, lady. I thank you for your hospitillity and I'll be back in the morning," he said, and as he turned toward the door he glanced aside at Tilly and saw that her mouth quivered into the shape of a slight smile—a knowing smile. "I will!" he said defiantly. "I'll be back here at ten o'clock to-morrow morning. You'll see!"

But when the door closed behind him, Tilly laughed aloud—and was at once reproved by her mistress. "We always ought to have faith that the better side of people will conquer, Tilly. I really think he'll come."

"Yes'm, like that last one 't said he was comin' back, and stole the knife and fork he ate with," said Tilly, laughing again.

"But this one didn't steal anything."

"No'm, but he'll never come back, to work," said Tilly. "He said 'You'll see,' and you will, but you won't see him!"

They had a mild argument upon the point, and then Mrs. Pinney returned to her husband, who was waiting for her to put on her Sunday wrap and hat, and go with him to spend their weekly afternoon among the babies at their son's house. She found her husband to be strongly of Tilly's opinion, and when they came home that evening, she renewed the argument with both of them; so that this mild and orderly little household was slightly disturbed (a most uncommon thing in its even life) over the question of the vagrant's return. Thus, Mrs. Pinney prepared a little triumph for herself;—at ten o'clock the next morning Tuttle opened the door of Tilly's bright kitchen and inquired:

"Where's that lawn-mower?"

He was there. He had defeated the skeptic and proved himself a worthy man, but at a price; for again he was far from well, and every movement he made increased well-founded inward doubts of

18

his constitution. Unfortunately, he had taken his flask of White Mule to bed with him in his limousine, and in that comfortable security moderation had seemed useless to the verge of absurdity. The point of knowing when to say no rests in the "when;" and when a man is already at home and safe in bed, "Why, my Glory!" he had reasoned it, "Why, if they ever is a time to say yes, it must be then!" So he had said "Yes," to the White Mule and in the morning awoke feeling most perishable. Even then, as in the night, from time to time he had vagrant thoughts of Tilly and her noble build, of the white and shining kitchen, and of those disbelieving cool blue eyes that seemed to triumph over him and indict him, accusing him of things she appeared to think he would do if he had the chance. There was something in her look that provoked him, as if she would stir his conscience, and though his conscience disturbed him no more than a baby's disturbs a baby, he was indeed somewhat disquieted by that cold look of hers. And so, when he had collected his mind a little, upon waking, he muttered feebly. "I'll show her!" Something strange and forgotten worked faintly within him, fluttered a little; and so, walking carefully, he kept his word and came to her door.

She looked at him in a startled way. Unquestionably he caused her to feel something like an emotion, and she said not a word, but went straightway and brought him the lawn-mower. He looked in her eyes as he took it from her hand.

"You thought I wouldn't come," he said.

"Yes," she admitted gravely.

"Well," he said, and smiled affably, "you certainly got a fine build on you!" And with that, pushing the lawn-mower before him, he went out to his work, leaving her visibly not offended.

"You showed her!" he said to himself.

In the yard he looked thoughtfully upon the grass, which was rather long and had not been cut since the spring had enlivened it to a new growing. The lot seemed longer than it had the day before; he saw that it must be two hundred feet from the street on which it fronted to the alley in the rear; it was a hundred feet wide, at least, and except for the area occupied by the house, which was of modest proportions, all of this was grass. He sighed profoundly: "Oh, Gosh!" he mourned. But he meant to do the work, and began it manfully.

With the mower rolling before him, reversed, the knives upward, he went to the extreme front of the lot, turned the machine over, and, surveying the prospect, decided to attack the lawn with long straight swathes, running from the front clear through to the alley—though, even before he began, the alley seemed far, far away.

However, he turned up the sleeves of his ancient coat an inch or two, and went at his task with a good heart. That is to say, he started with a good heart, but the lawn-mower was neither new nor sharp; the grass was tough, the sun hot, and his sense of unwellness formidable. When he had gone ten feet, he paused, wiped his forehead with a sleeve, and leaned upon the handle of the mower in an attitude not devoid of pathos. But he was yet determined; he thought of the blue eyes in the kitchen and resolved that they should not grow scornful again. Once more he set the mower in motion.

Mrs. Pinney heard the sound of it in her room upstairs, looked from the window, and with earnest pleasure beheld the workman at his toil. Her heart rejoiced her to have been the cause of a reformation, and presently she went down to the kitchen to gloat gently over a defeated antagonist in argument.

"Yes'm," Tilly admitted meekly. "He fooled me."

"You see I was right, Tilly. We always ought to have faith that the best part of our natures will conquer."

"Yes'm; it looks so."

"Have we some buttermilk in the refrigerator, Tilly?"

"Yes'm."

"Then I think you might have some ready for him, if he gets too hot. I don't think he looks very well and you might ask him if he'd like some. You might ask him now, Tilly."

"Now?" Tilly asked, and coloured a little. "You mean right now, Mrs. Pinney?"

"Yes. It might do him good and help keep him strong for his work."

"All right," Tilly said, and turned toward the ice-box; but at a thought she paused. "I don't hear the lawn-mower," she said. "It seems to me I ain't heard it since we began talking."

"Perhaps he's resting," Mrs. Pinney suggested, but her voice trembled a little with foreboding. "We might just go out and see."

They went out and saw. Down the full length of the yard, from the street to the alley, there was one long swathe of mowed grass; and but one, though it was perfect. Particularly as the trail of a fugitive it was perfect, and led straight to the alley, which, being paved with brick, offered to the searchers the complete bafflement of a creek to the bloodhound. A brick alley shows no trace of a reversed lawn-mower hurrying over it—yet nothing was clearer than that such a hurrying must have taken place. For Arthur T. De Morris was gone, and so was the lawn-mower.

"Mr. Pinney'll laugh at me I guess, too!" Mrs. Pinney said, swallowing, as she stood with Tilly, staring at the complete vacancy of the brick alley.

"Yes'm, he will," said Tilly, and laughed again, a little harshly.

****

The fugitive, already some blocks distant, propelled the ravished mower before him, and went so openly through the streets in the likeness of an honest toiler seeking lawns to mow that he had to pause and decline several offers, on his hurried way. He took note of these opportunities, however, remembering the friend he was on his way to see, and, after some difficulty, finding him in a negro pool-room, proffered him the lawn-mower in exchange for five dollars, spot cash.

"I ain' got it," replied Bojus, flaccid upon a bench. "I ain' feelin' like cuttin' nobody's grass to-day, nohow, an' besides I'm goin' stay right here till coas' clear. Mamie ain' foun' out who make all her trouble, 'cause I clim' out the window whiles she was engage' kickin' on celluh do'; but neighbours say she mighty s'picious who 'twas. I don' need no lawn-mo' in a pool-room."

"Well, you ain't goin' to stay in no pool-room forever; you got to git out and earn your livin' some time," Tuttle urged him. "Every man that's got the gumption of a man, he's got to do that!" And upon Bojus's lifeless admission of the truth of this statement, the bargaining began. It ended with Bojus's becoming the proprietor of the lawn-mower and Tuttle's leaving the pool-room after taking possession of everything in the world that Bojus owned except a hat, a coat, a pair of trousers, a shirt, two old shoes and four safety-pins. The spoil consisted of seventy-eight cents in money, half of a package of bent cigarettes, a pair of dice, a "mouth-organ" and the peculiar diamond ring.

This latter Mr. Tuttle placed upon his little finger, and as he walked along he regarded it with some pleasure; but he decided to part with it, and carried it to a pawn-shop he knew, having had some acquaintance with the proprietor in happier days.

He entered the place with a polite air, removing his hat and bowing, for the shop was a prosperous one.

"Golly!" said the proprietor, who happened to be behind a counter, instructing a new clerk. "I believe it's old George the hackman."

"That's who, Mr. Breitman," Tuttle responded. "Many's the cold night I yousta drive you all over town and—"

"Never mind, George," the pawnbroker interrupted crisply. "You payin' me just a social call, or you got some business you want to do?"

21

"Business," said Tuttle. "If the truth must be told, Mr. Breitman, I got a diamon' ring worth somewheres along about five or six thousand dollars, I don't know which."

Breitman laughed, "Oh, you got a ring worth either five or six thousand, you don't know which, and you come in to ask me to settle it. Is that it?"

"Yes. I don't want to hock her; I jest want to git a notion if I ever do decide to sell her." He set the ring upon the glass counter before Breitman. "Ain't she a beauty?"

Breitman glanced at the ring and laughed, upon which the owner hastily protested: "Oh, I know the ring part ain't gold: you needn't think I don't know that much! It's the diamon' I'm talkin' about. Jest set your eye on her."

The pawnbroker set his eye on her—that is, he put on a pair of spectacles, picked up the ring and looked at it carelessly, but after his first glance his expression became more attentive. "So you say I needn't think you don't know the 'ring part' ain't gold, George? So you knew it was platinum, did you?"

"Of course, I knowed it was plapmun," Tuttle said promptly, rising to the occasion, though he had never before heard of this metal. "I reckon I know plapmun when I see it."

"I think it's worth about ten or twelve dollars," Breitman said. "I'll give you twelve if you want to sell it."

Eager acceptance rushed to Tuttle's lips, but hung there unspoken as caution checked him. He drew a deep breath and said huskily, "Why, you can't fool me on this here ring, Mr. Breitman. I ain't worryin' about what I can git fer the plapmun part; all I want to know is how much I ought ast fer the diamon'. I ain't fixin' to sell it to you; I'm fixin' to sell it to somebody else."

"Oh, so that's it," said Breitman, still looking at the ring. "Where'd you get it?"

Tuttle laughed ingratiatingly. "It's kind of funny," he said, "how I got that ring. Yet it's all open and above-board, too. If the truth must be told, it belonged to a lady-cousin o' mine in Auburndale, Wisconsin, and her aunt-by-marriage left it to her. Well, this here lady-cousin o' mine, I was visitin' her last summer, and she found I had a good claim on the house and lot she was livin' in, account of my never havin' knowed that my grandfather—he was her grandfather, too—well, he never left no will, and this house and lot come down to her, but I never made no claim on it because I thought it had be'n willed to her till I found out it hadn't, when I went up there. Well, the long and short of it come out like this: the house and lot's worth about nine or ten thousand dollars, but she didn't have no money, so she handed me over this ring to settle my

22

claim. Name's Mrs. Moscoe, Mrs. Wilbur N. Moscoe, three-thirty-two South Liberty Street, Auburndale, Wisconsin."

"I see," Breitman said absently. "Just wait here a minute, George; I ain't going to steal it." And, taking the ring with him, he went into a room behind the shop, remaining there closeted long enough for Tuttle to grow a little uneasy.

"Hay!" he called. "You ain't tryin' to eat that plapmun ring are you, Mr. Breitman?"

Breitman appeared in the doorway. There was a glow in his eyes, and although he concealed all other traces of a considerable excitement, somehow Tuttle caught a vibration out of the air, and began to feel the presence of Fortune. "Step in here and sit down, George," the pawnbroker said. "I wanted to look at this stone a little closer, and of course I had to go over my lists and see if it was on any of 'em."

"What lists?" Tuttle asked as he took a chair.

"From the police. Stolen goods."

"Looky here! I told you how that ring come to me. My cousin ain't no crook. Her name's Mrs. Wilbur N. Moscoe, South Liberty Street, Auburnd—"

"Never mind," Breitman interrupted. "I ain't sayin' it ain't so. Anyway, this ring ain't on any of the lists and—"

"I should say it ain't!"

"Well, don't get excited. Now look here, George"—Breitman seated himself close to his client and spoke in a confidential tone—"George, you know I always took a kind of interest in you, and I want to tell you what you need. You ought to go get yourself all fixed up. You ought to go to a barber's and get your hair cut and your whiskers trimmed. Don't go to no cheap barber's; go to a good one, and tell 'em to fix your whiskers so's you'll have a Van Dyke—"

"A what?"

"A Van Dyke beard. It's swell," said Breitman. "Then you go get you a fine pearl-gray Fedora hat, with a black band around it, and a light overcoat, and some gray gloves with black stitching, and a nice cane and a nobby suit o' clo'es and some fancy top shoes—"

"Listen here!" Tuttle said hoarsely, and he set a shaking hand on the other's knee, "how much you willin' to bid on my plapmun ring?"

"Don't go so fast!" Breitman said, but his eyes were becoming more and more luminous. He had the hope of a great bargain; yet feared that Tuttle might have a fairly accurate idea of the value of the diamond. "Hold your hosses a little, George! You don't need so awful much to go and get yourself fixed up like I'm tellin' you, and you'll have a lot o' money left to go around and see high life with. I'll send right over to the bank and let you have it in cash, too, if you meet my views."

"How much?" Tuttle gasped. "How much?"

Breitman looked at him shrewdly. "Well, I'm takin' chances: the market on stones is awful down these days, George. Your cousin must have fooled you bad when she talked about four or five thousand dollars! That's ridiculous!"

"How much?"

"Well, I'll say!—I'll say seven hundred and fifty dollars."

Tuttle's head swam. "Yes!" he gasped.

****

No doubt as he began that greatest period in his whole career, half an hour later, he thought seriously of a pair of blue eyes in a white kitchen;—seven hundred and fifty dollars, with a competent Swedish wife to take care of it and perhaps set up a little shop that would keep her husband out of mischief and busy— But there the thought stopped short and his expression became one of disillusion: the idea of orderliness and energy and profit was not appetizing. He had seven hundred and fifty dollars in his pocket; and Tuttle knew what romance could come to him instantly at the bidding of this illimitable cash: he knew where the big crap games were; he knew where the gay flats and lively ladies were; he knew where the fine liquor gurgled—not White Mule; he knew how to find the lights, the lights and the music!

Forthwith he approached that imperial orgy of one heaped and glorious week, all of high-lights, that summit of his life to be remembered with never-failing pride when he went back, after it was all over, to his limousine and the shavings.

It was glorious straight through to the end, and the end was its perfect climax: the most dazzling memory of all. He forgave automobiles, on that last day, and in the afternoon he hired a splendid, red new open car, with a curly-haired chauffeur to drive it. Then driving to a large hardware store he spent eighteen dollars, out of his final fifty, upon the best lawn-mower the store could offer him. He had it placed in the car and drove away, smoking a long cigar in a long holder. Such was his remarkable whim; and it marks him as an extraordinary man.

That nothing might be lacking, his destiny arranged that Mrs. Pinney was superintending Tilly in the elimination of dandelions from the front yard when the glittering equipage, to their surprise, stopped at the gate. Seated beside the lawn-mower in the tonneau they beheld a superb stranger, portly and of notable presence. His pearl-gray hat sat amiably upon his head; the sleeves of his fawn-coloured overcoat ran pleasantly down to pearl gloves; his Van Dyke beard, a little grizzled, conveyed an impression of distinction not contradicted by a bagginess of the eyelids; for it is strangely true that dissipation sometimes even adds distinction to certain types of faces. All in all, here was a man who might have recalled to a student of courts some aroma of the entourage of the late King Edward at Hombourg. There was just that about him.

He alighted slowly—he might well have been credited with the gout—and entering the yard, approached with a courteous air, being followed by the chauffeur, who brought the lawn-mower.

"Good afternoon, lady and Tilly," he said, in a voice unfortunately hoarse; and he removed his pearl-gray hat with a dignified gesture.

They stared incredulously, not believing their eyes.

"I had a little trouble with your lawn-mower, so I up and got it fixed," he said. "It's the same one. I took and got it painted up some."

"Oh, me!" Tilly said, in a whisper. "Oh, me!" And she put her hand to her heart.

He perceived that he dazzled her; that she felt deeply; and almost he wished, just for this moment, to be sober. He was not—profoundly not—yet he maintained his dignity and his balance throughout the interview. "I thought you might need it again some day," he said.

"Mis-ter De Mor-ris!" Mrs. Pinney cried, in awed recognition. "Why, what on earth—"

"Nothin'," he returned lightly. "Nothin' at all." He waved his hand to the car. "One o' my little automobiles," he said.

With that he turned, and, preceded by the chauffeur, walked down the path to the gate. Putting his whole mind upon it, he contrived to walk without wavering; and at the gate, he paused and looked wistfully back at Tilly. "You certainly got a good build on you," he said.

Then beautifully and romantically he concluded this magnificent gesture—this unsolvable mystery story that the Pinneys' very grandchildren were to tell in after years, and that kept Tilly a maiden for many months in the hope of the miraculous stranger's return—at least to tell her who and what he was!

He climbed into the car, placed the long holder of the long cigar in his mouth, and, as the silent wheels began to turn, he took off his hat again and waved it to them graciously.

"I kept the pledge!" he said.

THE PARTY

THE thoughts of a little girl are not the thoughts of a little boy. Some will say that a little girl's thoughts are the gentler; and this may be, for the boy roves more with his tribe and follows its hardier leaders; but during the eighth or ninth year, and sometimes a little earlier, there usually becomes evident the beginning of a more profound difference. The little girl has a greater self-consciousness than the boy has, but conceals hers better than he does his; moreover, she has begun to discover the art of getting her way indirectly, which mystifies him and outrages his sense of justice. Above all, she is given precedence and preference over him, and yet he is expected to suppress what is almost his strongest natural feeling, and be polite to her! The result is that long feud between the sexes during the period running from the ages of seven and eight to fifteen, sixteen and seventeen, when reconciliation and reconstruction set in—often rapidly.

Of course the period varies with individuals;—however, to deal in averages, a male of five will play with females of similar age almost as contentedly as with other males, but when he has reached eight, though he may still at times "play with girls," he feels a guilt, or at least a weakness, in doing so; for within him the long hatred has begun to smoulder.

Many a parent and many an aunt will maintain that the girls are passive, that it is the boys who keep the quarrel alive, though this is merely to deny the relation between cause and result, and the truth is that the boys are only the noisier and franker in the exchange of reciprocal provocations. And since adults are but experienced children, we find illumination upon such a point in examples of the feud's revival in middle age; for it is indeed sometimes revived, even under conditions of matrimony. A great deal of coldness was shown to the suburban butcher who pushed his wife into his sausage vat. "Stay!" the philosopher protested. "We do not know what she had said to him."

The feud is often desultory and intermittent; and of course it does not exist between every boy and every girl; a Montagu may hate the Capulets with all his vitals, yet feel an extraordinary kindness toward one exceptional Capulet. Thus, Master Laurence Coy, nine, permitted none to surpass him in hating girls. He proclaimed his bitterness, and made the proclamation in public. (At a party in his own house and given in his own honour, with girls for half his guests, he went so far as to state—not in a corner, whispering, but in the centre of the largest room and shouting—that he hated every last thing about 'em. It seemed that he wished to avoid ambiguity.) And yet, toward one exceptional little girl he was as water.

Was what he felt for Elsie Threamer love? Naturally, the answer must depend upon a definition of the word; and there are definitions varying from the frivolous mots tossed off by clergymen to the fanatical dogmas of coquettes. Mothers, in particular, have their own definitions, which are so often different from those of their sons that no one will ever be able to compute the number of mothers who have informed sons, ranging in age from fourteen to sixty-two, that what those sons mistook for love, and insisted was love, was not love. Yet the conclusion seems to be inevitable that behind all the definitions there is but one actual thing itself; that it may be either a force, or a condition produced by a force, or both; and that although the phenomena by which its presence may be recognized are of the widest diversity, they may be somewhat roughly classified according to the ages of the persons affected. Finally, a little honest research will convince anybody that these ages range from seven months to one hundred and thirty-four years; and if scriptural records are accepted, the latter figure must be much expanded.

Hence there appears to be warranted accuracy in the statement that Laurence Coy was in a state of love. When he proclaimed his hatred of all girls and every last thing about 'em, that very proclamation was produced by his condition—it was a phenomenon related to the phenomena of crime, to those uncalled-for proclamations of innocence that are really the indications of guilt. He was indeed inimical to all other girls; but even as he declared his animosity, he hoped Elsie was noticing him.

Whenever he looked at her, he swallowed and had a warm but sinking sensation in his lower chest. If he continued to be in her presence for some time—that is, for more than four or five minutes—these symptoms were abated but did not wholly disappear; the neck was still a little uneasy, moving in a peculiar manner at intervals, as if to release itself from contact with the collar, and there was a feeling of looseness about the stomach.

In absence, her image was not ever and always within his doting fancy shrined; far from it! When he did think of her, the image was fair, doubtless; yet he had in mind nothing in particular he wished to say to its original. And when he heard that she had the scarlet fever, he did not worry. No, he only wondered if she could see him from a window as he went by her house, and took occasion to pass that way with a new kite. Truth to say, here was the gist of

27

his love in absence; it consisted almost entirely of a wish to have her for an audience while he performed; and that's not so far from the gist of divers older loves.

In her presence it was another matter; self-consciousness expanded to the point of explosion, for here was actually the audience of his fragmentary day-dreams, and great performances were demanded. Just at this point, however, there was a difficulty;— having developed neither a special talent nor even a design of any kind, he was forced back upon the more rudimentary forms of self-expression. Thus it comes about that sweet love itself will often be found the hidden cause of tumults that break up children's parties.

The moment of Elsie's arrival at Laurence's party could have been determined by an understanding person even if Elsie had been invisible to that person. Until then Laurence was decorous, greeting his arriving guests with a little arrogance natural to the occasion, since this was his own party and on his own premises; but the instant his glance fell upon the well-known brazen glow of apparently polished curls, as Elsie came toward him from the hall where she had left her pretty hat and little white coat, his decorum vanished conspicuously.

The familiar symptoms had assailed him, and automatically he reacted to prevent their unmanning him. Girls, generically, had been mentioned by no one, and he introduced the topic without prelude, stating at the top of his voice that he hated every last thing about 'em. Then, not waiting for Elsie to greet him, not even appearing to be aware of her approach, or of her existence, he ran across the room, shouting, "Hay, there, Mister!" and hurled himself against a boy whose back was toward him. Rebounding, he dashed upon another, bumping into him violently, with the same cry of "Hay, there, Mister!" and went careening on, from boy to boy, repeating the bellow with the bumping as he went.

Such easy behaviour on the part of the host immediately dispersed that formal reticence which characterizes the early moments of most children's parties; the other boys fell in with Laurence's idea and began to plunge about the room, bumping one another with a glad disregard of little girls who unfortunately got in their way. "Hay, there, Mister!" was the favoured cry, shouted as loudly as possible; and the bumping was as vigorous as the slogan. Falls were many and uproarious; annoyed little girls were upset; furniture also fell; the noise became glorious; and thus Laurence Coy's party was a riot almost from the start.

Now when boys at a party get this mob mood going, the state of mind of the little girls is warrantably that of grown ladies among drunken men. There is this difference, of course: that the adult

28

ladies leave the place and go home as soon as they can extricate themselves, whereas the little girls are incapable of even imagining such a course of action; they cannot imagine leaving a party before the serving of "refreshments," at the earliest. For that matter, children of both sexes sometimes have a miserable time at a party yet remain to the bitter end for no reason except that their minds are not equal to the conception of a departure. A child who of his own impulse leaves a party before it is over may be set down as either morbid or singularly precocious—he may be a genius.

When the bumping and bellowing broke out at Laurence's party, most of the little girls huddled discontentedly close to the walls or in corners, where they were joined by those who had been overturned; and these last were especially indignant as they smoothed down their rumpled attire. It cannot be said, however, that the little girls reduced the general clamour; on the contrary, they increased it by the loudest criticism.

Every one of the rumpled naturally singled out the bellowing bumper who had overturned herself, and declared him to be the worst of the malefactors bent upon "spoiling the party." But as the rioting continued, the ladies' criticism shifted in a remarkable way, and presently all of it became hotly concentrated upon one particular rioter. The strange thing about this was that the individual thus made the centre of odium was not Laurence, the founder of the objectionable game and the ringleader of the ruffians; not fat Bobby Eliot, the heaviest and most careless of his followers; not Thomas Kimball, the noisiest; not any of the boys, indeed, but on the peculiar contrary, a person of the resentful critics' own sex.

One little girl alone, among those overturned, had neither fled to the wall nor sought the protection of a corner; she remained upon the floor where Laurence, too blindly bumping, had left her; and it must be related that, thus recumbent, she kicked repeatedly at all who happened to pass her way. "Hay there, Mister!" she said. "I'll show you!"

Her posture had no dignity; her action lacked womanliness; she seemed unconventional and but little aware of those qualities which a young female appearing in society should at least affect to possess. Hence it is no wonder that even before she decided to stop kicking and rise from the floor, she was already being censured. And what indeed was the severity of that censure, when after rising, she bounced herself violently against Laurence, ricocheted upon Thomas Kimball, and shrilling, "Hay, there, Mister! I'll show you!" proceeded to enter into the game with an enthusiasm surpassing that of any other participant!

29

It cannot be said that she was welcomed by the male players; they made it as clear as possible that they considered her enthusiasm gratuitous. "Here, you!" the fat Eliot boy objected sternly, as she caromed into him. "You ole Daisy Mears, you! You ought to know you might ruin a person's stummick, doing like that with your elbow."

But Miss Mears was not affected by his severity; she projected herself at him again. "Hay, there, Mister!" she whooped. "I'll show you!" And so bounced on to the next boy.

Her voice, shrill beyond compare, could be heard—and by a sensitive ear heard painfully—far above the bellowing and the criticism. Her "Hay-there-Mister-I'll-show-you!" was both impetuous and continuous; and she covered more ground than any of the boys. Floored again, not once but many times, she recovered herself by a method of her own; the feet were quickly elevated as high as possible, then brought down, while a simultaneous swing of the shoulders threw the body forward; and never for an instant did she lose her up-and-at-'em spirit. She devised a new manner of bumping—charging upon a boy, she would turn just at the instant of contact, and back into him with the full momentum acquired in the charge. Usually they both fell, but she had the advantage of being the upper, which not only softened the fall for her but enabled her to rise with greater ease because of her opponent's efforts to hoist her from him.

Now, here was a strange thing: the addition of this blithe companion seemed to dull the sport for those who most keenly loved it. In proportion as her eagerness for it increased, their own appeared to diminish. Dozens of times, probably, she was advised to "cut it out," and with even greater frankness requested to "get on out o' here!" Inquiries were directed to her, implying doubts of her sanity and even of her consciousness of her own acts. "Hay, listen!" several said to her. "Do you think you know what you're doin'?"

Finally she was informed, once more by implication, that she was underweight—though here was a paradox, for her weight was visibly enough to have overthrown the informer, who was Laurence. But this was the second time she had done it, and his warmth of feeling was natural.

"Get off o' me," he said, and added the paradoxical appraisement of her figure. His words were definite, but to the point only as reprisal for her assault; Daisy Mears was properly a person, not a "thing"; neither was she "old," being a month or so younger than Laurence; nor did his loose use of another adjective do credit to his descriptive accuracy. It was true that Daisy's party manners had lacked suavity, true that her extreme vivacity had been uncalled-for, true that she was not beautiful; but she was no thinner than she was stout, and she must have wished to insist upon a recognition of this fact.

She was in the act of rising from a sitting posture upon Laurence when he used the inaccurate word; and he had struggled to his hands and knees, elevating her; but at once she sat again, with violence, flattening him. "Who's skinny?" she inquired.

"You get up off o' me!" he said fiercely.

She rose, laughing with all her shrillness, and Laurence would have risen too, but Miss Mears, shouting, "Hay, there, Mister!" easily pushed him down, for the polished floor was slippery and gave no footing. Laurence tried again, and again the merry damsel aided him to prostrate himself. This mortifying process was repeated and repeated until it attracted the attention of most of the guests, while bumping stopped and the bumpers gathered to look on; even to take an uproarious part in the contest. Some of them pushed Daisy; some of them pushed Laurence; and the latter, furious and scarlet, with his struggling back arched, and his head lowering among his guests' shoes and slippers, uttered many remonstrances in a strangled voice.

Finally, owing to the resentful activity of the fat Eliot boy, who remembered his stummick and pushed Daisy with ungallant vigour, the dishevelled Laurence once more resumed the upright position of a man, but only to find himself closely surrounded by rosily flushed faces, all unpleasantly mirthful at his expense. The universe seemed to be made of protuberant, taunting eyes and noisy open mouths.

"Ya-a-a-ay, Laur-runce!" they vociferated.

A lock of his own hair affected the sight of one of his eyes; a single hair of his late opponent was in his mouth, where he considered a hair of anybody's out of place, and this one peculiarly so, considering its source. Miss Mears herself, still piercing every tympanum with her shrillness, rolled upon the floor but did not protract her hilarity there. Instead she availed herself of him, and with unabated disrespect, came up him hand-over-hand as if he had been a rope.

Then, as he strove to evade her too-familiar grasp, there fell a sorry blow. Beyond the nearer spectators his unhampered eye caught the brazen zigzag gleam of orderly curls moving to the toss of a dainty head; and he heard the voice of Elsie, incurably sweet in tone, but oh, how destroying in the words! Elsie must have heard some grown person say them, and stored them for effective use.

"Pooh! Fighting with that rowdy child!"

"Fightin'?" shouted Miss Mears. "That wasn't fightin'!"

"It wasn't?" Thomas Kimball inquired waggishly. "What was

31

it?" And he added with precocious satire: "I s'pose you call it makin' love!"

To Laurence's horror, Master Kimball's waggish idea spread like a virulent contagion, even to Laurence's most intimate friends. "Ya-a-ay, Laur-runce!" they shouted. "Daisy Mears is your girl! Daisy Mears is Laurunce's girl! Oh, Laur-runce!"

He could only rage and bellow. "She is not! You hush up! I hate her! I hate her worse'n I do anybody!"

But his protests were disallowed and shouted down; the tormentors pranced, pointing at him with hateful forefingers, making other dreadful signs, sickening him unutterably. "Day-zy Mears and Laur-runce Coy! Daisy Mears is Laurunce's girl!"

"She is not!" he bawled. "You hush opp! I hate her! I hate her worse'n I do—worse'n I do—I hate her worse'n I do garbidge!"

It may have been that this comparison, so frankly unbowdlerized, helped to inspire Miss Daisy Mears. More probably what moved her was merely a continuation of the impulse propelling her from the moment of her first fall to the floor upon being accidentally bumped by Laurence. Surprisingly enough, in view of her present elations, Daisy had always been thought a quiet and unobtrusive little girl; indeed, she had always believed herself to be that sort of little girl. Never, until this afternoon, had she attracted special notice at a party, or anywhere else. Her nose, in particular, was almost unfortunately inconspicuous, her hair curled so temporarily, even upon artificial compulsion, that two small pigtails were found to be its best expression. She was the most commonplace of little girls; yet it has never been proved that commonplace people are content with their condition. Finding herself upon the floor and kicking, this afternoon, Daisy Mears discovered, for the first time in her life, that she occupied a prominent position and was being talked about. Then and there rose high the impulse to increase her prominence. What though comment were adverse, she was for once and at last the centre of it! And for some natures, to taste distinction is to determine upon the whole drunken cup: Daisy Mears had entered upon an orgy.

Laurence's choice of a phrase to illustrate the disfavour in which he held her had a striking effect upon all his guests: the little girls were shocked, said "Oh!" and allowed their mouths to remain open indefinitely; the boys were seemingly maddened by their host's free expression—they howled, leaped, beat one another; but the most novel course of action was that adopted by the newly ambitious Daisy. She ran upon Laurence from behind, and threw her arms about him in a manner permitting some question whether

32

her intention might be an embrace or a wrestling match. Her indiscreet words, however, dismissed the doubt.

"He's my dear little pet!" she shouted.

For a moment Laurence was incredulous; then in a dazed way he began to realize his dreadful position. He knew himself to be worse than compromised: a ruinous claim to him seemed upon the point of being established; and all the spectators instantly joined in the effort to establish it. They circled about him, leaping and pointing. They bawled incessantly within the very cup of his ear.

"She is! She is too your girl! She says so herself!"

To Laurence the situation was simply what it would have been to Romeo had an unattractive hoyden publicly claimed him for her own, embracing him in Juliet's presence, with the entire population of Verona boisterously insisting upon the hoyden's right to him. Moreover, Romeo's experience would have given him an advantage over Laurence. Romeo would have known how to point out that it takes two to make a bargain, would have requested the claimant to set forth witnesses or documents; he could have turned the public in his favour, could have extricated himself, and might have done so even with some grace. The Veronese would have respected his argument.

Not so with Laurence's public—for indeed his whole public now surrounded him. This was a public upon whom evidence and argument were wasted; besides, he had neither. He had only a dim kind of reasoning, very hurried—a perception that his only way out was to make his conduct toward Daisy Mears so consistently injurious that neither she nor the public could pretend to believe that anything so monstrous as affection existed between them. And since his conception of the first thing to be done was frankly elemental, it was well for his reputation as a gentleman and a host that his mother and his Aunt Ella happened to come into the living-room just then, bringing some boxes of games and favours. The mob broke up, and hurried in that direction.

Mrs. Coy looked benevolently over their heads, and completely mistaking a gesture of her son, called to him smilingly: "Come, Laurence; you can play tag with little Daisy after a while. Just now we've got some other games for you." Then, as he morosely approached, attended by Daisy, Mrs. Coy offered them a brightly coloured cardboard box. "Here's a nice game," she said, and continued unfortunately: "Since you want to play with Daisy, you can amuse yourselves with that. It's a game for just two."

"I won't!" Laurence returned, and added distinctly: "I rather die!"

"But I thought you wanted to play with little Daisy," Mrs. Coy explained in her surprise. "I thought—"

"I rather die!" said Laurence, speaking so that everybody might hear him. "I rather die a hunderd times!" And that no one at all might mistake his meaning, he concluded: "I'd rather eat a million boxes of rat-poison than play with her!"

So firm and loud a declaration of preference, especially in the unpreferred person's presence, caused a slight embarrassment to Mrs. Coy. "But Laurence, dear," she began, "you mustn't—"

"I would!" he insisted. "I rather eat a million, million boxes of rat-poison than play with her! She—"

"She's your girl!"

The sly interruption stopped him. It came from a person to be identified only as one of a group clustering about his Aunt Ella's boxes; and it was accompanied by a general giggle but half-suppressed in spite of the adult presences.

"You hush opp!" Laurence shouted.

"Laurence! Laurence!" said Mrs. Coy. "What is the matter, dear? It seems to me you're really not at all polite to poor little Daisy."

Laurence pursued the line of conduct he had set for himself as his only means of safety. "I wouldn't be polite to her," he said; "I wouldn't be polite to her if I had to eat a million—"

"Laurence!"

"I wouldn't!" he stoutly maintained. "Not if I had to eat a million, million—"

"Never mind!" his mother said with some emphasis. "Plenty of the other boys will be delighted to play with dear little Daisy."

"No," said Daisy brightly, "I got to play with Laurence."

Laurence looked at her. When a grown person looks at another in that way, it is time for the police, and Mrs. Coy was conscious of an emergency. She took Laurence by the shoulders, faced him about and told him to run and play with some one else; then she turned back to Daisy. "We'll find some nice little boy—" she began. But Daisy had followed Laurence.

She gave him a lively tap on the shoulder. "Got your tag!" she cried, and darted away, but as he did not follow, she returned to him. "Well, what are we goin' to play?" she inquired.

Laurence gave her another look. "You hang around me a little longer," he said, "an' I'll—I'll—I'll—"

Again came the giggled whisper:

"She's your girl!"

Laurence ran amuck. Head down, he charged into the group whence came the whisper, and successfully dispersed it. The component parts fled, squawking; Laurence pursued; boys tripped one another, wrestled, skirmished in groups; and, such moods being instantly contagious among males under twelve, many joined in the assault with a liveliness not remote, at least in appearance, from lunacy.

"Laurence! Laurence!" his mother exclaimed in vain, for he was the chief disturber; but he was too actively occupied in that capacity to be aware of her. She and Aunt Ella could only lament and begin to teach the little girls and two or three of the older and nobler boys to "play games," while troups of gangsters swept out of the room, then through it and out again, through other rooms, through halls and then were heard whooping and thumping on the front stairway.

One little girl was not with the rather insulted players of the cardboard games in the living-room. She accompanied the gangsters, rioting with the best, her little muslin skirt fluttering with the speed of her going; while ever was heard, with slight intermission, her piercing battle-cry: "Hay, there, Mister! I'll show you!" But the male chorus had a new libretto to work from, evidently: all through the house, upstairs, downstairs and in my lady's chamber, their merciless gaieties resounded:

"Ya-a-ay, Laur-runce! Wait for your girl! Your girl wants you, Laurunce!"

"What a curious child that Daisy Mears is!" Aunt Ella said to Laurence's mother. "I'd always thought she was such a quiet little girl."

"'Quiet!'" Mrs. Coy exclaimed. And then as a series of shocks overhead noticeably jarred the ceiling, she started. "Good heavens! They're upstairs—they'll have the roof on us!"

She hurried into the hall, but the outlaws were already descending. Just ahead of them plunged Laurence, fleeing like some rabid thing. Behind him, in the ruck of boys, Daisy Mears seemed to reach for him at the full length of her extended arms; and so the rout went on and out through the open front doors to the yard, where still was heard above all other cries, "Hay, there, Mister! I'll show you!"

Mrs. Coy returned helplessly to the guests of sweeter behaviour, and did what she could to amuse them, but presently she was drawn to a window by language without.

It was the voice of her son in frenzy. He stood on the lawn, swinging a rake about him circularly. "Let her try it!" he said. "Let her try it just once more, an' I'll show her!"

For audience, out of reach of the rake, he had Daisy Mears and all his male guests save the two or three spiritless well-mannered at feeble play in the living-room; and this entire audience, including Miss Mears, replied in chanting chorus: "Daisy Mears an' Laurunce Coy! She's your girl!" Such people are hard to convince.

Laurence swung the rake, repeating:

"Just let her try it; that's all I ast! Just let her try to come near me again!"

"Laurence!" said his mother from the window.

He looked up, and there was the sincerest bitterness in his tone as he said: "Well, I stood enough around here this afternoon!"

"Put down the rake," she said. "The idea of shaking a rake at a little girl!"

The idea she mentioned seemed reasonable to Laurence, in his present state of mind, and in view of what he had endured. "I bet you'd shake it at her," he said, "if she'd been doin' to you what she's been doin' to me!"

Now, from Mrs. Coy's standpoint, that was nothing short of grotesque; yet actually there was something in what he said. Mrs. Coy was in love with Mr. Coy; and if another man—one whom she disliked and thought homely and unattractive—had bumped into her at a party, upsetting her frequently, sitting on her, pushing her over repeatedly as she attempted to rise, then embracing her and claiming her as his own, and following her about, and pursuing her even when she fled, insisting upon his claim to her and upon embracing her again and again, causing Mr. Coy to criticize her with outspoken superiority—and if all this had taken place with the taunting connivance of absolutely every one of the best people she knew—why, under such parallel circumstances, Mrs. Coy might or might not have armed herself with a rake, but this would have depended, probably, on whether or not there was a rake handy, and supposing there was, upon whether or not she became too hysterical to use it.

Mrs. Coy had no realization whatever that any such parallel could be drawn; she coldly suggested that the party was being spoiled and that Laurence might well be ashamed of himself. "It's really very naughty of you," she said; and at a word from Aunt Ella, she added: "Now you've all had enough of this rough romping and you must come in quietly and behave yourselves like little gentlemen—and like a little lady! The pianist from the dancing-school has come, and dear little Elsie Threamer is going to do her fancy dance for us."

With that, under her eye, the procession filed into the house—and took seats in the living-room without any renewal of undesirable demonstrations. Laurence had the brooding air of a person who has been dangerously trifled with; but he seated himself in an orderly manner, and unfortunately did not observe which of his guests just afterward came to occupy the next chair. Elsie, exquisitely dainty, a lovely sight, was standing alone in the open space in the centre of the room.

The piano rippled out a tinkling run of little bells, and the graceful child began to undulate and pirouette. Her conscientious eyes she kept all the while downcast, with never a glance to any spectator, least of all to the lorn Laurence; but he had a miserable sense of what those veiled eyes thought about him, and he felt low and contaminated by the repulsive events connected with another of his guests. As he dumbly looked at Elsie, while she danced so prettily, beautiful things seemed to be floating about him in a summer sky: angels like pigeons with lovely faces, large glass globes in rainbow colours, and round, pure white icing cakes. His spiritual nature was uplifted; and almost his sufferings had left him, when his spine chilled at a sound behind him—a choked giggle and a hoarse but piercing whisper.

"Look at who Laurence is sittin' by! Oh, oh!"

He turned and found Daisy in the chair next to his. Her small bright eyes were fixed upon him in an intolerable mirth; her shoulders were humped with the effect to control that same, and her right hand tensely covered her mouth. From behind him came further gurgles and the words:

"Sittin' by his girl!"

At this moment Elsie was just concluding her dance with a series of charming curtseys. Laurence could not wait for them to be finished; he jumped from his chair, and crossed before the lovely dancer to a seat on the other side of the room, a titter following him. More than the titter followed him, in fact. Daisy walked on tiptoe just behind him.

But when she reached the centre of the room, she was suddenly inspired by the perception of a new way to increase her noticeableness. She paused before the curtseying danseuse and also sank in curtseys as deep, though not so adept. Then she too began to dance, and the piano having stopped, accompanied herself by singing loudly, "Ti-didy-um-tum, dee-dee-dee!" She pirouetted, undulated, hopped on one leg with the other stiff and rather high before her; she pranced in a posture of outrageous convexity from one point of view, of incredible concavity from the other. Then she curtsied again, in recognizable burlesque of the original, and flounced into the chair next to Laurence's, for he had been so shortsighted as to leave a vacancy beside him. This time his Aunt Ella had to take him out into the hall by force and talk to him.

A little later, when ice-cream, paper caps, and favours had been distributed, the party was over; and among those who presented themselves in the polite formalities of leavetaking was, naturally, Daisy Mears. On account of continued surveillance on the part of his Aunt Ella, Laurence was unable to respond in words, but his expression said a thousand eloquent things for him.

Daisy curtsied demurely. "G'by. Thank you for a wunnaful time, Laurence," she said; and went out of the house with a character that had changed permanently during the brief course of a children's party.

As for Laurence, he had been through a dog's time; and he showed it. Every night, after he said his bedside prayers, there was an additional rite his mother had arranged for him; he was to say: "I know that I have a character, and I know that I am a soul." But to-night he balked.

"Go on," his mother bade him. "Say it, Laurence."

"I doe' want to," he said dully.

Mrs. Coy sighed. "I don't know what's the matter with you: you behave so queerly sometimes! Don't you know you ought to appreciate what your mamma does for you—when she went to all the trouble to give you a nice party just to make you happy? Oughtn't you to do what she wants you to, to pay her for all that happiness?"

"I guess so." The poor child somehow believed it—but as he went through his formula and muttered that he knew he had a character, it is probable that he felt a strong doubt in the matter. This may have caused his aversion to saying it.

THE ONE-HUNDRED-DOLLAR BILL

THE new one-hundred-dollar bill, clean and green, freshening the heart with the colour of springtime, slid over the glass of the teller's counter and passed under his grille to a fat hand, dingy on the knuckles, but brightened by a flawed diamond. This interesting hand was a part of one of those men who seem to have too much fattened muscle for their clothes: his shoulders distended his overcoat; his calves strained the sprightly checked cloth, a little soiled, of his trousers; his short neck bulged above the glossy collar. His hat, round and black as a pot, and appropriately small, he wore slightly obliqued; while under its curled brim his small eyes twinkled surreptitiously between those upper and nether puffs of flesh that mark the too faithful practitioner of unhallowed gaieties. Such was the first individual owner of the new one-hundred-dollar bill, and he at once did what might have been expected of him.

Moving away from the teller's grille, he made a cylindrical packet of bills smaller in value—"ones" and "fives"—then placed round them, as a wrapper, the beautiful one-hundred-dollar bill, snapped a rubber band over it; and the desired inference was plain: a roll all of hundred-dollar bills, inside as well as outside. Something more was plain, too: obviously the man's small head had a sportive plan in it, for the twinkle between his eye-puffs hinted of liquor in the offing and lively women impressed by a show of masterly riches. Here, in brief, was a man who meant to make a night of it; who would feast, dazzle, compel deference, and be loved. For money gives power, and power is loved; no doubt he would be loved. He was happy, and went out of the bank believing that money is made for joy.

So little should we be certain of our happiness in this world: the splendid one-hundred-dollar bill was taken from him untimely, before nightfall that very evening. At the corner of two busy streets he parted with it to the law, though in a mood of excruciating reluctance and only after a cold-blooded threatening on the part of the lawyer. This latter walked away thoughtfully, with the one-hundred-dollar bill, now not quite so clean, in his pocket.

Collinson was the lawyer's name, and in years he was only twenty-eight, but already had the slightly harried appearance that marks the young husband who begins to suspect that the better part of his life has been his bachelorhood. His dark, ready-made clothes, his twice-soled shoes and his hair, which was too long for a neat and businesslike aspect, were symptoms of necessary economy; but he did not wear the eager look of a man who saves to "get on for himself": Collinson's look was that of an employed man who only deepens his rut with his pacing of it.

An employed man he was, indeed; a lawyer without much hope of ever seeing his name on the door or on the letters of the firm that employed him, and his most important work was the collection of small debts. This one-hundred-dollar bill now in his pocket was such a collection, small to the firm and the client, though of a noble size to himself and the long-pursued debtor from whom he had just collected it.

The banks were closed; so was the office, for it was six o'clock, and Collinson was on his way home when by chance he encountered the debtor: there was nothing to do but to keep the bill over night. This was no hardship, however, as he had a faint pleasure in the unfamiliar experience of walking home with such a thing in his pocket; and he felt a little important by proxy when he thought of it.

Upon the city the November evening had come down dark and moist, holding the smoke nearer the ground and enveloping the buildings in a soiling black mist. Lighted windows and street lamps appeared and disappeared in the altering thicknesses of fog, but at intervals, as Collinson walked on northward, he passed a small shop, or a cluster of shops, where the light was close to him and bright, and at one of these oases of illumination he lingered a moment, with a thought to buy a toy in the window for his three-year-old little girl. The toy was a gaily coloured acrobatic monkey that willingly climbed up and down a string, and he knew that the "baby," as he and his wife still called their child, would scream with delight at the sight of it. He hesitated, staring into the window rather longingly, and wondering if he ought to make such a purchase. He had twelve dollars of his own in his pocket, but the toy was marked "35 cents" and he decided he could not afford it. So he sighed and went on, turning presently into a darker street.

Here the air was like that of a busy freight-yard, thick with coal-dust and at times almost unbreathable so that Collinson was glad to get out of it even though the exchange was for the early-evening smells of the cheap apartment house where he lived.

His own "kitchenette" was contributing its share, he found, the baby was crying over some inward perplexity not to be explained; and his wife, pretty and a little frowzy, was as usual, and as he had expected. That is to say, he found her irritated by cooking, bored by the baby, and puzzled by the dull life she led. Other women, it appeared, had happy and luxurious homes, and, during the malnutritious dinner she had prepared, she mentioned many such women by name, laying particular stress upon the achievements of their husbands. Why should she ("alone," as she put it) lead the life she did in one room and a kitchenette, without even being able to afford to go to the movies more than once or twice a month? Mrs. Theodore Thompson's husband had bought a perfectly beautiful little sedan automobile; he gave his wife everything she wanted. Mrs. Will Gregory had merely mentioned that her old Hudson seal coat was wearing a little, and her husband had instantly said, "What'll a new one come to, girlie? Four or five hundred? Run and get it!" Why were other women's husbands like that—and why, oh, why! was hers like this? An eavesdropper might well have deduced from Mrs. Collinson's harangue that her husband owned somewhere a storehouse containing all the good things she wanted and that he withheld them from her out of his perverse wilfulness. Moreover, he did not greatly help his case by protesting that the gratification of her desires was beyond his powers.

"My goodness!" he said. "You talk as if I had sedans and sealskin coats and theatre tickets on me! Well, I haven't; that's all!"

"Then go out and get 'em!" she said fiercely. "Go out and get 'em!"

"What with?" he inquired. "I have twelve dollars in my pocket, and a balance of seventeen dollars at the bank; that's twenty-nine. I get twenty-five from the office day after to-morrow—Saturday; that makes fifty-four; but we have to pay forty-five for rent on Monday; so that'll leave us nine dollars. Shall I buy you a sedan and a sealskin coat on Tuesday out of the nine?"

Mrs. Collinson began to weep a little. "The old, old story!" she said. "Six long, long years it's been going on now! I ask you how much you've got, and you say, 'Nine dollars,' or 'Seven dollars,' or 'Four dollars'; and once it was sixty-five cents! Sixty-five cents; that's what we have to live on! Sixty-five cents!"

"Oh, hush!" he said wearily.

"Hadn't you better hush a little yourself?" she retorted. "You come home with twelve dollars in your pocket and tell your wife to hush! That's nice! Why can't you do what decent men do?"

"What's that?"

"Why, give their wives something to live for. What do you give me, I'd like to know! Look at the clothes I wear, please!"

"Well, it's your own fault," he muttered.

"What did you say? Did you say it's my fault I wear clothes any woman I know wouldn't be seen in?"

"Yes, I did. If you hadn't made me get you that platinum ring—"

"What!" she cried, and flourished her hand at him across the table. "Look at it! It's platinum, yes; but look at the stone in it, about

41

the size of a pin-head, so't I'm ashamed to wear it when any of my friends see me! A hundred and sixteen dollars is what this magnificent ring cost you, and how long did I have to beg before I got even that little out of you? And it's the best thing I own and the only thing I ever did get out of you!"

"Oh, Lordy!" he moaned.

"I wish you'd seen Charlie Loomis looking at this ring to-day," she said, with a desolate laugh. "He happened to notice it, and I saw him keep glancing at it, and I wish you'd seen Charlie Loomis's expression!"

Collinson's own expression became noticeable upon her introduction of this name; he stared at her gravely until he completed the mastication of one of the indigestibles she had set before him; then he put down his fork and said:

"So you saw Charlie Loomis again to-day. Where?"

"Oh, my!" she sighed. "Have we got to go over all that again?"

"Over all what?"

"Over all the fuss you made the last time I mentioned Charlie's name. I thought we settled it you were going to be a little more sensible about him."

"Yes," Collinson returned. "I was going to be more sensible about him, because you were going to be more sensible about him. Wasn't that the agreement?"

She gave him a hard glance, tossed her head so that the curls of her bobbed hair fluttered prettily, and with satiric mimicry repeated his question: "'Agreement! Wasn't that the agreement?' Oh, my, but you do make me tired, talking about 'agreements'! As if it was a crime my going to a vaudeville matinée with a man kind enough to notice that my husband never takes me anywhere!"

"Did you go to a vaudeville with him to-day?"

"No, I didn't!" she said. "I was talking about the time when you made such a fuss. I didn't go anywhere with him to-day."

"I'm glad to hear it," Collinson said. "I wouldn't have stood for it."

"Oh, you wouldn't?" she cried, and added a shrill laugh as further comment. "You 'wouldn't have stood for it!' How very, very dreadful!"

"Never mind," he returned doggedly. "We went over all that the last time, and you understand me: I'll have no more foolishness about Charlie Loomis."

"How nice of you! He's a friend of yours; you go with him yourself; but your wife mustn't even look at him just because he happens to be the one man that amuses her a little. That's fine!"

"Never mind," Collinson said again. "You say you saw him to-day. I want to know where."

"Suppose I don't choose to tell you."

"You'd better tell me, I think."

"Do you? I've got to answer for every minute of my day, do I?"

"I want to know where you saw Charlie Loomis."

She tossed her curls again, and laughed. "Isn't it funny!" she said. "Just because I like a man, he's the one person I can't have anything to do with! Just because he's kind and jolly and amusing and I like his jokes and his thoughtfulness toward a woman, when he's with her, I'm not to be allowed to see him at all! But my husband—oh, that's entirely different! He can go out with Charlie whenever he likes and have a good time, while I stay home and wash the dishes! Oh, it's a lovely life!"

"Where did you see him to-day?"

Instead of answering his question, she looked at him plaintively, and allowed tears to shine along her lower eyelids. "Why do you treat me like this?" she asked in a feeble voice. "Why can't I have a man friend if I want to? I do like Charlie Loomis. I do like him—"

"Yes! That's what I noticed!"

"Well, but what's the good of always insulting me about him? He has time on his hands of afternoons, and so have I. Our janitor's wife is crazy about the baby and just adores to have me leave her in their flat—the longer the better. Why shouldn't I go to a matinée or a picture-show sometimes with Charlie? Why should I just have to sit around instead of going out and having a nice time when he wants me to?"

"I want to know where you saw him to-day!"

Mrs. Collinson jumped up. "You make me sick!" she said, and began to clear away the dishes.

"I want to know where—"

"Oh, hush up!" she cried. "He came here to leave a note for you."

"Oh," said her husband. "I beg your pardon. That's different."

"How sweet of you!"

"Where's the note, please?"

She took it from her pocket and tossed it to him. "So long as it's a note for you it's all right, of course!" she said. "I wonder what you'd do if he'd written one to me!"

"Never mind," said Collinson, and read the note.

Dear Collie: Dave and Smithie and Old Bill and Sammy Hoag and maybe Steinie and Sol are coming over to the shack about eight-

43

thirt. Home-brew and the old pastime. You know! Don't fail.— Charlie.

"You've read this, of course," Collinson said. "The envelope wasn't sealed."

"I have not," his wife returned, covering the prevarication with a cold dignity. "I'm not in the habit of reading other peoples's correspondence, thank you! I suppose you think I do so because you'd never hesitate to read any note I get; but I don't do everything you do, you see!"

"Well, you can read it now," he said, and gave her the note.

Her eyes swept the writing briefly, and she made a sound of wonderment, as if amazed to find herself so true a prophet. "And the words weren't more than out of mouth! You can go and have a grand party right in his flat, while your wife stays home and gets the baby to bed and washes the dishes!"

"I'm not going."

"Oh, no!" she said mockingly. "I suppose not! I see you missing one of Charlie's stag-parties!"

"I'll miss this one."

But it was not to Mrs. Collinson's purpose that he should miss the party; she wished him to be as intimate as possible with the debonair Charlie Loomis; and so, after carrying some dishes into the kitchenette in meditative silence, she reappeared with a changed manner. She went to her husband, gave him a shy little pat on the shoulder and laughed good-naturedly. "Of course you'll go," she said. "I do think you're silly about my never going out with him when it would give me a little innocent pleasure and when you're not home to take me, yourself; but I wasn't really in such terrible earnest, all I said. You work hard the whole time, honey, and the only pleasure you ever do have, it's when you get a chance to go to one of these little penny-ante stag-parties. You haven't been to one for ever so long, and you never stay after twelve; it's really all right with me. I want you to go."

"Oh, no," said Collinson. "It's only penny-ante, but I couldn't afford to lose anything at all."

"But you never do. You always win a little."

"I know," he said. "I've figured out I'm about sixteen dollars ahead at penny-ante on the whole year. I cleaned up seven dollars and sixty cents at Charlie's last party; but of course my luck might change, and we couldn't afford it."

"If you did lose, it'd only be a few cents," she said. "What's the difference, if it gives you a little fun? You'll work all the better if you go out and enjoy yourself once in a while."

"Well, if you really look at it that way, I'll go."

"That's right, dear," she said, smiling. "Better put on a fresh collar and your other suit, hadn't you?"

"I suppose so," he assented, and began to make the changes she suggested. He went about them in a leisurely way, played with the baby at intervals, while Mrs. Collinson sang cheerfully over her work; and when he had completed his toilet, it was time for him to go. She came in from the kitchenette, kissed him, and then looked up into his eyes, letting him see a fond and brightly amiable expression.

"There, honey," she said. "Run along and have a nice time. Then maybe you'll be a little more sensible about some of my little pleasures."

He held the one-hundred-dollar bill, folded, in his hand, meaning to leave it with her, but as she spoke a sudden recurrence of suspicion made him forget his purpose. "Look here," he said. "I'm not making any bargain with you. You talk as if you thought I was going to let you run around to vaudevilles with Charlie because you let me go to this party. Is that your idea?"

It was, indeed, precisely Mrs. Collinson's idea, and she was instantly angered enough to admit it in her retort. "Oh, aren't you mean!" she cried. "I might know better than to look for any fairness in a man like you!"

"See here—"

"Oh, hush up!" she said. "Shame on you! Go on to your party!" With that she put both hands upon his breast, and pushed him toward the door.

"I won't go. I'll stay here."

"You will, too, go!" she cried shrewishly. "I don't want to look at you around here all evening. It'd make me sick to look at a man without an ounce of fairness in his whole mean little body!"

"All right," said Collinson, violently, "I will go!"

"Yes! Get out of my sight!"

And he did, taking the one-hundred-dollar bill with him to the penny-ante poker party.

The gay Mr. Charlie Loomis called his apartment "the shack" in jocular depreciation of its beauty and luxury, but he regarded it as a perfect thing, and in one way it was; for it was perfectly in the family likeness of a thousand such "shacks." It had a ceiling with false beams, walls of green burlap spotted with coloured "coaching prints," brown shelves supporting pewter plates and mugs, "mission" chairs, a leather couch with violent cushions, silver-framed photographs of lady-friends and officer-friends, a drop-light of pink-shot imitation alabaster, a papier-mâché skull tobacco-jar

45

among moving-picture magazines on the round card-table; and, of course, the final Charlie Loomis touch—a Japanese man-servant.

The master of all this was one of those neat, stoutish young men with fat, round heads, sleek, fair hair, immaculate, pale complexions and infirm little pink mouths—in fact, he was of the type that may suggest to the student of resemblances a fastidious and excessively clean white pig with transparent ears. Nevertheless, Charlie Loomis was of a free-handed habit in some matters, being particularly indulgent to pretty women and their children. He spoke of the latter as "the kiddies," of course, and liked to call their mothers "kiddo," or "girlie." One of his greatest pleasures was to tell a woman that she was "the dearest, bravest little girlie in the world." Naturally he was a welcome guest in many households, and would often bring a really magnificent toy to the child of some friend whose wife he was courting. Moreover, at thirty-three, he had already done well enough in business to take things easily, and he liked to give these little card-parties, not for gain, but for pastime. He was cautious and disliked high stakes in a game of chance.

That is to say, he disliked the possibility of losing enough money to annoy him, though of course he set forth his principles as resting upon a more gallant and unselfish basis. "I don't consider it hospitality to have any man go out o' my shack sore," he was wont to say. "Myself, I'm a bachelor and got no obligations; I'll shoot any man that can afford it for anything he wants to. Trouble is, you never can tell when a man can't afford it, or what harm his losin' might mean to the little girlie at home and the kiddies. No, boys, penny-ante and ten-cent limit is the highest we go in this ole shack. Penny-ante and a few steins of the ole home-brew that hasn't got a divorce in a barrel of it!"

Penny-ante and the ole home-brew had been in festal operation for half an hour when the morose Collinson arrived this evening. Mr. Loomis and his guests sat about the round table under the alabaster drop-light; their coats were off; cigars were worn at the deliberative poker angle; colourful chips and cards glistened on the cloth; one of the players wore a green shade over his eyes; and all in all, here was a little poker party for a lithograph. To complete the picture, several of the players continued to concentrate upon their closely held cards, and paid no attention to the newcomer or to their host's lively greeting of him.

"Ole Collie, b'gosh!" Mr. Loomis shouted, humorously affecting the bucolic. "Here's your vacant cheer; stack all stuck out for you 'n' ever'thin'! Set daown, neighbour, an' Smithie'll deal you in, next hand. What made you so late? Helpin' the little girlie at home get the kiddy to bed? That's a great kiddy of yours, Collie. I got a little Christmas gift for her I'm goin' to bring around some day soon. Yes, sir, that's a great little kiddy Collie's got over at his place, boys."

Collinson took the chair that had been left for him, counted his chips, and then as the playing of a "hand" still preoccupied three of the company, he picked up a silver dollar that lay upon the table near him. "What's this?" he asked. "A side bet? Or did somebody just leave it here for me?"

"Yes; for you to look at," Mr. Loomis explained. "It's Smithie's."

"What's wrong with it?"

"Nothin'. Smithie was just showin' it to us. Look at it."

Collinson turned the coin over and saw a tiny inscription that had been lined into the silver with a point of steel. " 'Luck,' " he read;—" 'Luck hurry back to me!' " Then he spoke to the owner of this marked dollar. "I suppose you put that on there, Smithie, to help make sure of getting our money to-night."

But Smithie shook his head, which was a large, gaunt head, as it happened—a head fronted with a sallow face shaped much like a coffin, but inconsistently genial in expression. "No," he said. "It just came in over my counter this afternoon, and I noticed it when I was checkin' up the day's cash. Funny, ain't it: 'Luck hurry back to me!' "

"Who do you suppose marked that on it?" Collinson said thoughtfully.

"Golly!" his host exclaimed. "It won't do you much good to wonder about that!"

Collinson frowned, continuing to stare at the marked dollar. "I guess not, but really I should like to know."

"I would, too," Smithie said. "I been thinkin' about it. Might 'a' been somebody in Seattle or somebody in Ipswich, Mass., or New Orleans or St. Paul. How you goin' to tell? Might 'a' been a woman; might 'a' been a man. The way I guess it out, this poor boob, whoever he was, well, prob'ly he'd had good times for a while, and maybe carried this dollar for a kind of pocket piece, the way some people do, you know. Then he got in trouble—or she did, whichever it was—and got flat broke and had to spend this last dollar he had— for something to eat, most likely. Well, he thought a while before he spent it, and the way I guess it out, he said to himself, he said, 'Well,' he said, 'most of the good luck I've enjoyed lately,' he said, 'it's been while I had this dollar on me. I got to kiss 'em good-bye now, good luck and good dollar together; but maybe I'll get 'em both back some day, so I'll just mark the wish on the dollar, like this: Luck hurry back to me! That'll help some, maybe, and anyhow I'll know my luck dollar if I ever do get it back.' That's the way I guess it out, anyhow. It's funny how some people like to believe luck depends on some little thing like that."

"Yes, it is," Collinson assented, still brooding over the coin.

The philosophic Smithie extended his arm across the table, collecting the cards to deal them, for the "hand" was finished. "Yes, sir, it's funny," he repeated. "Nobody knows exactly what luck is, but the way I guess it out, it lays in a man's believin' he's in luck, and some little object like this makes him kind of concentrate his mind on thinkin' he's goin' to be lucky, because of course you often know you're goin' to win, and then you do win. You don't win when you want to win, or when you need to; you win when you believe you'll win. I don't know who was the dummy that said, 'Money's the root of all evil'; but I guess he didn't have too much sense! I suppose if some man killed some other man for a dollar, the poor fish that said that would let the man out and send the dollar to the chair. No, sir; money's just as good as it is bad; and it'll come your way if you feel it will; so you take this marked dollar o' mine—"

But here this garrulous and discursive guest was interrupted by immoderate protests from several of his colleagues. "Cut it out!" "My Lord!" "Do something!" "Smithie! Are you ever goin' to deal?"

"I'm goin' to shuffle first," he responded, suiting the action to the word, though with deliberation, and at the same time continuing his discourse. "It's a mighty interesting thing, a piece o' money. You take this dollar, now: Who's it belonged to? Where's it been? What different kind o' funny things has it been spent for sometimes? What funny kind of secrets do you suppose it could 'a' heard if it had ears? Good people have had it and bad people have had it: why, a dollar could tell more about the human race—why, it could tell all about it!"

"I guess it couldn't tell all about the way you're dealin' these cards," said the man with the green shade. "You're mixin' things all up."

"I'll straighten 'em all out then," said Smithie cheerfully. "I knew of a twenty-dollar bill once; a pickpocket prob'ly threw it in the gutter to keep from havin' it found on him when they searched him, but anyway a woman I knew found it and sent it to her young sister out in Michigan to take some music lessons with, and the sister was so excited she took this bill out of the letter and kissed it. That's where they thought she got the germ she died of a couple o' weeks later, and the undertaker got the twenty-dollar bill, and got robbed of it the same night. Nobody knows where it went then. They say, 'Money talks.' Golly! If it could talk, what couldn't it tell? Nobody'd be safe. I got this dollar now, but who's it goin' to belong to next, and what'll he do with it? And then after that! Why for years

48

and years and years it'll go on from one pocket to another, in a millionaire's house one day, in some burglar's flat the next, maybe, and in one person's hand money'll do good, likely, and in another's it'll do harm. We all want money; but some say it's a bad thing, like that dummy I was talkin' about. Lordy! Goodness or badness, I'll take all anybody—"

He was interrupted again, and with increased vehemence. Collinson, who sat next to him, complied with the demand to "ante up," then placed the dollar near his little cylinders of chips, and looked at his cards. They proved unencouraging, and he turned to his neighbour. "I'd sort of like to have that marked dollar, Smithie," he said. "I'll give you a paper dollar and a nickel for it."

But Smithie laughed, shook his head, and slid the coin over toward his own chips. "No, sir. I'm goin' to keep it—awhile, anyway."

"So you do think it'll bring you luck, after all!"

"No. But I'll hold onto it for this evening, anyhow."

"Not if we clean you out, you won't," said Charlie Loomis. "You know the rules o' the ole shack: only cash goes in this game; no I. O. U. stuff ever went here or ever will. Tell you what I'll do, though, before you lose it: I'll give you a dollar and a quarter for your ole silver dollar, Smithie."

"Oh, you want it, too, do you? I guess I can spot what sort of luck you want it for, Charlie."

"Well, Mr. Bones, what sort of luck do I want it for?"

"You win, Smithie," one of the other players said. "We all know what sort o' luck ole Charlie wants your dollar for—he wants it for luck with the dames."

"Well, I might," Charlie admitted, not displeased. "I haven't been so lucky that way lately—not so dog-gone lucky!"

All of his guests, except one, laughed at this; but Collinson frowned, still staring at the marked dollar. For a reason he could not have put into words just then, it began to seem almost vitally important to him to own this coin if he could, and to prevent Charlie Loomis from getting possession of it. The jibe, "He wants it for luck with the dames," rankled in Collinson's mind: somehow it seemed to refer to his wife.

"I'll tell you what I'll do, Smithie," he said. "I'll bet two dollars against that dollar of yours that I hold a higher hand next deal than you do."

"Here! Here!" Charlie remonstrated. "Shack rules! Ten-cent limit."

"That's only for the game," Collinson said, turning upon his host with a sudden sharpness. "This is an outside bet between

Smithie and me. Will you do it, Smithie? Where's your sporting spirit?"

So liberal a proposal at once roused the spirit to which it appealed. "Well, I might, if some o' the others'll come in too, and make it really worth my while."

"I'm in," the host responded with prompt inconsistency; and others of the party, it appeared, were desirous of owning the talisman. They laughed and said it was "crazy stuff," yet they all "came in," and, for the first time in the history of this "shack," what Mr. Loomis called "real money" was seen upon the table as a stake. It was won, and the silver dollar with it, by the largest and oldest of the gamesters, a fat man with a walrus moustache that inevitably made him known in this circle as "Old Bill." He smiled condescendingly, and would have put the dollar in his pocket with the "real money," but Mr. Loomis protested.

"Here! What you doin'?" he shouted, catching Old Bill by the arm. "Put that dollar back on the table."

"What for?"

"What for? Why, we're goin' to play for it again. Here's two dollars against it I beat you on the next hand."

"No," said Old Bill calmly. "It's worth more than two dollars to me. It's worth five."

"Well, five then," his host returned. "I want that dollar!"

"So do I," said Collinson. "I'll put in five dollars if you do."

"Anybody else in?" Old Bill inquired, dropping the coin on the table; and all of the others again "came in." Old Bill won again; but once more Charlie Loomis prevented him from putting the silver dollar in his pocket.

"Come on now!" Mr. Loomis exclaimed. "Anybody else but me in on this for five dollars next time?"

"I am," said Collinson, swallowing with a dry throat; and he set forth all that remained to him of his twelve dollars. In return he received a pair of deuces, and the jubilant Charlie won.

He was vainglorious in his triumph. "Didn't that little luck piece just keep on tryin' to find the right man?" he cried, and read the inscription loudly. " 'Luck hurry back to me!' Righto! You're home where you belong, girlie! Now we'll settle down to our reg'lar little game again."

"Oh, no," said Old Bill. "You wouldn't let me keep it. Put it out there and play for it again."

"I won't. She's mine now."

"I want my luck piece back myself," said Smithie. "Put it out and play for it. You made Old Bill."

"I won't do it."

50

"Yes, you will," Collinson said, and he spoke without geniality. "You put it out there."

"Oh, yes, I will," Mr. Loomis returned mockingly. "I will for ten dollars."

"Not I," said Old Bill. "Five is foolish enough." And Smithie agreed with him. "Nor me!"

"All right, then. If you're afraid of ten, I keep it. I thought the ten'd scare you."

"Put that dollar on the table," Collinson said. "I'll put ten against it."

There was a little commotion among these mild gamesters; and someone said, "You're crazy, Collie. What do you want to do that for?"

"I don't care," said Collinson. "That dollar's already cost me enough, and I'm going after it."

"Well, you see, I want it, too," Charlie Loomis retorted cheerfully; and he appealed to the others. "I'm not askin' him to put up ten against it, am I?"

"Maybe not," Old Bill assented. "But how long is this thing goin' to keep on? It's already balled our game all up, and if we keep on foolin' with these side bets, why, what's the use?"

"My goodness!" the host exclaimed. "I'm not pushin' this thing, am I? I don't want to risk my good old luck piece, do I? It's Collie that's crazy to go on, ain't it?" He laughed. "He hasn't showed his money yet, though, I notice, and this ole shack is run on strickly cash principles. I don't believe he's got ten dollars more on him!"

"Oh, yes, I have."

"Let's see it then."

Collinson's nostrils distended a little; but he said nothing, fumbled in his pocket, and then tossed the one-hundred-dollar bill, rather crumpled, upon the table.

"Great heavens!" shouted Old Bill. "Call the doctor: I'm all of a swoon!"

"Look at what's spilled over our nice clean table!" another said, in an awed voice. "Did you claim he didn't have ten on him, Charlie?"

"Well, it's nice to look at," Smithie observed. "But I'm with Old Bill. How long are you two goin' to keep this thing goin'? If Collie wins the luck piece, I suppose Charlie'll bet him fifteen against it, and then—"

"No, I won't," Charlie interrupted. "Ten's the limit."

"Goin' to keep on bettin' ten against it all night?"

"No," said Charlie. "I tell you what I'll do with you, Collinson; we both of us seem kind o' set on this luck piece, and you're already

51

out some on it. I'll give you a square chance at it and at catchin' even. It's twenty minutes after nine. I'll keep on these side bets with you till ten o'clock, but when my clock hits ten, we're through, and the one that's got it then keeps it, and no more foolin'. You want to do that, or quit now? I'm game either way."

"Go ahead and deal," said Collinson. "Whichever one of us has it at ten o'clock, it's his, and we quit."

But when the little clock on Charlie's green-painted mantel shelf struck ten, the luck piece was Charlie's and with it an overwhelming lien on the one-hundred-dollar bill. He put both in his pocket; "Remember this ain't my fault; it was you that insisted," he said, and handed Collinson four five-dollar bills as change.

Old Bill, platonically interested, discovered that his cigar was sparkless, applied a match, and casually set forth his opinion. "Well, I guess that was about as poor a way of spendin' eighty dollars as I ever saw, but it all goes to show there's truth in the old motto that anything at all can happen in any poker game! That was a mighty nice hundred-dollar bill you had on you, Collie; but it's like what Smithie said: a piece o' money goes hoppin' around from one person to another—it don't care!—and yours has gone and hopped to Charlie. The question is, Who's it goin' to hop to next?" He paused to laugh, glanced over the cards that had been dealt him, and concluded: "My guess is 't some good-lookin' woman'll prob'ly get a pretty fair chunk o' that hundred-dollar bill out o' Charlie. Well, let's settle down to the ole army game."

They settled down to it, and by twelve o'clock (the invariable closing hour of these pastimes in the old shack) Collinson had lost four dollars and thirty cents more. He was commiserated by his fellow gamesters as they put on their coats and overcoats, preparing to leave the hot little room. They shook their heads, laughed ruefully in sympathy, and told him he oughtn't to carry hundred-dollar bills upon his person when he went out among friends. Old Bill made what is sometimes called an unfortunate remark.

"Don't worry about Collie," he said jocosely. "That hundred-dollar bill prob'ly belonged to some rich client of his."

"What!" Collinson said, staring.

"Never mind, Collie; I wasn't in earnest," the joker explained. "Of course I didn't mean it."

"Well, you oughtn't to say it," Collinson protested. "People say a thing like that about a man in a joking way, but other people hear it sometimes and don't know he's joking, and a story gets started."

"My goodness, but you're serious!" Old Bill exclaimed. "You look like you had a misery in your chest, as the rubes say; and I don't blame you! Get on out in the fresh night air and you'll feel better."

He was mistaken, however; the night air failed to improve Collinson's spirits as he walked home alone through the dark and chilly streets. There was indeed a misery in his chest, where stirred a sensation vaguely nauseating; his hands were tremulous and his knees infirm as he walked. In his mind was a confusion of pictures and sounds, echoes from Charlie Loomis's shack: he could not clear his mind's eye of the one-hundred-dollar bill; and its likeness, as it lay crumpled on the green cloth under the drop-light, haunted and hurt him as a face in a coffin haunts and hurts the new mourner. Bits of Smithie's discursiveness resounded in his mind's ear, keeping him from thinking. "In one person's hands money'll do good likely, and in another's it'll do harm."—"The dummy that said, 'Money's the root of all evil!' "

It seemed to Collinson then that money was the root of all evil and the root of all good, the root and branch of all life, indeed. With money, his wife would have been amiable, not needing gay bachelors to take her to vaudevilles. Her need of money was the true foundation of the jealousy that had sent him out morose and reckless to-night; of the jealousy that had made it seem, when he gambled with Charlie Loomis for the luck dollar, as though they really gambled for luck with her.

It still seemed to him that they had gambled for luck with her: Charlie had wanted the talisman, as Smithie said, in order to believe in his luck—his luck with women—and therefore actually be lucky with them; and Charlie had won. But as Collinson plodded homeward in the chilly midnight, his shoulders sagging and his head drooping, he began to wonder how he could have risked money that belonged to another man. What on earth had made him do what he had done? Was it the mood his wife had set him in as he went out that evening? No; he had gone out feeling like that often enough, and nothing had happened.

Something had brought this trouble on him, he thought; for it appeared to Collinson that he had been an automaton, having nothing to do with his own actions. He must bear the responsibility for them; but he had not willed them. If the one-hundred-dollar bill had not happened to be in his pocket— That was it! And at the thought he mumbled desolately to himself: "I'd been all right if it hadn't been for that." If the one-hundred-dollar bill had not happened to be in his pocket, he'd have been "all right." The one-hundred-dollar bill had done this to him. And Smithie's romancing again came back to him: "In one person's hands money'll do good, likely; in another's it'll do harm." It was the money that did harm or

53

good, not the person; and the money in his hands had done this harm to himself.

He had to deliver a hundred dollars at the office in the morning, somehow, for he dared not take the risk of the client's meeting the debtor. There was a balance of seventeen dollars in his bank, and he could pawn his watch for twenty-five, as he knew well enough, by experience. That would leave fifty-eight dollars to be paid, and there was only one way to get it. His wife would have to let him pawn her ring. She'd have to!

Without any difficulty he could guess what she would say and do when he told her of his necessity: and he knew that never in her life would she forego the advantage over him she would gain from it. He knew, too, what stipulations she would make, and he had to face the fact that he was in no position to reject them. The one-hundred-dollar bill had cost him the last vestiges of mastery in his own house; and Charlie Loomis had really won not only the bill and the luck, but the privilege of taking Collinson's wife to vaudevilles. But it all came back to the same conclusion: the one-hundred-dollar bill had done it to him. "What kind of a thing is this life?" Collinson mumbled to himself, finding matters wholly perplexing in a world made into tragedy at the caprice of a little oblong slip of paper.

Then, as he went on his way to wake his wife and face her with the soothing proposal to pawn her ring early the next morning, something happened to Collinson. Of itself the thing that happened was nothing, but he was aware of his folly as if it stood upon a mountain top against the sun—and so he gathered knowledge of himself and a little of the wisdom that is called better than happiness.

His way was now the same as upon the latter stretch of his walk home from the office that evening. The smoke fog had cleared, and the air was clean with a night wind that moved briskly from the west; in all the long street there was only one window lighted, but it was sharply outlined now, and fell as a bright rhomboid upon the pavement before Collinson. When he came to it he paused at the hint of an inward impulse he did not think to trace; and, frowning, he perceived that this was the same shop window that had detained him on his homeward way, when he had thought of buying a toy for the baby.

The toy was still there in the bright window; the gay little acrobatic monkey that would climb up or down a red string as the string slacked or straightened; but Collinson's eye fixed itself upon the card marked with the price: "35 cents."

He stared and stared. "Thirty-five cents!" he said to himself. "Thirty-five cents!"

Then suddenly he burst into loud and prolonged laughter.

The sound was startling in the quiet night, and roused the interest of a meditative policeman who stood in the darkened doorway of the next shop. He stepped out, not unfriendly.

"What you havin' such a good time over, this hour o' the night?" he inquired. "What's all the joke?"

Collinson pointed to the window. "It's that monkey on the string," he said. "Something about it struck me as mighty funny!"

So, with a better spirit, he turned away, still laughing, and went home to face his wife.

JEANNETTE

THE nurses at the sanitarium were all fond of the gentlest patient in the place, and they spoke of him as "Uncle Charlie," though he was so sweetly dignified that usually they addressed him as "Mr. Blake," even when it was necessary to humour his delusion. The delusion was peculiar and of apparently interminable persistence; he had but the one during his sixteen years of incarceration—yet it was a misfortune painful only to himself (painful through the excessive embarrassment it cost him) and was never for an instant of the slightest distress to any one else, except as a stimulant of sympathy. For all that, it closed him in, shutting out the moving world from him as completely as if he had been walled up in concrete. Moreover, he had been walled up overnight— one day he was a sane man, and the next he was in custody as a lunatic; yet nothing had happened in this little interval, or during any preceding interval in his life, to account for a seizure so instantaneous.

In 1904 no more commonplace young man could have been found in any of the great towns of our Eastern and near-Eastern levels. "Well brought up," as we used to say, he had inherited the quiet manner, the good health, and the moderate wealth of his parents; and not engaging in any business or profession, he put forth the best that was in him when he planned a lunch for a pretty "visiting girl," or, again, when he bought a pair of iron candle-snuffers for what he thought of as his "collection." This "collection," consisting of cheerless utensils and primitive furniture once used by woodsmen and farmers, and naturally discarded by their descendants, gave him his principal occupation, though he was sometimes called upon to lead a cotillion, being favourably regarded in the waltz and two-step; but he had no eccentricities, no habitual vices, and was never known to exhibit anything in the nature of an imagination.

It was in the autumn of the year just mentioned that he went for the first time to Europe, accompanying his sister, Mrs. Gordon Troup, an experienced traveller. She took him through the English cathedrals, then across the Channel; and they arrived unfatigued at her usual hotel in Paris after dark on a clear November evening—the fated young gentleman's last evening of sanity. Yet, as Mrs. Troup so often recalled later, never in his life had her brother been more "absolutely normal" than all that day: not even the Channel had disturbed him, for it was as still as syrup in a pantry jug; he slept on

56

the French train, and when he awoke, played gently with Mrs. Troup's three-year-old daughter Jeannette who, with a nurse, completed the small party. His talk was not such as to cause anxiety, being in the main concerned with a tailor who had pleased him in London, and a haberdasher he made sure would please him in Paris.

They dined in the salon of their apartment; and at about nine o'clock, as they finished their coffee, flavoured with a little burnt cognac, Mrs. Troup suggested the theatre—a pantomime or ballet for preference, since her brother's unfamiliarity with the French language rapidly spoken might give him a dull evening at a comedy. So, taking their leisure, they went to the Marigny, where they saw part of a potpourri called a "revue," which Mrs. Troup declared to be at once too feeble and too bold to detain them as spectators; and they left the Marigny for the Folies Bergères, where she had once seen a fine pantomime; but here they found another "revue," and fared no better. The "revue" at the Folies Bergères was even feebler, she observed to her brother, and much bolder than that at the Marigny: the feebleness was in the wit, the boldness in the anatomical exposures, which were somewhat discomfiting—"even for Paris!" she said.

She remembered afterward that he made no response to her remark but remained silent, frowning at the stage, where some figurantes just then appeared to be dressed in ball gowns, until they turned, when they appeared to be dressed almost not at all. "Mercy!" said Mrs. Troup; and presently, as the costume designer's ideas became less and less reassuring, she asked her brother if he would mind taking her back to the hotel: so much dullness and so much brazenness together fatigued her, she explained.

He assented briefly, though with some emphasis; and they left during the entr'acte, making their way through the outer room where a "Hungarian" band played stormily for a painted and dangerous-looking procession slowly circling like torpid skaters in a rink. The bang-whang of the music struck full in the face like an impulsive blow from a fist; so did the savage rouging of the promenaders; and young Mr. Blake seemed to be startled: he paused for a moment, looking confused. But Mrs. Troup pressed his arm. "Let's get out to the air," she said. "Did you ever see anything like it?"

He replied that he never did, went on quickly; they stepped into a cab at the door; and on the way to the hotel Mrs. Troup expressed contrition as a courier. "I shouldn't have given you this for your first impression of Paris," she said. "We ought to have waited until morning and then gone to the Sainte Chapelle. I'll try to make up for to-night by taking you there the first thing to-morrow."

He murmured something to the effect that he would be glad to see whatever she chose to show him, and afterward she could not remember that they had any further conversation until they reached their apartment in the hotel. There she again expressed her regret, not with particular emphasis, of course, but rather lightly; for to her mind, at least, the evening's experience was the slightest of episodes; and her brother told her not to "bother," but to "forget it." He spoke casually, even negligently, but she was able to recall that as he went into his own room and closed the door, his forehead still showed the same frown, perhaps of disapproval, that she had observed in the theatre.

The outer door of the apartment, giving entrance to their little hallway, opened upon a main corridor of the hotel; she locked this door and took the key with her into her bedchamber, having some vague idea that her jewels were thus made safer; and this precaution of hers later made it certain that her brother had not gone out again, but without doubt passed the night in his own room—in his own room and asleep, so far as might be guessed.

Her little girl's nurse woke her the next morning; and the woman's voice and expression showed such distress, even to eyes just drowsily opening, that Mrs. Troup jumped up at once. "Is something wrong with Jeannette?"

"No, ma'am. It is Mr. Blake."

"Is he ill?"

"I think so. That is, I don't know, ma'am. A valet-de-chambre went into his room half an hour ago, and Mr. Blake hid himself under the bed."

"What?"

"Perhaps you'd better come and see, ma'am. The valet-de-chambre is very frightened of him."

But it was poor young Mr. Blake who was afraid of the valet-de-chambre, and of everybody else, for that matter, as Mrs. Troup discovered. He declined to come out from under the bed so long as she and the nurse and the valet were present, and in response to his sister's entreaties, he earnestly insisted that she should leave the room at once and take the servants with her.

"But what's the matter, Charlie dear?" she asked, greatly disturbed. "Why are you under the bed?"

In his voice, as he replied, a pathetic indignation was audible: "Because I haven't got any clothes on!"

At this her relief was manifest, and she began to laugh. "Good heavens—"

"But no, madame!" the valet explained. "He has his clothes on. He is dressed all entirely. If you will stoop and look—"

58

She did as he suggested, and saw that her brother was fully dressed and making gestures as eloquently plaintive as the limited space permitted. "Can't you take these people away?" he cried pettishly. "Do you think it's nice to stand around looking at a person that's got nothing on?"

He said the same thing an hour later to the doctor Mrs. Troup summoned, though by that time he had left his shelter under the bed and had locked himself in a wardrobe. And thus, out of a clear sky and with no premonitory vagaries, began his delusion—his long, long delusion, which knew no variation in the sixteen years it possessed him. From first to last he was generally regarded as a "strange case;" yet his state of mind may easily be realized by anybody who dreams; for in dreams, everybody has undergone, however briefly, experiences similar to those in which Mr. Blake fancied himself so continuously involved.

He was taken from the hotel to a private asylum near Paris, where he remained until the following year, when Mrs. Troup had him quietly brought home to a suburban sanitarium convenient for her to visit at intervals; and here he remained, his condition changing neither for the better nor for the worse. He was violent only once or twice in the whole period, and, though he was sometimes a little peevish, he was the most tractable patient in the institution, so long as his delusion was discreetly humoured; yet it is probable that the complete records of kleptomania would not disclose a more expert thief.

This was not a new form of his disease, but a natural by-product and outgrowth of it, which within a year or two had developed to the point of fine legerdemain; and at the end of ten years Doctor Cowrie, the chief at the sanitarium, declared that his patient, Uncle Charlie Blake, could "steal the trousers off a man's legs without the man's knowing it." The alienist may have exaggerated; but it is certain that "Uncle Charlie" could steal the most carefully fastened and safety-pinned apron from a nurse, without the nurse's being aware of it. Indeed, attendants, nurses and servants who wore aprons learned to remove them before entering his room; for the most watchful could seldom prevent what seemed a miraculous exchange, and "Uncle Charlie" would be wearing the apron that had seemed, but a moment before, to be secure upon the intruder. It may be said that he spent most of his time purloining and collecting aprons; for quantities of them were frequently discovered hidden in his room, and taken away, though he always wore several, by permission. Nor were other garments safe from him: it was found that he could not be allowed to take his outdoor exercise except in those portions of the grounds remotest from the laundry yard; and even then as he was remarkably deft in concealing himself behind trees and among shrubberies, he was sometimes able to strip a whole length of clothesline, to don many of the damp garments, and to hide the others, before being detected.

He read nothing, had no diversions, and was immersed in the sole preoccupation of devising means to obtain garments, which, immediately after he put them on, were dissolved into nothingness so far as his consciousness was concerned. Mrs. Troup could not always resist the impulse to argue with him as if he were a rational man; and she made efforts to interest him in "books and the outside world," kindly efforts that only irritated him. "How can I read books and newspapers?" he inquired peevishly from under the bed, where he always remained when he received her. "Don't you know any better than to talk about intellectual pursuits to a man that hasn't got a stitch of clothes to his name? Try it yourself if you want to know how it feels. Find yourself totally undressed, with all sorts of people likely to drop in on you at any minute, and then sit down and read a newspaper! Please use your reason a little, Frances!"

Mrs. Troup sighed, and rose to depart—but found that her fur cloak had disappeared under the bed.

In fact, though Mrs. Troup failed to comprehend this, he had explained his condition to her quite perfectly: it was merely an excessive protraction of the nervous anxiety experienced by a rational person whose entire wardrobe is missing. No sensitive gentleman, under such circumstances, has attention to spare from his effort to clothe himself; and all information not bearing upon that effort will fail of important effect upon his mind. You may bring him the news that the Brooklyn Bridge has fallen with a great splash, but the gravity of the event will be lost upon him until he has obtained trousers.

Thus, year after year, while Uncle Charlie Blake became more and more dextrous at stealing aprons, history paced on outside the high iron fence inclosing the grounds of the sanitarium, and all the time he was so concerned with his embarrassment, and with his plans and campaigns to relieve it, that there was no room left in his mind for the plans and campaigns of Joffre and Hindenburg and Haig and Foch. Armistice Day, as celebrated by Uncle Charlie, was the day when, owing to some cheerful preoccupation on the part of doctors and attendants, he stole nine aprons, three overcoats, a waistcoat and seventeen pillow-slips.

Rip Van Winkle beat Uncle Charlie by four years. The likeness between the two experiences is pathetically striking, and the difference between them more apparent than actual; for though Rip Van Winkle's body lay upon the hill like a stone, the while his slumber was vaguely decorated with thousands of dreams, and although Uncle Charlie Blake had the full use of his body, and was all the time lost in one particular and definite dream, still if Rip Van Winkle could wake, so could Uncle Charlie. At least, this was the view of the younger alienist, Doctor Morphy, who succeeded Doctor Cowrie in 1919.

In the course of some long and sympathetic talks with his patient, Doctor Morphy slightly emphasized a suggestion that of late tin had come to be considered the most desirable clothing material: the stiffness and glitter of tin, as well as the sound of it, enabled a person to be pretty sure he had something over him, so long as he wore one of the new tin suits, the Doctor explained. Then he took an engraving of Don Quixote in armour to a tinsmith, had him make a suit of armour in tin, and left it in Uncle Charlie's corridor to be stolen.

The awakening, or cure, began there; for the patient accepted the tin armour as substance, even when it was upon him, the first apparel he had believed to be tangible and opaque enough for modesty since the night his sister had taken him to the Folies Bergères in 1904. The patient's satisfaction when he had put on this Don Quixote armour was instant, but so profound that at first he could express it only in long sighs, like those of a swimmer who has attained the land with difficulty and lies upon the bank flaccid with both his struggle and his relief. That morning, for the first time, he made no dive under his bed at the sound of a knock upon the door, and when he went out for his exercise, he broke his long habit of darting from the shelter of one tree to another. He was even so confident as to walk up to a woman nurse and remark that it was a pleasant day.

Thence onward, the measures to be taken for his restoration to society were obvious. The tin greaves pinched him at the joints when he moved, and Doctor Morphy pointed out that silver cloth, with rows of tiny bells sewed upon it here and there, would glitter and sound even better than tin. Then, when the patient had worn a suit of this silver cloth, instead of tin, for a few weeks, the bells were gradually removed, a row at a time, until finally they were all gone, and Uncle Charlie was convinced by only the glitter that he went apparelled. After that, the silver was secretly tarnished, yet the patient remained satisfied. Next a woollen suit of vivid green and red plaid was substituted; and others followed, each milder than its predecessor, until at last Uncle Charlie grew accustomed to the daily thought that he was clothed, and, relieved of his long anxiety, began to play solitaire in his room. His delusion had been gradually worn away, but not to make room for another; moreover, as it lost actuality to him, he began to forget it. His intelligence cleared, in fact, until upon Thanksgiving Day, 1920, when Mrs. Troup came to take him away, he was in everything—except a body forty-six years old—the same young man who had arrived in Paris on a November evening in 1904. His information, his point of view and his convictions were those of a commonplace, well-brought-up, conventional young American of that period; he had merely to bridge the gap.

Doctor Morphy advised Mrs. Troup that the bridging must be done with as little strain as possible upon the convalescent's mind— a mind never too hardily robust—and therefore the devoted lady took her brother to a mountain health resort, where for a month they lived in a detached cottage, walked footpaths in the woods, went to bed at nine, and made no acquaintances. Mrs. Troup dispensed with newspapers for the time (her charge did not appear to be aware of their absence) but she had brought such books as she thought might be useful; and every day she talked to him, as instructively as she could, of the terrific culminations history had seen during the latter part of his incarceration.

Of Bolshevism he appeared unable to make anything at all, though Mrs. Troup's explanations struck out a single spark from his memory. "Oh, yes," he said, "I remember a rather talky chap—he was one of the guests at that queer place where I used to live, you know—well, he used to make speeches the whole day long. He said the doctors got all the money and it was our money. If it wasn't for us, the doctors wouldn't have a cent, he said; and since we produced all the wealth, we ought to organize, and lock the doctors up in the cellar, and get the money ourselves. I remember some of the other guests seemed to think there was a good deal in the talky chap's speeches, and I suppose it must be something of this sort that's happened in Russia. It's very confusing, though."

And when her lessons, as mild as she could make them, had proceeded somewhat further, he passed his hand over his brow, professing himself more confused than ever.

"I declare!" he said. "No sensible person could make head or tail of it, if I may use such an expression. I never dreamed anything could actually come of all these eccentricities—women's rights, socialism, blue Sundays, prohibition and what not. I've heard of such people—heard jokes about 'em—but never in my life met a person that went in seriously for any of 'em, except that speechifying chap I told you about. How on earth did it all happen?"

Upon this she was able to enlighten him but feebly, and he rubbed his forehead again.

"It's no use," he told her. "There's no reason behind these

62

things: the only thing to do is to realize that the world's gone crazy. We used to think that civilization was something made of parts working together as they do in an engine; but from what you tell me, it must have been trying to split itself up, all the time. The nations split up and began to fight one another; and as soon as they'd all got so crippled and in debt that they couldn't fight any more, the other splits began. Everybody had to be on the side of the women or on the side of the men, and the women won. Now everybody has to be either a capitalist or a labourer, it seems, no matter what else he is; and even if he doesn't know which he is, he'll have to fight, because somebody's sure to hit him. And besides that, the people have gone and split themselves into those that drink and the others that won't let 'em. How many more splits are there going to be, with the people on each side just bound to run the world their way? There are plenty of other kinds of splits that could be made, and I suppose we might as well expect 'em; for instance, we can have all the married people on one side in a 'class-conscious class,' as you were explaining, and all the unmarried ones on the other. Or all the parents on one side and all the children on the other." He paused, and laughed, adding: "However, I don't suppose it's gone quite so far as children versus parents yet, has it?"

Mrs. Troup looked thoughtful. "I suppose it always has been 'children versus parents' at least, in a sense," she said. "I've been thinking lately, though, that since all revolts are more apt to take place against feeble governments than against strong ones, if the children are in revolt, it must be because the parents are showing greater laxity than they used to."

Mr. Blake went to his afternoon nap, shaking his head, but in silence. Naturally he was confused by what he heard from her, and once or twice he was confused by some things he saw, though in their seclusion he saw little. One mistake he made, however, amazed his sister.

From their pleasant veranda a rounded green slope descended slowly to the level lawn surrounding the Georgian upheavings of an endless hotel; and at a porte cochère of this hotel a dozen young women, come from a ride on the hills, were getting down from their saddles. Mr. Blake, upon the veranda of the cottage a hundred yards distant, observed them thoughtfully.

"It may be only the difference in fashions," he remarked; "but people's figures look very queer to me. The actual shapes seem to have changed as much as the clothes. You're used to them, I suppose, and so they don't surprise you, but down there at that porte cochère, for instance, the figures all look odd and—well, sort of bunchy. To me, every single one of those boys seems to be either knock-kneed or bow-legged."

" 'Boys!' " Mrs. Troup cried.

He stared at her. "What are they?"

"Good gracious! Don't you see? They're women!"

He still stared at her, while his incredulous expression slowly changed to one of troubled perplexity. But he said nothing at all, and after a moment more, turned away and went to his room, where he remained until dinner-time. When he appeared at the table, he made no reference to his mistake, but reverted to the topic of which they had been speaking that afternoon before his attention wandered to the horsewomen at the porte cochère.

"Prohibition must have altered a great many people's lives quite violently," he said. "I suppose it was quite a shock for people who'd always had wine or Scotch at dinner—giving it up so suddenly."

"I suppose so—I don't know—" A little colour showed below Mrs. Troup's eyes. "Of course, quite a number of people had supplies on hand when the day came."

"But most of that must be gone by this time."

"Quite a good deal of it is gone, yes; you don't see wine very often any more. People who have any left are getting very piggish about it, I believe."

"It must be odd," he said contemplatively, "the whole country's being absolutely sober and dry, like this."

"Well—" she began; then, after a pause, went on: "It isn't like that—exactly. You see—"

"Oh, of course there would be a few moonshine stills and low dives," he interrupted. "But people of our circle—"

"Aren't exactly 'dry,' Charles."

"But if they have no wine or—"

"It's my impression," said Mrs. Troup, "that certain queer kinds of whisky and gin—"

"But we were speaking of 'our circle'—the kind of people we—"

"Yes, I know," she said. "They carry these liquids about with them in the most exquisite flasks. Jeannette has one—a boy friend gave it to her—and it must have been made by a silversmith who is a real artist. It must have been fearfully expensive."

Mr. Blake's open mouth remained distended for a moment. "Your Jeannette!" he exclaimed. "Why, she's only—"

"Oh, she's nineteen," his sister informed him soothingly.

"But was it exactly nice for her to receive such a gift from a young man?"

"Oh, he's one of the nicest boys we know," Mrs. Troup explained. "They swim together every day."

" 'Swim together'?" her brother inquired feebly.

"Yes," said Mrs. Troup. "His aunt has a tank."

" 'His aunt has a tank,' " the convalescent repeated in a low voice, as if he wished to get the sentence by heart. " 'His aunt has a tank.' "

Mrs. Troup coughed placatively. "It may be a little difficult for you to understand," she said. "Of course, even I feel obliged to have something in the house at home—a certain amount of whisky. I don't approve of such things, naturally, but Jeannette feels it's necessary on account of the young men and the other girls. She doesn't like whisky and never touches it herself."

Jeannette's uncle uttered a sigh of relief. "I should think not! I was afraid, from what you told me of her flask—"

"Oh, in that," said Mrs. Troup, "she keeps gin."

"Gin?" he said in a whisper. "Gin?"

"She's rather fond of gin," Mrs. Troup informed him. "She makes it herself from a recipe; it's quite simple I believe."

"And she carries this flask—"

"Oh, not all the time!" Mrs. Troup protested, laughing. "Only to dances and girls' lunches." And, observing her brother's expression, she added: "Of course, she never takes too much; you mustn't get a wrong idea of Jeannette. She and all the girls of her set don't believe in that, at all—I'm positive none of them has ever been intoxicated. They have the very highest principles."

"They have?"

"Yes; you see, Jeannette has read Wells and Shaw since she was twelve. When we go home and you meet Jeannette, you must try to understand that she belongs to a different generation, Charles. You see, Jeannette has had so many influences that didn't affect your own youth at all. For instance, she always insisted on going to the movies even when she was a little girl, and I rather enjoy them myself, when I'm tired; and then there's the new stage— and the new novel—you know, we have everything on the stage and in books that we used to think could only be in books and on the stage in France, because here the police—"

"But in France," he interrupted, "—in France they didn't let the jeune fille read the books or go to the theatre."

"No," she agreed. "But of course over here we've had feminism—"

"What's that?"

"I don't know exactly, but I think it's something to do with the emancipation of women." She paused, then added thoughtfully: "Of course, Jeannette smokes."

"What!"

"Oh, that's nothing at all," she said hastily. "They've had to permit it in nearly all the restaurants."

He rose, leaning heavily upon his chair, as if for support, and looking rather more pallid than usual. In fact, his brow was damp from the exertion its interior workings had undergone in the effort to comprehend his sister's conversation. "I think, if you don't mind," he murmured, "I'll go directly to bed and rest."

"Do," she said sympathetically. "We'll talk some more about Jeannette to-morrow. She's the most lovably pretty thing in the world, and you'll be cra—" She changed the phrase hastily. "You'll be delighted to have such a niece."

But, as it happened, when she began to speak of Jeannette the next day, he gently protested, asking her to choose another topic. "I'm sure I couldn't understand," he said, "and the effort rather upsets me. It would be better to wait and let me form my own impressions when I see her."

His sister assented without debate; and nothing more was said about Jeannette until a week later when they were on the train, and half the way home. A telegram was handed to Mrs. Troup by the porter, and after reading it, she glanced rather apprehensively toward her brother, who, in the opposite seat, was so deeply attentive to a book that he had not noticed the delivery of the telegram; in fact, he did not observe it, still in her hand, when he looked up vaguely, after a time, to speak a thought suggested by his reading.

"So many of these books about the war and the after-effects of the war say that there is to be a 'new world.' All the young people have made up their minds that the old world was a failure and they're going to have something different. I don't know just what they mean by this 'new world' the writers talk so much about, because they never go into the details of the great change. It's clear, though, that the young people intend the new world to be much more spiritual than the old one. Well, I'm anxious to see it, and, of course, it's a great advantage to me, because I stayed so long at that queer place—where the doctors were—it will be easier to start in with a new world than it would be, maybe, to get used to the changes in the old one. I'm mighty anxious to see these new young people who—"

His sister interrupted him. "You'll see some of them soon enough, it appears. I really think Jeannette shouldn't have done this." And she handed him the telegram to read.

THOUGHT I BETTER LET YOU KNOW IN CASE YOU
PREFER TAKING UNCLE CHARLES TO HOTEL FOR FIRST
NIGHT AT HOME AS AM THROWING TODDLE ABOUT FORTY
COUPLES AT HOUSE SAUSAGE BREAKFAST AT FOUR AM TO
FINISH THE SHOW AND BLACKAMALOO BAND MIGHT
DISTURB UNCLE CHARLES.

Uncle Charles was somewhat disturbed, in fact, by the
telegram itself. " 'Am throwing toddle'—" he murmured.

"She means she's giving a dance," his sister explained,
frowning. "It's really not very considerate of her, our first evening at
home; but Jeannette is just made of impulses. She's given I don't
know how many dances since I went away with you, and she might
have let this one drop. I'm afraid it may be very upsetting for you,
Charles."

"You could send her a telegram from the next station," he
suggested. "You could ask her to telephone her friends and
postpone the—"

"Not Jeannette!" Mrs. Troup laughed. "I could wire, but she
wouldn't pay any attention. I have no influence with her."

"You haven't?"

"No." And upon this Mrs. Troup became graver. "I don't think
her father would have had any either, if he had lived; he was so
easy-going and used to sing so loudly after dinner. Jeannette always
seemed to think he was just a joke, even when she was a child. The
truth is, she's like a great many of her friends: they seem to lack the
quality of respect. When we were young, Charles, we had that, at
least; our parents taught us to have that quality."

"But haven't you taught Jeannette to have it?"

"Indeed I have," Mrs. Troup sighed. "I've told her every day
for years that she hadn't any. I noticed it first when she was thirteen
years old. It seemed to break out on her, as it were, that year."

"How did it happen?"

"Why, we were staying at a summer hotel, a rather gay place,
and I'm afraid I left her too much to her governess—I was feeling
pretty blue that summer and I wanted distraction. I liked tangoing—
"

" 'Tangoing'?" he said inquiringly. "Was it a game?"

"No; a dance. They called it 'the tango'; I don't know why. And
there was 'turkey-trotting,' too—"

" 'Turkey-trotting'?" he said huskily.

"Well, that," she explained, "was really the machiche that
tourists used to see in Paris at the Bal Bullier. In fact, you saw it
yourself, Charles. A couple danced the machiche that night at the

Folies Ber—" She checked herself hastily, bit her lip, and then, recovering, she said: "I got quite fond of all those dances after we imported them."

"You mean you got used to looking at them?" he asked slowly. "You went to see them at places where they were allowed?"

At this she laughed. "No, of course not! I danced them myself."

"What!"

"Why, of course!"

"No one—" He faltered. "No one ever saw you do it?"

"Why, of course. It's a little difficult to explain this to you, Charles, but all those dances that used to seem so shocking to us when we went to look on at them in foreign places—well, it turned out that they were perfectly all right and proper when you dance them yourself. Of course I danced them, and enjoyed them very much; and besides, it's a wholesome exercise and good for the health. Everybody danced them. People who'd given up dancing for years—the oldest kind of people—danced them. It began the greatest revival of dancing the world's ever seen, Charles, and the—"

He interrupted her. "Go a little slower, please," he said, and applied a handkerchief to his forehead. "About your seeming to lose your authority with Jeannette—"

"Yes; I was trying to tell you. She used to sit up watching us dancing in the hotel ballroom that summer, and I just couldn't make her go to bed! That was the first time she deliberately disobeyed me, but it was a radical change in her; and I've never since then seemed to have any weight with her—none at all; she's just done exactly what she pleased. I've often thought perhaps that governess had a bad influence on her."

He wiped his forehead again, and inquired: "You say she's given dances while you've been away with me?"

"Oh, she asks plenty of married people, of course."

"And it wouldn't be any use to telegraph her to postpone this one?"

"No. She'd just go ahead, and when we got home, she'd be rather annoyed with me for thinking a dance could be postponed at the last minute. We must make the best of it."

"I suppose so."

"We won't reach the house till almost nine, and you can go straight to bed, Charles. I'm afraid the music may disturb you; that's all. Dance music is rather loudish, nowadays."

"I was thinking," he said slowly, "—I was thinking maybe I'd dress and look on for a while; I do want to see these new young people. It might be a good thing for me to begin to get accustomed-"

"So it might," she agreed, brightening. "I was only bothered on your account, and if you take it that way, it will be all right." She laughed. "The truth is, I enjoy Jeannette's dances myself. I like to enter into things with her and be more like a sisterly companion than a mother in the old-fashioned strict sense. That's the modern spirit, Charles; to be a hail-fellow of your children—more a wise comrade than a parent. So, if you feel that you would be interested in looking on, and won't be disturbed—well, that's just too lovely! And you'll adore Jeannette!"

He was sure of that, he said; and added that as he was Jeannette's uncle he supposed it would be proper to kiss her when she met them at the station.

"Oh, she won't be at the station," said his sister. "In fact, I'll be surprised if she remembers to send the car for us."

But as it happened, Mrs. Troup was surprised: Jeannette sent the car, and they were comfortably taken homeward through a city that presented nothing familiar to Charles Blake, though he had spent his youth in it. The first thing he found recognizable was the exterior of his sister's big house, for she had lived in it ever since her marriage; but indoors she had remodelled it, and he was as lost as he had been under the great flares of light down-town. Mrs. Troup led him up to his room and left him there. "Jeannette's dressing, they tell me," she said. "Hurry and dress, yourself, so as to see her a minute before she gets too busy dancing. It's late."

In spite of her instruction, he was too nervous to dress quickly, and several times decided to get into bed instead of proceeding with his toilet; but an ardent curiosity prevailed over his timidity, and he continued to prepare himself for a state appearance, until a strange event upset him.

There were a few thin squeaks and low blats of warning—small noises incomprehensible to him, and seemingly distant—when suddenly burst forth the most outrageous uproar he had ever heard, and he thought it just outside his door. When it happened, he was standing with his right foot elevated to penetrate the orifice of that leg of his trousers, but the shock of sound overturned him; his foot became entangled, and he fell upon the floor.

Lying there, helpless, he heard a voice sweet as silver bells, even when it screamed, as it had to scream now to make itself heard. "No, no! I don't want 'The Maiden's Dream'! Stop it; dam it!" And the outrage became silence, murmurously broken by only the silvery voice which was itself now indistinguishable, except as ineffable sound; he could not make out the words.

Fingers tapped on his door. "Do hurry, Charles dear," Mrs. Troup said. "Jeannette's arguing with the musicians, but she might

69

have a moment or two to see you now. People are just beginning to come."

"With whom?" he asked hoarsely, not attempting to move.

"'With whom' what? I don't understand," his sister inquired, shouting through the closed door.

"You said she's arguing. With whom?"

"With the musicians."

"With whom?"

"The musicians. They began to play 'The Maiden's Dream,' but she doesn't like it: she wants something livelier."

"Livelier?"

"I must run," Mrs. Troup shouted. "Do hurry, Charles."

In spite of this departing urgency, Charles remained inert for some time, his cheek upon a rug, his upper eye contemplating the baseboard of the wall, and his right foot shackled in his trousers. Meanwhile, voices began to rise without in an increasing strident babble, until finally they roused him. He rose, completed his toilet and stepped outside his door.

He found himself upon a gallery which looked down upon a broad hall floored in wood now darkly lustrous with wax. He had a confused impression of strewn and drifting great tropical flowers in haphazard clusters and flaring again, in their unfamiliar colours, from the reflecting darkness of the polished floor; such dresses as he had never seen; and flesh-tints, too, of ivory and rose so emphasized and in such profusion as likewise he had never seen. And from these clusters and from the short-coated men among them, the shouting voices rose to him in such uproarious garbling chorus that though he had heard choruses not very different, long ago, it increased his timidity; and a little longing floated into his emotion—a homesickness for the old asylum, where everything had been so orderly and reasonable.

Suddenly he jumped: his hands were clutched upon the railing of the gallery, and they remained there; but his feet leaped inches into the air with the shock; for the crash that so startled him came from directly beneath the part of the gallery where he stood. In his nervousness, he seemed about to vault over the railing, but as his feet descended, he recognized the sound: it was of a nature similar to that which had overcome him in his room, and was produced by those whom his sister had defined as "the musicians:" they had just launched the dance music. The clusters of tropical flowers were agitated, broke up. The short black coats seized upon them, and they seized upon the short black coats; something indescribable began.

The dance music did not throb—the nervous gentleman in the

70

gallery remembered dance music that throbbed, dance music that tinkled merrily, dance music that swam, dance music that sang, and sometimes sang sadly and perhaps too sweetly of romantic love—but this was incredible: it beat upon his brain with bludgeons and blackjacks, rose in hideous upheavals of sound, fell into chaos, squawked in convulsions, seemed about to die, so that eighty pairs of shoes and slippers were heard in husky whispers against the waxed floor; then this music leaped to life again more ferociously than ever.

The thumping and howling of it brought to the gallery listener a dim recollection: once, in his boyhood, he had been taken through a slaughter-house; and this was what came back to him now. Pigs have imaginations, and as they are forced, crowding against one another, through the chute, their feet pounding the thunderous floor, the terrible steams they smell warn them of the murderers' wet knives ahead: the pigs scream horror with their utmost lungs; and the dumfounded gentleman recalled these mortal squealings now, though there was more to this music. There should be added, among other noises, all the agony three poisoned cats can feel in their entrails, the belabourings of hollow-log tomtoms by Aruwimi witch-doctors, and incessant cries of passion from the depths of negroes ecstasized with toddy.

A plump hand touched Mr. Blake's shoulder, and lifting his pale glance from below he found that his sister had ascended the gallery stairs to speak to him.

"What are they doing down there?" he shouted.

"Toddling."

"You mean dancing?"

"Yes; toddling. It's dancing—great fun, too!"

He was still incredulous, and turned to look again. To his perturbed mind everybody seemed bent upon the imitation of an old coloured woman he had once seen swaying on the banks of a creek, at a baptism. She jiggled the upper portions of her, he remembered, as if she were at once afflicted and uplifted by her emotions; and at the same time she shuffled slowly about, her very wide-apart feet keeping well to the ground. All of these couples appeared to have studied some such ancient religious and coloured person anxiously; but this was not all that interested the returned Mr. Blake. Partners in the performance below him clung to each other with a devotion he had never seen except once or twice, and then under chance circumstances which had cost him a hurried apology. Some, indeed, had set their cheeks together for better harmony; moreover, the performers, who in this exhibition of

71

comedy abandoned forever all hope of ever being taken seriously by any spectator, were by no means all of the youthfulness with which any such recklessness of dignity had heretofore been associated in Mr. Blake's mind: heads white as clouds moved here and there among the toddlers; so did dyed heads, and so did portly figures.

"I came up to point Jeannette out to you," Mrs. Troup explained, shouting in her brother's ear. "I wanted you to see her dancing: she looks so beautiful. There she is! See! Doesn't she look pretty?"

His eyes aimed along her extended forefinger and found Jeannette.

Jeannette did "look pretty" indeed, even when she toddled— there could be no test more cruel. She was a glowing, dark-eyed, dark-haired, exquisite young thing shimmering with innocent happiness. One of her childish shoulders bore a jewelled string; the other nothing. Most of her back and a part of each of her sides were untrammelled; and her skirt came several inches below the knee, unless she sat. Nothing her uncle had ever seen had been so pretty as Jeannette.

To her four grandparents, Jeannette would have been merely unbelievable. Her eight great-grandparents, pioneers and imaginative, might have believed her and her clothes possible, but they would have believed with horror. In fact, to find ancestors who would not be shocked at Jeannette, one would have to go back to the Restoration of Charles Stuart. At that time she had five hundred and twelve great-great-great-great-great-great-grandparents, and probably some of them were familiar with the court. They would have misunderstood Jeannette, and they would not have been shocked.

"I just wanted you to see her," Mrs. Troup shouted. "I must run back to my partner and finish this. Come down when this number is over and meet some people."

He did not attempt to reply, but stared at her blankly. As she turned away, more of her was seen than when she stood beside him; and a sculptor would have been interested. "Don't forget to come down," she called back, as she descended the stairway.

But he did not appear at the end of the dance; nor could she find him in the gallery or in his room; so, a little anxious, she sent a maid to look for him; and presently the maid came back and said that she had found him standing alone in the dining-room, but that when she told him Mrs. Troup was looking for him, he said nothing; he had walked away in the direction of the kitchen.

"How strange!" Mrs. Troup murmured; but as her troubled

eyes happened to glance downward, both of her hands rose in a gesture of alarm. "Jennie, where's your apron?" she cried.

"It's on me, ma'am," said Jennie; then she discovered that it wasn't. "Why, how in the world—"

But Mrs. Troup was already fluttering to the kitchen. She found trouble there between the caterer's people and her own: the caterer's chef was accusing Mrs. Troup's cook of having stolen a valuable apron.

Uncle Charles was discovered in the coal cellar. He had upon him both of the missing aprons, several others, a fur overcoat belonging to one of the guests, and most of the coal.

THE SPRING CONCERT

THE town was only about eighty years old, but it loved to think of itself as a "good old place," and it habitually spoke of the residence of its principal citizen as "that old-fashioned Ricketts property."

This was an under-statement: the Ricketts place was more than merely old-fashioned. So rapidly do fashions change in houses, nowadays, in small towns as well as in big, and so quickly does life become history, that the "Ricketts property" at fifty years of age was an actual archæological relic. Contemplating the place you contemplated a prevalent way of life already abandoned, and learned a bit of Midland history. The Ricketts place was a left-over from that period when every Midland townsman was his own farmer, according to his means; and if he was able, kept his cow and chickens, and raised corn and pigs at home.

The barn was a farm barn, with a barnyard about it; here were the empty pig-pens and the chicken house, the latter still inhabited. In summer, sweet corn was still grown in the acre lot adjoining the barnyard; and, between that lot and the driveway from the barn, there was a kitchen garden, there was an asparagus bed, and there was a strawberry patch fringed with currant-bushes. Behind the house were out-buildings: the storeroom, the washhouse, the smoke-house. Here was the long grape-arbour, and here stood the two pumps: one of iron, for the cistern; the other a wooden flute that sang higher and higher to an incredible pitch before it fetched the water.

The house was a large, pensive-looking, honest old brick thing, with a "front porch" all across it; and the most casual passer-by must have guessed that there was a great deal of clean oilcloth on the hall floors, and that cool mattings were laid, in summer, in all the rooms—mattings pleasant to the bare feet of children. It was a house that "smelled good": aromas at once sweet and spicy were wont to swim down the mild breezes of Pawpaw Street, whereon the Ricketts place fronted.

In the latter part of April the perfume of apple-blossoms was adrift on those breezes, too; for all the west side of the big yard was an apple orchard, and trees stood so close to the house that a branch of blossoms could be gathered from one of the "sitting-room" windows—and on a warm end-of-April day, when that orchard was full abloom, there sat reading a book, beneath the carnival clouds of blossom, an apple-blossom of a girl.

74

So she was informed by Mr. Lucius Brutus Allen. Mr. Allen came walking up Pawpaw Street from Main Street, about five o'clock in the afternoon; a broad, responsible figure with a broad, irresponsible face, and a good, solid, reddish-haired head behind the face. He was warm, it appeared; inclined to refresh his legs with a pause of leisure, his nose with the smell of the orchard, his eyes with the sight of its occupant. He halted, rested his stout forearms upon the top of the picket fence, and in his own way made the lady acquainted with his idea of her appearance.

"A generous soil makes a generous people, Miss Mary," he observed; and she looked up gravely from her book at the sound of his tremulous tenor voice. "You see, most of this country in the Ohio and Mississippi valleys is fertile. We don't have to scratch the rocks for our crops, so we have time to pronounce our r's. We've even got the leisure to drawl a little. A Yankee, now, he's too pinched for time, between his hard rocks and his hard winters, to pronounce his r's; so he calls his mother 'motha', and hurries on. But he's conscientious, Miss Mary; he knows he's neglected something, and so, to make up for it, he calls his sister 'Mariar.' Down South it's too hot for a fellow to trouble about the whole blame alphabet, so he says, 'Lessee, which lettuhs goin' to be the easies' to leave out?' he says. 'Well, the r's, I reckon,' he says. 'An' g,' he says. 'I'll leave r out most the time, an' g whenevuh I get the chance—an' sometimes d an' t. That'll be a heap easiuh,' he says, 'when I'm claimin' my little boy is the smahtis' chile in the worl'.'"

Mr. Allen paused genially, then concluded: "You see, Miss Mary, I've just been leading up logically to the question: Which is you and which is the rest of the apple-blossoms?"

Miss Ricketts made no vocal reply, but there was a slight concentration of the fine space between her eyebrows; decidedly no symptom of pleasure, though she might properly have enjoyed the loiterer's little extravagance, which was far from being inaccurate as extravagances go. Mr. Allen was forced to remind himself that "nobody loves a fat man," though he decided not to set his thoughts before the lady.

A smile of some ruefulness became just visible upon the ample surface of his face, then withdrew to the interior, and was transmuted into a quality of his odd and pleasant voice, which was distinctly rueful, as he said:

"It's the weather, Miss Mary. You mustn't mind what anybody says along during the first warm days in spring. People are liable to say anything at all."

"Yes," Miss Ricketts returned, not mollified. "I've just noticed." She gave him one dark glance, wholly unfavourable, as she spoke, and then looked down at her book again, allowing him no possible doubt that she wished to proceed with her reading.

"I'm a hard man to discourage," said Mr. Allen. "The band's going to play in the Square to-night. It's been practising 'Annie Laurie' and 'Tenting To-night' all winter, up in the storeroom over Tom Leggett's wall-paper and book emporium, and of course the boys are anxious to give their first concert. What I wanted to say was this: If I came by for you after supper, would you care to go?"

"No," said Miss Ricketts quietly, not looking up.

Before continuing and concluding the conversation, Lucius Brutus Allen paused to contemplate the top of her pink-and-white hat, which was significantly presented to his view as she bent over her book; and the pause was a wistful one on his part. "Seeing as that's the case," he said, finally, "I may be a hard man to discourage, and I was on my way home, but I believe I'll just turn right square around and go on back to the National House bar—and get me a drink of lemonade. I want to show people I'm as desperate as anybody, when I'm crossed."

Immediately, with an air of resolution, Mr. Allen set off upon the path by which he had come. He debouched upon Main Street, at the foot of Pawpaw, crossed the Square to the dismal brick pile much too plainly labelled, "National House, Will Wheen Propr," and passed between two swinging green doors on the ground floor. "George," he said to the bartender, "I'm not happy. Have you any lemons?"

The bartender rubbed the back of his neck, stooped, and poked and peered variously beneath the long bar. "Seems like I did have some, Lu," he said thoughtfully. "I remember seein' them lemons last Mon—"

"No," Mr. Allen interrupted, sighing. "I've been through this before with you, George. I'll take buttermilk."

"Oh, got plenty buttermilk!" the bartender said, brightening; and supplied his customer from a large, bedewed white pitcher. "Buttermilk goes good this weather, don't it, Lu?"

"It do," said Lucius gravely.

Glass in hand, he went to a small round table where sat the only other present patron of the bar—a young man well-favoured, but obviously in a state morbid if not moribund. He did not look up at Mr. Allen's approach; continuing to sit motionless with his far-away gaze marooned upon a stratum of amber light in his glass on the table before him.

He was a picturesque young man, and, with his rumpled black hair, so thick and wavy about his brooding white face, the picture he most resembled was that of a provincial young lawyer stricken with the stage-disease and bound to play Hamlet. This was no more than a resemblance, however; his intentions were different, as he roused himself to make clear presently, though without altering his attitude, or even the direction of his glance.

"What do you mean?" he inquired huskily, a moment after Mr. Allen had seated himself at the table. "What do you mean, slamming a glass of buttermilk down on my table, Lucius Brutus Allen?"

Mr. Allen put on a pair of eye-glasses, and thoughtfully examined the morose gentleman's countenance before replying, "I would consume this flagon of buttermilk in congenial melancholy, Joseph Pitney Perley."

Mr. Perley, still motionless, demanded: "Can't you see what I'm doing?"

"What are you doing, Joe?"

"Drinking!"

"Professionally?" Mr. Allen inquired. "Or only for the afternoon?"

"I don't want to be talked to!"

"I do," said Lucius. "Talk to me."

Here the bartender permitted himself the intervention of a giggle, and wiped his dry bar industriously—his favourite gesture. "You ain't goin' to git much talk out o' Joe, Lu!" he said. "All he's said sence he come in here was jest, 'Gimme same, George.' I tell him he ain't goin' to be in no condition to 'tend the band concert 's evening if he keeps on another couple hours or so. Me, I don't mind seein' a man drink some, but I like to see him git a little fun out of it!"

"Have you considered the band concert, Joe?" Mr. Allen inquired. "Do you realize what strange euphonies you'll miss unless you keep sober until seven-thirty?"

The sombre Perley relaxed his gaze, and uttered a fierce monosyllable of denunciation. "Sober!" he added, afterward. "I'm sober. That's my trouble. I've been trying to get tight for three hours!"

"I'll say this fer you," the bartender volunteered—"you been tryin' good, too!"

"Ever experiment any?" Lucius suggested. "Why don't you go over to Doc Willis's Painless Dental Parlours? He's got a tank of gas there, and all you do is put a rubber thing over your nose and breathe. Without any trouble at all you'll be completely out of business in forty-five seconds."

"Yeh," said the bartender. "But it don't last more'n about four minutes."

"No; that's true," Lucius admitted. "But maybe Joe could hire Doc to tap him behind the ear with one of those little lead mallets when he sees him coming out of the gas. Joe'd feel just about the same to-morrow as he will if he stays here running up a bill with you. Fact is, I believe he'd feel better."

"I tell you," said Mr. Perley, with emphasis, "I'm drinking!" And for further emphasis he rattled his glass. "Give me the same, George," he said.

George held a bottle to the light. He meditated, rubbing the back of his head; then spoke: "Tell you what I'll do. The wife's waitin' supper fer me now; I want to git back up-town early fer the trade before the concert, because I look fer quite a rush—"

"Yes," interrupted Mr. Allen musingly. "Our community is going to see a night of wine and music, George."

"I'll jest open a fresh bottle fer you, Joe," the bartender continued; "and when I git back I'll charge you with how many drinks you take out of it. I'm goin' on home to supper. You want any more buttermilk, Lu?"

"Bring the pitcher," said Mr. Allen. "I will sup upon it."

"All right." And George brought to the table the pitcher of buttermilk, a dim saucer of crackers and cheese, a brown bottle, ice-water, and fresh glasses. After that he doffed his apron, put on his hat, but no coat, and went to the door, where he turned to say: "If anybody else comes in here before I git back—"

"And calls for liquor," Mr. Allen took up the sentence, as George paused in thought, "we shall be glad to—"

"Tell 'em," said George, "they don't git it!" He departed.

Mr. Allen helped himself to buttermilk, ate a cracker, leaned back in his chair, and began to hum "Annie Laurie."

"Stop that!" said Perley sharply.

"Certainly," said Lucius. "I'll whistle instead."

"If you do," the troubled young man warned him, apparently in good faith, "I'll kill you!"

"What can I do to entertain you, Joe?"

"You might clear out," his friend suggested darkly. "God knows I haven't asked for your society!"

"No," said Lucius. "Our fairest gifts do oft arrive without petition. What an unusual thought! Have you noticed—"

But the other burst out suddenly in a tragic fury: "Shut up! What's the matter with you? Can't you see I want to be alone?"

Mr. Allen remained placid. "What difference do I make?" he asked. "I thought you said you were 'drinking'? If you're really in earnest about it you don't care who's here or anywhere else."

"Don't you see I'm in misery?" cried Perley.

"The ayes have it."

"Well, then, why in Heaven's name can't you—"

"I'll tell you," said Lucius. "I'm in misery, too. Terrible!"

"Well, what the devil do I care for that?"

"Haven't I got a right to sit here?" Lucius inquired mildly. "Haven't I got a right to sit here and drink, and cuss inside my innards, and take on the way you're doing? Mary Ricketts just told me that she wouldn't go to the band concert with me."

"Oh, do dry up!"

"Well, you're responsible for Mary's treatment of me, aren't you?" said Lucius. "I thought probably there'd be trouble when I saw you headed this way this afternoon."

"You do beat any ordinary lunatic!" the distressed young man protested. "I 'headed this way' this afternoon because I got one of my spells. You know well enough how it is with me, and how it was with my father before me—every so often the spell come on me, and I've got to drink. What in the Lord's name has that to do with Mary Ricketts? I don't suppose I've even seen her for a month. Never did see anything of her, to speak of, in my life."

Mr. Allen replenished his glass from the pitcher of buttermilk before replying, and appeared to muse sorrowfully. "Well, maybe I was mistaken," he said. "But I—" He broke off a line of thought; then sighed and inquired: "When this 'spell' comes on you, Joe, you feel that you've 'got' to go on until—"

"You know I do! I don't want to talk about it."

"But suppose," said Lucius, "suppose something took your mind off of it."

"Nothing could. Nothing on earth!"

"But just suppose something did turn up—right in the start of a spell, say—something you found you'd rather do. You know, Joe, I believe if it did and you found something else was really pleasanter, it might be you'd never start in again. You'd understand it wasn't the fun you think it is, maybe."

"Fun!" Joe cried. "I don't want to drink!"

And at that his stocky companion burst into outright laughter. "I know you think so, Joe," he said apologetically, when his hilarity was sufficiently diminished. "Of course you believe it. I'm not denying that."

"By George!" the unfortunate young man explained. "You do make me sick! I suppose if I had smallpox you'd say you weren't denying I believed I had it! You sit there and drink your buttermilk, and laugh at me like a ninny because you can't understand! No man on earth can understand, unless he has the thirst come on him the way mine does on me! And yet you tell me I only 'believe' I have it!"

"Yes, I ought to explain," said Mr. Allen soothingly. "It did sound unfeeling. One of the reasons you drink, Joe, is because this is a small town;—you have an active mind, a lot of the time there's nothing much to do, and you get bored."

"I told you nobody could understand such a thirst as mine—nobody except the man that's got one like it!"

"This hankering is something inside you, isn't it, Joe?"

"What of that?"

"It comes on you about every so often?"

"Yes."

"If there weren't any liquor in the world, you'd have the thirst for it just the same, would you?"

"Just the same," Perley answered. "And go crazy from it."

"Whereas," Mr. Allen returned, "since liquor's obtainable you prefer to go crazy from the imbibing of it instead of from the hanker for it. You find that more ossedalious, and nobody can blame you. But suppose alcohol had never been discovered, would you have the hanker?"

"No, because I wouldn't have inherited it from my father. You know as well as I do, how it runs in my family."

"So I do, Joe; so I do!" Mr. Allen sighed reminiscently. "Both your father and your Uncle Sam went that way. I remember them very well, and how they enjoyed it. That's different from you, Joe."

"Different!" Joe laughed bitterly. "Do you suppose I get any 'enjoyment' out of it? Three days I'll drink now; then I'll be in hell—and I've got to go on. I've got to!"

"Funny about its being hereditary," said Lucius, musing aloud. "I expect you rather looked forward to that, Joe?"

His companion stared at him fiercely. "What do you mean by that?" he demanded.

"You always thought it was going to be hereditary, didn't you, Joe? From almost when you were a boy?"

"Yes, I did. What of it?"

"And maybe—" Lucius suggested, with the utmost mildness—"just possibly, say about the time you began to use liquor a little at first, you decided that this hereditary thing was inevitable, and the idea made you melancholy about yourself, of course; but after all, you felt that the hereditary thing made a pretty fair excuse to yourself, didn't you?"

"See here," Joe said angrily, "I'm not in any mood to stand—"

"Pshaw!" Lucius interrupted. "I was only going on to say that it's more and more curious to me about this hereditary notion. I'm thirty-five, and you're only twenty-six. I remember well when your father began to drink especially. I was seventeen years old, and you

80

were about eight. You see you were already born then, and so I can't understand about the thirst being heredi—"

"Damn it all!" Joe Perley shouted; and he struck the table with his fist. "I told you I don't want to talk, didn't I? Didn't you hear me say I was drinking!"

The amiable man across the table produced two cigars from his coat pocket. "We'll change the subject," he said. "Smoke, Joe?"

"No, thank you."

"We'll change the subject," Lucius repeated. "I gather that this one is painful to you. You don't mind my staying here if we talk about something else?"

"No—not much."

"I mentioned that I asked Mary Ricketts to go with me to the band concert to-night, didn't I?" Mr. Allen inquired, as he lit his cigar. "I was telling you about that, wasn't I, Joe?"

"You said something about it," Mr. Perley replied with evident ennui.

"You know, Joe," said Lucius, his tone becoming confidential, "I walk past the old Ricketts property every afternoon on my way home. It's quite considerable out of my way, but I always do. Fact is," he chuckled ruefully, "I can't help it."

"I suppose you want me to ask you why," said his gloomy companion, with sincere indifference.

"Yes, Joe, will you?"

"All right. Why can't you help it?"

"Well, there's something about that old place so kind of pleasant and healthy and reliable. This is a funny world: there's a lot of things a fellow's got to be afraid of in it, and the older he gets the more he sees to scare him. I think what I like best about that old Ricketts property is the kind of safe look it has. It looks as if anybody that belonged in there was safe from 'most any kind of disaster—bankruptcy, lunacy, 'social ambition,' money ambition, evil thoughts, or turning into a darn fool of any kind. You don't happen to walk by there much, do you, Joe?"

"No, I don't."

"Well, sir, you ought to!" said Lucius genially. "The orchard's in bloom, and you ought to see it. The Ricketts orchard is the show of this county. The good old judge has surely looked after those old apple-trees of his; they're every one just solid blossom. Yes, sir, every last one! Why, it made me feel like a dryad!"

"Like a who?"

"You mean that I'm thirty-five"—so Mr. Allen thought fit to interpret this question—"and that I'm getting a little fat, some baldish and a whole lot reddish. So I am; but I'll tell you something, young Joseph: romance is a thing inside a person, just the same as your thirst. It doesn't matter what his outside is like. My trousers always bag at the knees, even when they're new, but my knees themselves are pure Grecian. It's the skinny seamstress of forty that dreams the most of marquises in silver armour; and darky boys in school forget the lesson in reveries about themselves—they think of themselves on horseback as generals with white faces and straight blond hair. And everybody knows that the best poets are almost always outrageously ordinary to look at. This is springtime, Joseph; and the wren lays an egg no bigger than a fairy's. The little birds—"

"By George!" Mr. Perley exclaimed, in real astonishment. "See here!" he said. "Had you been drinking, yourself, before you came in? If not, it's the first time I knew a person could get a talking jag on buttermilk."

"No," said Lucius, correcting him. "It's on apple-blossoms. She was sitting under 'em pretending to read a book, but I suppose she was thinking about you, Joe."

"Who was?"

"Mary," Mr. Allen replied quietly. "Mary Ricketts."

"You say she was thinking about me?"

"Probably she was, Joe. She was sitting there, and the little birds—"

"I know you're a good lawyer," Joe interrupted, shaking his head in gloomy wonder, "but everybody in town thinks you're a nut, except when you're on a law case, and I guess they're about right. You certainly talk like one!"

Mr. Allen nodded. "A reputation like that is mighty helpful sometimes."

"Well, if you like it you're free to refer all inquirers to me," said Joe heartily. "You're trying to tell me Mary Ricketts was 'thinking' about me, and I don't suppose I've seen her as much as five times this year; and I haven't known her—not to speak of—since we were children. I don't suppose I've had twenty minutes' talk with her, all told, since I got back from college. The only girl I ever see anything of at all is Molly Baker, and that's only because she happens to live next door. I don't see even Molly to speak to more than once or twice a month. I don't have anything to do with any of the girls. I keep away from 'em, because a man with the curse I've got hanging over me—"

"Thought you didn't want to talk about that, Joe."

"I don't," the young man said angrily. "But I want to know what you mean by this nonsense about Mary Ricketts and me."

"I don't know if I ought to tell you—exactly." Here Lucius

frowned as with a pressure of conscience. "I'm not sure I ought to. Do you insist on it, Joe?"

"Not if you've got to talk any more about 'the little birds!'" Joe returned with sour promptness. "But if you can leave them out and talk in a regular way, I'd like to hear you."

"Have you ever noticed," Mr. Allen began, "that Mary Ricketts is a beautiful girl?"

"She's not," said Joe. "She's not anything like 'beautiful.' Everybody in town knows and always has known that Mary Ricketts is an ordinarily good-looking girl. You can call her pretty if you want to stretch it a little, but that's all."

"That all, you think?"

"Certainly!"

"You ought to see her in the orchard, Joe!"

"Well, I'm not very likely to."

"Well, just why not, now?"

"Well, why should I?"

"You mean you've never given much thought to her?"

"Certainly I haven't," said Joe. "Why should I?"

"Isn't it strange now!" Mr. Allen shook his head wistfully. "I mentioned that I asked her to go to the band concert with me, didn't I, Joe?"

"You did."

"And did I tell you that she refused?"

"Lord, yes!"

"Well, that was it," said Mr. Allen gently. "She just said, 'No!' She didn't say 'No, thank you.' No, sir, nothing like that; just plain 'No!' 'Well,' I thought to myself, 'now why is that? Naturally, she'd want to go to the concert, wouldn't she? Why, of course she would; it's the first public event that's happened since the lecture on "Liquid Air" at Masonic Hall, along back in February. Certainly she'd want to go. Well, then, what's the matter? It must be simply she doesn't want to go with you, Lucius Brutus Allen!' That's what I said to myself, Joe. 'You're practically a fat old man from her point of view,' I said to myself. 'She wants to go, but you aren't the fellow she wants to go with. Well, who is it? Evidently,' I reasoned, 'evidently he hasn't turned up, because she's just the least bit snappish the way she tells me she isn't pining for my escort.' Well, sir, I began to cast around in my mind to think who on earth it could be. 'It isn't Henry Wheen,' I thought, 'because she discouraged Henry so hard, more than a year ago, that Henry went and married that waitress here at his father's hotel. And it isn't Bax Lewis,' I thought, 'because she showed Bax he didn't stand any chance from the first. And it isn't Charlie McGregor or Cal Veedis,' I thought, 'because she just wouldn't have anything to do with either of them, though they both tried to make her till the judge pretty near had to tell 'em right out that they'd better stay away. Well, it isn't Doc Willis, and it isn't Carlos Bollingbroke Thompson, nor Whit Connor,' I thought, 'because they're old bachelors like me—and that just about finishes the list.' Well, sir, there's where I had to scratch my head. 'It must be somebody,' I thought, 'somebody that hasn't been coming around the Ricketts property at all, so far, because she's never gone any place she could help with those that have been coming around there.' Then I thought of you, Joe. 'By George!' I thought. 'By George, it might be Joe Perley! He's the only young man in town not married, engaged, or feeble-minded, that hasn't ever showed any interest in Miss Mary. There's no two ways about it: likely as not it's liable to be Joe Perley!' "

"I never heard anything crazier in my life!" Joe said. "I don't suppose Mary Ricketts has given me two thoughts in the last five years."

Mr. Allen tilted back in his chair, his feet upon a rung of the table. He placed his cigar at the left extremity of his mouth, gazed at the ceiling, and waved his right hand in a take-it-or-leave-it gesture.

"Well, why would she?" Joe demanded. "There's nothing about me that—"

"No," said his friend. "Nothing except she doesn't know you very well."

At that Joe Perley laughed. "You are the funniest old Lucius!" he said. "Just because I've never been around there and the rest have, you say that proves—"

Mr. Allen waved his hand again. "I only say there's somebody could get her to go to that concert with him. Absolutely! Why absolutely? It's springtime; she's twenty-three. Of course, if it is you, she isn't very liable to hear the music except along with her family— not when you've got such pressing engagements here, of course! I'm thinking of going up there again pretty soon myself, to see if maybe Judge and Mrs. Ricketts aren't going to walk up-town for the concert, and maybe I can sort of push myself in among the family so that I can walk anyway in the same group with Mary! It's going to be moonlight, and as balmy as a night in a piece of poetry! By George! you can smell apple-blossoms from one end of the town to the other, Joe!"

"How you hate talking!" Mr. Perley remarked discouragingly.

"I hear the band is going to try 'Schubert's Serenade,' " Lucius continued. "The boys aren't so bad as we make out, after all; the truth is, they play almighty well. I expect you'll be able to hear some of it from in here, Joe; but take me now—I want to be out in the moonlight in that apple-blossom smell when they play 'Schubert's Serenade!' I want to be somewhere where I can see the moonshine shadow of Mary Ricketts's hat fall across her cheek, so I can spend my time guessing whether she's listening to the music with her eyes shut or open. It's a pink-and-white hat, and she's wearing a pink-and-white dress, too, to-day, Joe. She was sitting under those apple-blossoms, and the little bir—"

Sudden, loud and strong expressions suffered him not to continue for several moments.

"Certainly, Joe," Mr. Allen then resumed. "I will not mention them again. I was only leading to the remark that nightingales serenading through the almond-groves of Sicily probably have nothing particular on our enterprising little city during a night in apple-blossom time. My great trouble, Joe, is never getting used to its being springtime. Every year when it comes around again it hits me just the same way—maybe a little more so each year that I grow older. And this has been the first plumb genuine spring day we've had. At the present hour this first true blue spring day is hushing itself down into the first spring evening, and in a little while there'll be another miracle: the first scented and silvered spring night. All over town the old folks are coming out from their suppers to sit on their front porches, and the children are beginning to play hi-spy in and out among the trees. Pretty soon they'll all, old and young, be strolling up-town to hear the band play on the courthouse steps. I expect some of the young couples already have started; they like to walk slowly and not say much, on the way to the spring concert, you know."

Mr. Allen drank another glass of buttermilk, smiled, then murmured with repletion and the pathos of a concluding bit of enthusiasm. "Oh, Lordy, Lordy!" he said, "What it is to be twenty or twenty-five in springtime!"

"Not for me," Mr. Perley rejoined, shaking his head.

"No, I suppose not. It does seem pretty rough," said Lucius, sympathetically, "to think of you sitting here in this reeky hole, when pretty nearly every other young fellow in town will be strolling through the apple-blossom smell in the moonlight with a girl on his arm, and the band playing, and all. Old soak Beeslum'll probably be in here to join you after while, though; and four or five farm hands, and some of the regular Saturday-night town drunks, and maybe two or three Swedes. Oh, I expect you'll have company enough, Joe!"

"I guess so. Anyhow, I haven't much choice! This thing's got me, and I've got to go through with it, Lucius."

"I see. Yes, sir, it's too bad! Too bad!" And Lucius looked

sympathetically down, then cheerfully up again, as the swinging-doors parted to admit the entrance of the returned bartender. "Hello, George!"

"Back a'ready," said George self-approvingly. "Ham, fried potatoes, coffee, and griddle-cakes, all tucked inside o' me, too! Didn't miss any customers, did I?"

"No."

George came to the table. "Lemme look how many drinks you owe me fer sence I went out, Joe," he said. "I had the place where she come to in the neck of the bottle marked with my thumb." He lifted the bottle, regarded it thoughtfully at first, then with some surprise. He set it down upon the table without comment, began to whistle "Little Annie Rooney," went behind the bar, doffed his hat, resumed his apron, and continued to whistle.

Mr. Allen rose, dusting some crumbs of cracker from his attire. "I guess I must have won the buttermilk record, George," he said, as he placed a silver dollar upon the bar. "If buttermilk were intoxicating there wouldn't be a sober creature on the face of the earth. Trouble with your other stuff, George, it tastes so rotten!"

"I take buttermilk sometimes myself, Lu," said George as he made change. "I guess there ain't nobody seen me carryin' much hard liquor sence my second child was born. That was the time they had to jug me, and—whoo, gosh! you'd ought to seen what I went through when I got home that night! She's little and she was sick-abed, too, but that didn't git in her way none! No, sir!"

"Good night," said Lucius cheerily. "I'm going to stroll along Pawpaw Street before the band starts. Moon'll be 'way up in a little while now, and on such a night as this is going to be did Jessica, the Jew's daughter— You know what I mean, George."

"Yep," said George blankly. "I gotcha, Lu."

"I'm going," said Lucius, "to go and push in with some folks to listen to the band with. Good night, Joe."

Joe Perley did not turn his head, but sat staring fixedly at the table, his attitude being much the same as that in which Lucius had discovered him.

"Good night, Joe," the departing gentleman paused to repeat.

"What?"

"Nothing," said Lucius. "I only said 'good night.'"

"All right," said Joe absently. "Good night."

Mr. Allen took a musical departure. "Oh, as I strolled out one summer evening," he sang, "for to meet Miss Nellie Green, all the birds and the flow'rs was singing sweetly, wherev-urr they was to be seen!"

Thus, singing heartily, he passed between the swinging-doors and out to the street. Here he continued his euphonic mood, but moderated his expression of it to an inconspicuous humming. Dusk had fallen, a dusk as scented and as alive with spring as he had claimed it would be; and a fair shaft of the rising moon already struck upon the white cupola of the courthouse.

. . . Mary Ricketts was leaning upon the front gate of the Ricketts place when he came there.

"Good evening, Miss Mary," he said. "Are the Judge and your mother at home?"

"They're right there on the front porch, Mr. Allen," she said cordially. "Won't you come in?"

"In a minute," he responded. "It does me good to hear you answer when I ask for your parents, Miss Mary."

"How is that?"

"Why," he said, "you always sound so friendly when I ask for them!"

She laughed, and explained her laughter by saying, "It's funny you don't always ask for them!"

"Just so," he agreed. "I've been thinking about that. Are you all going up to the Square pretty soon, to hear the concert?"

"Father and mother are, I think," she said. "I'm not."

"Just 'waiting at the gate'?"

"Not for any one!"

Lucius took off his hat and fanned himself, a conciliatory gesture. "I tell you I feel mighty sorry for one young man in this town to-night," he said.

"Who's that, Mr. Allen?"

"Well—" he hesitated. "I don't know if I ought to tell you about it."

"Why not me?" she asked, not curiously.

"Well—it's that young Joe Perley."

Miss Ricketts was mildly amused; Lucius's tone was serious, and if she had any interest whatever in Mr. Perley it was of a quality most casual and remote. "Why should you either tell me or not tell me anything about him?" she asked.

"You know he's such a good-looking young fellow," said Lucius. "And he's going to make a fine lawyer, too; I've had him with me in a couple of cases, and I've an idea he might have something like a real career, if—" He paused.

"Yes?" she said idly. "If what? And why is it you feel so sorry for him, and why did you hesitate to tell me? What's it all about, Mr. Allen?"

"I suppose I'd better explain, now I've gone this far," he said, a little embarrassed. "I was talking with Joe to-day, and—well, the fact is we got to talking about you."

"You did?" Her tone betokened an indifference unmistakably genuine. "Well?"

Lucius laughed with increased embarrassment. "Well—the fact is we talked about you a long while."

"Indeed?" she said coldly, but there was a slight interest now perceptible under the coldness; for Miss Mary Ricketts was not unhuman. "Was there a verdict?"

"It—it wasn't so much what he said, exactly—no, not so much that," Lucius circumlocuted. "It was more the—the length of time we were talking about you. That was the thing that struck me about it, because I didn't know—that is, I'd never heard—I—"

"What are you trying to say, Mr. Allen?"

"Well, I mean," said Lucius, "I mean I hadn't known that he came around here at all."

"He doesn't."

"That's why I was so surprised."

"Surprised at what?" she said impatiently.

"Why," said Lucius, "surprised at the length of time that we were talking about you!"

"What nonsense!" she cried. "What nonsense! I don't suppose he's said two words to me or I to him in two years!"

"Yes," Lucius assented. "That's what makes it all the more remarkable! I supposed the only girl he ever thought anything about was Molly Baker, but he told me the only reason he ever goes there is just because she lives next door to him."

"Not very polite to Molly!" said Miss Ricketts, and she laughed with some indulgence for this ungallantry.

"Still, Molly's a determined girl," Lucius suggested; "and she might—"

"She might what?"

"Nothing," said Lucius. "I was only remembering I'd always heard she was such a—such a grasping sort of girl."

"Had you?"

"Yes, hadn't you?"

She was thoughtful for a moment. "Oh, I don't know."

"So it seemed to me—well—" He laughed hesitatingly. "Well, it certainly was curious, the length of time we were talking about you to-day!" And he paused again as if awaiting her comment; but she offered none. "Well," he said, finally, "I expect I better go join the old folks on the porch where I belong."

He was heartily received and made welcome in that sedate retreat, where, as he said, he belonged; but throughout the greetings and the subsequent conversation he kept a corner of his eye upon the dim white figure in the shadow of the maple trees down by the gate.

Presently another figure, a dark one, graceful and young, came slowly along the sidewalk—slowly, and rather hesitatingly. This figure paused, took a few steps onward again; then definitely halted near the gate.

"Who is that young man out there, talking to Mary?" asked Mary's mother. "Can you make out, father?"

"It's that young Joe Perley."

"I've heard he drinks a good deal sometimes," said Mrs. Ricketts thoughtfully. "His mother says he tries not to, but that it comes over him, and that he's afraid he'll turn out like his father."

Mr. Allen laughed cheerfully. "Anybody at Joe's age can turn out any way he wants to," he said. "Mrs. Perley needn't worry about Joe any more. I just sat with him an hour down at the National House, and there was an open whisky bottle on the table before us, and he never once touched it all the time I was talking with him."

"Well, I'm glad of that," said Mrs. Ricketts. "That ought to show he has plenty of will-power, anyhow."

"Plenty," said Lucius.

Then Mary's young voice called from the spaces of night. "I'm going to walk up-town to the concert with Mr. Perley, mother. You'd better wear your shawl if you come."

And there was the click of the gate as she passed out.

"We might as well be going along then, I suppose," said Mrs. Ricketts, rising. "You'll come with us old folks, Lucius?"

As the three old folks sauntered along the moon-speckled sidewalk the two slim young figures in advance were faintly revealed to them, likewise sauntering. And Lucius was right: you could smell apple-blossoms from one end of the town to the other.

"I hope our boys will win the band tournament at the county fair next summer," said Mrs. Ricketts. "Don't you think there's a pretty good chance of it, Lucius?"

For a moment he appeared not to have heard her, and she gently repeated her question:

"Don't you think there's a pretty good chance of it?"

"Yes, more than a chance," he dreamily replied. "It only takes a hint in springtime. They'll do practically anything you tell 'em to. It's mostly the apple-blossoms and the little birds."

WILLAMILLA

MASTER LAURENCE COY, aged nine, came down the shady sidewalk one summer afternoon, in a magnificence that escaped observation. To the careless eye he was only a little boy pretending to be a drummer; for although he had no drum and his clenched fingers held nothing, it was plain that he drummed. But to be merely a drummer was far below the scope of his intentions; he chose to employ his imagination on the grand scale, and to his own way of thinking, he was a full drum-corps, marching between lines of tumultuous spectators. And as he came gloriously down the shouting lane of citizenry he pranced now and then; whereupon, without interrupting his drumming, he said sharply: "Whoa there, Jenny! Git up there, Gray!" This drum-corps was mounted.

He vocalized the bass drums and the snare drums in a staccato chant, using his deepest voice for the bass, and tones pitched higher, and in truth somewhat painfully nasal, for the snare; meanwhile he swung his right arm ponderously on the booms, then resumed the rapid employment of both imaginary sticks for the rattle of the tenor drums. Thus he projected and sketched, all at the same time, every detail of this great affair.

"Boom!" he said. "Boom! Boomety, boomety, boom!" Then he added:

> *"Boom! Boom!*
> *Boom bought a rat trap,*
> *Bigger than a bat trap,*
> *Bigger than a cat trap!*
> *Boom! Boom!*
> *Boomety, boomety, boom!"*

So splendid was the effect upon himself of all this pomp and realism, that the sidewalk no longer contented him. Vociferating for the moment as a bugle, the drum-corps swung to the right and debouched to the middle of the street, where such a martial body was more in place, and thenceforth marched, resounding. "Boom! Boom! Boomety, boomety, boom!" There followed repetitions of the chant concerning the celebrated trap purchased by Mr. Boom.

A little girl leaned upon a gate that gave admission to a pleasant yard, shaded by a vast old walnut tree, and from this point she watched the approach of the procession. She was a homely little girl, as people say; but a student of small affairs would have guessed

90

that she had been neatly dressed earlier in the day; and even now it could be seen that the submergence of her right stocking into its own folds was not due to any lack of proper equipment, for equipment was visible. She stood behind the gate, eagerly looking forth, and by a coincidence not unusual in that neighbourhood, a beautiful little girl was at the gate of the next yard, some eighty or a hundred feet beyond; but this second little girl's unspotted attire had suffered no disarrangements, and her face was clean; even her hands were miraculously clean.

When the sonorous Laurence came nearer, the homely little girl almost disappeared behind her gate; her arms rested upon the top of it, and only her hair, forehead and eyes could be seen above her arms. The eyes, however, had become exceedingly sharp, and they shone with an elfin mirth that grew even brighter as the drum-corps drew closer.

"Boom!" said Laurence. "Boomety, boomety, boom!" And again he gave an account of Mr. Boom's purchase; but he condescended to offer no sign betokening a consciousness of the two spectators at their gates. He went by the first of these in high military order, executing a manœuvre as he went—again briefly becoming a trumpeter, swinging to the right, then to the left, and so forward once more, as he resumed the drums. "Boom! Boom! Boomety, boomety, boom!

> "Boom! Boom!
> Boom bought a rat trap,
> Bigger than a bat trap—"

But here he was profoundly annoyed by the conduct of the homely little girl. She darted out of her gate, ran to the middle of the street and pranced behind him in outrageous mockery. In a thin and straining voice, altogether inappropriate for the representation of a drum-corps, she piped:

> "Boom bought a rat trap,
> Bigger than a bat trap,
> Bigger than a cat trap!
> Boom!"

Laurence turned upon her. "For heavenses' sakes!" he said. "My good-nuss, Daisy Mears, haven't you got any sense? For heavenses' sakes, pull up your ole stockin's!"

"I won't," Miss Mears returned with instant resentment. "I guess you can't order me around, Mister Laurence Coy! I doe' know

91

who ever 'pointed you to be my boss! Besides, only one of 'em's fell down."

"Well, pull it up, then," he said crossly. "Or else don't come hangin' around me!"

"Oh, you don't say so!" she retorted. "Thank you ever so kinely an' p'litely for your complimunts just the same, but I pull up my stockin's whenever I want to, not when every person I happen to meet in the street goes an' takes an' tells me to!"

"Well, you better!" said Laurence, at a venture, for he was not absolutely certain of her meaning. "Anyway, you needn't hang around me unless—"

He stopped, for Daisy Mears had begun, not to hang around him indeed, but to dance around him, and indecorously at that! She levelled her small, grimy right forefinger at him, appearing to whet it with her left forefinger, which was equally begrimed, and at the same time she capered, squealing triumphantly: "Ya-ay, Laurunce! Showin' off! Showin' off 'cause Elsie Threamer's lookin' at you! Showin' off for Elsie! Showin' off for Elsie!"

"I am not!" Laurence made loud denial, but he coloured and glanced wretchedly at the other little girl, who had remained at her own gate. Her lovely, shadowy eyes appeared to be unaware of the dispute in the street; and, crooning almost soundlessly to herself, she had that perfect detachment from environment and events so often observed in Beauties.

"I am not!" Laurence repeated. "If I was goin' to show off before anybody, I wouldn't show off before Elsie!" And on the spur of the moment, to prove what he said, he made a startling misrepresentation of his sentiments. "I hate her!" he shouted.

But his tormentress was accustomed to deal with wild allegations of this sort, and to discount them. "Ya-ay, Laur-runce!" she cried. "Showin' off for Elsie! Yes, you were! Showin' off for Elsie! Show-win' off for Ell-see!" And circling round him in a witch dance, she repeated the taunt till it nauseated him, his denials became agonized and his assertions that he hated Elsie, uproarious. Thus within the space of five minutes a pompous drum-corps passed from a state of discipline to one of demoralization.

"Children! Children!" a woman's voice called from an open window. "Get out of the street, children. Look out for the automobiles!"

Thereupon the witch dance stopped, and the taunting likewise; Daisy returned to the sidewalk with a thoughtful air; and Master Coy followed her, looking rather morbid, but saying nothing. They leaned against the hedge near where the indifferent and dreamy Elsie stood at her gate; and for some time none of the three spoke: they had one of those apparently inexplicable silences that come upon children. It was Laurence who broke it, with a muttering.

"Anyways, I wasn't," he said, seemingly to himself.

"You was, too," Daisy said quietly.

"Well, how you goin' to prove it?" Laurence inquired, speaking louder. "If it's so, then you got to prove it. You either got to prove it or else you got to take it back."

"I don't either haf to!"

"You do too haf to!"

"All right, then," said Daisy. "I'll prove it by Elsie. He was, wasn't he, Elsie?"

"What?" Elsie inquired vaguely.

"Wasn't Laurence showin' off out in the street? He was showin' off, wasn't he?"

"I was not!"

"You was, too! Wasn't he, Elsie?"

"I doe' know," Elsie said, paying no attention to them; for she was observing a little group that had made its appearance at the next corner, a few moments earlier, and now came slowly along the sidewalk in the mottled shade of the maple trees. "Oh, look!" she cried. "Just look at that darling little coloured baby!"

Her companions turned to look where she pointed, and Daisy instantly became as ecstasized as Elsie. "Oh, look at the precious, darling, little thing!" she shouted.

As for Laurence, what he saw roused little enthusiasm within his bosom; on the contrary, he immediately felt a slight but distinct antipathy; and he wondered as, upon occasion he had wondered before, why in the world little girls of his own age, and even younger girls, as well as older girls and grown-up women, so often fell into a gesticular and vocal commotion at the sight of a baby. However, he took some interest in the dog accompanying this one.

The baby sat in a small and rickety wooden wagon which appeared to be of home manufacture, since it was merely a brown box on small wheels or disks of solid wood. A long handle projected behind as a propelling device, but the course of the vehicle was continually a little devious, on account of a most visible eccentricity of the front wheels. The infant was comfortable among cushions, however, and over its head a little, ancient, fringed red parasol had been ingeniously erected, probably as much for style as for shade. Moreover, this note of fashion was again touched in the baby's ribboned cap, and in the embroidered scarf that served as a coverlet, and, though plainly a relic, still exhibited a lively colour.

An unevenly ponderous old coloured woman pushed the

wagon; but her complexion was incomparably darker than the occupant's, which was an extremely light tan, so that no one would have guessed them to be as nearly related as they really were. And although this deeply coloured woman's weight was such a burden to her that she advanced at a slow, varying gait, more a sag-and-shuffle than a walk, she was of an exuberantly gracious aspect. In fact, her expression was so benevolent that it was more than striking; it was surprising. Her eyes, rolling and curiously streaked, were visibly moist with kindness; her mouth was murmurous in loving phrases addressed sometimes to life generally, sometimes to the baby, and sometimes to the dog accompanying the cortège.

This dog was one of those dogs who feel themselves out of place in the street, and show that they do by the guardedness of their expressions. Their relief when they reach an alley is evident; then they relax at once; the look of strain vanishes from their eyes, and their nerves permit them once more to sit when they massage their ears. They seem intended to be white, but the intention appears to have become early enfeebled, leaving them the colour of a pale oyster;—and they do not wear collars, these dogs. A collar upon one of them would alter his status disturbingly, and he would understand that, and feel confused and troubled. In a word, even when these dogs are seen in an aristocratic environment, for some straying moment, they are dogs instantly recognizable as belonging to coloured persons.

This one was valued highly by his owners; at least that was implied by what the benevolent old woman said to him as they moved slowly along the sidewalk toward the three children at Elsie Threamer's gate.

"Hossifer," she said, addressing the dog, "Hossifer, I b'lieve my soul you the fines' dog in a worl'! I feel the lovin'es' to you I ever feel any dog. You wuff fo', fi' hunnud dolluhs, Hossifer. You wuff fousan' dolluhs; yes, you is! You a lovin' dog, Hossifer!" Then she spoke to the baby, but affection and happiness almost overcame her coherence. "Dah-li-dah-li-dah-li-deedums!" she said. "Oh, but you the lovin', lovin', lovin' baby, honey! You is my swee', swee', li'l dee-dee-do! Oh, oh, oh, bless Lawd, ain' it a fine day! Fine day fer my honey lovin' baby! Fine day f'um lovin' heaven! Oh, oh, oh, I'm a-happy! Swee' lovin' livin', lem me sing! Oh, lem me sing!"

She sang, and so loudly that she astonished the children; whereupon, observing their open mouths and earnestly staring eyes, she halted near them and laughed.

"Why all you look at me so funny?" she inquired hilariously. "Li'l whi' boy, what fer you open you' mouf at me, honey?"

"I didn't," Laurence said.

"Yes'm, indeed you did, honey," she gaily insisted. "You all free did. Open you' moufs and look so funny at me—make me laugh an' holler!" And with unconventional vivacity she whooped and cackled strangely.

Finding her thus so vociferously amiable, Daisy felt encouraged to approach the wagon; and bending down over it, she poked the mulatto baby repeatedly in an affectionate manner. "Oh!" she exclaimed. "I do think this is the darlingest baby!"

"Ain' it!" the coloured woman cried. "Ain' it! Yes'm, you say what's so! Ain' it!"

"Does it belong to you?" Daisy inquired.

"Yes'm, indeed do! I'm baby' grammaw. Baby my li'l lovin' gran'chile."

It was plain that all three children thought the statement remarkable; they repeatedly looked from the light tan grandchild to the dark brown grandmother and back again, while Daisy, in particular, had an air of doubt. "Are you sure?" she asked. "Are you sure you're its gran'ma?"

"Yes'm indeed!"

"Honest?"

"Yes'm indeed!"

"Well—" Daisy began, and was about to mention the grounds of her doubt; but tact prevailed with her, and she asked a question instead.

"What's its name?"

"Name Willamilla."

"What?"

"Name Willamilla."

"Willamilla?" said Daisy. "I never heard it before, but it's a right pretty name."

"Yes'm indeed!" the coloured woman agreed enthusiastically. "Willamilla lovin', happy, gran' name!"

"What's the dog's name?" Laurence asked.

"Hossifer."

Laurence frowned importantly. "Is he full-blooded?" he inquired.

"Is he who?"

"I guess he isn't very full-blooded," Laurence said. "Will he bite?"

"Hossifer?" she said. "Hossifer, he a mighty lovin' dog! Bite? He ain' bite nobody. Hossifer, he a lovin'-hearted dog."

Elsie had come out of her gate, and she bent over the wagon with Daisy. "Oh, my!" she said wistfully. "I do wish we could have this baby to play with."

95

"Couldn't we?" Daisy asked of the baby's grandmother. "Would you be willing to sell it to us?"

"No'm," the coloured woman replied, though she manifested no surprise at the question. "No'm; my son-'law, he wouldn' lem me sell no Willamilla."

"Well, would you give it to us, then?"

"No'm. Can' give Willamilla 'way."

"Oh, my!" Daisy exclaimed. "I do wish we could have this baby to play with awhile, anyway."

The woman appeared to consider this, and her processes of considering it interested the children. Her streaked eyes were unusually large and protuberant; she closed them, letting the cumbrous lids roll slowly down over them, and she swayed alarmingly as she did this, almost losing her balance, but she recovered herself, opened her eyes widely, and said:

"How long you want play with Willamilla, honey?"

"Oh!" Daisy cried. "Will you let us? Oh, all afternoon!"

"Listen me," said Willamilla's grandmother. "I got errand I love to go on. Wagon push ri' heavy, too. I leave Willamilla with you lovin' li'l whi' chillun, an' come back free o'clock."

"Oh, lovely!" Daisy and Elsie both shouted.

"Free o'clock," said the coloured woman.

"That'll give us lots o' time," said Elsie. "Maybe almost an hour!"

The woman took a parcel from the wagon; it was wrapped in an old newspaper, and its shape was the shape of a bottle, though not that of an infant's milk-bottle. Also, the cork was not quite secure, and the dampened paper about the neck of this bottle gave forth a faint odour of sweet spirits of niter mingled with the spicy fragrance of a decoction from juniper, but naturally neither the odour nor the shape of the parcel meant anything to the children. It meant a great, great deal to Willamilla's grandma, however; and her lovingness visibly increased as she took the parcel in her arms.

"I'm go' take this nice loaf o' bread to some po' ole sick folks whut live up the alley ovuh yonnuh," she said. "Hossifer he go' stay with Willamilla an' li'l wagon." She moved away, but paused to speak to Hossifer, who followed her. "Hossifer, you the lovin'est dog in a wide worl', but you go on back, honey!" She petted him, then waved him away. "Go on back, Hossifer!" And Hossifer returned to the wagon, while she crossed the street toward the mouth of an alley.

The children stared after her, being even more interested just then in her peculiar progress than they were in their extraordinary new plaything. When the coloured woman reached a point about half way across the street, she found a difficulty in getting forward; her feet bore her slowly sidewise for some paces; she seemed to wander and waver; then, with an effort at concentration, she appeared to see a new path before her, followed it, and passed from sight down the alley.

Behind her she left a strongly favourable impression. Never had Daisy and Elsie met an adult more sympathetic to their wishes or one more easily persuaded than this obliging woman, and they turned to the baby with a pleasure in which there was mingled a slight surprise. They began to shout endearing words at Willamilla immediately, however, and even Master Coy looked upon the infant with a somewhat friendly eye, for he was warmed toward it by a sense of temporary proprietorship, and also by a feeling of congeniality, due to a supposition of his in regard to Willamilla's sex. But of course Laurence's greater interest was in Hossifer, though the latter's manner was not encouraging. Hossifer's brow became furrowed with lines of suspicion; he withdrew to a distance of a dozen yards or so, and made a gesture indicating that he was about to sit down, but upon Laurence's approaching him, he checked the impulse, and moved farther away, muttering internally.

"Good doggie!" Laurence said. "I won't hurt you. Hyuh, Hossifer! Hyuh, Hossifer!"

Hossifer's mutterings became more audible, his brow more furrowed, and his eyes more undecided. Thus by every means he sought to make plain that he might adopt any course of action whatever, that he but awaited the decisive impulse, would act as it impelled, and declined responsibility for what he should happen to do on the spur of the moment. Laurence made a second effort to gain his confidence, but after failing conspicuously he thought best to return to Willamilla and the ladies.

"My goodness!" he said. "What on earth you doin' to that baby?"

Chattering in the busiest and most important way, they had taken Willamilla from the wagon and had settled which one was to have the "first turn." This fell to Daisy, and holding Willamilla in her arms rather laboriously—for Willamilla was fourteen months old and fat—she began to walk up and down, crooning something she no doubt believed to be a lullaby.

"It's my turn," Elsie said. "I've counted a hunderd."

"No fair!" Daisy protested at once. "You counted too fast." And she continued to pace the sidewalk with Willamilla while Elsie walked beside her, insisting upon a rightful claim.

"Here!" Laurence said, coming up to them. "Listen! You're holdin' him all sprawled out and everything—you better put him back in the wagon. I bet if you hold him that way much longer you'll spoil somep'm in him."

"Him?" Both of his fair friends shouted; and they stared at Laurence with widening eyes. "Well, I declare!" Elsie said pettishly. "Haven't you even got sense enough to know it's a girl, Laurence Coy?"

"It is not!"

"It is, too!" they both returned.

"Listen here!" said Laurence. "Look at his name! I guess that settles it, don't it?"

"It settles it he's a girl," Daisy cried. "I bet you don't even know what her name is."

"Oh, I don't?"

"Well, what is it, then?"

"Willie Miller."

"What?"

"Willie Miller!" Laurence said. "That's what his own gran'mother said his name was. She said his name's Willie Miller."

Upon this the others shouted in derision; and with the greatest vehemence they told him over and over that Willamilla's name was Willamilla, that Willamilla was a girl's name, that Willamilla was consequently a girl, that she was a girl anyhow, no matter what her name was, but that her name actually was Willamilla, as her own grandmother had informed them. Grandmothers, Daisy and Elsie explained pityingly, are supposed to know the names of their own grandchildren.

Laurence resisted all this information as well as he was able, setting forth his own convictions in the matter, and continuing his argument while they continued theirs, but finally, in desperation, he proposed a compromise.

"Go on an' call him Willamilla," he said bitterly, "—if you got to! I doe' care if you haven't got any more sense'n to call him Willamilla when his real name's Willie Miller an' his own gran'mother says so! I'm goin' to call him Willie Miller till I die; only for heavenses' sake, hush up!"

The ladies declined to do as he suggested; whereupon he withdrew from the dispute, and while they talked on, deriding as well as instructing him, he leaned upon the gate and looked gloomily at the ground. However, at intervals, he formed with his lips, though soundlessly, the stubborn words, "His name's Willie Miller!"

"Oh, I tell you what'd be lovely!" Daisy cried. "Maybe she knows how to walk! Let's put her down and see—and if she doesn't know how already, why, we can teach her!"

Elsie gladly fell in with her friend's idea, and together they endeavoured to place Willamilla upon her feet on the ground. In this they were confronted with insuperable difficulties: Willamilla proved unable to comprehend their intentions; and although Daisy knelt and repeatedly placed the small feet in position, the experiment was wholly unsuccessful. Nevertheless the experimenters, not at all discouraged, continued it with delight, for they played that Willamilla was walking. They heaped praises upon her.

"My darling baby!" Daisy cried. "Doesn't she walk beautiful?"

"The precious little love!" Elsie echoed. "She just walks beautiful!"

At this the gloomy person in the background permitted himself to sneer. "That ain't walkin'," he said.

"It is, too! You doe' know what you're talkin' about!" the chorus of two retorted, not interrupting their procedure.

"He ain't walkin'," Laurence maintained.

"She is, too!" said Elsie.

"She's walkin' now," said Daisy. "She's walkin' all the time."

"No, he's not," Laurence said. "His feet are sort of curly, and they're 'way too wide apart. I bet there's somep'm the matter with him."

"There is not!" The two little girls looked round at him indignantly; for this unwarranted intimation of some structural imperfection roused them. "Shame on you!" Daisy said; and to Willamilla: "Show mamma how beautiful she walks."

"He can't do it," Laurence said obdurately. "I bet there is somep'm the matter with him."

"There is not!"

"Yes, sir," said Laurence, and he added, with conviction: "His legs ain't fixed on him right."

"Shame on you, Laurence Coy!"

But Laurence persisted in his view.

"Listen!" he said, arguing. "Look at my legs. Look at anybody's legs that can walk. Well, are they fixed on 'em the way his are?"

"Yes, they are!" Daisy returned sharply. "Only hers are fixed on better than yours!"

"They ain't," said Laurence. "Mine are fixed on like other people's, and his are—well, they're terrable!"

"Oh, isn't he tiresome?" Elsie said pettishly. "Do be quiet about your ole legs!"

"Yes, do!" said Daisy; and then she jumped up, a new idea lighting her eyes. "I tell you what let's do," she cried. "Let's put her back in the wagon, an' play we're takin' a walk on Sunday with our baby an' all the family."

"How'll we play it?" Elsie asked.

"Well, I'll be the mamma and push the wagon," Daisy said excitedly. "Elsie, you be some lady that's visitin' us, an' sort of walk along with us, an'—"

"No," Elsie interrupted. "I want to be the mamma and push the wagon, an' you be some lady that's visitin' us."

Daisy looked a little annoyed, but she compromised. "Well, we'll go a long walk, and I'll be the mamma the first block, an' then the next block you can be the mamma, and I'll be the lady that's visitin' us, an' then the next block it'll be my turn again."

"All right," said Elsie. "What'll we have Laurence be?"

"We'll have him be the father."

Laurence frowned; the idea was rather distasteful to him, and for some reason a little embarrassing. "Listen!" he said. "What do I haf to do?"

"Oh, just walk along and kind of talk an' everything."

"Well—" he said uncertainly; then he brightened a little. "I'll be smokin' cigars," he said.

"All right, you can." And having placed Willamilla in the wagon, Daisy grasped the handle, pushing the vehicle before her. Laurence put a twig in his mouth, puffing elaborately; Elsie walked beside Willamilla; and so the procession moved—Hossifer, still in a mood of indecision, following at a varying distance. And Daisy sang her lullaby as they went.

This singing of hers had an unfavourable effect upon Laurence. For a few minutes after they started he smoked his twig with a little satisfaction and had a slight enjoyment in the thought that he was the head of a family—but something within him kept objecting to the game; he found that really he did not like it. He bore it better on the second and fourth blocks, for Elsie was the mother then, but he felt a strong repulsion when Daisy assumed that relation. He intensely disliked being the father when she was the mother, and he was reluctant to have anybody see him serving in that capacity. Daisy's motherhood was aggressive; she sang louder and louder, and even without the singing the procession attracted a great deal of attention from pedestrians. Laurence felt that Daisy's music was in bad taste, especially as she had not yet pulled up her stocking.

She made up the tune, as well as the words, of her lullaby; the tune held beauty for no known ears except her own and these were the words:

100

"Oh, my da-ar-luh-un baby,
My-y lit-tull baby!
Go to sleep! Go to slee-heep!
Oh, my dear lit-tull baby!
My baby, my dar-luh-un bay-bee,
My bay-bee, my bay-hay-bee!"

As she thus soothed the infant, who naturally slumbered not, with Daisy's shrill voice so near, some people on the opposite side of the street looked across and laughed; and this caused a blush of mortification to spread over the face of the father.

"Listen!" he remonstrated. "You don't haf to make all that noise."

She paid no attention but went on singing.

"Listen!" said Laurence nervously. "Anyways, you don't haf to open your mouth so wide when you sing, do you? It looks terrable!"

She opened it even wider and sang still louder:

"My lit-tull baby, my da-ar-luh-un bay-bee!
My bay-bee! My bay-hay-bee!"

"Oh, my!" Laurence said, and he retired to the rear; whereupon Hossifer gave him a look and fell back a little farther. "Listen!" Laurence called to Daisy. "You scared the dog!"

Daisy stopped singing and glanced back over her shoulder. "I did not!" she said. "You scared her yourself."

"Who?" Laurence advanced to the side of the wagon, staring incredulously. "Who you talkin' about?"

"She was walkin' along nice only a little way behind us," Daisy said, "until you went near her."

"I went near who?" Laurence asked, looking very much disturbed. "Who was walkin' along nice?"

"Hossifer was. You said I scared her, and all the time she—"

"Listen!" said Laurence, breathing rapidly. "I won't stand it. This dog isn't a girl!"

"Hossifer's a girl's name," said Daisy placidly. "I bet you never heard of a boy by that name in your life!"

"Well, what if I never?"

"Well," said Daisy authoritatively, "that proves it. Hossifer's a girl's name and you just the same as said so yourself. Elsie, didn't he say Hossifer isn't a boy's name, an' doesn't that prove Hossifer's a girl?"

"Yes, it does," Elsie returned with decision.

Laurence looked at them; then he shook his head. "Oh, my!"

he said morosely, for these two appeared set upon allowing him no colleagues or associates whatever, and he felt himself at the end of his resources.

Daisy began to sing again at once.

"Oh, my dar-lun lit-tull bay-hay-bee-hee!" she sang; and she may have been too vehement for Willamilla, who had thus far remained remarkably placid under her new circumstances; Willamilla began to cry.

She began in a mild way, with a whimper, inaudible on account of the lullaby; then she slightly increased her protest, making use of a voice like the tinnier tones of a light saxophone; and having employed this mild mechanism for some time, without securing any relief from the shrillness that bothered her, she came to the conclusion that she was miserable. Now, she was of this disposition: once she arrived at such a conclusion, she remained at it, and nothing could convey to her mind that altered conditions had removed what annoyed her, until she became so exhausted by the protraction of her own protests that she slept, forgot and woke to a new life.

She marked the moment of her decision, this afternoon, by the utterance of a wail that rose high over the singing; she lifted up her voice and used the full power of lungs and throat to produce such a sound that even the heart of the father was disquieted, while the mamma and the visiting lady at once flung themselves on their knees beside the wagon.

"Whassa matta? Whassa matta?" Daisy and Elsie inquired some dozens of times, and they called Willamilla a "peshus baby" even oftener, but were unable to quiet her. Indeed, as they shouted their soothing endearments, her tears reached a point almost torrential, and she beat the coverlet with her small fat hands.

"He's mad about somep'm, I guess," the father observed, looking down upon her. "Or else he's got a spasm, maybe."

"She hasn't either," Daisy said. "She'll stop in a minute."

"Well, it might not be spasms," Laurence said. "But I bet whatever it is, it happened from all that singin'."

Daisy was not pleased with his remark. "I'll thank you not to be so kinely complimentary, Mister Laurence Coy!" she said, and she took up Willamilla in her arms, and rather staggeringly began to walk to and fro with her, singing:

"Oh, my peshus litt-tull bay-hay-bee-hee!"

Elsie walked beside her, singing too, while Willamilla beat upon the air with desperate hands and feet, closed her effervescent eyes as tightly as she could, opened her mouth till the orifice appeared as the most part of her visage, and allowed the long-sustained and far-reaching ululations therefrom to issue. Laurence began to find his position intolerable.

"For heavenses' sakes!" he said. "If this keeps up much longer, I'm goin' home. Everybody's a-lookin' at us all up an' down the street! Whyn't you quit singin' an' give him a chance to get over whatever's the matter with him?"

"Well, why don't you do somep'm to help stop her from cryin', yourself?" Elsie asked crossly.

"Well, I will," he promised, much too rashly. "I'd stop him in a minute if I had my way."

"All right," Daisy said unexpectedly, halting with Willamilla just in front of him. "Go on an' stop her, you know so much!"

"He'll stop when I tell him to," Laurence said, in the grim tone his father sometimes used, and with an air of power and determination, he rolled up the right sleeve of his shirtwaist, exposing the slender arm as far as the elbow. Then he shook his small fist in Willamilla's face.

"You quit your noise!" he said sternly. "You hush up! Hush up this minute! Hush opp!"

Willamilla abated nothing.

"Didn't you hear me tell you to hush up?" Laurence asked her fiercely. "You goin' to do it?" And he shook his fist at her again.

Upon this, Willamilla seemed vaguely to perceive something personal to herself in his gesture, and to direct her own flagellating arms as if to beat at his approaching fist.

"Look out!" Laurence said threateningly. "Don't you try any o' that with me, Mister!"

But the mulatto baby's squirmings were now too much for Daisy; she staggered, and in fear of dropping the lively burden, suddenly thrust it into Laurence's arms.

"Here!" she gasped. "I'm 'most worn out! Take her!"

"Oh, golly!" Laurence said.

"Don't drop her!" both ladies screamed. "Put her back in the wagon."

Obeying them willingly for once, he turned to the wagon to replace Willamilla therein; but as he stooped, he was forced to pause and stoop no farther. Hossifer had stationed himself beside the wagon and made it clear that he would not allow Willamilla to be replaced. He growled; his upper lip quivered in a way that exhibited almost his whole set of teeth as Laurence stooped, and when Laurence went round to the other side of the wagon, and bent over it with his squirming and noisy bundle, Hossifer followed, and repeated the demonstration. He heightened its eloquence, in fact, making feints and little jumps, and increasing the visibility of his teeth, as well as the poignancy of his growling. Thus menaced, Laurence straightened up and moved backward a few steps, while his two friends, some distance away, kept telling him, with unreasonable insistence, to do as they had instructed him.

"Put her in the wagon, and come on!" they called. "We got to go back! It's after three o'clock! Come on!"

Laurence explained the difficulty in which he found himself. "He won't let me," he said.

"Who won't?" Daisy asked, coming nearer.

"This dog. He won't let me put him back in the wagon; he almost bit me when I tried it. Here!" And he tried to restore Willamilla to Daisy. "You take her an' put her in."

But Daisy, retreating, emphatically declined—which was likewise the course adopted by Elsie when Laurence approached her. Both said that Hossifer "must want" Laurence to keep Willamilla, for thus they interpreted Hossifer's conduct.

"Well, I won't keep her," Laurence said hotly. "I don't expect to go deaf just because some old dog don't want her in the wagon! I'm goin' to slam her down on the sidewalk and let her lay there! I'm gettin' mighty tired of all this."

But when he moved to do as he threatened, and would have set Willamilla upon the pavement, the unreasonable Hossifer again refused permission. He placed himself close to Laurence, growling loudly, displaying his teeth, bristling, poising dangerously, and Laurence was forced to straighten himself once more without having deposited the infant, whom he now hated poisonously.

"My goodnuss!" he said desperately.

"Don't you see?" Daisy cried, and her tone was less sympathetic than triumphant. "It's just the way we said; Hossifer wants you to keep her!"

Elsie agreed with her, and both seemed pleased with themselves for having divined Hossifer's intentions so readily, though as a matter of fact they were entirely mistaken in this intuitional analysis. Hossifer cared nothing at all about Laurence's retaining Willamilla; neither was the oyster-coloured dog's conduct so irrational as the cowed and wretched Laurence thought it. In the first place, Hossifer was never quite himself away from an alley; he had been upon a strain all that afternoon. Then, when the elderly coloured woman had forbidden him to accompany her, and he found himself with strangers, including a white boy, and away from everything familiar, except Willamilla, in whom he had never taken any personal interest, he became uneasy and fell into a querulous mood. His uneasiness naturally concerned itself with the boy, and was deepened by two definite attempts of this boy to approach him.

When the family Sunday walk was undertaken, Hossifer followed Willamilla and the wagon; for of course he realized that this was one of those things about which there can be no question: one does them, and that's all. But his thoughts were constantly upon the boy, and he resolved to be the first to act if the boy made the slightest hostile gesture. Meanwhile, his nerves were unfavourably affected by the strange singing, and they were presently more upset by the blatancies of Willamilla. Her wailing acted unpleasantly upon the sensitive apparatus of his ear—the very thing that made him so strongly dislike tinny musical instruments and brass bands. And then, just as he was feeling most disorganized, he saw the boy stoop. Hossifer did not realize that Laurence stooped because he desired to put Willamilla into the wagon; Hossifer did not connect Willamilla with the action at all. He saw only that the boy stooped. Now, why does a boy stoop? He stoops to pick up something to throw at a dog. Hossifer made up his mind not to let Laurence stoop.

That was all; he was perfectly willing for Willamilla to be put back in the wagon, and the father, the mother and the visiting lady were alike mistaken—especially the father, whose best judgment was simply that Hossifer was of a disordered mind and had developed a monomania for a very special persecution. Hossifer was sane, and his motives were rational. Dogs who are over two years of age never do anything without a motive; Hossifer was nearing seven.

Daisy and Elsie, mistaken though they were, insisted strongly upon their own point-of-view in regard to him. "She wants you to keep her! She wants you to keep her!" they cried, and they chanted it as a sort of refrain; they clapped their hands and capered, adding their noise to Willamilla's, and showing little appreciation of the desperate state of mind into which events had plunged their old friend Laurence.

"She wants you to keep her!" they chanted. "She wants you to keep her. She wants you to keep her, Laurence!"

Laurence piteously entreated them to call Hossifer away; but the latter was cold to their rather sketchy attempts to gain his attention. However, they succeeded in making him more excited, and he began to bark furiously, in a bass voice. Having begun, he barked without intermission, so that with Hossifer's barking, Willamilla's relentless wailing, and the joyous shouting of Daisy and Elsie, Laurence might well despair of making himself heard. He seemed to rave in a pantomime of oral gestures, his arms and hands being occupied.

A man wearing soiled overalls, with a trowel in his hand, came from behind a house near by and walking crossly over the lawn, arrived at the picket fence beside which stood the abandoned wagon.

"Gosh, I never did!" he said, bellowing to be audible. "Git away from here! Don't you s'pose nobody's got no ears? There's a sick lady in this house right here, and she don't propose to have you kill her! Go on git away from here now! Go on! I never did!"

Annoyed by this labourer's coarseness, Elsie and Daisy paused to stare at him in as aristocratic a manner as they could, but he was little impressed.

"Gosh, I never did!" he repeated. "Git on out the neighbourhood and go where you b'long; you don't b'long around here!"

"I should think not," Daisy agreed crushingly. "Where we live, if there's any sick ladies, they take 'em out an' bury 'em!" Just what she meant by this, if indeed she meant anything, it is difficult to imagine, but she felt no doubt that she had put the man in his ignoble and proper place. Tossing her head, she picked up the handle of the wagon and moved haughtily away, her remarkably small nose in the air. Elsie went with her in a similar attitude.

"Go on! You hear me?" The man motioned fiercely with his trowel at Laurence. "Did you hear me tell you to take that noise away from here? How many more times I got to—"

"My gracious!" Laurence interrupted thickly. "I doe' want to stay here!"

He feared to move; he was apprehensive that Hossifer might not like it, but upon the man's threatening to vault over the fence and hurry him with the trowel, he ventured some steps; whereupon Hossifer stopped barking and followed closely, but did nothing worse. Laurence therefore went on, and presently made another attempt to place Willamilla upon the pavement—and again Hossifer supported the ladies' theory that he wanted Laurence to keep Willamilla.

"Listen!" Laurence said passionately to Hossifer. "I never did anything to you! What's got the matter of you, anyway? How long I got to keep all this up?"

Then he called to Elsie and Daisy, who were hurrying ahead and increasing the distance between him and them, for Willamilla's weight made his progress slow and sometimes uncertain. "Wait!" he called. "Can' chu wait? What's the matter of you? Can' chu even wait for me?"

But they hurried on, chattering busily together, and his troubles were deepened by his isolation with the uproarious Willamilla and Hossifer. Passers-by observed him with hearty amusement; and several boys, total strangers to him, gave up a game of marbles and accompanied him for a hundred yards or so, speculating loudly upon his relationship to Willamilla, but finally deciding that Laurence was in love with her and carrying her off to a minister's to marry her.

He felt that his detachment from the rest of his party was largely responsible for exposing him to these insults, and when he had shaken off the marble-players, whose remarks filled him with horror, he made a great effort to overtake the two irresponsible little girls.

"Hay! Can' chu wait?" he bawled. "Oh, my good-nuss! For heavenses' sakes! Dog-gone it. Can' chu wait! I can't carry this baby all the way!"

But he did. Panting, staggering, perspiring, with Willamilla never abating her complaint for an instant, and Hossifer warning him fiercely at every one of his many attempts to set her down, Laurence struggled on, far behind the cheery vanguard. Five blocks of anguish he covered before he finally arrived at Elsie Threamer's gate, whence this unfortunate expedition had set out.

Elsie and Daisy were standing near the gate, looking thoughtfully at Willamilla's grandmother, who was seated informally on the curbstone, and whistling to herself.

Laurence staggered to her. "Oh, my! Oh, my!" he quavered, and would have placed Willamilla in her grandmother's arms, but once more Hossifer interfered—for his was a mind bent solely upon one idea at a time—and Laurence had to straighten himself quickly.

"Make him quit that!" he remonstrated. "He's done it to me more than five hunderd times, an' I'm mighty tired of all this around here!"

But the coloured woman seemed to have no idea that he was saying anything important, or even that he was addressing himself to her. She rolled her eyes, indeed, but not in his direction, and continued her whistling.

"Listen! Look!" Laurence urged her. "It's Willie Miller! I wish he was dead; then I wouldn't hold him any longer, I bet you! I'd just throw him away like I ought to!" And as she went on whistling, not even looking at him, he inquired despairingly: "My goodness, what's the matter around here, anyways?"

"Elsie!" a voice called from a window of the house.

"Yes, mamma."

"Come in, dear. Come in quickly."

"Yes'm."

She had no more than departed when another voice called from a window of the house next door, "Daisy! Come in right away! Do you hear, Daisy?"

"Yes, mamma." And Daisy went hurriedly upon the summons.

Laurence was left alone in a world of nightmare. The hated Willamilla howled within his ear and weighed upon him like a house; his arms ached, his head rang; his heart was shaken with the fear of Hossifer; and Willamilla's grandmother sat upon the curbstone, whistling musically, with no apparent consciousness that there was a busy world about her, or that she had ever a grandchild or a dog. His terrible and mystifying condition began to appear to Laurence as permanent, and the accursed Willamilla an Old-Man-of-the-Sea to be his burden forever. A weariness of life—a sense of the futility of it all—came upon him, and yet he could not even sink down under it.

Then, when there was no hope beneath the sky, out of the alley across the street came a delivering angel—a middle-aged, hilarious coloured man seated in an enfeebled open wagon, and driving a thin gray antique shaped like a horse. Upon the side of the wagon was painted, "P. SkoNe MoVeiNG & DeLiVRys," and the cheerful driver was probably P. Skone himself.

He brought his wagon to the curb, descended giggling to Willamilla's grandmother, and by the exertion of a muscular power beyond his appearance, got her upon her feet. She became conscious of his presence, called him her lovin' Peter, blessed and embraced him, and then, consenting to test the tensile strength of the wagon, reclined upon him while he assisted her into it. After performing this feat, he extended his arms for Willamilla.

"He won't let me," Laurence said, swallowing piteously. "He wants me to keep him, an' he'll bite me if I—"

"Who go' bite you, white boy?" the cheerful coloured man inquired. "Hossifer?" Laughing, he turned to the faithful animal, and swept the horizon with a gesture. "Hossifer, you git in nat wagon!"

With the manner of a hunted fugitive, Hossifer instantly obeyed; the man lifted Willamilla's little vehicle into the wagon, took Willamilla in his arms, and climbed chuckling to the driver's seat. "Percy," he said to the antique, "you git up!"

Then this heavenly coloured man drove slowly off with Willamilla, her grandmother, Hossifer and the baby-wagon, while Laurence sank down upon the curbstone, wiped his face upon his polka-dotted sleeve and watched them disappear into the dusty alley. Willamilla was still crying; and to one listener it seemed that she had been crying throughout long, indefinite seasons, and would probably continue to cry forever, or at least until a calamity should arrive to her, in regard to the nature of which he had a certain hope.

He sat, his breast a vacancy where lately so much emotion had been, and presently two gay little voices chirped in the yard behind him. They called his name; and he turned to behold his fair friends. They were looking brightly at him over the hedge.

"Mamma called me to come in," Daisy said.

"So'd mine," said Elsie.

"Mamma told me I better stay in the house while that ole coloured woman was out here," Daisy continued. "Mamma said she wasn't very nice."

"So'd mine," Elsie added.

"What did you do, Laurence?" Daisy asked.

"Well—" said Laurence. "They're gone down that alley."

"Come on in," Daisy said eagerly. "We're goin' to play I-Spy. It's lots more fun with three. Come on!"

"Come on!" Elsie echoed. "Hurry, Laurence."

He went in, and a moment later, unconcernedly and without a care in the world, or the recollection of any, began to play I-Spy with the lady of his heart and her next neighbour.

THE ONLY CHILD

THE little boy was afraid to go into the dark room on the other side of the hall, and the little boy's father was disgusted with him. "Aren't you ashamed of yourself, Ludlum Thomas?" the father called from his seat by the library lamp. "Eight years old and scared! Scared to step into a room and turn the light on! Why, when I was your age I used to go out to the barn after dark in the winter-time, and up into the loft, all by myself, and pitch hay down to the horse through the chute. You walk straight into that dining-room, turn on the light, and get what you want; and don't let's have any more fuss about it. You hear me?"

Ludlum disregarded this speech. "Mamma," he called, plaintively, "I want you to come and turn the light on for me. Please, mamma!"

Mrs. Thomas, across the library table from her husband, looked troubled, and would have replied, but the head of the house checked her.

"Now let me," he said. Then he called again: "You going in there and do what I say, or not?"

"Please come on, mamma," Ludlum begged. "Mamma, I lef' my bow-an'-arry in the dining-room, an' I want to get it out o' there so's I can take it up to bed with me. Mamma, won't you please come turn the light on for me?"

"No, she will not!" Mr. Thomas shouted. "What on earth are you afraid of?"

"Mamma—"

"Stop calling your mother! She's not coming. You were sitting in the dining-room yourself, not more than an hour ago, at dinner, and you weren't afraid then, were you?"

Ludlum appeared between the brown curtains of the library doorway—the sketch of a rather pale child-prince in black velvet. "No, but—" he said.

"But what?"

"It was all light in there then. Mamma an' you were in there, too."

"Now look here!" Mr. Thomas paused, rested his book upon his knee, and spoke slowly. "You know there's nothing in that dining-room except the table and the chairs and the sideboard, don't you?"

Ludlum's eyes were not upon his father but upon the graceful figure at the other side of the table. "Mamma," he said, "won't you please come get my bow-an'-arry for me?"

"Did you hear what I said?"

"Yes, sir," the boy replied, with eyes still pleadingly upon his mother.

"Well, then, what is there to be afraid of?"

"I'm not afraid," said Ludlum. "It's dark in there."

"It won't be dark if you turn on the light, will it?"

"Mamma—"

"Now, that's enough!" the father interrupted testily. "It's after eight. You go on up to bed."

Ludlum's tone began to indicate a mental strain. "I don't want to go to bed without my bow-an'-arry!"

"What do you want your bow and arrow when you're in bed for?"

"I got to have it!"

"See here!" said Mr. Thomas. "You march up to bed and quit talking about your bow and arrow. You can take them with you if you go in there right quick and get them; but whether you do that or not you'll march to bed inside of one minute from now!"

"I got to have my bow-an'-arry. I got to, to go upstairs with."

"You don't want your bow and arrow in bed with you, do you?"

"Mamma!" Thus Ludlum persisted in his urgent appeal to that court in whose clemency he trusted. "Mamma, will you please come get my bow-an'—"

"No, she won't."

"Then will you come upstairs with me, mamma?"

"No, she won't! You'll go by yourself, like a man."

"Mamma—"

Mrs. Thomas intervened cheerily. "Don't be afraid, dearie," she said. "Your papa thinks you ought to begin to learn how to be manly; but the lights are lit all the way, and I told Annie to turn on the one in your room. You just go ahead like a good boy, and when you're all undressed and ready to jump in bed, then you just whistle for me—"

"I don't want to whistle," said Ludlum irritably. "I want my bow-an'-arry!"

"Look here!" cried his father. "You start for—"

"I got to have my bow-an'—"

"You mean to disobey me?"

"I got to have my—"

Mr. Thomas rose; his look became ominous. "We'll see about that!" he said; and he approached his son, whose apprehensions were expressed in a loud cry.

"Mamma!"

"Don't hurt his feel—" Mrs. Thomas began.

"Something's got to be done," her husband said grimly, and his hand fell upon Ludlum's shoulder. "You march!"

Ludlum muttered vaguely.

"You march!"

"I got to have my bow-an'-arry! I can't go to bed 'less mamma comes with me! She's got to come with me!"

Suddenly he made a scene. Having started it, he went in for all he was worth and made it a big one. He shrieked, writhed away from his father's hand, darted to his mother, and clung to her with spasmodic violence throughout the protracted efforts of the sterner parent to detach him.

When these efforts were finally successful, Ludlum plunged upon the floor, and fastened himself to the leg of a heavy table. Here, for a considerable time, he proved the superiority of an earnest boy's wind and agility over those of a man: as soon as one part of him was separated from the leg of the table another part of him became attached to it; and all the while he was vehemently eloquent, though unrhetorical.

The pain he thus so powerfully expressed was undeniable; and nowadays few adults are capable of resisting such determined agony. The end of it was, that when Ludlum retired he was accompanied by both parents, his father carrying him, and Mrs. Thomas following close behind with the bow-an'-arry.

They were thoughtful when they returned to the library.

"I would like to know what got him into such a state," said the father, groaning, as he picked up his book from the floor. "He used to march upstairs like a little man, and he wasn't afraid of the dark, or of anything else; but he's beginning to be afraid of his own shadow. What's the matter with him?"

Mrs. Thomas shook her head. "I think it's his constitution," she said. "I don't believe he's as strong as we thought he was."

" 'Strong!' " her husband repeated incredulously. "Have I been dreaming, or were you looking on when I was trying to pry him loose from that table-leg?"

"I mean nervously," she said. "I don't think his nerves are what they ought to be at all."

"His nerve isn't!" he returned. "That's what I'm talking about! Why was he afraid to step into our dining-room—not thirty feet from where we were sitting?"

"Because it was dark in there. Poor child, he did want his bow and arrow!"

"Well, he got 'em! What did he want 'em for?"

"To protect himself on the way to bed."

112

"To keep off burglars on our lighted stairway?"

"I suppose so," said Mrs. Thomas. "Burglars or something."

"Well, where'd he get such ideas from?"

"I don't know. Nearly all children do get them."

"I know one thing," Mr. Thomas asserted, "I certainly never was afraid like that, and none of my brothers was, either. Do you suppose the children Ludlum plays with tell him things that make him afraid of the dark?"

"I don't think so, because he plays with the same children now that he played with before he got so much this way. Of course he's always been a little timid."

"Well, I'd like to know what's at the root of it. Something's got into his head. That's certain, isn't it?"

"I don't know," Mrs. Thomas said musingly. "I believe fear of the dark is a sort of instinct, don't you?"

"Then why does he keep having it more and more? Instinct? No, sir! I don't know where he gets this silly scaredness from, nor what makes it, but I know that it won't do to humour him in it. We've got to be firmer with him after this than we were to-night. I'm not going to have a son of mine grow up to be afraid!"

"Yes; I suppose we ought to be a little firmer with him," she said dreamily.

However, for several days and nights there was no occasion to exercise this new policy of firmness with Ludlum, one reason being that he was careful not to leave his trusty bow and arrow in an unlighted room after dark. Three successive evenings, weapon in hand, he "marched" sturdily to bed; but on the fourth he was reluctant, even though equipped as usual.

"Is Annie upstairs?" he inquired querulously, when informed that his hour had struck.

"I'm not sure, dearie," said his mother. "I think so. It's her evening out, but I don't think she's gone."

Standing in the library doorway, Ludlum sent upward a series of piercing cries: "Annie! Annee! Ann-ee! Oh, Ann-nee-ee!"

"Stop it!" Mr. Thomas commanded fiercely. "You want to break your mother's ear-drums?"

"Ann-nee-eeee!"

"Stop that noise!"

"Ann—"

"Stop it!" Mr. Thomas made the gesture of rising, and Ludlum, interrupting himself abruptly, was silent until he perceived that his father's threat to rise was only a gesture, whereupon he decided that his vocalizations might safely be renewed.

"Ann-nee-ee!"

"What is the matter with him?"

"Ludlum, dear," said Mrs. Thomas, "what is it you want Annie for?"

"I want to know if she's upstairs."

"But what for?"

Ludlum's expression became one of determination. "Well, I want to know," he replied. "I got to know if Annie's upstairs."

"By George!" Mr. Thomas exclaimed suddenly. "I believe now he's afraid to go upstairs unless he knows the housemaid's up there!"

"Martha's probably upstairs if Annie isn't," Mrs. Thomas hurriedly intervened. "You needn't worry about whether Annie's up there, Luddie, if Martha is. Martha wouldn't let anything hurt you any more than Annie would, dear."

"Great heavens!" her husband cried. "There's nothing up there that's going to hurt him whether a hundred cooks and housemaids are upstairs or downstairs, or in the house or out of it! That's no way to talk to him, Jennie! Ludlum, you march straight—"

"Ann-nee-ee!"

"But, dearie," said Mrs. Thomas, "I told you that Martha wouldn't let anything hurt—"

"She isn't there," Ludlum declared. "I can hear her chinkin' tin and dishes around in the kitchen." And, again exerting all his vocal powers of penetration, "Oh, Ann-ee-ee!" he bawled.

"By George!" Mr. Thomas exclaimed. "This is awful! It's just awful!"

"Don't call any more, darling," the mother gently urged. "It disturbs your papa."

"But, Jennie, that isn't the reason he oughtn't to call. It does disturb me, but the real reason he oughtn't to do it is because he oughtn't to be afraid to—"

"Ann-ee-EE!"

Mr. Thomas uttered a loud cry of his own, and, dismissing gestures, rose from his chair prepared to act. But his son briskly disappeared from the doorway; he had been reassured from the top of the stairs. Annie had responded, and Ludlum sped upward cheerfully. The episode was closed—except in meditation.

There was another one during the night, however. At least, Mr. Thomas thought so, for at the breakfast table he inquired: "Was any one out of bed about half-past two? Something half woke me, and I thought it sounded like somebody knocking on a door, and then whispering."

Mrs. Thomas laughed. "It was only Luddie," she explained. "He had bad dreams, and came to my door, so I took him in with me

114

for the rest of the night. He's all right, now, aren't you, Luddie? Mamma didn't let the bad dream hurt her little boy, did she?"

"It wasn't dreams," said Ludlum. "I was awake. I thought there was somep'm in my room. I bet there was somep'm in there, las' night!"

"Oh, murder!" his father lamented. "Boy nine years old got to go and wake up his mamma in the middle of the night, because he's scared to sleep in his own bed with a hall-light shining through the transom! What on earth were you afraid of?"

Ludlum's eyes clung to the consoling face of his mother. "I never said I was afraid. I woke up, an' I thought I saw somep'm in there."

"What kind of a 'something'?"

Ludlum looked resentful. "Well, I guess I know what I'm talkin' about," he said importantly. "I bet there was somep'm, too!"

"I declare I'm ashamed," Mr. Thomas groaned. "Here's the boy's godfather coming to visit us, and how's he going to help find out we're raising a coward?"

"John!" his wife exclaimed. "The idea of speaking like that just because Luddie can't help being a little imaginative!"

"Well, it's true," he said. "I'm ashamed for Lucius to find it out."

Mrs. Thomas laughed, and then, finding the large eyes of Ludlum fixed upon her hopefully, she shook her head. "Don't you worry, darling," she reassured him. "You needn't be afraid of what Uncle Lucius will think of his dear little Luddie."

"I'm not," Ludlum returned complacently. "He gave me a dollar las' time he was here."

"Well, he won't this time," his father declared crossly. "Not after the way you've been behaving lately. I'll see to that!"

Ludlum's lower lip moved pathetically and his eyes became softly brilliant—manifestations that increased the remarkable beauty he inherited from his mother.

"John!" cried Mrs. Thomas indignantly.

Ludlum wept at once, and between his gulpings implored his mother to prevent his father from influencing Uncle Lucius against the giving of dollars. "Don't let him, mamma!" he quavered. "An' 'fif Uncle Lucius wuw-wants to give me a dollar, he's got a right to, hasn't he, mamma? Hasn't he got a right to, mamma?"

"There, dearie! Of course!" she comforted him. "Papa won't tell Uncle Lucius. Papa is sorry, and only wants you to be happy and not cry any more."

Papa's manner indicated somewhat less sympathy than she implied; nevertheless, he presently left the house in a condition vaguely remorseful, which still prevailed, to the extent of a slight preoccupation, when he met Uncle Lucius at the train at noon.

Uncle Lucius—Lucius Brutus Allen, attorney-at-law of Marlow, Illinois, population more than three thousand, if you believed him—this Uncle Lucius was a reassuring sight, even to the eyes of a remorseful father who had been persecuting the beautiful child of a lovely mother.

Mr. Allen was no legal uncle to Ludlum: he was really Mrs. Thomas's second cousin, and, ever since she was eighteen and he twenty-four, had been her favoured squire. In fact, during her young womanhood, Mrs. Thomas and others had taken it as a matter of course that Lucius was in love with her; certainly that appeared to be his condition.

However, with the advent of Mr. John Thomas, Lucius Brutus Allen gave ground without resistance, and even assisted matters in a way which might have suggested to an outsider that he was something of a matchmaker as well as something of a lover. With a bravery that touched both the bride and bridegroom, he had stood up to the functions of Best Man without a quaver—and, of course, since the day of Ludlum's arrival in the visible world, had been "Uncle Lucius."

He was thirty-five; of a stoutish, stocky figure; large-headed and thin-haired; pinkish and cheerful and warm. His warmth was due partly to the weather, and led to a continuous expectancy on the part of Ludlum, for it was the habit of Uncle Lucius to keep his handkerchief in a pocket of his trousers. From the hour of his arrival, every time that Uncle Lucius put his hand in his pocket and drew forth a handkerchief to dry his dewy brow, Ludlum suffered a disappointment.

In fact, the air was so sticky that these disappointments were almost continuous, with the natural result that Ludlum became peevish; for nobody can be distinctly disappointed a dozen or so times an hour, during the greater part of an afternoon, and remain buoyantly amiable.

Finally he could bear it no longer. He had followed his parents and Uncle Lucius out to the comfortable porch, which gave them ampler air and the pretty sight of Mrs. Thomas's garden, but no greater coolness; and here Uncle Lucius, instead of bringing forth from his pocket a dollar, produced, out of that storage, a fresh handkerchief.

"Goodness me, but you got to wipe your ole face a lot!" said Ludlum in a voice of pure spitefulness. "I guess why you're so hot mus' be you stuff yourself at meals, an' got all fat the way you are!"

Wherewith, he emitted a shrill and bitter laugh of self-applause for wit, while his parents turned to gaze upon him—Mrs. Thomas with surprise, and Mr. Thomas with dismay. To both of them his rudeness crackled out of a clear sky; they saw it as an effect detached from cause; therefore inexplicable.

"Ludlum!" said the father sharply.

"Dearie!" said the mother.

But the visitor looked closely at the vexed face. "What is it you've decided you don't like about me, Luddie?" he asked.

"You're too fat!" said Ludlum.

Both parents uttered exclamations of remonstrance, but Mr. Allen intervened. "I'm not so very fat," he said. "I've just realized what the trouble between us is, Luddie. I overlooked something entirely, but I'll fix it all right when we're alone together. Now that I've explained about it, you won't mind how often I take my handkerchief out of my pocket, will you?"

"What in the world!" Mrs. Thomas exclaimed. "What are you talking about?"

"It's all right," said Lucius.

Ludlum laughed; his face was restored to its serene beauty. Obviously, he again loved his Uncle Lucius, and a perfect understanding, mysterious to the parents, now existed between godfather and godson. In celebration, Ludlum shouted and ran to caper in the garden.

"By George!" said John Thomas. "You seem to understand him! I don't. I don't know what the dickens is in his mind, half the time."

Mrs. Thomas laughed condescendingly. "No wonder!" she said. "You're down-town all the daytime and never see him except at breakfast and in the evenings."

"There's one thing puzzles me about it," said John. "If you understand him so well, why don't you ever tell me how to? What made him so smart-alecky to Lucius just now?"

Again she laughed with condescension. "Why, Luddie didn't mean to be fresh at all. He just spoke without thinking."

But upon hearing this interpretation, Mr. Allen cast a rueful glance at his lovely cousin. "Quite so!" he said. "Children can't tell their reasons, but they've always got 'em!"

"Oh, no, they haven't," she laughed. And then she jumped, for there came a heavy booming of thunder from that part of the sky which the roof of the porch concealed from them. The sunshine over the pink-speckled garden vanished; all the blossoms lost colour and grew wan, fluttering in an ominous breeze; at once a high wind whipped round the house and the row of straight poplars beyond the garden showed silver sides.

117

"Luddie!" shrieked Mrs. Thomas; and he shrieked in answer; came running, just ahead of the rain. She seized his hand, and fled with him into the house.

"You remember how afraid they are of lightning," said John apologetically. "Lightning and thunder. I never could understand it, but I suppose it's genuine and painful."

"It's both," the visitor remarked. "You wouldn't think I'm that way, too, would you?"

"You are?"

"Makes me nervous as a cat."

"Did you inherit it?"

"I don't think so," said Lucius; and he waved his host's silent offer of a cigar. "No, thanks. Never want to smoke in a thunderstorm. I—Whoo!" he interrupted himself, as a flare of light and a catastrophe of sound came simultaneously. "Let's go in," he said mildly.

"Not I. I love to watch it."

"Well—" Lucius paused, but at a renewal of the catastrophe, "Excuse me!" he said, and tarried no longer.

He found Mrs. Thomas and Ludlum in the centre of the darkened drawing-room. She was sitting in a gilt chair with her feet off the floor and upon a rung of the chair; and four heavy, flat-bottomed drinking-glasses were upon the floor, each of them containing the foot of a leg of the gilt chair. Ludlum was upon her lap.

"Don't you believe in insulation, Lucius?" she asked anxiously. "As long as we sit like this, we can't be struck, can we?"

He put on his glasses and gave her a solemn stare before replying. "I don't know about that," he said. "Of course John is safer out on the porch than we are in here."

"Oh, no, no!" she cried. "A porch is the most dangerous place there is!"

"I don't know whether or not he's safe from the lightning," Lucius explained. "I mean he's safe from being troubled about it the way we are."

"I don't call that being safe," his lady-cousin began. "I don't see what—"

But she broke off to find place for a subdued shriek, as an admiral's salute of great guns jarred the house. Other salutes followed, interjected, in spite of drawn shades and curtains, with spurts of light into the room, and at each spurt Mrs. Thomas shivered and said "Oh!" in a low voice, whereupon Ludlum jumped and said "Ouch!" likewise in a low voice. Then, at the ensuing crash,

Mrs. Thomas emitted a little scream, and Ludlum emitted a large one.

"Ouch! Ow!" he vociferated. "Mamma, I want it to stop! Mamma, I can't stand it! I can't stand it!"

"It's odd," said Lucius, during an interregnum. "The thunder frightens us more than the lightning, doesn't it?"

"They're both so horrible," she murmured. "I'm glad they affect you this way, too, Lucius. It's comforting. Do you think it's almost over?"

"I'll see," he said; and he went to a window, whither Ludlum, having jumped down, followed him.

"Don't open the curtains much," Mrs. Thomas begged, not leaving her chair. "Windows are always dangerous. And come away from the window, Luddie. The lightning might—"

She shrieked at a flash and boom, and Luddie came away from the window. Voiceless—he was so startled—he scrambled toward his mother, his arms outstretched, his feet slipping on the polished floor; then, leaping upon her lap, he clung to her wildly; gulped, choked, and found his voice. He howled.

"That was about the last, I think," observed Lucius, from the window. "It's beginning to clear already. Nothing but a shower to make things cooler for us. Let's go play with old John again. Come on, Luddie."

But Ludlum clung to his mother, remonstrating. "No!" he cried. "Mamma, you got to stay in the house. I don't want to go out there. It might begin again!"

She laughed soothingly. "But Uncle Lucius says it's all over now, darling. Let's go and—"

"I d'wawn' to! I won't go out of the house. You tell me a story."

"Well," she began, "once upon a time there was a good fairy and there was a bad fairy—"

"Where'd they live?"

"Oh, in a town—under some flowers in a garden in the town."

"Like our garden?"

"I suppose so," she assented. "And the good fairy—"

"Listen, mamma," said Ludlum. "If they lived in the garden like those fairies you were tellin' me about yesterday, they could come in the windows of the house where the pretty little boy lived, couldn't they?"

"I suppose so."

At this Ludlum's expression became apprehensive and his voice peevish. "Well, then," he complained, "if there was a window open at night, or just maybe through a crack under the door, the bad fairy could slip up behind the pretty little boy, or into the pretty little boy's bedroom, an'—"

"No, no!" his mother laughed, stroking his head. "You see, the good fairy would always be watching, too, and the good fairy wouldn't let the bad fairy hurt the pretty little boy."

The apprehensive expression was not altogether soothed from the pretty little boy's face. However, he said: "Go on. Tell what happened. Did the pretty little boy—"

"Lucius!" Mrs. Thomas exclaimed, "don't stay here to be bored by Luddie and me. I've got to tell him this story—"

"Yes," Ludlum eagerly agreed. "An' then afterward she has to read me a chapter in our book."

"So you go and make John tell you a story, Lucius. I have to be polite to Luddie because he's had such a fright, poor blessed child!"

Lucius was obedient: he rejoined John upon the porch, and the two men chatted for a time.

"What book is Jennie reading to the boy?" Mr. Allen inquired, after a subsequent interval of silence.

"I don't know just now. Classic fiction of some sort, probably. She's great on preparing his mind to be literary; reads an hour to him every day, and sometimes longer—translations—mythology— everything. All about gods and goddesses appearing out of the air to heroes, and Medusa heads and what not. Then standard works: Cooper, Bulwer, Scott, Hugo—some of the great romances."

"I see," said Lucius. "She always did go at things thoroughly. I remember," he went on, with a musing chuckle, "I remember how I got hold of Bulwer's 'Zanoni' and 'Strange Story' when I was about ten years old. By George! I've been afraid to go home in the dark ever since!"

"You have?" John smiled; then sent a serious and inquiring glance at the visitor, who remained placid. "Of course Jennie doesn't read 'Zanoni' to Ludlum."

"No, she wouldn't," said Lucius. "Not till he's older. She'd read him much less disturbing things at his age, of course."

His host made no additional comment upon the subject, but appeared to sit in some perplexity.

Mr. Allen observed him calmly; then, after a time, went into the house—to get a cigar of his own, he said.

In the hall he paused, listening. From the library came Mrs. Thomas's voice, reading with fine dramatic fire:

" 'What! thou frontless dastard, thou—thou who didst wait for opened gate and lowered bridge, when Conrad Horst forced his way over moat and wall, must thou be malapert? Knit him up to the

120

stanchions of the hall-window! He shall beat time with his feet while we drink a cup to his safe passage to the devil!'

" 'The doom was scarce sooner pronounced than accomplished; and in a moment the wretch wrestled out his last agonies, suspended from the iron bars. His body still hung there when our young hero entered the hall, and, intercepting the pale moonbeam, threw on the castle-floor an uncertain shadow, which dubiously yet fearfully intimated the nature of the substance which produced it.

" 'When the syndic—' "

Ludlum interrupted. "Mamma, what's a stanchion?" His voice was low and a little husky.

"It's a kind of an iron bar, or something, I think," Mrs. Thomas answered. "I'm not sure."

"Well, does it mean—mamma, what does it mean when it says 'he wrested out his last annogies?' "

" 'Agonies,' dear. It doesn't mean anything that little boys ought to think about. This is a very unpleasant part of the book, and we'll hurry on to where it's all about knights and ladies, and pennons fluttering in the sunshine and—"

"No; I don't want you to hurry. I like to hear this part, too. It's nice. Go on, mamma."

She continued, and between the curtains at the door, Lucius caught a glimpse of them. Sunlight touched them through a window; she sat in a high-backed chair; the dark-curled boy, upon a stool, huddling to her knee; and, as they sat thus, reading "Quentin Durward," they were like a mother and son in stained glass—or like a Countess, in an old romance, reading to the Young Heir. And Lucius Brutus Allen had the curious impression that, however dimly, both of them were conscious of some such picturesque resemblance.

Unseen, he withdrew from the renewed sound of the reading, and again went out to sit with John upon the porch, but Mrs. Thomas and Ludlum did not rejoin them until the announcement of dinner. When the meal was over, Lucius and his hostess played cribbage in the library; something they did at all their reunions—a commemoration of an evening habit of old days. But to-night their game was interrupted, a whispering in the hall becoming more and more audible as it increased in virility; while protests on the part of a party of the second part punctuated and accented the whispering:

"I d'wawn' to!" . . . "I won't!" . . . "I will ast mama!" . . . "Leggo!"

The whispering became a bass staccato, though subdued, under the breath; protests became monosyllabic, but increased in passion; short-clipped squealings and infantile grunts were heard—and then suddenly, yet almost deliberately, a wide-mouthed roar of human agony dismayed the echoing walls.

The cavern whence issued the horrid sound was the most conspicuous thing in the little world of that house, as Ludlum dashed into the library. Even in her stress of sympathy, the mother could not forbear to cry: "Don't, Luddie! Don't stretch your mouth like that! You'll spoil the shape of it."

But Ludlum cared nothing for shape. Open to all the winds, he plunged toward his mother; and cribbage-board, counters, and cards went to the floor.

"Darling!" she implored. "What has hurt mamma's little boy so awfully? Tell mamma!"

In her arms, his inclement eyes salting his cheeks, the vocal pitch of his despair rose higher and higher like the voice of a reluctant pump.

"Papa twissud my wrist!" he finally became coherent enough to declare.

"What!"

"He did!" All in falsetto Ludlum sobbed his version of things. "He—he suss-said I had to gug-go up to bed all—all alone. He grabbed me! He hurt! He said I couldn't interrup' your ole gug-game! 'N' he said, 'I'll show you!' 'N' then—then—then—he twissud my wrist!"

At that she gathered him closer to her, and rose, holding him in her arms. Her face was deeply flushed, and her shining eyes avoided her husband, who stood near the doorway.

"Put him down, Jennie," he said mildly. "I—"

Straightway she strode by him, carrying her child. She did not pause, nor speak aloud, yet Lucius and John both heard the whispered word that crumpled the latter as the curtains waved with the angry breeze of her passing. "Shame!"

Meanwhile, Lucius, on his knees—for he never regarded his trousers seriously—began to collect dispersed cards and pegs. "What say?" he inquired, upon some gaspings of his unfortunate friend, John.

"She believed it!" (These stricken words came from a deep chair in the shadows.) "She thought I actually did twist his wrist!"

"Oh, no," said Lucius. "She didn't believe anything of the kind. Darn that peg!" With face to the floor and in an attitude of Oriental devotion, he appeared to be worshipping the darkness under a divan. "She was merely reacting to the bellow of her offspring. She knew he invented it, as well as you did."

"It's incredible!" said John. "The cold-blooded cunning of it!

122

He was bound to have his way, and make her go up with him; and I'd turned him toward the stairway by his shoulders, and he tried to hold himself back by catching at one of those big chairs in the hall. I caught his wrist to keep him from holding to the chair—and I held him a second or two, not moving. The little pirate decided on the thing then and there, in his mind. He understood perfectly well he could make it all the more horrible because you were here, visiting us. I swear it appals me! What sort of a nature is that?"

"Oh," said Lucius, "just natural nature. Same as you and me."

"I'd hate to believe that!"

"You and I got ashamed long ago of the tricks that came in our minds to play," said Lucius, groping under the divan. "We got ashamed so often that they don't come any more."

"Yes, but it ought to be time they stopped coming into that boy's mind. He was eight last month."

"Yes—darn that peg!—there seems to be something in what you say. But of course Luddie thought he was in a fix that was just as bad to him as it would be to me if somebody were trying to make me walk into Pancho Villa's camp all alone. I'd make a fuss about that, if the fuss would bring up the whole United States Army to go with me. That's what it amounted to with Luddie."

"I suppose so," groaned the father. "It all comes down to his being a coward."

"It all comes down to the air being full of queer things when he's alone," said Lucius.

"Well, I'd like to know what makes it full of queer things. Where does his foolishness come from?"

"And echo answers—" Lucius added, managing to get his head and shoulders under the divan, and thrusting with arms and legs to get more of himself under.

But a chime of laughter from the doorway answered in place of echo. "What are you doing, Lucius?" Mrs. Thomas inquired. "Swimming lessons? I never saw anything—" And laughter so overcame her that she could speak no further, but dropped into a chair, her handkerchief to her mouth.

Lucius emerged crabwise, and placed a cribbage-peg upon the table, but made no motion to continue the game. Instead he dusted himself uselessly, lit a cigar, and sat.

"Luddie's all right," said the lady, having recovered her calmness. "I think probably something he ate at dinner upset him a little. Anyhow, he was all right as soon as he got upstairs. Annie's sitting with him and telling him stories."

"I wonder if that lightning struck anything this afternoon," Lucius said absently. "Some of it seemed mighty near."

"It was awful."

"Do you remember," Lucius asked her, "when you first began to be nervous about it?"

"Oh, I've always been that way, ever since I was a little child. I haven't the faintest idea how it got hold of me. Children just get afraid of certain things, it seems to me, and that's all there is to it. You know how Luddie is about lightning, John."

John admitted that he knew how Luddie was about lightning. "I do," was all he said.

Mrs. Thomas's expression became charmingly fond, even a little complacent. "I suppose he inherits it from me," she said.

"My mother has that fear to this day," Lucius remarked. "And I have it, too, but I didn't inherit it from her."

"How do you know?" his cousin asked quickly. "What makes you think you didn't inherit it?"

"Because my father used to tell me that when I was three and four years old he would sit out on the porch during a thunder-storm, and hold me in his lap, and every time the thunder came both of us would laugh, and shout 'Boom!' Children naturally like a big noise. But when I got a little bit older and more imaginative, and began to draw absurd conclusions from things, I found that my mother was frightened during thunder-storms—though she tried her best to conceal it—and, of course, seeing her frightened, I thought something pretty bad must be the matter. So the fear got fastened on me, and I can't shake it off though I'm thirty-five years old. Curious thing it is!"

Mrs. Thomas's brilliant eyes were fixed upon her cousin throughout this narrative with an expression at first perplexed, then reproachful, finally hostile. A change, not subtle but simple and vivid, came upon her face, while its habitual mobility departed, leaving it radiantly still, with a fierce smoldering just underneath. How deep and fast her breathing became, was too easily visible.

"Everything's curious, though, for the matter o' that," Lucius added. And without looking at his cousin—without needing to look at her, to understand the deadliness of her silence—he smoked unconcernedly. "Yes, sir, it's all curious; and we're all curious," he continued, permitting himself the indulgence of a reminiscent chuckle. "You know I believe my father and mother got to be rather at outs about me—one thing and another, goodness knows what!—and it was years before they came together and found a real sympathy between them again. Truth is, I suspect where people aren't careful, their children have about twice as much to do with driving 'em apart as with drawing 'em together—especially in the case of an only child. I really do think that if I hadn't been an only child my father and mother might have been—"

A sibilant breath, not a word and not quite a hiss, caused Lucius to pause for a moment, though not to glance in the direction of the lips whence came the sound. He appeared to forget the sentence he had left incomplete; at all events he neglected to finish it. However, he went on, composedly:

"Some of my aunts tell me I was the worst nuisance they ever knew. In fact, some of 'em go out of their way to tell me that, even yet. They never could figure out what was the matter with me— except that I was spoiled; but I never meet Aunt Mira Hooper on the street at home, to this day, that she doesn't stop to tell me she hasn't learned to like me, because she got such a set against me when I was a child—and I meet her three or four times a week! She claims there was some kind of a little tragedy over me, in our house, every day or so, for years and years. She blames me for it, but Lord knows it wasn't my fault. For instance, a lot of it was my father's."

"What did he do?" asked John.

Lucius chuckled again. "The worst he did was to tell me stories about Indians and pioneer days. Sounds harmless enough, but father was a good story-teller, and that was the trouble. You see, the foundation of nearly all romance, whether it's Indian stories or fairy-stories—it's all hero and villain. Something evil is always just going to jump out of somewhere at the hero, and the reader or the listener is always the hero. Why, I got so I wouldn't go into a darkened room, even in the daytime! As we grow older we forget the horrible visions we had when we were children; and what's worse, we forget there's no need for children to have 'em. Children ought to be raised in the real world, not the dream one. Yes, sir, I lay all my Aunt Mira Hooper's grudge against me to my father's telling me stories so well and encouraging me to read the classics and—"

"Lucius," Mrs. Thomas spoke in a low voice, but in a tone that checked him abruptly.

"Yes, Jennie?"

"Don't you think that's enough?"

"I suppose it is tiresome," he said. "Too much autobiography. I was just rambling on about—"

"You meant me!" she cried.

"You, Jennie?"

"You did! And you meant Ludlum was a 'nuisance'; not you. And I don't think it's very nice! Do you?"

"Why, I nev—"

But his cousin's emotions were no longer to be controlled. She rose, trembling. "What a fool I was this afternoon!" she exclaimed

125

bitterly. "I didn't suspect you; yet I never remembered your being nervous in a thunder-storm before. I thought you were sympathetic, and all the time you were thinking these cruel, wicked things about Luddie and me!"

Lucius rose, too. "You know what I think about you, all the time, Jennie," he said genially. "John, if you can remember where you put my umbrella when we came in, it's about time for me to be catching a street-car down to the station."

She opposed him with a passionate gesture. "No!" she cried fiercely. "You can't say such things to me and then slip out like that! You tell me I've taught my child to be a coward and that I've made a spoilt brat of him—"

"Jennie!" he protested. "I was talking about me!"

"Shame on you to pretend!" she said. "You think I'm making John hate Luddie—"

"Jennie!" he shouted in genuine astonishment.

"You do! And you come here pretending to be such a considerate, sympathetic friend—and every minute you're criticizing and condemning me in your heart for all my little stories to my child—all because—because—" suddenly she uttered a dry sob— "because I want to raise my boy to be a—a poet!"

"John," said Lucius desperately, "do you think you can find that umbrella?"

With almost startling alacrity John rose and vanished from the room, and Lucius would have followed, but the distressed lady detained him. She caught a sagging pocket of his coat, and he found it necessary to remain until she should release him.

"You sha'n't!" she cried. "Not till you've taken back that accusation."

"But what accusa—"

"Shame on you! Ah, I didn't think you'd ever come here and do such a thing to me. And this morning I was looking forward to a happy day! It's a good thing you're a bachelor!"

With which final insult she hurled his pocket from her—at least that was the expression of her gesture—and sank into a chair, weeping heart-brokenly. "You don't understand!" she sobbed. "How could any man understand—or any woman not a mother! You think these hard things of me, but—but John doesn't always love Luddie. Don't you get even a little glimpse of what that means to me? There are times when John doesn't even like Luddie!"

"Take care," said Lucius gently. "Take care that those times don't come oftener."

She gasped, and would have spoken, but for a moment she

126

could not, and was able only to gaze at him fiercely through her tears. Yet there was a hint of fear behind the anger.

"You dare to say such a thing as that to a mother?" she said, when she could speak.

Lucius's eyes twinkled genially; he touched her upon the shoulder, and she suffered him. "Mother," he said lightly, "have pity on your child!" Somehow, he managed to put more solemnity into this parting prayer of his than if he had spoken it solemnly; and she was silent.

Then he left the room, and, on his way, stumbled over a chair, as he usually did at the dramatic moments in his life.

John was standing in the open doorway, Lucius's umbrella in his hand. "I think I hear a car coming, old fellow," he said.

"Got to get my hat," Mr. Allen muttered. He had been reminded of something; a small straw hat, with a blue ribbon round it, was upon the table, and he fumbled with it a moment before seizing his own and rushing for the door at the increasing warning of a brass gong in the near distance. Thus, when he had gone, a silver dollar was pocketed within the inside band of the small straw hat with the blue ribbon. . . . John Thomas, returning in sharp trepidation to the lovely, miserable figure in the library, encountered one of the many surprises of his life.

"He never could tell the truth to save his life!" she said. "He doesn't know what truth means! Did you hear him sitting up there and telling us he was 'an only child'? He has a brother and four sisters living, and I don't know how many dead!"

"You don't mean it!" said John, astounded. "That certainly was pecu—"

He lost his breath at that moment. She rose and threw her arms round him with the utmost heartiness. "He's such an old smart Aleck!" she cried, still weeping. "That's why I married you instead of him. I love you for not being one! If you want to spank Luddie for telling that story about his wrist I wish you'd go and wake him up and do it!"

"No," said John. "Lucius called to me as he was running for the car that he's going to be married next week. I'll wait and spank one of his children. They'll be the worst spoiled children in the world!"

LADIES' WAYS

TWO young people, just out of college and pleasing to the eye, ought to appreciate the advantage of living across the street from each other: but Miss Muriel Eliot's mood, that summer, was so advanced and intellectual that she found all round about her only a cultural desert, utterly savourless. This was her own definition of her surroundings, and when she expressed herself thus impressively to Mr. Renfrew Mears, the young gentleman who lived directly opposite her, he was granted little choice but to suppose himself included among the unspiced vacancies she mentioned. "The whole deadly environment crushes me," she told him, as they paused at her gate on returning from a walk. "This town is really a base thing."

"Do you think so, Muriel?" he said. "Well, I don't know; around here it's a right pleasant place to live—nice big yards and trees and all. And you know the population is increasing by fifteen to twenty thousand every year. The papers say—"

"Listen, Renfrew," she interrupted, and then said deliberately: "It is a cultural desert, utterly savourless!"

When she had spoken in this way, the first feeling of young Mr. Mears appeared to be one of admiration, and perhaps she understood, or even expected, that some such sensation on his part would be inevitable, for she allowed her eyes to remain uplifted gloomily toward the summer sky above them, so that he might look at her a little while without her seeming to know it. Then she repeated slowly, with a slight shake of the head: "Yes—a cultural desert, utterly savourless!"

But Renfrew now became uneasy. "You mean the looks of the place and the—"

"I mean the whole environment," she said. "These Victorian houses with their Victorian interiors and the Victorian thoughts of the people that live in 'em. It's all, all Victorian!"

" 'Victorian?' " said Renfrew doubtfully, for he was far from certain of her meaning. His vague impression was that the word might in some remote way bear upon an issue of bonds with which he had some recent familiarity through an inheritance from his grandfather. "You think it's—Victorian—do you, Muriel?" he thought best to inquire.

"Absolutely!" she said. "Culturally it's a Victorian desert and utterly savourless."

"But you don't mean all of it?" he ventured, being now certain that "Victorian" meant something unfavourable. "That is, not the people?"

"It's the people I'm talking about," explained Muriel coldly.

"Well—but not all of 'em?"

"Yes, everybody!"

"You don't mean every last one of 'em, though, do you, Muriel?" he asked plaintively.

"Yes, I do."

"Well, but look here," he said. "You couldn't mean that. It would include your own family, and all your old family neighbours. Why, it might include some of your very best friends!"

She sighed. "Since I've come home, I've felt that really I had nothing in common with a single soul in the place. I don't live on the same plane. I don't think the same thoughts. I don't speak the same language."

He appeared to swallow a little air and to find some difficulty in doing so. "I know," he said, "you do talk a lot more intellectually than the rest of us dubs around here. It's because you've got a more intellectual nature, and everything like that; and that's one of the reasons I look up to you the way I do. I always used to think that a girl that usually had an intellectual nature had to wear horn spectacles and have her dress higher on one side than it was on the other, and wear these sensible-looking shoes, and everything like that. But you've showed me I was mistaken, Muriel. You made me see that a girl could have an intellectual nature and be prettier and dress niftilier than all the brainless ones put together. But what worries me is—" He paused uncomfortably, and repeated, "What worries me is—" then paused again, and, with his head on one side, moved his forefinger to and fro between his collar and his neck as if he felt a serious tightness there.

"Well?" Muriel said, after waiting for some time. "Do you wish me to understand it's your neckwear that worries you, Renfrew?"

"No," he said absently, and frowning in his pained earnestness, again repeated: "What worries me is—" Once more he stopped.

"Well, well!"

"It's simply this," he said. "What worries me is simply this. It's like this. For instance, do you think it's absolutely necessary for them both to have an intellectual nature?"

" 'Both?' " she inquired. "What do you mean—'both?' "

"I mean the man and the woman," he said. "Do you think they both have to have—"

"What man and woman?"

"I mean," said Renfrew, "I mean the husband and the wife."

"Why, what in the world—"

"Would they both have to have one?" he asked hopefully.

"They wouldn't both have to have an intellectual nature, would they?"

"I haven't the slightest idea what you're talking about," she said with emphasis, though a delicate colour had risen in her cheeks, and people seldom blush on account of being puzzled. "I don't believe you know what you mean, yourself."

"Yes, I do," he insisted, his earnestness constantly increasing. "I mean, for instance, wouldn't it be all right for the woman to go on following her intellectual nature in her own way, if the man provided the house and the food and everything like that? Even if he didn't have an intellectual nature himself, don't you think they could get along together all right, especially if he respected hers and looked up to it and was glad she had one, and so—well, and so they could go on and on together—and on and on—"

"Renfrew!" she cried. "How long are you going 'on and on' about nothing?"

He looked depressed. "I only meant—did you—did you really mean everybody, Muriel?"

"When?"

"When you said that about—about the savage desert that didn't have any culture or anything."

"That wasn't what I said, Renfrew," she reminded him, and her expression became one of cold disapproval. "I said, 'A cultural!—'"

"Well, anyway," he urged, "you didn't really mean everybody, did you?"

"Seriously, Renfrew," she said; "—seriously, I don't understand how you can live the life you do."

"Why, I'm not living any life," he said reproachfully. "I never did do anything very dissipated."

"I don't mean that," she returned impatiently. "I mean what are you doing with your mind, your soul, your spirit? You never have a thought that the common herd around us doesn't have. You never read a book that the common herd doesn't read, and you don't even read many of them! What do you do with your time? I'm asking you!"

"Well, the truth is," he said meekly, "if you come right down to it: why, most of the time I loaf around in our front yard waiting to see if you're not coming out or anything."

His truthfulness did little to appease her. "Yes!" she said. "You sit hours and hours under that walnut tree over there in a perfect vacuum!"

"Well, it is like that," he agreed, "when you don't come out, Muriel."

130

"I'm not talking about anything of that sort!" she said quickly. "I mean, how can you bear to stay on such a plane? You don't have to just sit down and live on what your grandfather left you, do you?"

"Well, but," he protested, "I told you I was thinking of trying to run for the legislature!"

She stared at him. "Good heavens!" she said. "Do you think that would be rising to a higher plane?"

"A person has to begin," he ventured to remind her. "Even at that, they tell me I probably couldn't get nominated till I tried for it two or three times. They tell me I have to keep on going around till I get well known."

"Renfrew!"

"Well, I haven't made up my mind about it," he said. "I see you don't think much of it, and I'm not sure I do, myself. What do you think I ought to do?"

"What do I think you ought to do?" she cried. "Why, do anything—anything rather than be one of the commonplace herd on the commonplace plane!"

"Well, what do I have to do to get off of it?"

"What?"

"I mean, what's the best way for me to get on some other plane, the kind you mean? If you think it's no good my trying for the legislature, what do you think I had better do?"

He asked for information; in all honesty he simply wanted to be told. "I just don't know how to go about it," he added; "I don't know how to even start; that's the trouble. What had I better do first?"

Muriel stared at him; for in truth, she found herself at a loss. Faced with a request for grovelling details of the lofty but somewhat indefinite processes she had sketched, she was as completely a vacancy as could be found in all the cultural desert about her.

"Really!" she said. "If you don't know such things for yourself, I don't believe you could ever find out from anybody else!"

In this almost epigrammatic manner she concealed from him—and almost from herself—that she had no instructions to give him; nor was she aware that she had employed an instinctive device of no great novelty. Self-protection inspires it wherever superiority must be preserved; it has high official and military usages, but is most frequently in operation upon the icier intellectual summits. Yet, like a sword with a poisonous hilt, it always avenges its victim, and he who employs it will be irritable for some time afterward—he is really irritated with himself, but naturally prefers to think the irritation is with the stupidity that stumped him.

Thus Muriel departed abruptly, clashing the gate for all her expression of farewell, and left startled young Mr. Mears standing there, a figure of obvious pathos. She went indoors, and, having ascended to her own room, presently sat down and engaged herself with writing materials. Little shadows of despondency played upon her charming forehead as she wrote:

> "Life is so terrible!
> Far off—far, far—oh, infinitely distant—oh,
> Where far-flung fleets and argosies
> Of nobler thoughts abound
> Than those I find around me
> In this crass, provincial town,
> I must go!
> For I am lonely here,
> One lonely, lonely little figure
> Upbearing still one white, white light invisible.
> How could those see whose thoughts are all
> Of marts and churches, dancing, and the links?"

She paused to apply the blotter upon a tiny area of ink, oozed from the pen to her forefinger, which had pressed too ardently, being tense with creative art; and having thus broken the spell of composition, she glanced frowningly out of the window beside her desk. Across the way, she could see Renfrew Mears sitting under the walnut tree in his own yard. He was not looking toward her, but leaned back in a wicker chair, and to a sympathetic observation his attitude and absent skyward gaze might have expressed a contemplative bafflement. However, this was not Muriel's interpretation, for she wrote:

> "Across the street, ignoble in content,
> Under a dusty walnut tree,
> A young man flanneled sits,
> And dreams his petty burgher dreams
> Of burghers' petty offices.
> He's nothing.
> So, lonely in the savourless place, I find
> No comrade for my white, white light,
> No single soul that understands,
> Or glimpses just, my meanings."

Again the lonely girl looked out of the window, but this time with the sharpest annoyance, and wished herself even lonelier and more remote than her poem declared. Half a dozen lively children, including her own fat little brother Robert, had begun to play in the yard across the street, where the young man flanneled sat; and sometimes one of them came to hide behind his chair, though Renfrew was so immersed in his petty burgher dreams that he did not appear to know it. The shouting of the children interfered with composition, however, and while the poetess struggled on, the interference grew so poignant that it became actually a part of the texture of her poem:

> *"Oh, I am lonely in this world of noises,*
> *This world of piercing senseless outcries,*
> *I hate it so! I hear the shrill,*
> *Malignant yowls of children,*
> *Growing up like all the rest*
> *Without the power of thinking.*
> *Oh, noises how accursed—"*

Here her poem came to an end forever—that is to say, it had no end, was never completed, remained a fragment. Muriel jumped up, and the expressions she employed were appropriate for a maddened poet's use, though they befitted not a maiden's. The accursed noises across the street had become unbearable; they roused Renfrew from his petty dreams, and he straightened up in his chair to see what was going on.

"Here, here!" he said. "This isn't the Fourth of July. Quiet down a little, will you?"

Four boys, Masters Robert Eliot, Laurence Coy, Thomas Kimball and Freddie Mears, an eight-year-old cousin of Renfrew's, were advancing upon him, each evidently operating an imaginary machine-gun. "Bang! Bang! Bang! Bangity, Bangity, Bang! Bang!" they shouted with the utmost violence of their lungs.

"Stop it!" Renfrew commanded, and as the machine-guns seemed to be levelled straight at himself, he added: "Let me alone. I haven't done anything to you. What do you want to kill me for?"

He mistook their meaning, as he discovered immediately. "Ping! Ping! Ping!" a shrill voice cried out from the ground just behind his chair—another machine-gun, or else an "ottomatick."

"Pingity, pingity, ping. Ur-r-r-r-ping!"

The voice was that of Renfrew's nine-year-old sister Daisy; and looking round and down, he discovered her crouching low behind his chair, firing continuously. Renfrew perceived that he was a fortification of some sort; for although the presence of a grown person has naturally a stultifying effect upon children, they readily forget him if he remains in his own sphere; then he becomes but part of their landscape; they will use him as a castle, or perhaps as a distant Indian. Renfrew was now a log cabin.

"Ping! Ping! Pingety ur-r-r-r-ping!" Daisy shrieked from behind him. "You're all dead! Lay down!"

"You're dead yourself," Robert Eliot retorted. "I guess all us four filled you fuller o' wounds than you did us, didn't we? Lay down yourself!"

"I won't!" And Daisy, rising, began to argue the question vehemently. "I saw you all the time when you came around the house. I shot you first, didn't I? Wasn't I sayin' 'Ping,' before ever any one of you said 'Bang?'"

"No, you wasn't," Laurence Coy hotly replied. "Why, if we'd of had real guns, they wouldn't be enough left o' you to bury in a hen's nest."

"They would, too!" Daisy shouted. "If I'd had a real gun, they wouldn't be enough left of you to bury in half a hen's nest!"

"They would, too!" Laurence retorted, and his comrades in arms loudly echoed him. "They would, too!" they shouted.

"You're dead!" Daisy insisted. "You got to all four lay down. You got to!"

But upon this they raised such a chorus of jeering that she stamped her foot. "You got to!" she cried.

"Listen!" said Laurence. "Listen here! I killed you myself, first thing when we came around the house. I leave it to Elsie Threamer."

He referred to the one other little girl who was present, though she took no part in these military encounters and seemed, in fact, to disapprove of them. Fastidiously remaining at a distance from the belligerents, she sat alone upon the steps of the large front porch—a dainty little figure in strong contrast to the strident Daisy. Elsie was in smooth and unspotted white linen; and Daisy, too, had been in smooth and unspotted white linen—for a few minutes—but this one point of resemblance was now lost. Elsie was a beautiful child, whereas even the fonder of Daisy's two grandmothers had never gone so far as to say that Daisy was a beauty. Elsie was known for her sweet disposition, though some people thought that living next door to Daisy was injuring it. When Elsie came into a room where grown people were, they looked pleased; when Daisy came into a room where grown people were, they looked at their watches.

"Yes," said Robert Eliot, confirming Master Coy's choice of an umpire. "I leave it to Elsie. Whoever Elsie says is dead, why, they got to be dead."

"Leave it to Elsie," the other boys agreed. "Daisy's dead, isn't she, Elsie?"

"I am not!" Daisy cried. "I don't care what Elsie says. I killed every last one of you, and if you don't lay down, I'll make you."

"You will?" the bulky Robert inquired. "How you goin' to make us?"

"I'll frow you down," said the determined Daisy; and she added vindictively: "Then I'll walk all over you!"

The enemy received this with unanimous hootings. "Yes, you will!" Laurence Coy boasted satirically. "Come on and try it if you don't know any better!" And he concluded darkly: "Why, you wouldn't live a minute!"

"Anyway," Daisy insisted, "I won't leave it to Elsie, whether I'm dead or not."

"You got to," said Laurence, and walking toward Elsie, he pointed to Daisy, and spoke with some deference. "Tell her she's dead, Elsie."

Elsie shook her head. "I doe' care 'nything about it," she said coldly. "I doe' care whether she's dead or whether she isn't."

"But she didn't kill us, did she, Elsie?" Laurence urged her. "Our side's alive, isn't it, Elsie?"

"I doe' care whether you are or whether you're not," the cold and impartial Miss Threamer returned. "I doe' care 'nything about it which you are."

"I am not dead!" Daisy shouted, jumping up and down as she pranced toward the steps where sat the indifferent judge. "I doe' care if Elsie says I'm dead a thousan' times, I guess I got my rights, haven't I?"

"No, you haven't," Robert Eliot informed her harshly.

"I have, too!" she cried. "I have, too, got my rights."

"You haven't, either," Laurence said. "You haven't got any rights. Whatever Elsie says is goin' to be the rights."

Daisy strained her voice to its utmost limits: "I got my Rights!" she bawled.

They crowded about Elsie, arguing, jeering, gesticulating, a shrill and active little mob; meanwhile Elsie, seated somewhat above them, rested her chin on her clean little hand, and looked out over their heads with large, far-away eyes that seemed to take no account of them and their sordid bickerings. And Renfrew, marking how aloof from them she seemed, was conscious of a vague resemblance; Elsie, like Muriel, seemed to dwell above the common herd.

Then, as she watched the clamorous group, he noticed that whenever Laurence Coy appealed to Elsie, his voice, though loud, betrayed a certain breathlessness, while frequently after speaking to her he opened his mouth and took in a little air, which he then

135

swallowed with some difficulty, his neck becoming obviously uneasy. Indeed, this symptom was so pronounced that Renfrew, observing it with great interest, felt that there was something reminiscent about it—that is, it reminded him of something; he could not think just what. But he began to feel that Laurence perceived that Elsie was on a higher plane.

Elsie seemed to think so herself. "I doe' care 'nything about it," remained her unaltered verdict. "I doe' care a thing which is dead or which isn't."

"Well, then," said Laurence Coy, "we might as well play somep'm else."

"All right," Daisy agreed. "Le's play I'm a grea' big Injun woyer, an' all the rest of you are children I got to come an' scalp."

Her proposal met with no general favour—with no favour at all, in fact. "For heaven's sakes!" Thomas Kimball said. "I'd like to know what you take us for!" And in this scornful view he was warmly seconded by all his fellows.

"Well, this is my yard," Daisy reminded them severely. "I guess as long as you're in my yard, you'll please be p'lite enough to play what I say. I guess I got some rights in my own yard, haven't I?"

"I guess you better remember you ast us over here to play with you," Laurence Coy retorted, and his severity was more than equal to hers. "We never came an' ast you if we could, did we? You better learn sense enough to know that long as you ast us, we got a right to play what we want to, because we're company, an' we aren't goin' to play have you scalp us!"

"You haf to," Daisy insisted. "I got a perfect right to play what I want to in my own yard."

"You go on play it, an' scalp yourself, then," Laurence returned ungallantly. "Elsie, what you want to play?"

"I doe' want to play rough games," Elsie said. "I doe' like those fighting games."

"Well, what do you like?"

"Well, nice quiet games," she replied. "I'd be willing to play school."

"How do you play it?"

"Well, I'd be willing to be the teacher," she said. "You all sit down in a row, an' I'll say what punishments you haf to have."

Daisy instantly objected. "No, I'll be the teacher!"

"You won't!" Laurence said. "Elsie's got to be the teacher because she's company, an' anyway she said so first." And the majority agreeing to this, it was so ordered; whereupon Daisy, after some further futile objections, took her place with the boys. They sat

136

in a row upon the grass, facing Elsie, who stood on the steps confronting them.

"Now, the first thing to do," she said, "I better find out who's the worst; because you every one been very, very naughty an' deserve the terrablest punishments I can think of. I haf to think what I'm goin' to do to you." She paused, then pointed at Laurence. "Laurence Coy, you're the very worst one of this whole school."

"What did I do?" Laurence inquired.

"You said you hated girls."

"Well, I did say that," he admitted; and then, lest his comrades suspect him of weakening, he added: "I hate every last thing about 'em!"

"I bet you don't," said Daisy Mears, giggling.

Laurence blushed. "I do!" he shouted. "I hate every last—"

"Hush!" said the teacher. "That's very, very, very naughty, and you haf to be punished. You haf to be—well, I guess you haf to be spanked."

"I doe' care!" Laurence said, seeming to forget that this was only a game. "I hate girls and every last thing about 'em!"

"Hush!" Elsie said again. "I 'point Robert Eliot and Freddie Mears monitors. Robert must hold you while Freddie spanks you."

But Daisy jumped up, uncontrollably vociferous. "No, no!" she shouted. "I'm goin' to be a monitor! This is my yard, an' I guess I got some rights around here! Robert can hold him, but I got to spank him."

"Very well," said Elsie primly. "I 'point Daisy in Freddie's place."

Master Coy did not take this well; he rose and moved backward from the enthusiastic Daisy. "I won't do it," he said. "I won't let her spank me."

"You haf to," Daisy told him, clapping her hands. "You haf to do whatever Elsie says. You said so yourself; you said she had to be the teacher, an' we haf to do whatever she tells us."

"I won't!" he responded doggedly, for now he felt that his honour was concerned. "I won't do it!"

"Robert Eliot!" Elsie said reprovingly. "Did you hear me 'point you a monitor to hold Laurence while he's punished?"

"You better keep away from me," Laurence warned Robert, as the latter approached, nothing loth. "I won't do it!"

"I'm goin' to do it," said Daisy. "All you haf to do is hold still."

"I won't!" said Laurence.

"I guess I better do it with this," Daisy remarked, and, removing her left slipper as she and Robert continued their advance upon Laurence, she waved it merrily in the air. "What you so 'fraid

137

of, Laurence?" she inquired boastingly. "This isn't goin' to hurt you—much!"

"No, it isn't," he agreed. "And you better put it back where it was if you ever want to see it again. I'll take that ole slipper, an' I'll—"

"Teacher!" Daisy called, looking back to where Elsie stood. "Didn't you say this naughty boy had to be spanked?"

"Yes, I did," Elsie replied. "You hurry up and do it!"

Her voice was sweet; yet she spoke with sharpness, even with a hint of acidity, which the grown-up observer, forgotten by the children, noted with some surprise. Renfrew had been sure that he detected in Master Coy the symptoms of a tender feeling for Elsie. Laurence had deferred to her, had been the first to appeal to her when she sat aloof, had insisted that she should choose the game to play, and when she had chosen, hotly championed her claim to be the "teacher." Above all was the difference in his voice when he spoke to her, and that swallowing of air, that uneasiness of the neck. Renfrew was sure, too, that Elsie herself must be at least dimly aware of these things, must have some appreciation of the preference for her that they portended—and yet when she was given authority, her very first use of it was to place Master Coy in a position unspeakably distasteful to himself. Sometimes children were impossible to understand, Renfrew thought—and so were some grown people, he added, in his mind, with a despondent glance across the street.

Having glanced that way, his eyes came to rest upon the open window of a room upstairs, where the corner of a little satinwood writing-table was revealed—Muriel's, he knew. Branches of a tall maple tree gave half the window a rococo frame, and beyond this bordering verdure sometimes he had caught glimpses of a graceful movement, shadowy within the room—a white hand would appear for an instant moving something on the desk, or adjusting the window-shade for a better light; or at the best, it might be half revealed, half guessed, that Muriel was putting on her hat at a mirror. But this befell only on days when she was in a gentle mood with him, and so it was seldom. Certainly it was not to-day, though she might be there; for when she was gloomiest about her environment (of which he was so undeniably a part) she might indeed sit at that charming little satinwood table to write, but sat invisible to him, the curtains veiling her. Of course, at such times, there was only one thing left for Renfrew to do, and legend offers the parallel of the niggardly mother who locked up the butter in the pantry, but let her children rub their dry bread on the knob of the pantry door. Renfrew could look at the window.

The trouble was that when he looked at it, he was apt to continue to look at it for an indefinite period of time, during which his faculties lost their usefulness; people whom he knew might pass along the sidewalk, nod graciously to him, and then, not realizing his condition, vow never to speak again to so wooden a young snob. And into such a revery—if revery it were that held no thoughts, no visions, but only the one glamorous portrait of an empty window— he fell to-day. The voices of the children, sharp with purpose, shrill with protest, but died in his tranced ear as if they came from far away. The whole summer day, the glancing amber of the sunshine, the white clouds ballooning overhead between the tree-tops, the warm touch and smell of the air—these fell away from his consciousness. "He's nothing," the lonely poetess brusquely wrote of him; and now, for the time, it was almost true, since he was little more than a thought of a vacant window.

When Renfrew was in this jellied state, something rather unusual was needed to rouse him—though a fire-department ladder-truck going by, with the gong palavering, had done it. What roused him to-day were sounds less metallic, but comparable in volume and in certain ways more sensational. As he stood, fixed upon the window, he slowly and vaguely became aware that the children seemed to be excited about something. Like some woodland dreamer who discovers that a crow commune overhead has been in hot commotion for some time without his noticing it, he was not perturbed, but gradually wakened enough to wonder what the matter was. Then he turned and looked mildly about him.

His sister Daisy still held her slipper, but it was now in her left hand; in her right she had a shingle. Accompanied by Robert Eliot, she was advancing in a taunting manner upon Laurence Coy; and all three, as well as the rest of the children, may be described as continuously active and poignantly vociferous. Master Coy had armed himself with a croquet mallet, and his face expressed nothing short of red desperation; he was making a last stand. He warned the world that he would not be responsible for what he did with this mallet.

Master Eliot also had a mallet; he and Daisy moved toward Laurence, feinting, charging and retreating, while the other children whooped, squealed, danced and gave shrill advice how the outlaw might best be taken.

Daisy was the noisiest of all. "I'll show you, Mister Laurence Coy!" she cried. "You went an' tore my collar, an' you hit me with your elbow on my nose, an'—"

"I'm glad I did!" Laurence returned.

"It hurts me, too!" Daisy proclaimed.

"I'm glad it does! You had no business to grab me, an' I'm glad I—"

"We'll show you!" she promised him. "Soon as we get hold of you I'm goin' to spank you till this shingle's all wore out, an' then I'm goin' to keep on till my slipper's all wore out, an' then I'm goin' to take off my other slipper an'—"

"Look, Daisy!" Elsie Threamer cried. "While Robert keeps in front of him, why don't you go round behind him? Then you could grab his mallet, and Robert could throw him down."

At this the dreamy Renfrew looked at Elsie in a moderate surprise. Elsie, earlier so aloof upon her higher plane, was the lady who had objected to roughness; it was she who said she didn't like "those fighting games." Yet here she was now, dancing and cheering on the attack, as wolfish as the rest, as intent as any upon violence to the unfortunate Laurence. Nay, it was she who had devised and set in motion the very engine for his undoing.

"Get behind him, Daisy," she squealed. "That'll fix him!"

"She better not get behind me!" the grim Laurence warned them. "Her ole nose got one crack already to-day, an' if it gets another—"

"I'll take care o' that, Mister Laurence Coy!" Daisy assured him. "I'll look after my own nose, I kinely thank you."

"Yes, you will!" he retorted bitterly. "It ain't hardly big enough to see it, an' I bet if it comes off on this mallet, nobody could tell it was gone."

"I'll—I'll show you!" Daisy returned, finding no better repartee, though she evidently strove. "I'll pay you with this paddle for every one of your ole insulks!"

"Run behind him!" Elsie urged her. "Why didn't you run behind and grab him?"

"You watch!" Daisy cried. "You keep pokin' at him in front, Robert." And she darted behind Laurence, striking at the swinging mallet with her shingle.

But Laurence turned too, pivoting; and as he did, Robert Eliot, swinging his own weapon, rushed forward. The two mallets clattered together; there was a struggle—a confused one, for there were three parties to it, Daisy seeming to be at once the most involved and the most vigorous of the three. Her left arm clung about Laurence's neck, with the sole of her slipper pressed against his face, which he strove hard to disengage from this undesirable juxtaposition; her right arm rose and fell repeatedly, producing a series of muffled sounds.

"I'll show you!" she said. "I'll show you whose nose you better talk about so much!"

140

"Ya-a-ay, Laurence!" the other children shouted. "Gettin' spanked by a girl! Ya-ay, Laur-runce!"

They uproariously capered between Renfrew and the writhing group; but it struck him that the two mallets, which were both moving rather wildly, might do damage; and he moved toward the mêlée.

"Here!" he called. "What's all this nonsense? Put down those mallets."

He spoke too late. The maddened Laurence's feelings differed little from those of a warrior manhandled by a squaw in the midst of the taunting tribe; and in his anguish his strength waxed exceedingly. His mallet described a brief arc in the air, and not Daisy's nose, but the more evident nose of fat Robert Eliot, was the recipient. Contact was established audibly.

Robert squawked. He dropped his mallet, clasped his nose, and lay upon the good earth. Then when he looked at his ensanguined fingers, he seemed to feel that his end was hard upon him. He shrieked indeed.

Daisy also complained, an accident having befallen her, though she took it for no accident. "Ooh!" she said. "You made your elbow hit me in the stummick, Laurence Coy!" She stood as a semicircle, and clasped herself, while the noise of the other children was hushed—except the extreme noise of Robert—and the discomfort of sudden calamity fell upon them. Their silent mouths were all open, particularly that of Laurence Coy, whom Daisy did little to reassure.

"I bet I haf to have the doctor," she prophesied ominously; and then, pointing to the fallen, she added: "An' I bet Robert's goin' to die."

"Nonsense!" her brother said, bending over Robert. "Nonsense!"

But Laurence Coy did not hear this optimistic word. Laurence had no familiarity with mortal wounds;—to his quaking eye, Robert bore a fatal appearance, and Daisy's chill prophecy seemed horribly plausible. Laurence departed. One moment he stood there, pallid and dumfounded, but present; and the next, no one could have defined his whereabouts with certainty. All that could be known was that he had gone, and from the manner of his going, it might well be thought that he was shocked to find himself forgetting a rendezvous appointed for this very moment at some distant spot;—he had a hurried air.

Others were almost as deeply affected by Daisy's gloomy prophecy. As soon as she put the thought in their minds, Thomas Kimball, Freddie Mears and the remarkable Elsie were all convinced that Robert was near his passing, and with natural solicitude they had but the one thought in common: to establish an alibi.

"Well, I never went anywhere near him," Elsie said. "I never even touched a mallet!"

"Neither'd I!" said Thomas Kimball. "I wasn't in ten feet of him."

"I wasn't in a hunderd!" said Freddie.

"It wasn't me!" Thomas protested. "I didn't have anything to do with it."

"It was Laurence Coy," said Freddie. "That's who it was."

"It was every bit Laurence Coy," said Elsie. "I told them not to play such rough games."

Thus protesting, the three moved shyly toward various exits from the yard, and protesting still, went forth toward their several dwelling-places—and went unnoticed, for Robert was the centre of attention. The volume of sound he produced was undiminished, though the tone had elevated somewhat in pitch, and he seemed to intend words, probably of a reproachful nature; but as his excess of emotion enabled him to produce only vowels, the effect was confused, and what he wished to say could be little more than guessed.

"Hush, hush!" said Renfrew, trying to get him to stand up. "You'll bring the whole town here!"

Robert became more coherent. "He him me om my mose!"

"I know," said Renfrew. "But you're not much hurt."

Appearing to resent this, Robert cried the louder. "I am, too!" he wailed. "I bet I do die!"

"Nonsense!"

"I bet he does," said the gloomy Daisy. "He is goin' to die, Renfrew."

Pessimism is useful sometimes, but this was not one of the times. When Robert heard Daisy thus again express her conviction, he gave forth an increased bellowing; and it was with difficulty that Renfrew got him to a hydrant in the side yard. Here, plaintively lowing, with his head down, Robert incarnadined Renfrew's trousers at intervals, while the young man made a cold compress of a handkerchief and applied it to the swelling nose.

"If I—'f I—'f I die," the patient blubbered, during this process, "they got to ketch that lull-little Lull-Laurence Coy and huh-hang him!"

"Nonsense!" said Renfrew. "Stand still; your nose isn't even broken."

"Well, my stummick is," Daisy said, attending upon them and still in the semicircular attitude she had assumed for greater comfort. "I guess he broke that, if he never broke anything else, and whether he gets hung or not, I bet my mother'll tell his mother she's got to whip him, when she finds out."

"When she finds out what?" Renfrew asked.

"When she finds out what he did to my stummick!"

"Pooh," said Renfrew. "Both of you were teasing Laurence, and worrying him till he hardly knew what he was doing. Besides, there isn't really anything to speak of the matter with either of you."

Both resented his making light of injuries so sensational as theirs; and Robert released his voice in an intolerable howl. "There is, too! An' if I got to die—"

"Stop that!" Renfrew commanded. "How many times must I tell you? You're not any more likely to die than I am!"

With that he was aware of a furious maiden entering the gate and running toward them across the lawn, and even as she sped, completing a hasty "putting up" of her hair.

"If he isn't 'likely to die,'" she cried, "I'd be glad to know whose fault it is! Not yours, I think, Renfrew Mears!"

At sight of his sister, Master Eliot bellowed anew; he wanted to tell his troubles all over again; but emotion in the presence of sympathy was too much for him; and once more he became all vowels, so that nothing definite could be gathered. Muriel clasped him to her. "Poor darling Bobby!" she said. "Don't cry, darling! Sister'll take care of you!"

"Here," said Renfrew, proffering a fresh handkerchief. "Be careful. His nose isn't quite—"

She took the handkerchief and applied it, but gave the donor no thanks. "I never in all my life saw anything like it!" she exclaimed. "I never saw anything to compare with it!"

"Why, it didn't amount to so very much," Renfrew said mildly, though he was surprised at her vehemence. "The children were playing, and they got to teasing, and Robert got tapped on the—"

"'Tapped!'" she cried. "He might have been killed! But what I meant was you!"

"Me?"

"Certainly! You! I never saw anything like your behaviour, and I saw it all from the sofa in my room. If I hadn't had to dress, I'd have been over here in time to stop it long before you did, Renfrew Mears!"

"Why, I don't understand at all," he protested feebly. "You seem angry with me! But all I've done was to put cold water on Robert's nose."

"That's it!" she cried. "You stood there—I saw you. You stood there, and never lifted a finger while those children were having the most dreadful fight with croquet mallets, not forty feet from you! They might all have been killed; and my poor darling little brother almost was killed—"

At this, Robert interrupted her with fresh outcries, and clung to her pitifully. She soothed him, and turned her flashing and indignant eyes upon Renfrew.

"You stood there, not like a man but like a block of wood," she said. "You didn't even look at them!"

"Why, no," said Renfrew. "I was looking at your window."

Apparently he felt that this was an explanation that explained everything. He seemed to imply that any man would naturally demean himself like a block of wood while engaged in the act of observation he mentioned, even though surrounded by circumstances of murder.

It routed Muriel. She had no words to express her feeling about a person who talked like that; and giving him but one instant to take in the full meaning of her compressed lips, her irate colour and indignant breathing, she turned pointedly away. Then, with Robert clinging to her, she went across the lawn and forth from the gate, while Mr. Mears and his small sister watched in an impressed silence.

Some one else watched Muriel as she supported the feeble steps of the weeping fat boy across the street; and this was the self-styled woman-hater and celebrated malleteer, Master Laurence Coy. He was at a far distance down the street, and in the thorny middle of a hedge where no sheriff might behold him; but he could see, and he was relieved (though solely on his own account) to discover that Robert was still breathing. He was about to come out from the hedge when the disquieting afterthought struck him: Robert might have expressed a wish to be taken to die in his own home. Therefore Laurence remained yet a while where he was.

By the hydrant, Daisy was so interested in the departure of the injured brother and raging sister that she had forgotten her broken stummick and the semicircular position she had assumed to assuage it, or possibly to keep the broken parts together. She stood upright, watching the two emotional Eliots till they had disappeared round their own house in the direction of their own hydrant. Then she turned and looked up brightly at her brother.

"She's fearful mad, isn't she?" Daisy said, laughing. "She treats you awful, don't she?"

"Never mind," Renfrew said, and then he remembered something that had puzzled him not so painfully; and he wondered if Daisy might shed a light on this. "Daisy, what in the world made you pick on poor little Laurence the way you did?"

"Me?" she asked, surprised. "Why, it was Elsie told us to."

"That's it," Renfrew said. "That's what I want to know. Laurence was just as nice to her as he could be; he did everything he could think of to please her, and the first chance she got, she set the whole pack of you on him. What did she do a thing like that for?"

Daisy picked a dandelion from the grass and began to eat it. "What?" she inquired.

"What makes Elsie so mean to poor little Laurence Coy?"

"Oh, well," said Daisy casually, "she likes him best. She likes him best of all the boys in town." And then, swallowing some petals of the dandelion, she added: "She treats him awful."

Renfrew looked at her thoughtfully; then his wondering eyes moved slowly upward till they rested once more upon the maple-embowered window over the way, and into his expression there came a hint of something almost hopeful.

"So she does!" he said.

MAYTIME IN MARLOW

IN MAY, when the maple leaves are growing large, the Midland county seat and market town called Marlow so disappears into the foliage that travellers, gazing from Pullman windows, wonder why a railroad train should stop to look at four or five preoccupied chickens in a back yard. On the other hand, this neighbourly place is said to have a population numbering more than three thousand. At least, that is what a man from Marlow will begin to claim as soon as he has journeyed fifteen or twenty miles from home; but to display the daring of Midland patriotism in a word, there have been Saturdays (with the farmers in town) when strangers of open-minded appearance have been told, right down on the Square itself, that Marlow consisted of upwards of four thousand mighty enterprising inhabitants.

After statistics so dashing, it seems fairly conservative to declare that upon the third Saturday of last May one idea possessed the minds and governed the actions of all the better bachelors of Marlow who were at that time between the ages of seventeen and ninety, and that the same idea likewise possessed and governed all the widowers, better and worse, age unlimited.

She was first seen on the Main Street side of the Square at about nine o'clock in the morning. To people familiar with Marlow this will mean that all the most influential business men obtained a fair view of her at an early hour, so that the news had time to spread to the manufacturers and professional men before noon.

Mr. Rolfo Williams, whose hardware establishment occupies a corner, was the first of the business men to see her. He was engaged within a cool alcove of cutlery when he caught a glimpse of her through a window; but in spite of his weight he managed to get near the wide-spread front doors of his store in time to see her framed by the doorway as a passing silhouette of blue against the sunshine of the Square. His clerk, a young married man, was only a little ahead of him in reaching the sidewalk.

"My goodness, George!" Mr. Williams murmured. "Who is that?"

"Couldn't be from a bit more'n half a mile this side o' New York!" said George, marvelling. "Look at the clo'es!"

"No, George," his employer corrected him gently. "To me it's more the figger."

The lady was but thirty or forty feet away, and though she did not catch their words, the murmur of the two voices attracted her

146

attention. Not pausing in her light stride forward, she looked back over her shoulder, and her remarkable eyes twinkled with recognition. She smiled charmingly, then nodded twice—first, unmistakably to Mr. Williams, and then, with equal distinctness, to George.

These dumfounded men, staring in almost an agony of blankness, were unable to return the salutation immediately. The attractive back of her head was once more turned to them by the time they recovered sufficiently to bow, but both of them did bow, in spite of that, being ultimately conscientious no matter how taken aback. Even so, they were no more flustered than was old Mr. Newton Truscom (Clothier, Hatter, and Gents' Furnisher), just emerging from his place of business next door; for Mr. Truscom was likewise sunnily greeted.

"My goodness!" Mr. Williams gasped. "I never saw her from Adam!"

Mr. Truscom, walking backward, joined the hardware men. "Seems like fine-lookin' girls liable to take considerable of a fancy to us three fellers," he said; "whether they know us or not!"

"Shame on you, Newt!" George returned. "Didn't you see her give me the eye? Of course, after that, she wanted to be polite to you and Mr. Williams. Thought him and you were prob'ly my pappy and gran'daddy!"

"Look!" said Mr. Truscom. "She's goin' in Milo Carter's drugstore. Sody-water, I shouldn't wonder!"

"It just this minute occurred to me how a nectar and pineapple was what I needed," said George. "Mr. Williams, I'll be back at the store in a few min—"

"No, George," his employer interrupted. "I don't mind your lollin' around on the sidewalk till she comes out again, because that's about what I'm liable to do myself, but if you don't contain yourself from no nectar and pineapple, I'm goin' to tell your little bride about it—and you know what Birdie will say!"

"Rolfo, did you notice them shoes?" Mr. Truscom asked, with sudden intensity. "If Baker and Smith had the enterprise to introduce a pattern like that in our community—"

"No, Newt, I didn't take so much notice of her shoes. To me," said Mr. Williams dreamily, "to me it was more the whole figger, as it were."

The three continued to stare at the pleasing glass front of Milo Carter's drug-store; and presently they were joined by two other men of business who had perceived from their own doorways that something unusual was afoot; while that portion of Main Street lying beyond Milo Carter's also showed signs of being up with the

147

times. Emerging from this section, P. Borodino Thompson and Calvin Burns, partners in Insurance, Real Estate, Mortgages and Loans, appeared before the drug-store, hovered a moment in a non-committal manner that was really brazen, then walked straight into the store and bought a two-cent stamp for the firm.

Half an hour later, Mortimer Fole was as busy as he could be. That is to say, Mortimer woke from his first slumber in a chair in front of the National House, heard the news, manœuvred until he obtained a view of its origin, and then drifted about the Square exchanging comment with other shirt-sleeved gossips. (Mortimer was usually unemployed; but there was a Mexican War pension in the family.)

"Heard about it?" he inquired, dropping into E. J. Fuller's (E. J. Fuller & Co., Furniture, Carpets and Wall-Paper).

"Yes, Mortimore," E. J. Fuller replied. "Anybody know anything?"

"Some of 'em claim they do," said Mortimer. "Couple fellers I heard says she must belong with some new picture theatre they claim an out-o'-town firm's goin' to git goin' here, compete with the Vertabena. Howk, he says thinks not; claims it's a lady he heard was comin' to settle here from Wilkes-Barry, Pennsylvania, and give embroidery lessons and card-playin'. Cousin of the Ferrises and Wheelers, so Howk claims. I says, 'She is, is she?' 'Well,' he says, 'that's the way I look at it.' 'Oh, you do, do you?' I says. 'Then what about her speakin' to everybody?' I ast him, right to his face; and you'd ought to seen him! Him and all of 'em are wrong."

"How do you know, Mortimore?" asked Mr. Fuller. "What makes you think so?"

"Listen here, Ed," said Mortimer. "What'd she do when she went into Charlie Murdock's and bought a paper o' pins? You heard about that, yet?"

"No."

"She went in there," said Mr. Fole, "and spoke right to Charlie. 'How are you, Mister Murdock?' she says. Charlie like to fell over backwards! And then, when he got the pins wrapped up and handed 'em to her she says, 'How's your wife, Mr. Murdock?' Well, sir, Charlie says his wife was just about the last woman in the world he had in his mind right then!"

"Where's she supposed to be now?" Mr. Fuller inquired, not referring to Mrs. Murdock. "Over at the hotel?"

"Nope," Mortimer replied. "She ain't puttin' up there. Right now she's went upstairs in the Garfield Block to Lu Allen's office. Haven't heard what Lu's got to say or whether she's come out. You git to see her yet?"

148

"No, sir," Mr. Fuller returned, rather indifferently. "What's she look like, Mortimore?"

"Well, sir, I can give you a right good notion about that," said Mortimer. "I expect I'm perty much the only man in town that could, too. You remember the time me and you went over to Athens City and took in the Athens City lodge's excursion to Chicago? Well, remember somebody got us to go to a matinée show without any much cuttin' up or singin' in it, but we got so we liked it anyhow—and went back there again same night?"

"Yes, sir. Maude Adams."

"Well, sir, it ain't her, but that's who she kind o' put me in mind of. Carryin' a blue parasol, too."

Mr. Fuller at once set down the roll of wall-paper he was measuring, and came out from behind his counter.

"Where goin', Ed?" Mortimer inquired, stretching himself elaborately, though somewhat surprised at Mr. Fuller's abrupt action—for Mortimer was indeed capable of stretching himself in a moment of astonishment.

"What?"

"Where goin'?"

Mr. Fuller, making for the open, was annoyed by the question. "Out!" he replied.

"I got nothin' much to do right now," said the sociable Mortimer. "I'll go with you. Where'd you say you was goin', Ed?"

"Business!" Mr. Fuller replied crossly.

"That suits me, Ed. I kind o' want to see Lu Allen, myself!"

Thereupon they set forth across the Square, taking a path that ran through the courthouse yard; but when they came out from behind the old, red brick building and obtained a fair view of the Garfield Block, they paused. She of the blue parasol was disappearing into the warm obscurity of Pawpaw Street; and beside her sauntered Mr. Lucius Brutus Allen, Attorney at Law, his stoutish figure and celebrated pongee coat as unmistakable from the rear as from anywhere. In the deep, congenial shade of the maple trees her parasol was unnecessary, and Lucius dangled it from his hand, or poked its ferule idly at bugs in shrubberies trembling against the picket fences that lined the way.

At any distance it could be seen that his air was attentive and gallant—perhaps more than that, for there was even a tenderness expressed in the oblique position of his shoulders, which seemed to incline toward his companion. Mr. Rolfo Williams, to describe this mood of Lucius Allen's, made free use of the word "sag." Mr. Williams stood upon the corner with his wife, that amiable matron, and P. Borodino Thompson, all three staring unaffectedly. "That's

149

Lu Allen's lady-walk," said Rolfo, as E. J. Fuller and Mortimer joined them. "He always kind o' sags when he goes out walkin' with the girls. Sags toe-ward 'em. I'll say this much: I never see him sag deeper than what he is right now. Looks to me like he's just about fixin' to lean on her!"

"Don't you worry!" his wife said testily. "Lucy'd slap him in a minute! She always was that kind of a girl."

" 'Lucy!' " Mortimer echoed. "Lucy who?"

"Lucy Cope."

"What on earth are you talkin' about, Miz Williams? That ain't Lucy Cope!"

Mrs. Williams laughed. "Just why ain't it?" she asked satirically. "I expect some o' the men in this town better go get the eye-doctor to take a look at 'em! Especially"—she gave her husband a compassionate glance—"especially the fat, old ones! Mrs. Cal Burns come past my house 'while ago; says, 'Miz Williams, I expect you better go on up-town look after your husband,' she says. 'I been huntin' fer mine,' she says, 'but I couldn't locate him, because he knows better than to let me to,' she says, 'after what P. Borodino Thompson's just been tellin' me about him! Lucy Cope Ricketts is back in town,' she says, 'and none the men reckanized her yet,' she says, 'and you better go on up to the Square and take a look for yourself how they're behavin'! I hear,' she says, 'I hear hasn't anybody been able to get waited on at any store-counter in town so far this morning, except Lucy herself.' "

"Well, sir," Mr. Williams declared. "I couldn't hardly of believed it, but it certainly is her." He shook his head solemnly at Mrs. Williams, and, gently detaching her palm-leaf fan from her hand, used it for his own benefit, as he continued: "Boys, what I'm always tellin' ma here is that there ain't nothin' on earth like bein' a widow to bring out the figger!"

"You hush up!" she said, but was constrained to laugh and add, "I guess you'd be after me all right if I was a widow!"

"No, Carrie," he said, "I wouldn't be after nobody if you was a widow."

"I mean if I was anybody else's," Mrs. Williams explained. "Look how George says you been actin' all morning about this one!"

Mr. Fuller intervened in search of information. He was not a native, and had been a citizen of Marlow a little less than four years. "Did you say this lady was one of the Ricketts family, Mrs. Williams?" he inquired.

"No. She married a Ricketts. She's a Cope; she's all there is left of the Copes."

"Did I understand you to say she was a widow?"

150

"I didn't say she was one," Mrs. Williams replied. "She is one now, though. Her and Tom Ricketts got married ten years ago and went to live in California. He's been dead quite some time—three-four years maybe—and she's come back to live in the Copes' ole house, because it belongs to her, I expect. Everybody knew she was comin' some time this spring—everybody'd heard all about it—but none you men paid any attention to it. I'll have to let you off, Mr. Fuller. You're a widower and ain't lived here long, and you needn't take what I'm sayin' to yourself. But the rest of all you rag-tag and bob-tail aren't goin' to hear the last o' this for some time! Mr. Fuller, if you want to know why they never took any interest up to this morning in Lucy Cope Ricketts' goin' to come back and live here again, it's because all they ever remembered her she was kind of a peakid girl; sort of thin, and never seemed to have much complexion to speak of. You wouldn't think it to look at her now, but that's the way she was up to when she got married and went away. Now she's back here, and a widow, not a one of 'em reckanized her till Mrs. Cal Burns come up-town and told 'em—and look how they been actin'!"

"It all goes to show what I say," said Rolfo. "She always did have kind of a sweet-lookin' face, but I claim that there's nothin' in the world like being a happy widow to bring out the complexion and the—"

"Listen to you!" his wife interrupted. "How you do keep out o' jail so long I certainly don't know!" She turned to the others. "That man's a born bigamist," she declared. "And at that I don't expect he's so much worse'n the rest of you!"

"You ought to leave me out along with E. J. Fuller, Mrs. Williams," Mr. Thompson protested. "I've never even been married at all."

But this only served to provoke Rolfo's fat chuckle, and the barbed comment: "It is a heap cheaper at mealtimes, Bore!"

"How's it happen Lu Allen's so thick with Mrs. Ricketts?" E. J. Fuller inquired. "How's it come that he—"

"He's her lawyer," Mrs. Williams informed him, "and he was executor of the Cope will, and all. Besides that, he used to be awful attentive to her, and nobody was hardly certain which she was goin' to take, Lu Allen or Tom Ricketts, right up to a year or two before she got married. Looks like Lu was goin' to get a second chance, and money throwed in!"

"Well, Lu's a talker, but he'll have to talk some now!" P. Borodino Thompson announced thoughtfully. "I used to know her, too, but I never expected she was going to turn out like this!"

"You and I been gettin' to be pretty fair friends, Bore," said

151

Mr. Fuller, genially, as the group broke up. "Think you could kind of slide me in along with you when you go up there to call?"

"No, sir!" Mr. Thompson replied emphatically. "Red-headed Lu Allen isn't much of a rival, but he's enough for me. If you think of starting in, first thing I do I'm going to tell her you're an embezzler. I'm going home now to get out my cutaway suit and white vest, and you can tell 'em all to keep out of my road! I'm going calling this evening, right after supper!"

"Never mind!" Fuller warned him. "I'll get up there some way!"

Meanwhile, in the sun-checkered shadow of a honeysuckle vine that climbed a green trellis beside an old doorway, Mr. Lucius Brutus Allen was taking leave of his lovely friend.

"Will you come this evening, Lucius, and help me decide on some remodeling for the house?" she asked; and probably no more matter-of-fact question ever inspired a rhapsody in the bosom of a man of thirty-five.

"No, thanks," said Mr. Allen. "I never could decide which I thought your voice was like, Lucy: a harp or a violin. It's somewhere between, I suspect; but there are pictures in it, too. Doesn't make any difference what you say, whenever you speak a person can't help thinking of wild roses shaking the dew off of 'em in the breezes that blow along about sunrise. You might be repeating the multiplication table or talking about hiring a cook, but the sound of your voice would make pictures like that, just the same. I had to hear it again to find out how I've been missing it. I must have been missing it every single day of these ten years whether I knew it or not. It almost makes me sorry you've come back, because if you hadn't I'd never have found out how I must have been suffering."

Mrs. Ricketts looked at him steadily from within the half-shadow of the rim of her pretty hat. "When will you come and help me with the plans?" she asked.

"I don't know," Mr. Allen returned absently; and he added with immediate enthusiasm: "I never in my life saw any girl whose hair made such a lovely shape to her head as yours, Lucy! It's just where you want a girl's hair to be, and it's not any place you don't want it to be. It's the one thing in the world without any fault at all—the only thing the Lord made just perfect—except your nose and maybe the Parthenon when it was new."

That brought a laugh from her, and Lucius, who was pink naturally and pinker with the warm day, grew rosy as he listened to Lucy's laughter. "By George!" he said. "To hear you laugh again!"

"You always did make me laugh, Lucius."

"Especially if I had anything the matter with me," he said. "If I had a headache or toothache I'd always come around to get you to laugh. Sometimes if the pain was pretty bad, it wouldn't go away till you laughed two or three times!"

She laughed the more; then she sighed. "Over ten years, almost eleven—and you saying things like this to every girl and woman you met, all the time!"

"Well," Mr. Allen said thoughtfully, "nobody takes much notice what a chunky kind of man with a reddish head and getting a little bald says. It's quite a privilege."

She laughed again, and sighed again. "Do you remember how we used to sit out here in the evenings under the trees, Lucius? One of the things I've often thought about since then was how when you were here, papa and mamma would bring their chairs and join us, and you'd talk about the moon, and astronomy, and the Hundred Years War, and—"

"Yes!" Lucius interrupted ruefully. "And then some other young fellow would turn up—some slim, dark-haired Orlando—and you'd go off walking with him while I stayed with the old folks. I'd be talking astronomy with them, but you and Orlando were strolling under the stars—and didn't care what they were made of!"

"No," she said. "I mean what I've thought about was that papa and mamma never joined us unless you were here. It took me a long while to understand that, Lucius; but finally I did." She paused, musing a moment; then she asked: "Do the girls and boys still sit out on front steps and porches, or under the trees in the yard in the evenings the way we used to? Do you remember how we'd always see old Doctor Worley jogging by in his surrey exactly as the courthouse bell rang nine, every night; his wife on the back seat and the old doctor on the front one, coming home from their evening drive? There are so many things I remember like that, and they all seem lovely now—and I believe they must be why I've come back here to live—though I didn't think much about them at the time. Do the girls and boys still sit out in the yards in the evening, Lucius?"

Lucius dangled the ferule of the long-handled blue parasol over the glowing head of a dandelion in the grass. "Not so much," he answered. "And old Doc Worley and his wife don't drive in their surrey in the summer evenings any more. They're both out in the cemetery now, and the surrey's somewhere in the air we breathe, because it was burnt on a trash-heap the other day, though I've seemed to see it driving home in the dusk a hundred times since it fell to pieces. Nowadays hardly any, even of the old folks, ride in surreys. These ten years have changed the world, Lucy. Money and gasoline. Even Marlow's got into the world; and in the evenings they go out snorting and sirening and blowing-out and smoking blue oil all over creation. Bore Thompson's about the only man in town that's still got any use for a hitching-post. He drives an old white horse to a phaeton, and by to-morrow afternoon at the latest you'll find that old horse and phaeton tied to the ring in the hand of that little old cast-iron stripe-shirted nigger-boy in front of your gate yonder."

Mrs. Ricketts glanced frowningly at the obsolete decoration he mentioned; then she smiled. "That's one of the things I want you to advise me about," she said. "I don't know how much of the place to alter and how much to leave as it is. And why will I find Mr. Thompson's horse tied to our poor old cast-iron darky boy?"

"He's seen you, hasn't he?"

"Yes, but he looked startled when I spoke to him. Besides, he used to see me when I was a girl, and he was one of the beaux of the town, and he never came then."

"He will now," said Lucius.

"Oh, surely not!" she protested, a little dismayed.

"He couldn't help it if he tried, poor thing!"

At that she affected to drop him a curtsey, but nevertheless appeared not over-pleased. "You seem to be able to help it, Lucius," she said; and the colour in his cheeks deepened a little as she went on: "Of course you don't know that the way you declined to come this evening is one of the things that make life seem such a curious and mixed-up thing to me. After I—when I'd gone away from here to live, you were what I always remembered when I thought of Marlow, Lucius. And I remembered things you'd said to me that I hadn't thought of at all when you were saying them. It was so strange! I've got to knowing you better and better all the long, long time I've been away from you—and I could always remember you more clearly than anybody else. It seems queer and almost a little wicked to say it, but I could remember you even more clearly than I could papa and mamma—and, oh! how I've looked forward to seeing you again and to having you talk to me about everything! Why won't you come this evening? Aren't you really glad I'm home again?"

"That's the trouble!" he said; and seemed to feel that he had offered a satisfactory explanation.

"What in the world do you mean?" she cried.

"I gather," he said slowly, "from what you've said, that you think more about me when I'm not around where you have to look at me! Besides—"

"Besides what?" she insisted, as he moved toward the gate.

"I'm afraid!" said Lucius; and his voice was husky and honest.

"I'm afraid," he repeated seriously, as he closed the gate behind him. "I'm afraid to meet Maud and Bill."

She uttered half of a word of protest, not more than that; and it went unheard. Frowning, she compressed her lips, and in troubled silence stood watching his departure. Then, all at once, the frown vanished from her forehead, the perplexity from her eyes; and she pressed an insignificant handkerchief to a charming mouth overtaken by sudden laughter. But she made no sound or gesture that would check Lucius Brutus Allen or rouse him to the realization of what he was doing.

The sturdy gentleman was marching up Pawpaw Street toward the Square, unconscious that he had forgotten to return the long-handled blue parasol to its owner—and that he was now jauntily carrying it over his right shoulder after the manner of a musket. Above the fence, the blue parasol and the head of Lucius bobbed rhythmically with his gait, and Mrs. Ricketts, still with her handkerchief to her lips, watched that steady bobbing until intervening shrubberies closed the exhibition. Then, as she opened the door of the old frame house, she spoke half-aloud:

"Nobody—not one—never anywhere!" she said; and she meant that Lucius was unparalleled.

When Mr. Allen debouched upon Main Street from Pawpaw, he encountered Mortimer Fole, who addressed him with grave interest:

"Takin' it to git mended, I suppose, Lu?"

"Get what mended?" asked Lucius, pausing.

"Her parasol," Mr. Fole responded. "If you'll show me where it's out of order, I expect I could get it fixed up about as well as anybody. Frank Smith that works over at E. J. Fuller's store, he's considerable of a tinker, and I reckon he'd do it fer nothin' if it was me ast him to. I'd be willin' to carry it up to her house for you, too. I go by there anyhow, on my way home."

"No, Mortimore, thank you." Lucius brought the parasol down from his shoulder and stood regarding it seriously. "No; it isn't out of order. I—I just brought it with me. What's the news?"

"Well, I don't know of much," said Mortimer, likewise staring attentively at the parasol. "Some wall-paperin' goin' on here and there over town, E. J. Fuller says. Ed says P. Borodino Thompson told him he was goin' to drop round and call this evening, he says; but afterwards I was up at the hardware store, and Bore come in there and Rolfo Williams's wife talked him out o' goin'. 'My heavens!' she says, 'can't you even give her a couple days to git unpacked and straighten up the house?' So Bore says he guessed he'd wait till to-morrow afternoon and ast her to go buggy-ridin' in that ole mud-coloured phaeton of his. Milo Carter's fixin' to go up there before long, and I hear Henry Ledyard says he's liable to start in mighty soon, too. You and Bore better look out, Lu. Henry's some years younger than what you and Bore are. He ain't as stocky as what you are, nor as skinny as what Bore is, and he certainly out-dresses the both of you every day in the week an' twicet on Sunday!"

"Thank you, Mortimore," Lucius responded, nodding. "I'd been calculating a little on a new necktie—but probably it wouldn't be much use if Henry Ledyard's going to—"

"No, sir," Mortimer interrupted to agree. "Henry buys 'em a couple or more at a time. Newt Truscom's goin' to be a rich man if Henry don't quit. So long, Lu!"

Mr. Allen, turning in at the entrance to the stairway that led to his office, waved his left hand in farewell, his right being employed in an oddly solicitous protection of the parasol—though nothing threatened it. But Mortimer, having sauntered on a few steps, halted, and returned to the stairway entrance, whence he called loudly upward:

"Lu! Oh, Lu Allen!"

"What is it?"

"I forgot to mention it. You want to be lookin' out your window along around three o'clock or half-past, to-morrow afternoon."

"What for?"

"Why, P. Borodino was talkin' and all so much, about that buggy-ride, you know, so Rolfo Williams bet him a safety-razor against three dollars' worth of accident insurance that he wouldn't git her to go with him, and Bore's got to drive around the Square, first thing after they start, to prove it. There's quite a heap of interest around town in all this and that; and you better keep your eye out your window from three o'clock on!"

Thus, at three o'clock, the next afternoon, Mr. Allen was in fact looking—though somewhat crossly—out of his office window. Below, P. Borodino Thompson was in view, seated in his slowly moving phaeton, exuberantly clad for a man of his special reputation for "closeness," and with his legs concealed by a new dust-robe, brilliantly bordered; but he was as yet unaccompanied.

A loud and husky voice ascended to the window: "On his way!" And Lucius marked the form and suspender of Mortimer upon the sidewalk below; whereupon Mortimer, seeing that Lucius observed him, clapped hand to mouth, and simulated a jocular writhing in mockery of P. Borodino. "Hay, Bore!" he bellowed. "Floyd Kilbert's wife's got a sewin'-machine she wants you to move

156

fer her in that empty seat you'll have in your phaeton when you git back here to the Square in a few minutes!"

Mr. Thompson waved his whip condescendingly, attempting no other retort; and turned into the maple shade of Pawpaw Street. Five minutes later, "General," the elderly white horse, was nosing the unyielding hand of the cast-iron darky boy, and the prophecy made by Mr. Allen on the preceding morning was fulfilled.

A neat young woman, descendant of vikings, but tamed in all except accent, showed Mr. Thompson into an Eighteen-Eighty parlour; went away, returned, and addressed him as "yentleman." Mrs. Ricketts would be glad to see him, she reported, adding: "Yust wait some minute."

The visitor waited some minutes, then examined his reflection in the glass over the Eastlake mantel; and a slight rustling in the hall, near the doorway, failed to attract his attention, for he was engaged in a fundamental rearrangement of his tie.

"Wookin' at himseff in the wookin'-gwass!"

This unfavourable comment caused him to tuck his tie back into the neck of his white waistcoat in haste, and to face the doorway somewhat confusedly. Two pretty little children stood there, starchy and fresh, and lustrously clean, dressed in white: a boy about seven and a girl about five—and both had their mother's blue eyes and amber hair.

"He's dressin' himself," said the boy.

"Wookin' at himseff in the wookin'-gwass!" the little girl repeated, and, pointing a curling forefinger, she asked: "Who? Who that man?"

"Well, tots," the visitor said, rather uncomfortably, but with proper graciousness, "who are you? What's your name, little girl?"

"Maud," the little girl replied, without any shyness.

"What's yours, little man?"

"Bill," said the boy. "Bill Ricketts. You got somep'm stickin' out of your vest at the top."

Mr. Thompson incautiously followed an impulse to turn again to the mirror, whereupon the child, Maud, instantly shouted:

"Wookin' at himseff in the wookin'-gwass!"

Her voice was so loud, and the information it imparted so discomfiting, that the visitor felt himself breaking out suddenly into a light perspiration. Foolishly, he attempted to defend himself against the accusation. "Why, no, I wasn't, little Maudie," he said, with an uneasy laugh.

To his horror, she responded by shouting at an even higher pitch than before:

"Wookin' at himseff in the wookin'-gwass!"

157

She did not stop at that, for children in such moods are terrible, and they have no pity. P. Borodino Thompson, substantial citizen, of considerable importance financially, not only in Marlow but throughout the county, and not without dignity to maintain, found himself at the mercy of this child who appeared to be possessed (for no reason whatever) by the old original Fiend of malice. She began to leap into the air repeatedly; leaping higher and higher, clapping her hands together, at arms'-length above her head, while she shrieked, squealed, and in all ways put pressure upon her lungs and vocal organs to distribute over the world the scandal that so horridly fascinated her:

"Caught him! Wookin' at himseff in the wookin'-gwass! Caught him wookin' at himseff in the wookin'-gwass! Wookin' at himseff in the wookin'-GWASS!"

Meanwhile, her brother did not escape infection. He, likewise, began to leap and to vociferate, so that it was not possible to imagine any part of the house, or of the immediate neighbourhood, to which the indictment was not borne.

"Stickin' out of his vest!" shouted Bill. "Got somep'n stickin' out of his vest! Out of his vest, vest, vest! Out of his vest, vest, VEST!"

Then, without warning, he suddenly slapped his sister heartily upon the shoulder. "Got your tag!" he cried; darted away, and out through the open front door to the green sunshiny yard, whither Maud instantly pursued him.

Round and round the front yard they went, the two little flitting white figures, and round the house, and round and round the old back yard with its long grape-arbour and empty stable. By and by, when each had fallen separately four or five times, they collided and fell together, remaining prone, as by an unspoken agreement. Panting, they thus remained for several minutes; then Bill rose and walked into the stable, until now unexplored; and Maud followed him.

When they came out, two minutes later, Bill was carrying, to the extreme damage of his white blouse, a large can of red paint, while Maud was swinging a paint-brush that had been reposing in the can; and the look upon their two flushed faces was studious but inscrutable.

Maud applied the brush to the side of the house, leaving a broad red streak upon the gray weather-boarding; but Bill indignantly snatched the brush from her hand.

"Shame!" he said. "You know what you got once!"

"When?" Maud demanded. "When did I got it?"

158

"You know!" her brother responded darkly. "For markin' on the nurs'ry wall with my little box o' paints."

"She did not!"

"She did, too!"

"Not!"

"Did!" said Bill. "And you'll get one now if she finds out you stuck paint on the house. You will!"

"I won't!"

"Will, too! You know it's wrong to stick paint on a house."

" 'Tisn't!" Maud insisted. "She spanks you more'n she spanks me."

"You wait an' see!"

He shook his head ominously, and for a moment Maud was depressed, but the signs of foreboding vanished from her angelic brow, and she made the natural inquiry:

"What we goin' to paint?"

To Bill also, it was evident that something had to be painted; but as he looked about him, the available material seemed sparse. As a being possessed of reason, he understood that a spanking applied to his sister in order to emphasize the immunity of houses, might well be thought to indicate that stables and fences were also morally unpaintable. Little appeared to remain at the disposal of a person who had just providentially acquired a can of red paint and a brush. Shrubberies were obviously impracticable, and Bill had his doubts about the trunks of trees: they were made of wood, he knew, like many houses and fences and stables.

As he stood, thinking profoundly, there came loudly through the still afternoon the sound of General, shaking his harness and stamping the ground, as a May fly persisted in annoying him.

Maud pointed with her curling forefinger. "Wet's paint that," she said.

"That" was the horse; Maud was pointing at General. And immediately Bill's eyes showed his relief from a great strain, and became eager and confident: nobody had ever told him not to paint a horse.

Hand-in-hand, the brother and sister approached General. The kind old horse, worried by the fly and the heat, was pleased to have the fly chased away; and after the first stroke of the cool wet brush on his right foreleg, he closed one eye in hushed ecstasy and stood motionless, lest he break the spell.

General's owner, meanwhile, in the quiet parlour, had not quite recovered his usual pallor; but the departure of the children mightily relieved him, and he found time to complete the bestowal of his tie. Thereafter, Mrs. Ricketts still not making her appearance,

159

he had leisure to acquaint himself with the design of romantic musical instruments inlaid in pearl upon the top of the centre-table; and with the two tall alabaster pitchers upon the mantelpiece, each bearing the carved word "Souvenir;" and with the Toreador burnt upon a panel of wood and painted, but obscure with years of standing in an empty house—though nothing was dusty, for plainly the daughter of vikings had been "over" everything thoroughly. Altogether, Mr. Thompson considered the room (which spoke of Lucy Cope's mother rather than of Lucy) a pleasant and comfortable one—that is, if those children—

A step descending the stair, a whispering of silk—and Mr. Thompson, after a last settling of his neck into his collar, coughed reassuringly, and faced the door with a slight agitation. More would have been warranted by the vision that appeared there.

She came quickly toward him and gave him her hand. "How kind of you to remember me and come to see me!" she said. "And how inhospitable you're thinking me to have kept you waiting so long in such a stuffy room!" She turned to the nearest window as she spoke, and began to struggle delicately with the catch of the old-fashioned "inside shutters." "We'll let some air in and some light, too; so that we can both see how little we've changed. The children were the reason I was so long: they were washed and dressed like little clean angels, but they're in rather high spirits—you know how children are for the first few days after coming to a new place—and they slipped down into the cellar, which we haven't had time to get put in order yet, and they found an old air-passage to the furnace, and crawled through it, and so they had to be all washed and dressed over again; and when I got through doing it, I had to be all washed and dressed over again! I hope they didn't annoy you, Mr. Thompson: I thought I heard them romping down here, somewhere. They're really not so wild as they must seem; it's only that coming to a place altogether strange to them has upset them a little, and— There!" The catch yielded, and she spread the shutters wide. "Now we can have a little more li—"

She paused in the middle of the word, gazing fixedly out of the window.

But the caller did not follow the direction of Mrs. Ricketts's gaze; he was looking at her with concentrated approval, and mentally preparing the invitation it was his purpose to extend. After coughing rather formally, "I have called," he said, "or, rather, I have stopped by on my way to take a drive, because I thought, perhaps, as the weather was warm, it might be cooler than sitting indoors to take a turn around the Square first and then drive out toward the Athens City Pike, and return by way of—"

"Mercy!" exclaimed Mrs. Ricketts in a tone so remarkable that he stopped short; and then his eyes followed the direction of hers.

He uttered a stricken cry.

All four of General's legs had been conscientiously painted, and Maud, standing directly under his stomach, so to speak, was holding the can of paint clasped in her arms, while the older artist began work on the under side of General's ribs. General's expression was one of dreamy happiness, though his appearance, and that of the children's clothes, hands, cheeks, and noses suggested a busy day at the abattoir.

"Don't move!" Mrs. Ricketts called suddenly, but not alarmingly, as she raised the window. "Stand still, Maud! Now walk straight this way—walk toward me. Instantly!"

And as Maud obeyed, her mother jumped out of the window, a proceeding that both children recognized as extraordinary and ill-omened. Bill instinctively began to defend himself.

"You never told us we couldn't paint horses!" he said hotly. "We haven't painted him much, we've only—"

"March!" said his mother in the tone that meant the worst. "Round to the kitchen—not through the house! Both of you! Quick!"

Bill opened his mouth to protest further, but, almost to his own surprise, a wail came forth instead of an argument, and at that sound, Maud dropped the sanguinary can and joined him in loud dole. Shouting with woe, holding their unspeakable hands far from them, with fingers spread wide, they marched. Round the corner of the house went the dread pageant, and the green grass looked like murder where it passed. But when Mrs. Ricketts returned, after delivering Maud and Bill into the hands of a despairing servitress, General and the phaeton were gone.

"Oh, oh, oh!" she murmured, and, overcome by the dreadful picture that rose before her imagination, she went droopingly into the house. In her mind's eye she saw Mr. Thompson in all his special dressiness and lemon-yellow tie, driving through the streets and explaining to people: "Yes, Lucy Ricketts has come back and her children did this!" She saw him telling Lucius—and she remembered what Lucius had said: "I'm afraid to meet Maud and Bill!"

She began to feel strickenly sure that Lucius would return her parasol by a messenger. If he did that (she thought) what was the use of coming all the way from California to live in a town like Marlow!

But the parasol was not sent, nor did Lucius bring it. It remained, as did Mr. Allen himself, obscured from her sight and from her knowledge. Nor was there brought to her any account of P.

Borodino's making a dreadful progress through the town as she had imagined. Mr. Thompson had, in fact, led General as hastily as possible into the nearest alley—so Mortimer Fole explained to Lucius one week later, almost to the hour.

Mortimer had dropped into Mr. Allen's office and had expressed surprise at finding its tenant in town. "I been up here two three times a day fer a week, Lu," he said, seating himself. "Where on earth you been?"

"Argument before the Federal court in Springfield," Lucius answered. "What did you want to see me about, Mortimer?"

"Well, they's been some talk about our pension goin' out the family," said Mortimer, "in case it happened my wife's stepmother was to die. It comes through that branch, you know, Lu."

"Is she ailing?"

"No," said Mortimer. "She gits the best of care. We were only talkin' it over, and some of 'em says, 'Suppose she was to go, what then?'"

"I wouldn't worry about it until she did," his legal adviser suggested. "Anything else?"

Mortimer removed his hat, and from the storage of its inner band took half of a cigar, which, with a reflective air, he placed in the corner of his mouth. Then he put his hat on again, tilted back against the wall, and hooked his heels over a rung of his chair. "Heard about Henry Ledyard yet?" he inquired.

"No."

"Well, sir, he went up there," said Mortimer. "He only went oncet!"

"What was the trouble?"

Mr. Fole cast his eyes high aloft, an ocular gesture expressing deplorable things.

"Maud and Bill," he said.

"What did they do?"

"Henry was settin' in the parlour talkin' to their mother, and, the way I heard it, all of a sudden they heard somep'n go 'Pop!' outside, in the hall, and when they come to look, it was that new, stiff, high-crowned straw hat he went and ordered from New York and had shipped out here by express. They got a woman up there cookin' and a Norwegian lady to do extra work, and I hear this here Norwegian tells some that the way it happened was Maud was settin' on it, kind of jouncin' around to see if it wouldn't bounce her up and down. Seems this Norwegian she says spankin' and shuttin' up in the closet don't do neither of 'em one little bit o' good. Says there ain't nothin' in the world'll take it out of 'em. Them two chuldern have just about got this town buffaloed, Lu!"

162

"Oh, only breaking a straw hat," said Lucius. "I don't see how that's—"

"The two of 'em come up-town," Mortimer interrupted firmly. "They come up-town to the Square, the next afternoon after they busted Henry's twelve-dollar hat, and they went into E. J. Fuller's store and Ed says they come mighty near drivin' him crazy, walkin' up and down behind him singin' 'Gran'-mammy Tipsytoe.' Then they went on over to Milo Carter's, and they had a dollar and forty cents with 'em that they'd went and got out of their little bank. They et seven big ice-cream sodies apiece and got sick right in the store. Milo had to telephone fer their mother, and her and the Norwegian come and had to about carry 'em home. And that ain't half of it!"

"What's the other half?" Lucius asked gravely.

"Well, you heard about Bore, of course."

"No, I haven't."

Mortimer again removed his hat, this time to rub his head. "I reckon that might be so," he admitted. "I guess you must of left town by the time it leaked out."

"By the time what leaked out?"

"Well, you remember how he started off, that day," Mortimer began, "to git her to go out buggy-ridin' in his phaeton with ole General?"

"Yes."

"Well, sir, you know he was goin' to drive back here and around the Square to win that bet off o' Rolfo, and he never come. 'Stead o' that he turned up at the hardware store about two hours later and settled the bet. Says he lost it because she wasn't feelin' too well when he got there, and so they just set around and talked, instead of ridin'. But Bore never went back there, and ain't goin' to, you bet, any more than what Henry Ledyard is! There ain't hardly a man in town but what Maud and Bill's got buffaloed, Lu."

Mr. Allen occupied himself with the sharpening of a pencil. "What did they do to Thompson?" he asked casually.

"Well, sir, fer the first few days I expect I was the only man in town knowed what it was." Mr. Fole spoke with a little natural pride. "You see, after he went up there and wasn't no sign of him on the Square fer awhile, why I didn't have nothin' much to do just then, and thinks I, 'Why not go see what's come of him?' thinks I. So I walked around there the back way, by Copes's alley, and just as I was turnin' in one end the alley, by Glory! here come P. Borodino Thompson leadin' ole General and the phaeton in at the other end, and walkin' as fur away from him as he could and yet still lead him.

"Well, sir, I almost let out a holler: first thing I thought was they must of been in the worst accident this town had ever saw.

163

Why, pore ole General—honest, he looked more like a slaughter-house than he did like a horse, Lu! 'What in the name of God is the matter, Bore!' I says, and you never hear a man take on the way he done.

"Seems Maud and Bill had painted ole General red, and they painted him thick, too, while Bore was in the house fixin' to take their mother out on this here buggy-ride. And, well, sir, to hear him take on, you'd of thought I was responsible for the whole business! Says it might as well be all over town, now he'd ran into me! Truth is, he talked like he was out of his mind, but I kind o' soothed him down, and last I fixed it up with him to give me credit fer a little insurance my wife's been wantin' to take out on her stepmother, if I'd put General and the phaeton in George Coles's empty barn, there in the alley, until after dark, and not say nothin' to George or anybody about it, and then drive him over to Bore's and unhitch him and wash him off with turpentine that night.

"Well, sir, we got it all fixed up, and I done everything I said I would, but of course you can't expect a thing like that not to leak out some way or other; so I'm not breakin' any obligation by tellin' you about it, because it got all over town several days ago. If I've told Bore Thompson once I've told him a hunderd times, what's the use his actin' the fool about it! 'What earthly good's it goin' to do,' I says, 'to go around mad,' I says, 'and abusin' the very ones,' I says, 'that done the most to help you out? The boys are bound to have their joke,' I says to him, 'and if it hadn't been you, why, like as not they might of been riggin' somep'n on Lu Allen or Cal Burns, or even me,' I says, 'because they don't spare nobody! Why, look,' I says. 'Ain't they goin' after Milo Carter almost as much as they are you and Henry,' I says, 'on account of what happened to Milo's store?' I says, 'And look at E. J. Fuller,' I says. 'Ain't the name o' Gran'-mammy Tipsytoe perty near fastened on him fer good? He don't go all up and down pickin' at his best friend,' I says. 'E. J. Fuller's got a little common sense!' I says. Yes, sir, that's the way I look at it, Lu."

Mortimer unhooked his heels, and, stretching himself, elevated his legs until the alternation thus effected in the position of his centre of gravity brought his tilted chair to a level—whereupon he rose, stretched again, sighed, and prepared to conclude the interview.

"Speakin' o' the devil, Lu," he said, as he moved to the door—"yes, sir, them two chuldern, Maud and Bill, have perty much got our whole little city buffaloed! They's quite some talk goin' on about the brain work you been showin' Lu. I expect your reputation never did stand no higher in that line than what it does right to-day. I shouldn't wonder it'd bring you a good deal extry law-practice, Lu:

Mrs. Rolfo Williams says she always did know you were the smartest man in this town!"

"Now what are you talking about?" Lucius demanded sharply, but he was growing red to the ears, and over them.

"Goin' out o' town," said Mortimer admiringly. "Keepin' out the way o' them chuldern and lettin' other fellers take the brunt of 'em. Yes, sir; there isn't a soul raises the question but what their mother is the finest-lookin' lady that ever lived here, or but what she does every last thing any mortal could do in the line o' disciplinn; but much as everybody'd enjoy to git better acquainted with her and begin to see somep'n of her, they all think she's liable to lead kind of a lonesome life in our community unless—" Mortimer paused with his hand upon the door-knob—"unless somep'n happens to Maud and Bill!"

He departed languidly, his farewell coming back from the stairway: "So long, Lu!"

But the blush that had extended to include Mr. Allen's ears, at the sound of so much praise of himself, did not vanish with the caller; it lingered and for a time grew even deeper. When it was gone, and its victim restored to his accustomed moderate pink, he pushed aside his work and went to a locked recess beneath his book-shelves. Therefrom he took the blue parasol, and a small volume in everything dissimilar to the heavy, calf-bound legal works that concealed all the walls of the room; and, returning to his swivel-chair, placed the parasol gently upon the desk. Then, allowing his left hand to remain lightly upon the parasol, he held the little book in his right and read musingly.

He read, thus, for a long time—in fact, until the setting in of twilight; and, whatever the slight shiftings of his position, he always kept one hand in light contact with the parasol. Some portions of the book he read over and over, though all of it was long since familiar to him; and there was one part of it in which his interest seemed quite unappeasable. Again and again he turned back to the same page; but at last, as the room had grown darker, and his eye-glasses tired him, he let the book rest in his lap, took off the glasses and used them to beat time to the rhythm of the cadences, as he murmured, half-aloud:

> *"The lamplight seems to glimmer with a flicker of surprise,*
> *As I turn it low to rest me of the dazzle in my eyes.*
> *And light my pipe in silence, save a sigh that seems to yoke*
> *Its fate with my tobacco and to vanish with the smoke.*
> *'Tis a fragrant retrospection—for the loving thoughts that start*

165

Into being are like perfume from the blossoms of the heart:
And to dream the old dreams over is a luxury divine—
When my truant fancy wanders with that old sweet-heart
of mine."

He fell silent; then his lips moved again:

"And I thrill beneath the glances of a pair of azure eyes
As glowing as the summer and as tender as the skies.
I can see—"

Suddenly he broke off, and groaned aloud: "My Lord!" he said all in a breath. "And thirty-five years old—blame near thirty-six!"

He needs interpretation, this unfortunate Lucius. He meant that it was inexplicable and disgraceful for a man of his age to be afraid of a boy of seven and a girl of five. He had never been afraid of anybody else's children. No; it had to be hers! And that was why he was afraid of them; he knew the truth well enough: he was afraid of them because they were hers. He was a man who had always "got on" with children beautifully; but he was afraid of Maud and Bill. He was afraid of what they would do to him and of what they would think of him.

There, in brief, is the overwhelming part that children can play in true romance!

"Lordy, Lordy!" sighed Lucius Brutus Allen. "Oh, Lordy!"

But at last he bestirred himself. He knew that Saruly, his elderly darky cook, must be waiting for him with impatience; she would complain bitterly of dishes overcooked because of his tardiness. Having glanced down into the Square and found it virtually devoid of life, for this was the universal hour of supper, he set his brown straw hat upon his head, and took the parasol under his arm—not because he meant to return it. He took it with him merely for the pleasure of its society.

Upon the bottom step of the flight of stairs that led down to the street, he found seated a small figure in a white "sailor suit." This figure rose and spoke politely.

"How do you do?" it said. "Are you Uncle Lucius?"

"Who— What's your name?"

"Bill. Bill Ricketts," said Bill.

Lucius made a hasty motion to reascend the stairs, but Bill confidingly proffered a small, clean hand that Mr. Allen was constrained to accept. Once having accepted it, he found himself expected to retain it.

"Mamma lef' me sittin' here to wait till you came downstairs,"

Bill explained. "That man that came out said he couldn't say but he was pretty sure you were up there. She told me to wait till either you came downstairs or she came back for me. She wants her parasol. Come on!"

"Come on where?"

"Up to your house," said Bill. "She lef' Maud waitin' up there for you."

It was the truth. And after a rather hurried walk, during which the boy spoke not once unless spoken to, but trotted contentedly at Lucius's side, confidingly hand-in-hand with him, when they came in sight of the small brick house in the big yard, where Lucius lived, a tiny white figure was discernible through the dusk, rocking patiently in a wicker rocking-chair on the veranda.

At sight of them she jumped up and came running to the gate to meet them. But there she paused, gravely.

She made a curtsey, formal but charming.

"How do do, Uncka Wucius?" she said. "Mamma would wike her paraso'."

Saruly, looming dark and large behind her, supplemented this information: "Miz Ricketts done lef' the little girl here to wait fer you, Mist' Allen. She tell me ask you please be so kine as to bring the chillun along home with you, an' her parasol with 'em. She tell me the chillun been a little upset, jest at first, 'count o' movin' to a new place, but they all quieted down now, an' she think it'll be safe fer you to stay to dinnuh. An' as ev'ything in my kitchen's plum done to a crisp 'count o' you bein' so late, Mist' Allen, if you leave it to me I think you bettuh."

"I'll leave it to you, Saruly," said Lucius, gently. "I think I'd better."

And then, with the parasol under his arm, and the hand of a child resting quietly in each of his, he turned with Bill and Maud, and, under the small, bright stars of the May evening, set forth from his own gate on his way to Lucy's.

"YOU"

MURIEL ELIOT'S friends and contemporaries were in the habit of describing her as "the most brilliant girl in town." She was "up on simply everything," they said, and it was customary to add the exclamation: "How on earth she finds the time!" And since Muriel also found time to be always charmingly dressed, in harmony with her notable comeliness, the marvel of so much upness in her infant twenties may indeed need a little explaining.

Her own conception was that she was a "serious" person and cared for "serious reading"—that is to say, after she left college, she read, not what is acceptably called literature, but young journalists' musings about what aspires to be called that; she was not at all interested in buildings or pictures or statues themselves, but thought she was, read a little of what is printed about such things in reviews, and spoke of "art" and "literature" with authoritative conviction. She was a kind-hearted girl, and she believed that "capitalism" was the cunning device of greedy men to keep worthy persons under heel; hence it followed that all "capital" should be taken away from the "capitalist class" by the "people;" and, not picturing herself as in any way uncomfortably affected by the process of seizure, she called herself a "socialist."

In addition to all this, Muriel's upness included "the new psychology" and the appropriate humorous contempt for the Victorian Period, that elastic conception of something-or-other which, according to the writing young ladies and gentlemen who were her authorities, seemed to extend from about the time of Custer's Last Fight to the close of President Wilson's first administration. Muriel, like her original sources of information, was just becoming conscious of herself as an authority at about the latter date—she was sixteen then; and at twenty she began to speak of having spent her youth in the Late Victorian Period. That obscure decade before her birth, that time so formless and dark between the years of our Lord 1890 and 1900, was Mid-Victorian; people still mistook Tennyson and Longfellow for poets.

Sometimes older women thought Muriel a little hard; she was both brilliant and scholarly, they admitted; but the papers she wrote for the women's clubs were so "purely intellectual," so icily scientific, so little reticent in the discussion of love, marriage and children, that these ladies shook their heads. The new generation, as expressed by Muriel, lacked something important, they complained; for nothing less than maidenliness itself had been lost, and with it the rosebud reveries, the twilight half-dreams of a coming cavalier, the embowered guitar at moonrise. In a word, the charm of maidenhood was lost because romance was lost. Muriel lacked the romantic imagination, they said, a quality but ill replaced by so much "new thought."

They made this mistake the more naturally because Muriel herself made it, though of course she did not think of her supposed lack of romance as a fault. She believed herself to be a severely practical person, and an originally thinking person, as a quotation from one of her essays may partly explain. "I face the actual world as it is; I face it without superstition, and without tradition. Despising both the nonsense and the misery into which former generations have been led by romance, I permit no illusions to guide my thinking. I respect nothing merely because it is established; I examine mathematically; I think mathematically; I believe nothing that I do not prove. I am a realist."

When she wrote this, she was serious and really thought it true; but as a matter of fact, what she believed to be her thinking was the occasional mulling over of scattered absorptions from her reading. Her conception of her outward appearance, being somewhat aided by mirrors, came appreciably near the truth, but her conception of her mind had no such guide. Her mind spent the greater part of its time adrift in half-definite dreaming, and although she did not even suspect such a thing, her romantic imagination was the abode in which she really dwelt.

There is an astronomer who knows as much about the moon as can yet be known; but when that moon is new in the sky, each month, he will be a little troubled if he fails to catch his first glimpse of it over the right shoulder. When he does fail, his disappointment is so slight that he forgets all about it the next moment, and should you ask him if he has any superstition he will laugh disdainfully, with no idea that he deceives both his questioner and himself. This is the least of the mistakes he makes about his own thoughts; he is mistaken about most of them; and yet he is a great man, less given to mistakes than the rest of us. Muriel Eliot's grandmother, who used to sing "Robin Adair," who danced the Spanish Fandango at the Orphan Asylum Benefit in 1877, and wrote an anonymous love-letter to Lawrence Barrett, was not actually so romantic as Muriel.

The point is that Muriel's dreaminess, of which she was so little aware, had a great deal more to do with governing her actions than had her mathematical examinings and what she believed to be her thinking. Moreover, this was the cause of her unkindness to young Renfrew Mears, who lived across the street. Even to herself

169

she gave other reasons for rejecting him; but the motive lay deep in her romanticism; for Muriel, without knowing it, believed in fairies.

Had she been truly practical, she would have seen that young Mr. Mears was what is called an "ideal match" for her. His grandfather, a cautious banker, had thought so highly of the young man's good sense as to leave him the means for a comfortable independence; yet Renfrew continued to live at home with his family and was almost always in bed by eleven o'clock. He was of a pleasant appearance; he was kind, modest, thoughtfully polite, and in everything the perfect material from which the equerry or background husband of a brilliant woman is constructed. No wonder her mother asked her what on earth she did want! Muriel replied that she despised the capitalistic institution of marriage, and she believed that she meant what she said; but of course what she really wanted was a fairy-story.

In those wandering and somewhat shapeless reveries that controlled her so much more than she guessed, there were various repetitions that had become rather definite, though never quite so. One of these was the figure of her Mate. Her revery-self never showed her this mystery clearly in contours and colours, but rather in shadowy outlines, though she was sure that her Mate had dark and glowing eyes. He was somewhere, and sometime she would see him. When she did see him, she would recognize him instantly; the first look exchanged would bring the full revelation to both of them—they would ever have little need of spoken words. But her most frequent picture of this mystic encounter was a painful one: she saw herself a bride upon the bridegroom's arm and coming down the steps of the church;—a passing stranger, halting abruptly upon the pavement, gave her one look from dark and glowing eyes, a look fateful with reproach and a tragic derision, seeming to say: "You did not wait till I came, but took that fool!"

Then he passed on, forever; and it was unfortunate for young Mr. Mears that the figure of the bridegroom in these foreshadowings invariably bore a general resemblance to his own. Renfrew had more to overcome than appeared upon the surface; he had shadows to fight; and so have other lovers—more of them than is guessed—when ladies are reluctant. For that matter, the thing is almost universal; and rare is the girl, however willing, who says "Yes," without giving up at least some faint little tremulous shadow of a dream—though she may forget it and deny it as honestly as that astronomer forgets and denies the moon and his right shoulder.

Renfrew's case with his pretty neighbour was also weakened by the liking and approval of her father and mother, who made the mistake of frequently praising him to her; for when parents do this, with the daughter adverse, the poor lover is usually ruined—the reasons being obvious to everybody except the praising parents. Mrs. Eliot talked Renfrew Mears and his virtues at her daughter till the latter naturally declared that she hated him. "I do!" she said one morning. "I really do hate him, mamma!"

"What nonsense!" her mother exclaimed. "When I heard the two of you chatting together on the front porch for at least an hour, only last evening!"

"Chatting!" Muriel repeated scornfully. "Chatting together! That shows how much you observe, mamma! I don't think he said more than a dozen words the whole evening."

"Well, don't you like a good listener?"

"Yes," Muriel replied emphatically. "Indeed, I do! A good listener is one who understands what you're saying. Renfrew Mears has just lately learned enough to keep quiet, for fear if he speaks at all, it'll show he doesn't understand anything!"

"Well, if he doesn't, why did you talk to him?"

"Good gracious!" Muriel cried. "We can't always express ourselves as we wish to in this life, mamma; I should think you'd know that by this time! I can't throw rocks at him and say, 'Go back home!' every time he comes poking over here, can I? I have to be polite, even to Renfrew Mears, don't you suppose?"

The mother, sighing, gave her daughter one of those little half-surreptitious glances in which mothers seem to review troubled scenes with their own mothers; then she said gently: "Your father and I do wish you could feel a little more kindly toward the poor boy, Muriel."

"Well, I can't, and I don't want to. What's more, I wouldn't marry him if I did."

"Not if you were in love?"

"Poor mamma!" Muriel said compassionately. "What has love to do with marrying? I expect to retain my freedom; I don't propose to enter upon a period of child-rearing—"

"Oh, good gracious!" Mrs. Eliot cried. "What a way to talk!"

"But if I did," Muriel continued, with some sharpness, "I should never select Renfrew Mears to be my assistant in the task. And as for what you call 'love,' it seems to me a rather unhealthy form of excitement that I'm not subject to, fortunately."

"You are so queer," her mother murmured; whereupon Muriel laughed.

No doubt her laughter was a little condescending. "Queer?" she said. "No—only modern. Only frank and wholesome! Thinking people look at life as it really is, nowadays, mamma. I am a child of the new age; but more than that, I am not the slave of my emotions;

I am the product of my thinking. Unwholesome excitement and queer fancies have no part in my life, mamma."

"I hope not," her mother responded with a little spirit. "I'm not exactly urging anything unwholesome upon you, Muriel. You're very inconsistent, it seems to me."

"I!" Muriel said haughtily. "Inconsistent!"

"Why, when I just mention that your father and I'd be glad if you could feel a little kinder toward a good-looking, fine young man that we know all about, you begin talking, and pretty soon it sounds as though we were trying to get you to do something criminal! And then you go on to say you haven't got any 'queer fancies!' Isn't it a queer fancy to think we'd want you to do anything unhealthy or excited? That's why I say you're inconsistent."

Muriel coloured; her breathing quickened; and her eyes became threateningly bright. "The one thing I won't be called," she said, "is 'inconsistent!' "

"Well, but—"

"I won't!" she cried, and choked. "You know it makes me furious; that's why you do it!"

"Did I understand you to say you never permitted your emotions to control you?" her mother asked dryly.

In retort, Muriel turned to the closet where she kept her hats; for her favourite way of meeting these persecutions was to go out of the house abruptly, leaving her mother to occupy it in full remorse; but this time Mrs. Eliot forestalled her. A servant appeared in the doorway and summoned her: "There's someone downstairs wants to see you; I took him in the library."

"I'll come," said Mrs. Eliot, and with a single dignified glance at her daughter, she withdrew, leaving Muriel to digest a discomfiture. For the art of domestic altercation lies almost wholly in the withdrawal, since here the field is won by abandoning it. In family embroilments she proves herself right, and the others wrong, who adroitly seizes the proper moment to make an unexpected departure either with dignity or in tears. People under stress of genuine emotion have been known to practice this art, seeming thereby to indicate the incompatible presence of a cool dramatist somewhere in the back of their heads; yet where is there anything that is not incompatible? Muriel, injured by the word "inconsistent," had meant to withdraw in silent pain, thus putting her mother in the wrong; but, in the sometimes invaluable argot of the race-course, Mrs. Eliot got away first. Muriel felt severely baffled.

There remained to her, however, a retreat somewhat enfeebled by her mother's successful withdrawal: Mrs. Eliot had gone out of the room; Muriel could still go out of the house.

Therefore she put on a hat, descended the stairs and went toward the front door in a manner intended to symbolize insulted pride taking a much more important departure than the mere walking out of a room.

Her mother, of course, was intended to see her pass the open double doors of the library, but Mrs. Eliot's back happened to be toward these doors, and she was denied the moving-picture of the daughter sweeping through the hall. The caller, however, suffered no such deprivation; he sat facing the doorway, and although Muriel did not look directly at him, she became aware of a distinguished presence. The library was shadowy, the hall much lighter; she passed the doors quickly; but she was almost startled by the impression made upon her by this young man whom she had never before seen. Then, as she went on toward the front door, she had suddenly a sensation queerly like dizziness; it seemed to her that this stranger had looked at her profoundly as she passed, and that the gaze he bent upon her had come from a pair of dark and glowing eyes.

She went out into the yard, but not, as she had intended, to the street; and turning the corner of the house, she crossed the sunny lawn to some hydrangea bushes in blossom, where she paused and stood, apparently in contemplation of the flowers. She was trembling a little, so strong was her queer consciousness of the stranger in the library and of his dark and glowing eyes. Such sensations as hers have often been described as "unreal;" that is to say, "she seemed to be in a dream." Her own eyes had not fully encountered the dark and glowing ones, but never had any person made so odd and instantaneous an impression upon her. What else was she to conclude but that there must have been "something psychic" about it? And how, except by telepathy, could she have so suddenly found in her mind the conviction that the distinguished-looking young man was a painter? For to her own amazement, she was sure of this.

After a time she went back into the house, and again passed through the hall and by the open doors, but now her bearing was different. In a sweet, low voice she hummed a careless air from Naples, while in her arms she bore a sheaf of splendid hydrangea blossoms, thus offering, in the momentary framing of the broad doorway, a composition rich in colour and also of no mean decorative charm in contour, it may be said. "The Girl from the Garden" might have been the title she wished to suggest to a painter's mind, but when she came into the view of her mother's caller, consciousness of him increased all at once so overwhelmingly that she forgot herself. She had meant to pass the doorway with a cool leisureliness and entirely in profile—a Girl from the Garden with no other thought than to enliven her room with an armful of hydrangea blossoms—but she came almost to a halt midway, and, for the greater part of a second packed with drama, looked full upon the visitor.

He was one of those black-and-white young men: clothes black, linen white, a black bow at the collar, thick black hair, the face of a fine pallor, and black eyes lustrously comprehending. What they must have comprehended now was at least a little of the significance of the arrested attitude beyond the doorway, and more than a little of what was meant by the dark and lustrous eyes that with such poignant inquiry met his own. For Muriel's fairly shouted at him the startled question: "Who are you?"

Time, life and love are made of seconds and bits of seconds: Muriel had gone on, carrying her question clamouring down the hall with her, before this full second elapsed. She ran up the stairs and into her own room, dropped the hydrangeas upon a table, and in two strides confronted a mirror. A moment later she took up the hydrangeas again, with a care to hold them as she had held them in the hall below, then walked by the mirror, paused, gave the glass a deep, questioning look and went on. After that she seated herself beside an open window that commanded a view of the front gate, and waited, the great question occupying her tumultuously.

By this time the great question had grown definite, and of course it was, "Is this He?" Other questions came tumbling after it: How did she know he was a painter, this young man of whom she had never heard? It is only in the moving pictures that a doctor must look like a doctor, a judge like a judge, an anarchist like an anarchist, a painter like a painter; the age of machines, hygiene and single-type clothing has so blurred men into indistinguishability that only a few musicians still look like musicians, a feat accomplished simply by the slight impoverishment of barbers. The young man in the library was actually a painter, but Muriel may well have been amazed that she knew it; for nowadays it is a commonplace that a Major General in mufti may reasonably be taken for a plumber, while an unimportant person soliciting alms at the door is shown into the house under the impression that a Senator is calling.

Why (Muriel asked herself) had her mother not mentioned such an appointment? But perhaps there had been no appointment; perhaps he had called without one. What for? To ask permission to paint the daughter's portrait? Had he seen her somewhere before to-day? Where did he live? In Paris?

The front door could be heard closing below, and she looked

174

down upon a white straw hat with a black band. This hat moved quickly down the path to the gate, and the young stranger was disclosed beneath the hat: a manly figure with an elastic step. Outside the gate he paused, looking back thoughtfully with his remarkable eyes; and Muriel, who had instantly withdrawn into the concealment of a window-curtain, marked that this look of his had the quality of covering the whole front of the house at a glance. It was a look, moreover, that seemed to comprehend the type of the house and even to measure its dimensions—a look of the kind that "takes in everything," as people say. Muriel trembled again. Did he say to himself: "This is Her house?" Did he think: "I should like to set my easel here by the gate and paint this house, because it is the house where She dwells"?

His pause at the gate was only a momentary one; he turned toward the region of commerce and hotels and walked quickly away, the intervening foliage of the trees almost immediately cutting him off from the observation of the girl at the window. Then she heard her mother coming up the stairs and through the upper hall; whereupon Muriel, still tremulous, began hastily to alter the position of the little silver implements upon her dressing-table, thus sketching a preoccupation with small housewifery, if Mrs. Eliot should come into the room. But to the daughter's acute disappointment, the mother passed the open door without even looking in, and retired to her own apartment.

Muriel most urgently wished to follow her and shower her with questions: "Who is he? Isn't he a painter? Why did he come to see you? What were you talking about? When is he coming again? What did he say when he saw me?" But remembering the terms upon which she and her mother had so recently parted, and that odious word "inconsistent," Muriel could not bend to the intimacy of such a questioning. In fact, her own thought took the form, "I'd rather die!"

She turned to the window again, looked out at that gate so lately made significant by the passage of the stranger—and there was young Mr. Renfrew Mears, just coming in. He was a neat picture of a summer young gentleman for any girl's eye; but to Muriel he was a too-familiar object, and just now about as interesting as a cup of tepid barley-water. She tried to move away before he saw her, but Renfrew had always a fatal quickness for seeing her. He called to her.

"Oh, Muriel!"

"Well—what?" she said reluctantly.

"There's something I want to ask you about. Will you come down a few minutes?"

"Oh, well—I suppose so," was her not too heartening response; but on the way downstairs a thought brightened her. Perhaps Renfrew might know something about a dark young man—a painter—lately come to town.

He was blank upon this subject, however, as she discovered when they had seated themselves upon a wicker settee on the veranda. "No," he said. "I haven't heard of any artist that's come here lately. Where'd you hear about one?"

"Oh, around," she said casually. "I'm not absolutely certain he's an artist, but I got that idea somewhere. The reason I wanted to know is because I thought he might be one of the new group that have broken away, like Matisse and Gaugin."

"Who?"

"Never mind. Haven't you heard of anybody at all that's a stranger here—visiting somebody, perhaps?"

"Not exactly," Renfrew replied, thinking it over conscientiously. "I don't believe I have, exactly."

"What do you mean, you don't think you have 'exactly'?" she asked irritably. "Have you, or haven't you?"

"Well," he said, "my Aunt Milly from Burnetsville is visiting my cousins, the Thomases, but she's an invalid and you probably wouldn't—"

"No, I wouldn't!" Muriel said. "Don't strain your mind any more, Renfrew."

"I could inquire around," he suggested. "I thought it wouldn't likely be my aunt, but you said 'anybody at all.' "

"Never mind! What was it you wanted to ask me?"

"Well, it's something that's rather important, but of course maybe you won't think so, Muriel. Anyway, though, I hope you'll think it's sort of important."

"But what is it? Don't hang fire so, Renfrew!"

"I just wanted to lead up to it a little," he explained mildly. "I've been thinking about getting a new car, and I wondered what sort you think I'd better look at. I didn't want to get one you wouldn't like."

Her lips parted to project that little series of sibilances commonly employed by adults to make children conscious of error. "Why on earth should you ask me?" she said sharply. "Is that your idea of an important question?"

Renfrew's susceptible complexion showed an increase of colour, but he was growing more and more accustomed to be used as a doormat, and he responded, without rancour: "I meant I hoped you'd sort of think it important, my not wanting to get one you wouldn't like."

"Now, what do you mean by that?"

"Well," he said, "I mean I hoped you'd think it was important, my thinking it was important to ask you."

"I don't," she returned as a complete answer.

"You say—"

"I say I don't," she repeated. "I don't. I don't think it's important. Isn't that clear enough, Renfrew?"

"Yes," he said, and looked plaintively away from her. "I guess I don't need any new car."

"Is there anything more this morning?" she was cruel enough to inquire.

"No," he answered, rising. "I guess that's all." Then, having received another of his almost daily rejections, he went away, leaving her to watch his departing figure with some exasperation, though she might well have admired him for his ingenuity: every day or two he invented a new way of proposing to her. In comparison, her refusals were commonplace, but of course she neither realized that nor cared to be brilliant for Renfrew; and also, this was a poor hour for him, when the electric presence of the black-and-white stranger was still vibrant in the very air. Muriel returned to her room and put the hydrangeas in a big silver vase; she moved them gently, with a touch both reverent and caressing, for they had borne a part in a fateful scene, and already she felt it possible that in the after years she would never see hydrangeas in blossom without remembering to-day and the First Meeting.

Impulsively she went to her desk and wrote:

"Is it true that You have come? My hand trembles, and I know that if I spoke to my mother about You, my voice would tremble. Oh, I could never ask her a question about You! A moment ago I sat upon the veranda with a dull man who wants to marry me. It seemed a desecration to listen to him—an offense to You! He has always bored me. How much more terribly he bored me when perhaps I had just seen You for the first time in my life! Perhaps it is not for the first time in eternity, though! Was I ever a Queen in Egypt and were You a Persian sculptor? Did we meet in Ephesus once?

"It is a miracle that we should meet at all. I might have lived in another century—or on another planet! Should we then have gone seeking, seeking one another always vainly? All my life I have been waiting for You. Always I have known that I was waiting, but until to-day I did not know it was for just You. My whole being trembled when I saw You—if it was You? I am trembling now as I think of You, as I write of You—write to You! A new life has possibly begun for me in this hour!

"And some day will I show You this writing? That thought is like fire and like ice. I burn with it and freeze with it, in terror of You! See! Here is my heart opened like a book for your reading!

"Oh, is it, is it You? I think that You are a painter; that is all I know of You—and why do I think it? It came to me as I stood in a garden, thrilling with my first quick glimpse of You. Was that the proof of our destiny, yours and mine? Yes, the miracle of my knowing that You are a painter when I do not even know your name—that is the answer! It must be You! I tremble with excitement as I write that word 'You' which has suddenly leaped into such fiery life and meaning: I tremble and I could weep! Oh, You—You—You! Is it?"

Twice, during the latter phases of this somewhat hasty record of ardour, she had been summoned to lunch, and after hurrying the final words upon the page, she put the paper into a notebook and locked it inside her desk. Then she descended the stairs and went toward the dining-room, but halted suddenly, unseen, outside the door. She had caught the word "painter," spoken by her father.

"Well, I'm glad you liked that painter."

"Yes," Mrs. Eliot said. "I talked it over with him, and I'm afraid he agreed with you instead of with me. Naturally, he would, though! I was quite interested in him."

"You were?"

"Yes—such an unexpected type."

"Well, no," Mr. Eliot said. "Nobody's an unexpected type nowadays. Isn't Muriel coming down at all?"

"Jennie's been up for her twice," his wife informed him. "I suppose she'll come eventually. She's cross this morning."

"What about?"

"Oh, I just asked her if she couldn't be a little fairer to a certain somebody. I suppose I'd better not have mentioned it, because it made her very peevish."

Upon this, Muriel made her entrance swiftly enough to let her mother know that the last words had been overheard, an advantage the daughter could not forego. She took her place at the table opposite to her gourmandizing little brother Robert, and in silence permitted her facial expression alone to mention what she thought of a mother who called her "peevish" when she was not present to defend herself.

Only a moment before, she had been thrilled inexpressibly: the black-and-white stranger, so mysteriously spoken of by her parents, was indeed a painter. That proved his You-ness, proved everything! Her whole being (as she would have said) shook with the revelation, and her anxiety to hear more of him was consuming;

178

but the word "peevish" brought about an instantaneous reversion. She entered the dining-room in an entirely different mood, for her whole being was now that of a daughter embattled with a parent who attacks unfairly—so intricately elastic are the ways of our whole beings!

Mrs. Eliot offered only the defense of a patient smile; Mr. Eliot looked puzzled and oppressed; and for a time there was no conversation during the further progress of this uncomfortable meal. Nothing was to be heard in the room except the movements of a servant and the audible eating of fat little Robert, who was incurably natural with his food.

It was Muriel who finally decided to speak. "I'm sorry to have interrupted your conversation," she said frostily. "Perhaps, though, you'd prefer not to say any more about me to papa and Robert while I'm here to explain what really happened, mamma."

"Oh, nonsense!" Mr. Eliot said. "I suppose even the Pope gets 'peevish' now and then; it's no deadly insult to say a person got a little peevish. We weren't having a 'conversation' about you at all. We were talking about other matters, and just barely mentioned you."

Muriel looked at him quickly. "What other things were you talking about?"

He laughed. "My! How suspicious you are!"

"Not at all; I simply asked you what other things you were talking about."

Instead of replying, "About a distinguished young painter who saw you on the street and wants to paint your portrait," Mr. Eliot laughed again and rose, having finished his coffee. He came round the table to her and pinched her ear on his way to the door. "Good gracious!" he said. "Don't you suppose your mother and I ever talk about anything except what a naughty daughter we have?" And with that he departed. Mrs. Eliot said, "Excuse me," rather coldly to Muriel, followed him to the front door, and failed to return.

Muriel did not see her mother again during the afternoon, and in the evening Mr. and Mrs. Eliot went out to a dinner of their bridge-club, leaving their daughter to dine in the too audible company of Robert. She dressed exquisitely, though not for Robert, whose naturalness at the table brought several annoyed glances from her. "Can't you manage it more quietly, Robert?" she asked at last, with the dessert. "Try!"

"Whaffor?" he inquired.

"Only because it's so hideous!"

"Oh, hush!" he said rudely, and, being offended, became more natural than ever, on purpose.

179

She sighed. With the falling of the dusk, her whole being, not antagonized by her mother's presence, had become an uplifted and mysterious expectation; and the sounds made by the gross child Robert were not to be borne. She left the table, went out into the starlight, and stood by the hydrangeas, an ethereal figure in draperies of mist.

"Oh, You!" she whispered, and let a bare arm be caressed by the clumps of great blossoms. "When are you coming again, You? To-night?"

She quivered with the sense of impending drama; it seemed to her certain that the next moment she would see him—that he would come to her out of the darkness. The young painter should have done so; he should have stepped out of the vague night-shadows, a poetic and wistful figure, melancholy with mystery yet ineffably radiant. "Mademoiselle, step lightly!" he should have said. "Do you not see the heart beneath your slipper? It was mine until I threw it there!"

"Ah, You!" she murmured to the languorous hydrangeas.

At such a moment the sound of peanuts being eaten, shells and all, could not fail to prove inharmonious. She shivered with the sudden anguish of a dislocated mood; but she was Robert's next of available kin and recognized a duty. She crossed the lawn to the veranda, where he sat, busy with a small paper sack upon his knee.

"Robert! Stop that!"

"I ain't doin' anything," he said crossly.

"You are. What do you mean, eating peanuts when you've just finished an enormous dinner?"

"Well, what hurt is that?"

"And with the shells on!" she cried.

"Makes more to 'em," he explained.

"Stop it!"

"I won't," Robert said doggedly. "I'm goin' to do what I please to-night, no matter how much trouble I get into to-morrow!"

"What 'trouble' do you expect to-morrow?"

"Didn't you hear about it?" he asked. "Papa and mamma were talkin' about it at lunch."

"I didn't hear them."

"I guess it was before you came down," Robert said; and then he gave her a surprise. "The painter was here this morning, and they got it all fixed up."

Muriel moved back from him a step, and inexplicably a dismal foreboding took her. "What?" she said.

"Well, the thing that bothers me is simply this," Robert informed her: "He told mamma he'd have to bring his little boy

180

along and let him play around here as long as the work went on. He said he has to take this boy along with him, because his wife's a dentist's 'sistant and can't keep him around a dentist office, and they haven't got any place to leave him. He's about nine years old, and I'll bet anything I have trouble with him before the day's over."

"Do you mean the—the painter is married, Robert?"

"Yes, and got this boy," Robert said, shaking his head. "I bet I do have trouble with him, if he's got to be around here until they get three coats o' paint on our house. Mamma thought they only needed two, but papa said three, and the painter talked mamma into it this morning."

"The house?" Muriel said. "We're going to have the—the house painted?"

Robert was rather surprised. "Why, don't you remember how much papa and mamma were talkin' about it, two or three weeks ago? And then they thought not and didn't say so much about it, but for a while papa was goin' to have every painter in town come up here and make a bid. Don't you remember?"

"I do now," Muriel said feebly; and a moment later she glanced toward the bright windows of the house across the street. "Robert," she said, "if you've finished those horrible peanuts, you might run and ask Mr. Renfrew Mears if he'd mind coming over a little while."

She had been deeply stirred by the subject that had occupied her all day, and it was a spiritual necessity for her (so to say) to continue upon the topic with somebody—even with Renfrew Mears! However, she rejected him again, though with a much greater consideration for his feelings than was customary; and when he departed, she called after him:

"Look out for your clothes when you come over to-morrow. We're going to have the house painted."

Then, smiling contentedly, she went indoors and up to her room. The great vase of hydrangeas stood upon a table; she looked at it absently, and was reminded of something. She took some sheets of written paper from a notebook in her desk, tossed them into a waste-basket, yawned, and went to bed.

"US"

"HIGHLAND PLACE" was one of those new little cross-streets in a new little bosky neighbourhood, that had "grown up over night," as we say, meaning grown up in four or five years; so that when citizens of the older and more solid and soiled central parts of the city come driving through the new part, of a Sunday afternoon in spring, they are pleased to be surprised. "My goodness!" they exclaim. "When did all this happen? Why, it doesn't seem more'n a year or so since we used to have Fourth o' July picnics out here! And now just look at it—all built up with bride-and-groom houses!"

"Highland Place" was the name given to this cross-street by the speculative land company that "developed" it, and they did not call it "Waverley Place" because they had already produced a "Waverley Place" a block below. Both "Places" were lined with green-trimmed small white houses, "frame" or stucco; and although the honeymoon suggestion was architecturally so strong, as a matter of fact most of the inhabitants held themselves to be "settled old married people," some of the couples having almost attained to a Tin Wedding Anniversary.

The largest of the houses in "Highland Place" was the "hollow-tile and stucco residence of Mr. and Mrs. George M. Sullender." Thus it had been defined, under a photographic reproduction, with the caption "New Highland Place Sullender Home," in one of the newspapers, not long after the little street had been staked out and paved; and since the "Sullender Home" was not only the largest house but the first to be built in the "Place," and had its picture in the paper, it naturally took itself for granted as being the most important.

Young Mrs. William Sperry, whose equally young husband had just bought the smallest but most conspicuously bride-and-groom cottage in the whole "Place," was not so deeply impressed with the Sullender importance as she should have been, since the Sperrys were the newcomers of the neighbourhood, had not yet been admitted to its intimacies, and might well have displayed a more amiable deference to what is established.

"No," Mrs. Sperry said to her husband, when they got home after their first experience of the "Place's" hospitality, a bridge-party at the Sullenders'—"I just can't stand those people, Will. They're really awful!"

"Why, what's the matter with 'em?" he inquired. "I thought

182

they were first rate. They seemed perfectly friendly and hospitable and—"

"Oh, yes! Lord and Lady of the Manor entertaining the tenantry! I don't mind being tenantry," young Mrs. Sperry explained;—"but I can't stand the Lord-and-Lady-of-the-Manor style in people with a nine-room house and a one-car garage."

"It may be one-car," her husband laughed; "but it has two stories. They have a chauffeur, you know, and he lives in the upstairs of the garage."

"So that entitles the Sullenders to the Manor style?"

"But I didn't notice any of that style," he protested. "I thought they seemed right nice and cordial. Of course Sullender feels that he's been making quite a success in business and it naturally gives him a rather condescending air, but he's really all right."

"He certainly was condescending," she grumbled, and went on with some satire: "Did you hear him allude to himself as a 'Realtor?' "

"Well, why shouldn't he? He is one. That's his business."

"My Lord the Realtor!" Mrs. Sperry cried mockingly. "There ought to be an opera written called 'Il Realtor' like the one there used to be with the title 'Il Janitor.' Those are such romantic words! 'Toreador,' 'Realtor,' 'Humidor'—"

"Here, here!" her husband said. "Calm down! You seem to have got yourself worked up into a mighty sarcastic mood for some reason. Those people only want to be nice to us and they're all right."

Mrs. Sperry looked at him coldly. "Did you hear Mr. Sullender saying that his company had sold seven 'homes' this month?" she inquired.

"Oh, you can't expect everybody to know all the purist niceties of the English language," he said. "Sullender's all right and his wife struck me as one of the nicest, kindest women I ever—"

"Kind!" Mrs. Sperry echoed loudly. "She doesn't stop at being 'kind'! She's so caressingly tender, so angelically loving, that she can't possibly pronounce a one-syllabled word without making two syllables of it! Did you notice that she said 'yay-yus' for 'yes', and 'no-oh' for 'no'? I do hate the turtle-dove style of talking, and I never met a worse case of it. Mrs. Sullender's the sweetest sweet-woman I ever saw in my life and I'm positive she leads her husband a dog's life!"

"What nonsense!"

"It serves him right for his Realtoring, though," Mrs. Sperry added thoughtfully. "He ought to have that kind of a wife!"

"But you just said she was the sweetest—"

"Yes, the sweetest sweet-woman I ever saw. I do hate the whole clan of sweet-women!"

The young husband looked perplexed. "I don't know what you're talking about," he admitted. "I always thought—"

"I'm talking about the sweet-woman type that Mrs. Sullender belongs to. They use intended sweetness. They speak to total strangers with sweetness. They wear expressions of saintly sweetness. Everybody speaks of a sweet-woman with loving reverence, and it's generally felt that it would be practically immoral to contradict one of 'em. To be actually sassy to a sweet-woman would be a cardinal sin! They let their voices linger beautifully on the air; and they listen, themselves, to the lovely sounds they make. They always have the most exquisitely self-sacrificing reasons for every action of their lives; but they do just exactly what they want to do, and everybody else has to do what a sweet-woman wants him to. That's why I'm sure Mr. Sullender, in spite of all his pomposity, leads a dog's life at home."

"Of all the foolish talk!" young Sperry exclaimed. "Why, everybody says they're the most ideally married couple and that they lead the happiest life together that—"

" 'Everybody says!' " she mocked him, interrupting. "How often have you known what 'everybody says' turn out to be the truth about anything? And besides, we don't know a thing about any of these people, and we don't know anybody else that does! Who is this 'everybody' that's told you how happy the Sullenders are?"

"Well, it's just a general impression I got," he admitted. "I think I heard someone down-town alluding to Sullender's domestic relations being very fortunate and pleasant."

"Oh, you think so? Is that all? You don't really know a thing about it, then."

"No matter. You're wrong this time, Bella. The Sullenders—"

But Bella shook her pretty young head, interrupting him again. "You'll see! I do hope there won't have to be too much intimacy but you can't live across the street from people very long, in a neighbourhood like this, without getting to know the real truth about 'em. You wait and see what we get to know about the Sullenders!"

"Yes, I'll wait," he laughed. "But how long?"

"Oh, I don't know; maybe a year, maybe a month—"

"Let's make it a month, Bella," he said, and put his arm about her. "If we don't find out in a month that the Sullenders are miserable together, will you admit you're wrong?"

"No, I won't! But you'll probably have to admit that I'm right before that long. I have a sense for these things, Will, and I never go

184

wrong when I trust it. Women know intuitively things that men never suspect. I know I'm right about Mrs. Sullender."

Her husband permitted the discussion to end with this, wisely fearing that if he sought further to defend his position Bella might plausibly accuse him of "always insisting upon the last word." And so, for that night, at least, the matter was dropped from their conversation, though not from the thoughts of Mrs. Sperry. Truth to tell, she was what is sometimes called an "obstinate little body," and, also, she appreciated the advisability of a young wife's building for future and lifelong use the foundations of infallibility. That is to say, she was young and therefore inexperienced, but she had foresight.

Moreover, she had attentively observed the matrimonial condition of her parents and aunts and uncles. Many and many a time had she heard a middle-aged husband speak to his wife of like years somewhat in this manner: "No, Fannie, you're wrong again. You're mistaken about this now, just as you were about James Thompson's adding machine in 1897. And you were wrong about painting the house, the year after that, too. Don't you remember how you insisted dark green was the right colour, and finally had to admit, yourself, that dark green was awful, and light yellow would have been just right, as I all along said it would?"

Thus, young Mrs. Sperry, looking to times far ahead, had determined to be wrong about nothing whatever during these early years of her matrimony. Moreover, since argument had arisen concerning the Sullenders, she had made up her mind to be right about them, and to "prove" herself right, "whether she really was or not!" And that is why, on the morning after her arraignment of sweet-women generally, and of her too gracious neighbour particularly, the pretty newcomer in "Highland Place" found herself most pleasurably excited by the naïve but sinister revelations of a stranger eight years of age.

At a little before nine o'clock, Mr. William Sperry had departed (in a young husband's car) for his place of business, some five miles distant in the smoky heart of the city; and not long afterward the thoughtful Bella, charmingly accoutred as a gardener, came forth with a trowel to uproot weeds that threatened a row of iris she had set out along the gravel path leading from the tiny white veranda to the white picket gate. Thus engaged, she became aware of a small presence fumbling at the latch of this gate, and she changed her position from that of one on all fours, who gropes intently in the earth, to that of one upright from the knees, but momentarily relaxed.

"Do you want to come in?" she inquired, looking out from the

185

shade of her broad hat to where the little figure in blue overalls was marked off into stripes of sunshine and shadow by the intervening pickets of the gate. "Is there something you want here, little boy?"

He succeeded in operating the latch, came in, and looked attentively over her excavations. "Have you found any nice worms?" he asked.

"No, I haven't found any at all," she said, somewhat surprised by his adjective. "But I don't think there are any 'nice' worms anywhere. Worms are all pretty horrid."

"No, they ain't," he returned promptly and seriously. "There's lots o' nice worms."

"Oh, I don't think so."

"Yes, there is."

"Oh, no."

"There is, too," he said stubbornly and with some asperity. "Everybody knows there's plenty of nice worms."

"Where did you get such nonsense in your head?" Bella asked, a little sharply. "Whoever told you there are nice worms?"

"Well, there is!"

"But what makes you think so?" she insisted.

"Well—" He hesitated, then said with a conclusive air, settling the question: "My mother. I guess she knows!"

Bella stared at him incredulously for a moment.

"What's your name?"

"My name's George. My name's George, the same as my papa," he replied somewhat challengingly.

"Don't you live just across the street?" she asked.

"Yes, I do." He turned, pointing to the "George M. Sullender residence"; and Bella thought she detected a note of inherited pride in his tone as he added, "That's where I live!"

"But, George, you don't mean," she insisted curiously;—"you don't mean that your mother told you there are nice worms? Surely not!"

"My mother did," he asserted, and then with a little caution, modified the assertion. "My mother just the same as did."

"How was that?"

And his reply, so unexpected by his questioner, sent a thrill of coming triumph through her. "My mother called my father a worm."

"What!"

"She did," said George. "She called him a worm over and over—"

"What!"

"And if he's a worm," George went on, stoutly, "well, I guess he's nice, isn't he? So there got to be plenty nice worms if he's one."

186

"George!"

"She calls him a worm most every little while, these days," said George, expanding, and he added, in cold blood, "I like him a great deal better than what I do her."

"You do?"

"She hit him this morning," George thought fit to mention.

"What?"

"With a cloe's-brush," he said, dropping into detail. "She hit him on the back of the head with the wooden part of it and he said, 'Ooh'!"

"But she was just in fun, of course!"

"No, she wasn't; she was mad and said she was goin' to take me with her and go back to my grampaw's. I won't go with her. She's mad all the time, these days."

Bella stared, her lips parted, and she wished him to continue, but remembered her upbringing and tried to be a lady. "Georgie," she said severely;—"you shouldn't tell such things. Don't you know better than to speak in this way of what happens between your poor papa and your mother?"

The effect upon George was nothing, for even at eight years of age a child is able to understand what interests an adult listener, and children deeply enjoy being interesting. In response to her admonition, he said simply: "Yesterday she threw a glass o' water at him and cut where his ear is. It made a big mark on him."

"Georgie! I'm afraid you're telling me a dreadful, dreadful story!" Bella said, though it may not be denied that in company with this suspicion there arrived a premonitory symptom of disappointment. "Why, I saw your papa yesterday evening, myself, and there wasn't any mark or anything like—"

"It don't show," George explained. "It took him a good while, but he got it fixed up so's it didn't show much. Then he brushed his hair over where it was."

"Oh!"

"My mother hates my papa," said George. "She just hates and hates him!"

"What for?" Bella couldn't stop this question.

"She wants him to have more money and he says what good would that do because she'd only throw it around."

"No!"

"Yes," said George. "And she's mad because once he got so mad at her he hit her."

"What!"

"He did, too," George informed her, nodding, his large eyes as honest as they were earnest. "She said she was goin' to see my grampaw and she left me at home, but my papa catched her at the Pitcher Show with Mr. Grumbaugh."

"Who?"

"Mr. Grumbaugh," George repeated, with the air of explaining everything. "So my papa made her come home and he hit her, and she hit him, too!"

"Before you!" Bella exclaimed, horrified.

"Sure!" George said, and looked upon her with some superiority. "They do it all before me. Last week they had a big fight—"

He would have continued willingly, but at this point he was interrupted. Across the street a door opened, and out of it came Mrs. Sullender, leading a five-year-old girl by the hand. She called loudly, though in a carefully sweet and musical tone:

"George? Jaw—aurge? Oh, Jaw-aur-gie?"

"Yes'm?" he shouted.

Mrs. Sullender nodded smilingly to Bella, and called across: "Georgie, you dear little naughty thing! Didn't I tell you half an hour ago to come indoors and play with poor dear little Natalie? She's been waiting and waiting so patiently!"

George looked morose, but began to move in the desired direction. "I'm comin'," he muttered, and was so gross as to add, under his breath, "Doggone you!"

However, he went across the street; and then Mrs. Sullender, benevolently leading the two children by the hand, nodded again to Bella with a sweetness that was evident even at a distance, and reëntered the house, taking George and the tiny Natalie with her.

Bella remained upon her knees, staring violently at the "Sullender Home," and her thoughts were centred upon her husband. "Just wait till he gets here!" she thought.

But she saved her triumph until after dinner, when he had made himself comfortable upon the lounge in their tiny "living-room" and seemed to be in good content with his briar pipe.

"I had a caller after you left, this morning," she informed him sunnily.

"Who was it?"

"Mr. George M. Sullender."

"So? That's odd," said Sperry. "I saw him starting down-town in his car just before I did. How did he happen to come back here?"

"He didn't. This was Mr. George M. Sullender, Junior."

"Who's that?"

"Their little boy," said Bella. "You've seen him playing in their yard with the little sister."

"Oh, yes. Did his mother send him over on an errand?"

"No. He came to see if I'd found any 'nice worms'," Bella said, and added, in a carefully casual tone, but with a flashing little glance from the corner of her eye: "He said some worms must be nice because Mrs. Sullender is in the habit of calling Mr. Sullender a worm, and Georgie thinks his father is nice."

Young Mr. Sperry took his pipe from his mouth and looked at his wife incredulously. "What did you say about Mrs. Sullender's calling Mr. Sullender—"

"A 'worm,' William," said Bella. "She calls him a 'worm,' William, because he doesn't make even more money than he does, poor man. The child really hates his mother: he never once spoke of her as 'mamma' but he always said 'my papa' when he mentioned Mr. Sullender. I think I must have misjudged that poor creature a little, by the way. Of course he is pompous, but I think his pomposity is probably just assumed to cover up his agony of mind. He has a recent scar that his wife put on his head, too, to cover up."

"Bella!"

"Yes," she said reflectively. "I think he's mainly engaged in covering things up, poor thing. Of course he does strike his sweet-woman, now and then, when he finds her at the movies with gentlemen he doesn't approve of; but one can hardly blame him, considering the life she leads him. It was last week, though, when they had their big fight, I understand—with the children looking on."

But at this, William rose to his feet and confronted her. "What on earth are you talking about, Bella?"

"The Sullenders," she said. "It was curious. It was like having the front of their house taken off, the way a curtain rolls up at the theatre and shows you one of those sordid Russian plays, for instance. There was the whole sickening actual life of this dreadful family laid bare before me: the continual petty bickerings that every hour or so grow into bitter quarrels with blows and epithets—and then, when other people are there, as we were, last night, the assumption of suavity, the false, too-sweet sweetness and absurd pomposities—oh, what an ugly revelation it is, Will! It's so ugly it makes me almost sorry you were wrong about them—as you're rather likely to be in your flash judgments, you poor dear!"

Bella (who was "literary" sometimes) delivered herself of this speech with admirable dramatic quality, especially when she made her terse little realistic picture of the daily life of the Sullenders, but there was just a shade of happy hypocrisy and covert triumph in the final sentence, and she even thought fit to add a little more on the point. "How strange it is to think that only last night we were arguing about it!" she exclaimed. "And that I said we'd not need to

189

wait a month to prove that I was right! Here it is only the next day, and it's proved I was a thousand times righter than I said I was!"

"Well, perhaps you'll enlighten me—" he began, and she complied so willingly that she didn't let him finish his request.

She gave him Georgie's revelation in detail, emphasizing and colouring it somewhat with her own interpretations of many things only suggested by the child's meagre vocabulary; and she was naturally a little indignant when, at first, her husband declined to admit his defeat.

"Why, it's simply not believable," he said. "Those people couldn't seem what they seemed to be last night, and be so depraved. They were genuinely affectionate in the tone they used with each other and they—"

"Good gracious!" Bella cried. "Do you think I'm making this up?"

"No, of course not," he returned hastily. "But the child may have made it up."

"About his own father and mother?"

"Oh, I know; yet some children are the most wonderful little story-tellers: they tell absolutely inexplicable lies and hardly know why themselves."

But at this, Bella looked at him pityingly. "Listen a moment! There was all the sordid daily life of these people laid out before me in the poor little child's prattle: a whole realistic novel, complete and consistent, and I'd like to know how you account for a child of seven or eight being able to compose such a thing—and on the spur of the moment, too! When children make up stories they make 'em up about extraordinary and absurd things, not about the sordid tragedies of everyday domestic life. Do you actually think this child made up what he told me?"

"Well, it certainly does seem peculiar!"

" 'Peculiar?' Why, it's terrible and it's true!"

"Well, if it is," he said gloomily, "we certainly don't want to get mixed up in it. We don't want to come into a new neighbourhood and get involved in a scandal—or even in gossiping about one. We must be careful not to say anything about this, Bella."

She looked away from him thoughtfully. "I suppose so, though of course these people aren't friends of ours; they're hardly acquaintances."

"No, but that's all the more reason for our not appearing to be interested in their troubles. We'll certainly be careful not to say anything about this, won't we, Bella?"

"Oh, I suppose so," she returned absently. "Since the people

190

are really nothing to us, though, I don't suppose it matters whether we say anything or not."

"Oh, but it does!" he insisted, and then, something in her tone having caught his attention, he inquired: "You haven't said anything to any one about it, have you, Bella?"

"What?"

"You haven't repeated to any one what the child told you, have you?"

"Oh, no," she said lightly. "Not to any one who would have any personal interest in it."

"Oh, my!" William exclaimed, dismayed. "Who'd you tell?"

"Nobody that has the slightest interest in the Sullenders," Bella replied, with cold dignity. "Nobody that cares the slightest thing about them."

"Well, then, what in the world did you tell 'em for?"

"Why, to pass the time, I suppose," Bella said, a little offended. "Cousin Ethel dropped in for a while this afternoon and the whole thing was so extraordinary I just sketched it to her. What are you making such a fuss about?"

"I'm not," he protested feebly. "But even if the thing's true, we don't want to get the name of people that gossip about their—"

"Oh, my!" she sighed impatiently. "I've told you Cousin Ethel hasn't the slightest personal interest in these people, and besides she'll never repeat what I told her."

"Well, if she doesn't, it'll be the first time!"

"Will, please!"

"Golly, I hope it won't get back to the Sullenders!"

"Such horrible people as that, what difference would it make?" Bella demanded. "And how could it get back? Cousin Ethel doesn't move in Sullender circles. Not precisely!"

"No, but her close friend, Mrs. Howard Peebles, is the aunt of Mrs. Frank Deem and Frank Deem is Sullender's business partner."

"Oh, a Realtor, is he?" Bella said icily.

William returned to the lounge, but did not recline. Instead, he sat down and took his head in his hands. "I do wish you hadn't talked about it," he said gloomily.

Bella was sensitive; therefore she began to be angry. "Do you think it's very intelligent," she asked, "to imply that I don't know enough not to make neighbourhood trouble? You may not recall that only last night you were sure that you were right and I was wrong about what sort of people these Sullenders are. Already, the very next day, you've had to confess that you were utterly mistaken and that your wife is wholly in the right. I suppose you may feel a little depressed about that and want to change the question to something else and claim I'm in the wrong about that. But don't you think it's a little bit childish of you, Will? Don't you think that the way you're taking your defeat is just a little bit—small?"

He was hurt, and looked up at her with an expression that showed the injury. "I'd hardly have expected you'd call me that," he said. "At least, not quite so soon after our wedding-trip!"

"Well, I might have expected you wouldn't be accusing me of gossiping harmfully," she retorted. "Not quite so soon!"

Young Mr. Sperry rose again. "Do you think that's as bad as using the epithet 'small' to your husband?"

"'Epithet'?" she echoed. "You charge me with using 'epithets'?"

"Well, but didn't—"

"I think I'll ask you to excuse me," Bella said, with an aspect of nobility in suffering. Thereupon, proudly, she betook herself from the room.

It was a tiff. Next day they were as polite to each other as if they had just been introduced, and this ceremonial formality was maintained between them until the third evening after its installation, when a calamity caused them to abandon it. After a stately dinner in their hundred square feet of dining-room, Bella had gone out into the twilight to refresh her strips of iris with fair water from the garden hose, and William reclined upon his lounge, solitary with a gloomy pipe. Unexpectedly, he was summoned: Bella looked in upon him from the door and spoke hastily. "Uh—Mr. and Mrs. Sullender—" she said. "Uh—" And as hastily she withdrew.

Perturbed, he rose and went out to the little veranda, where, with a slightly nervous hospitality, Bella was now offering chairs to Mrs. George M. Sullender and her husband. Mrs. Sullender smilingly, and in her angelic voice, declined the offer.

"Oh, no," she said. "We came in for a moment to admire your lovely irises at closer range; we're just passing on our way to some friends in Waverley Place."

"We'd be so glad—" Bella fluttered.

"No, no, no," Mrs. Sullender murmured caressingly. "We've only a moment—I'm so sorry you disturbed your husband—we're just going over for bridge. I suppose you know most of the people in Waverley Place?"

"No, I don't think I know any."

"Well, of course we don't think it compares to Highland Place," Mrs. Sullender said, with a little deprecatory laugh. "I'm afraid it's rather—well, gossipy."

"Oh—" Bella said. "Is it?"

"I'm afraid so," the gentle-mannered lady returned. "Of course that's a great pity, too, in such a new little community where people are bound to be thrown together a great deal. Don't you think it's a great pity, Mrs. Sperry?"

"Oh—naturally," Bella acquiesced. "Yes, indeed."

"I knew you would. Of course it's just thoughtlessness—most of the people who live there are so young—but we heard a really dreadful story only yesterday. It came from a very young newly-married couple, and my husband and I were so sorry to hear they'd started out by telling such dreadful things about their neighbours. Don't you think it's most unwise, Mrs. Sperry?"

Mrs. Sullender's voice, wholly unruffled, and as indomitably tender as ever, gave no intimation that she spoke with a peculiar significance; but William Sperry was profoundly alarmed, and, with a sympathy that held no triumph in it, he knew that Bella was in a similar or worse condition.

"Ye-es," Bella murmured. "Of—of course I do."

"I knew you would feel that way," said Mrs. Sullender soothingly. "It's unwise, because gossip travels so. It nearly always goes straight back to the people it's about. In fact, I don't believe I ever knew of one single case where it didn't. Did you, Mrs. Sperry?"

"I—I don't—that is, well, no," Bella stammered.

"No. It's so unwise!" Mrs. Sullender insisted, with a little murmur of tender laughter. Then she took the arm of her solemn and silent husband, and they turned together toward the gate, but paused. "Oh, I'd meant to tell you, Mrs. Sperry—"

"Uh—yes?"

"That dear little boy Georgie—the little boy you were chatting with the other morning when I called him in to play with my little girl—you remember, Mrs. Sperry?"

"Yes!" Bella gasped.

"I thought you made such friends with him you'd be sorry to know you won't see him any more."

"No?"

"No," Mrs. Sullender cooed gently. "Poor little Georgie Goble!"

"Georgie—who?"

"Georgie Goble," said Mrs. Sullender. "He was Goble, our chauffeur's little boy. They lived over our garage and had quite a distressing time of it, poor things! The wife finally persuaded Goble to move to another town where she thinks chauffeurs' pay is higher. I was sure you'd be sorry to hear the poor dear little boy had gone. They left yesterday. Good night. Good night, Mr. Sperry."

With that, followed by somewhat feeble good-nights from both the Sperrys, she passed through the gate with her husband,

and a moment later disappeared in the clean dusk of "Highland Place."

Then Bella turned to her troubled William. "She—she certainly made it pl-plain!"

"Yes," he said. "But after all, she really did let us down pretty easy."

" 'Us,' " the young wife demanded sharply. "Did you say 'Us?' "

"Yes," he answered. "I think she let us down about as easy as we could have expected."

Bella instantly threw herself in his arms. "Oh, William!" she cried. "William, do be the kind of husband that won't throw this up at me when we're forty and fifty! William, promise me you'll always say 'Us' when I get us in trouble!"

And William promised and William did.

THE TIGER

THE two little girls, Daisy Mears and Elsie Threamer, were nine years old, and they lived next door to each other; but there the coincidence came to an end; and even if any further similarity between them had been perceptible, it could not have been mentioned openly without causing excitement in Elsie's family. Elsie belonged to that small class of exquisite children seen on canvas in the days when a painter would exhibit without shame a picture called "Ideal Head." She was one of those rare little fair creatures at whom grown people, murmuring tenderly, turn to stare; and her childhood was attended by the exclamations not only of strangers but of people who knew her well. "Greuze!" they said, or "A child Saint Cecilia!" or "That angelic sweetness!" But whatever form preliminary admiration might take, the concluding tribute was almost always the same: "And so unconscious, with it all!" When some unobservant and rambling-minded person did wander from the subject without mentioning Elsie's unconsciousness, she was apt to take a dislike to him.

People often wondered what that ineffable child with the shadowy downcast eyes was thinking about. They would "give anything," they declared, to know what she was thinking about. But nobody wondered what Daisy Mears was thinking about—on the contrary, people were frequently only too sure they knew what Daisy was thinking about.

From the days of her earliest infancy, Elsie, without making any effort, was a child continually noticed and acclaimed; whereas her next neighbour was but an inconspicuous bit of background, which may have been more trying for Daisy than any one realized. No doubt it also helped great aspirations to sprout within her, and was thus the very cause of the abrupt change in her character during their mutual tenth summer. For it was at this time that Daisy all at once began to be more talked about than Elsie had ever been. All over the neighbourhood and even beyond its borders, she was spoken of probably dozens of times as often as Elsie was—and with more feeling, more emphasis, more gesticulation, than Elsie had ever evoked.

Daisy had accidentally made the discovery that the means of becoming prominent are at hand for anybody, and that the process of using them is the simplest in the world; for of course all that a person desirous of prominence needs to do is to follow his unconventional impulses. In this easy way prodigious events can be produced at the cost of the most insignificant exertion, as is well understood by people who have felt a temptation to step from the roof of a high building, or to speak out inappropriately in church. Daisy still behaved rather properly in church, but several times she made herself prominent in Sunday school; and she stepped off the roof of her father's garage, merely to become more prominent among a small circle of coloured people who stood in the alley begging her not to do it.

She spent the rest of that day in bed—for after all, while fame may so easily be obtained, it has its price, and the bill is inevitably sent in—but she was herself again the next morning, and at about ten o'clock announced to her mother that she had decided to "go shopping."

Mrs. Mears laughed, and, just to hear what Daisy would say, asked quizzically: " 'Go shopping?' What in the world do you mean, Daisy?"

"Well, I think it would be a nice thing for me to do, mamma," Daisy explained. "You an' grandma an' Aunt Clara, you always keep sayin', 'I believe I'll go shopping.' I want to, too."

"What would you do?"

"Why, I'd go shopping the way you do. I'd walk in a store an' say: 'Have you got any unb'eached muslin? Oh, I thought this'd be only six cents a yard! Haven't you got anything nicer?' Everything like that. I know, mamma. I know any amount o' things to say when I go shopping. Can't I go shopping, mamma?"

"Yes, of course," her mother said, smiling. "You can pretend our big walnut tree is a department store and shop all you want."

"Well—" Daisy began, and then realizing that the recommendation of the walnut tree was only a suggestion, and not a command, she said, "Well, thank you, mamma," and ran outdoors, swinging her brown straw hat by its elastic cord. The interview had taken place in the front hall, and Mrs. Hears watched the lively little figure for a moment as it was silhouetted against the ardent sunshine at the open doors; then she turned away, smiling, and for the rest of the morning her serene thought of Daisy was the picture of a ladylike child playing quietly near the walnut tree in the front yard.

Daisy skipped out to the gate, but upon the public sidewalk, just beyond, she moderated her speed and looked as important as she could, assuming at once the rôle she had selected in the little play she was making up as she went along. In part, too, her importance was meant to interest Elsie Threamer, who was standing in graceful idleness by the hedge that separated the Threamers' yard from the sidewalk.

"Where you goin', Daisy?" the angelic neighbour inquired.

Daisy paused and tried to increase a distortion of her face, which was her conception of a businesslike concentration upon "shopping." "What?" she inquired, affecting absent-mindedness.

"Where you goin'?"

"I haf to go shopping to-day, Elsie."

Elsie laughed. "No, you don't."

"I do, too. I go shopping almost all the time lately. I haf to."

"You don't, either," Elsie said. "You don't either haf to."

"I do, too, haf to!" Daisy retorted. "I'm almos' worn out, I haf to go shopping so much."

"Where?"

"Every single place," Daisy informed her impressively. "I haf to go shopping all the way down-town. I'll take you with me if you haf to go shopping, too. D'you want to?"

Elsie glanced uneasily over her shoulder, but no one was visible at any of the windows of her house. Obviously, she was interested in her neighbour's proposal, though she was a little timorous. "Well—" she said. "Of course I ought to go shopping, because the truth is I got more shopping to do than 'most anybody. I haf to go shopping so much I just have the backache all the time! I guess—"

"Come on," said Daisy. "I haf to go shopping in every single store down-town, and there's lots o' stores on the way we can go shopping in before we get there."

"All right," her friend agreed. "I guess I rilly better."

She came out to the sidewalk, and the two turned toward the city's central quarter of trade, walking quickly and talking with an accompaniment of many little gestures. "I rilly don't know how I do it all," said Elsie, assuming a care-worn air. "I got so much shopping to do an' everything, my fam'ly all say they wonder I don't break down an' haf to go to a sanitanarian or somep'm because I do so much."

"Oh, it's worse'n that with me, my dear!" said Daisy. "I declare I doe' know how I do live through it all! Every single day, it's like this: I haf to go shopping all day long, my dear!"

"Well, I haf to, too, my dear! I never get time to even sit down, my dear!"

Daisy shook her head ruefully. "Well, goodness knows the last time I sat down, my dear!" she said. "My fam'ly say I got to take some rest, but how can I, with all this terrable shopping to do?"

"Oh, my dear!" Elsie exclaimed. "Why, my dear, I haven't sat down since Christmus!"

Thus they enacted a little drama, improvising the dialogue, for of course every child is both playwright and actor, and spends most of his time acting in scenes of his own invention—which is one reason that going to school may be painful to him; lessons are not easily made into plays, though even the arithmetic writers do try to help a little, with their dramas of grocers and eggs, and farmers and bushels and quarts. A child is a player, and an actor is a player; and both "play" in almost the same sense—the essential difference being that the child's art is instinctive, so that he is not so conscious of just where reality begins and made-up drama ends. Daisy and Elsie were now representing and exaggerating their two mothers, with a dash of aunt thrown in; they felt that they were the grown people they played they were; and the more they developed these "secondary personalities," the better they believed in them.

"An' with all my trouble an' everything," Daisy said, "I jus' never get a minute to myself. Even my shopping, it's all for the fam'ly."

"So's mine," Elsie said promptly. "Mine's every single bit for the fam'ly, an' I never, never get through."

"Well, look at me!" Daisy exclaimed, her hands fluttering in movements she believed to be illustrative of the rush she lived in. "My fam'ly keep me on the run from the minute I get up till after I go to bed. I declare I don't get time to say my prayers! To-day I thought I might get a little rest for once in my life. But no! I haf to go shopping!"

"So do I, my dear! I haf to look at— Well, what do you haf to look at when we go in the stores?"

"Me? I haf to look at everything! There isn't a thing left in our house. I haf to look at doilies, an' all kinds embrawdries, an' some aperns for the servants, an' taffeta, an' two vases for the liberry mantelpice, an' some new towerls, an' kitchen-stove-polish, an' underwear, an' oilcloth, an' lamp-shades, an' some orstrich feathers for my blue vevvut hat. An' then I got to get some—"

"Oh, my dear! I got more'n that I haf to look at," Elsie interrupted. And she, likewise, went into details; but as Daisy continued with her own, and they both talked at the same time, the effect was rather confused, though neither seemed to be at all disturbed on that account. Probably they were pleased to think they were thus all the more realistically adult.

It was while they were chattering in this way that Master Laurence Coy came wandering along a side-street that crossed their route, and, catching sight of them, considered the idea of joining them. He had a weakness for Elsie, and an antipathy for Daisy, the latter feeling sometimes not unmingled with the most virulent repulsion; but there was a fair balance struck; in order to be with Elsie, he could bear being with Daisy. Yet both were girls, and, regarded in that light alone, not the company he cared to be thought of as deliberately choosing. Nevertheless, he had found no boys at home that morning; he was at a loss what to do with himself, and bored. Under these almost compulsory circumstances, he felt justified in consenting to join the ladies; and, overtaking them at the crossing, he stopped and spoke to them.

"Hay, there," he said, taking care not to speak too graciously. "Where you two goin', talkin' so much?"

They paid not the slightest attention to him, but continued busily on their way.

"My dear Mrs. Smith!" Daisy exclaimed, speaking with increased loudness. "I jus' pozzatively never have a minute to my own affairs! If I doe' get a rest from my housekeepin' pretty soon, I doe' know what on earth's goin' to become o' my nerves!"

"Oh, Mrs. Jones!" Elsie exclaimed. "It's the same way with me, my dear. I haf to have the doctor for my nerves, every morning at seven or eight o'clock. Why, my dear, I never—"

"Hay!" Laurence called. "I said: 'Where you goin', talkin' so much?' Di'n'chu hear me?"

But they were already at some distance from him and hurrying on as if they had seen and heard nothing whatever. Staring after them, he caught a dozen more "my dears" and exclamatory repetitions of "Mrs. Smith, you don't say so!" and "Why, Mis-suz Jones!" He called again, but the two little figures, heeding him less than they did the impalpable sunshine about them, hastened on down the street, their voices gabbling, their heads waggling importantly, their arms and hands incessantly lively in airy gesticulation.

Laurence was thus granted that boon so often defined by connoisseurs of twenty as priceless—a new experience. But he had no gratitude for it; what he felt was indignation. He lifted up his voice and bawled:

"Hay! Di'n'chu hear what I said? Haven't you got 'ny ears?"

Well he knew they had ears, and that these ears heard him; but on the spur of the moment he was unable to think of anything more scathing than this inquiry. The shoppers went on, impervious, ignoring him with all their previous airiness—with a slight accentuation of it, indeed—even when he bellowed at them a second time and a third. Stung, he was finally inspired to add: "Hay! Are you gone crazy?" But they were halfway to the next crossing.

A bitterness came upon Laurence. "What I care?" he muttered. "I'll show you what I care!" However, his action seemed to deny his words, for instead of setting about some other business to prove his indifference, he slowly followed the shoppers. He was driven by a necessity he felt to make them comprehend his displeasure with their injurious flouting of himself and of etiquette in general. "Got 'ny politeness?" he muttered, and replied morosely: "No, they haven't—they haven't got sense enough to know what politeness means! Well, I'll show 'em! They'll see before I get through with 'em! Oh, oh! Jus' wait a little: they'll be beggin' me quick enough to speak to 'em. 'Oh, Laur-runce, please!' they'll say. 'Please speak to us, Laur-runce. Won' chu please speak to us, Laurunce? We'd jus' give anything to have you speak to us, Laurunce! Won' chu, Laurunce, pull-lease?' Then I'll say: 'Yes, I'll speak to you, an' you better listen if you want to learn some sense!' Then I'll call 'em everything I can think of!"

It might have been supposed that he had some definite plan for bringing them thus to their knees in supplication, but he was only solacing himself by sketching a triumphant climax founded upon nothing. Meanwhile he continued morbidly to follow, keeping about fifty yards behind them.

"Poot!" he sneered. "Think they're wunnaful, don't they? You wait! They'll see!"

He came to a halt, staring. "Now what they doin'?"

Elsie and Daisy had gone into a small drug-store, where Daisy straightway approached the person in charge, an elderly man of weary appearance. "Do you keep taffeta?" she asked importantly. Since she and her friend were "playing" that they were shopping, of course they found it easily consistent to "play" that the druggist was a clerk in a department store; and no doubt, too, the puzzlement of the elderly man gave them a profound if secret enjoyment.

He moved toward his rather shabby soda-fountain, replying: "I got chocolate and strawb'ry and v'nilla. I don't keep no fancy syrups."

"Oh, my, no!" Daisy exclaimed pettishly. "I mean taffeta you wear."

"What?"

"I mean taffeta you wear."

" 'Wear'?" he said.

"I want to look at some taffeta," Daisy said impatiently. "Taffeta."

"Taffy?" the man said. "I don't keep no line of candies."

Daisy frowned, and shook her head. "I guess he's kind of deaf or somep'm," she said to Elsie; and then she shouted again at the elderly man: "Taffetah! It's somep'm you wear. You wear it on you!"

"What for?" he said. "I ain't deaf. You mean some brand of porous plaster? Mustard plaster?"

"Oh, my, no!" Daisy exclaimed, and turned to Elsie. "This is just the way it is. Whenever I go shopping, they're always out of everything I want!"

"Oh, it's exackly the same with me, my dear," Elsie returned. "It's too provoking! Rilly, the shops in this town—"

"Listen here," the proprietor interrupted, and he regarded these fastidious customers somewhat unfavourably. "You're wastin' my time on me. Say what it is you want or go somewheres else."

"Well, have you got some very nice blue-silk lamp-shades?" Daisy inquired, and she added: "With gold fringe an' tassels?"

"Lamp-shades!" he said, and he had the air of a person who begins to feel seriously annoyed. "Listen! Go on out o' here!"

But Daisy ignored his rudeness. "Have you got any very good unb'eached muslin?" she asked.

"You go on out o' here!" the man shouted. "You go on out o' here or I'll untie my dog."

"Well, I declare!" Elsie exclaimed as she moved toward the door. "I never was treated like this in all my days!"

"What kind of a dog is it?" Daisy asked, for she was interested.

"It's a biting dog," the drug-store man informed her; and she thought best to retire with Elsie. The two came out to the sidewalk and went on their way, giggling surreptitiously, and busier than ever with their chatter. After a moment the injured party in the background again followed them.

"They'll find out what's goin' to happen to 'em," he muttered, continuing his gloomy rhapsody. " 'Please speak to us, Laurunce,' they'll say. 'Oh, Laurunce, pull-lease!' An' then I'll jus' keep on laughin' at 'em an' callin' 'em everything the worst I ever heard, while they keep hollerin': 'Oh, Laur-runce, pull-lease!' "

A passer-by, a kind-faced woman of middle age, caught the murmur from his slightly moving lips, and halted inquiringly.

"What is it, little boy?" she asked.

"What?" he said.

"Were you speaking to me, little boy? Didn't you say 'Please'?"

"No, I didn't," he replied, colouring high; for he did not like to be called "little boy" by anybody, and he was particularly averse to this form of address on the lips of a total stranger. Moreover, no indignant person who is talking to himself cares to be asked what he is saying. "I never said a thing to you," he added crossly. "What's the matter of you, anyhow?"

"Good gracious!" she exclaimed. "What a bad, rude little boy! Shame on you!"

"I ain't a little boy, an' shame on your own self!" he retorted; but she had already gone upon her way, and he was again following the busy shoppers. As he went on his mouth was slightly in motion,

201

though it was careful not to open, and his slender neck was imperceptibly distended by small explosions of sound, for he continued his dialogues, but omitted any enunciation that might attract the impertinence of strangers. "It's none o' your ole biznuss!" he said, addressing the middle-aged woman in this internal manner. "I'll show you who you're talkin' to! I guess when you get through with me you'll know somep'm! Shame on your own self!" Then his eyes grew large as they followed the peculiar behaviour of the two demoiselles before him. "My goodness!" he said.

Daisy was just preceding Elsie into a barber-shop.

"Do you keep taffeta or—or lamp-shades?" Daisy asked of the barber nearest the door.

This was a fat coloured man, a mulatto. He had a towel over the jowl and eyes of his helpless customer, and standing behind the chair, employed his thumbs and fingers in a slow and rhythmic manipulation of the man's forehead. Meanwhile he continued an unctuous monologue, paying no attention whatever to Daisy's inquiry. "I dess turn roun' an' walk away little bit," said the barber. " 'N'en I turn an' look 'er over up an' down from head to foot. 'Yes,' I say. 'You use you' mouth full freely,' I say, 'but dess kinely gim me leave fer to tell you, you ain't got nothin' to rouse up no int'est o' mine in you. I make mo' money,' I say, 'I make mo' money in a day than whut Henry ever see in a full year, an' if you tryin' to climb out o' Henry's class an' into mine—' "

"Listen!" Daisy said, raising her voice. "Do you keep taffeta or—"

"Whut you say?" the barber asked, looking coldly upon her and her companion.

"We're out shopping," Daisy explained. "We want to look at some—"

"Listen me," the barber interrupted. "Run out o' here. Run out."

Daisy moved nearer him. "What you doin' to that man's face?" she asked.

"Nem mine! Nem mine!" he said haughtily.

"What were you tellin' him?" Daisy inquired. "I mean all about Henry's class an' usin' her mouth so full freely. Who was?"

"Run out!" the barber shouted. "Run out!"

"Well, I declare!" Daisy exclaimed, as she and Elsie followed his suggestion and emerged from the shop. "It's just this same way whenever I go shopping! I never can find the things I want; they act almos' like they don't care whether they keep 'em or not."

"It's dreadful!" Elsie agreed, and, greatly enjoying the air of annoyance they were affecting, they proceeded on their way. No one would have believed them aware that they were being followed; and neither had spoken a word referring to Master Coy; but they must have understood each other perfectly in the matter, for presently Daisy's head turned ever so slightly, and she sent a backward glance out of the very tail of her eye. "He's still comin'!" she said in a whisper that was ecstatic with mirth. And Elsie, in the same suppressed but joyous fashion, said: "Course he is, the ole thing!" This was the only break in their manner of being the busiest shoppers in the world; and immediately after it they became more flauntingly shoppers than ever.

As for Laurence, his curiosity was now almost equal to his bitterness. The visit to the drug-store he could understand, but that to the barber-shop astounded him; and when he came to the shop he paused to flatten his nose upon the window. The fat mulatto barber nearest the window was still massaging the face of the recumbent customer and continuing his narrative; the other barbers were placidly grooming the occupants of their chairs, while two or three waiting patrons, lounging on a bench, read periodicals of a worn and flaccid appearance. Nothing gave any clue to the errand of Laurence's fair friends; on the contrary, everything that was revealed to his staring eyes made their visit seem all the more singular.

He went in, and addressed himself to the fat barber. "Listen," he said. "Listen. I want to ast you somep'm."

"Dess 'bout when she was fixin' to holler," the barber continued, to his patron, "I take an' slap my money ri' back in my pocket. 'You talk 'bout tryin' show me some class,' I say. 'Dess lem me—' "

"Listen!" Laurence said, speaking louder. "I want to ast you somep'm."

" 'Dess lem me tell you, if you fixin' show me some class,' " the barber went on; " 'if you fixin' show me some class,' I say. 'Dess lem me tell you if—' "

"Listen!" Laurence insisted. "I want to ast you somep'm."

For a moment the barber ceased to manipulate his customer and gave Laurence a look of disapproval. "Listen me, boy!" he said. "Nex' time you flatten you' face on nat window you don' haf to breave on nat glass, do you? Ain' you' folks taught you no better'n go roun' dirtyin' up nice clean window?"

"What I want to know," Laurence said: "—What were they doin' in here?"

"What were who doin' in here?"

"Those two little girls that were in here just now. What did they come here for?"

203

"My goo'nuss!" the barber exclaimed. "Man'd think barber got nothin' do but stan' here all day 'nanswer questions! Run out, boy!"

"But, listen!" Laurence urged him. "What were they—"

"Run out, boy!" the barber said, and his appearance became formidable. "Run out, boy!"

Laurence departed silently, though in his mind he added another outrage to the revenge he owed the world for the insults and mistreatments he was receiving that morning. "I'll show you!" he mumbled in his throat as he came out of the shop. "You'll wish you had some sense, when I get through with you, you ole barber, you!"

Then, as he looked before him, his curiosity again surpassed his sense of injury. The busy shoppers were just coming out of a harness-shop, which was making a bitter struggle to survive the automobile; and as they emerged from the place, they had for a moment the hasty air of ejected persons. But this was a detail that escaped Laurence's observation, for the gestures and chatter were instantly resumed, and the two hurried on as before.

"My gracious!" said Laurence, and when he came to the harness-shop he halted and looked in through the open door; but the expression of the bearded man behind a counter was so discouraging that he thought it best to make no inquiries.

The bearded man was as irritable as he looked. "Listen!" he called. "Don't block up that door, d'you hear me? Go on, get away from there and let some air in. Gosh!"

Laurence obeyed morosely. "Well, doggone it!" he said.

He had no idea that the pair preceding him might have been received as cavalierly, for their air of being people engaged in matters of importance had all the effect upon him they desired, and deceived him perfectly. Moreover, the mystery of what they had done in the barber-shop and in the harness-shop was actually dismaying; they were his colleagues in age and his inferiors in sex; and yet all upon a sudden, this morning, they appeared to deal upon the adult plane and to have business with strange grown people. Laurence was unwilling to give them the slightest ground for a conceited supposition that he took any interest in them, or their doings, but he made up his mind that if they went into another shop, he would place himself in a position to observe what they did, even at the risk of their seeing him.

Four or five blocks away, the business part of the city began to be serious; buildings of ten or twelve stories, several of much more than that, were piled against the sky; but here, where walked the shoppers and their disturbed shadower, the street had fallen upon slovenly days. Farther out, in the quarter whence they had come, it led a life of domestic prosperity, but gradually, as it descended southward, its character altered dismally until just before it began to be respectable again, as a business street, it was not only shabby but had a covert air of underhand enterprise. And the shop windows had not been arranged with the idea of offering a view of the interiors.

Of course Elsie and Daisy did not concern themselves with the changed character of the street; one shop was as good as another for the purposes involved in the kind of shopping that engaged them this morning; and they were having too glorious a time to give much consideration to anything. Elsie had fallen under the spell of a daring leadership; she was as excited as Daisy, as intent as she upon preserving the illusion they maintained between them; and both of them were delightedly aware that they must be goading their frowning follower with a splendid series of mysteries.

"I declare!" Daisy said, affecting peevishness. "I forgot to look at orstrich feathers an' unb'eached muslin at both those two last places we went. Let's try in here."

By "in here" she referred to a begrimed and ignoble façade once painted dark green, but now the colour of street dust mixed with soot. Admission was to be obtained by double doors, with the word "Café" upon both of the panels. "Café" was also repeated upon a window, where a sign-painter of great inexperience had added the details: "Soft Drinks Candys Cigars & C." And upon three shelves in the window were displayed, as convincing proof of the mercantile innocence of the place, three or four corncob pipes, some fly-specked packets of tobacco, several packages of old popcorn and a small bottle of catsup.

Daisy tugged at the greasy brass knob projecting from one of the once green doors, and after some reluctance it yielded. "Come on," she said. The two then walked importantly into the place, and the door closed behind them.

Laurence immediately hurried forward; but what he beheld was discouraging. The glass of the double door was frankly opaque; and that of the window was so dirty and besooted, and so obstructed by the shelves of sparse merchandise, that he could see nothing whatever beyond the shelves.

"Well, dog-gone it!" he said.

Daisy and Elsie found themselves the only visible occupants of an interior unexampled in their previous experience. Along one side of the room, from wall to wall, there ran what they took to be a counter for the display of goods, though it had nothing upon it except a blackened little jar of matches and a short thick glass goblet, dimmed at the bottom with an ancient sediment. A brass rail extended along the base of the counter, and on the wall, behind, was a long mirror, once lustrous, no doubt, but now coated with a white substance that had begun to suffer from soot. Upon the wall opposite the mirror there were two old lithographs, one of a steamboat, the other of a horse and jockey; and there were some posters advertising cigarettes, but these decorations completed the invoice of all that was visible to the shoppers.

"Oh, dear!" Daisy said. "Wouldn't it be too provoking if they'd gone to lunch or somep'm!" And she tapped as loudly as she could upon the counter, calling: "Here! Somebody come an' wait on us! I want to look at some of your nicest unb'eached muslin an' some orstrich feathers."

There was a door at the other end of the room and it stood open, revealing a narrow and greasy passage, with decrepit walls that showed the laths, here and there, where areas of plaster had fallen. "I guess I better go call in that little hallway," said Daisy. "They don't seem to care how long they keep their customers waitin'!"

But as she approached the door, the sound of several muffled explosions came from the rear of the building and reached the shoppers through the funnel of the sinister passage.

"That's funny," said Daisy. "I guess somebody's shootin' off firecrackers back there."

"What for?" Elsie asked.

"I guess they think it must be the Fourth o' July," Daisy answered; and she called down the passageway: "Here! Come wait on us. We want to look at some unb'eached muslin an' orstrich feathers. Can't you hurry up?"

No one replied, but voices became audible, approaching;— voices in simultaneous outbursts, and manifesting such poignant emotion that although there were only two of them, a man's and a woman's, Daisy and Elsie at first supposed that seven or eight people were engaged in the controversy. For a moment they also supposed the language to be foreign, but discovered that some of the expressions used were familiar, though they had been accustomed to hear them under more decorous circumstances.

"They're makin' an awful fuss," Elsie said. "What are they talkin' about?"

"The way it sounds," said Daisy, "it sounds like they're talkin' about things in the Bible."

Then another explosion was heard, closer; it seemed to come from a region just beyond the passageway; and it was immediately followed by a clatter of lumber and an increase of eloquence in the vocal argument.

"You quit that!" the man's voice bellowed plaintively. "You don't know what you're doin'; you blame near croaked me that time! You quit that, Mabel!"

"I'm a-goin' to learn you!" the woman's voice announced. "You come out from under them boards, and I'll learn you whether I know what I'm doin' or not! Come out!"

"Please go on away and lea' me alone," the man implored. "I never done nothin' to you. I never seen a cent o' that money! Honest, George never give me a cent of it. Why'n't you go an ast him? He's right in yonder. Oh, my goodness, whyn't you ast him?"

"Come out from under them boards!"

The man's voice became the more passionate in its protesting. "Oh, my goodness! Mabel, can't you jest ast George? He ain't left the place; you know that! He can't show his face in daytime, and he's right there in the bar, and so's Limpy. Limpy'll tell you jest the same as what George will, if you'll only go and ast 'em. Why can't you go and ast 'em?"

"Yes!" the woman cried. "And while I'm in there astin' 'em, where'll you be? Over the alley fence and a mile away! You come out from under them boards and git croaked like you're a-goin' to!"

"Oh, my goodness!" the man wailed. "I wish I had somep'm on me to lam you with! Jest once! That's all I'd ast—jest one little short crack at you!"

"You come out from under them boards!"

"I won't! I'll lay here till—"

"We'll see!" the woman cried. "I'm a-goin' to dig you out. I'm a-goin' to take them boards off o' you and then I'm a-goin' to croak you. I am!"

Elsie moved toward the outer door. "They talk so—so funny!" she said with a little anxiety. "I doe' b'lieve it's about the Bible."

"I guess she's mad at somebody about somep'm," Daisy said, much amused; and stepping nearer the passageway, she called: "Here! We want to look at some unb'eached muslin an' orstrich feathers!"

But the room beyond the passage was now in turmoil: planks were clattering again, and both voices were uproarious. The man's became a squawk as another explosion took place; he added an incomplete Scriptural glossary in falsetto; and Elsie began to be nervous.

"That's awful big firecrackers they're usin'," she said. "I guess we ought to go home, Daisy."

"Oh, they're just kind of quarrellin' or somep'm," Daisy explained, not at all disturbed. "If you listen up our alley, you can hear coloured people talkin' like that lots o' times. They do this way, an' they settle down again, or else they're only in fun. But I do wish these people'd come, because I just haf to finish my shopping!" And, as yet another explosion was heard, she exclaimed complacently: "My! That's a big one!"

Then, beyond the passage, there seemed to be a final upheaval of lumber; the discussion reached a climax of vociferation, and a powerful, bald-headed man, without a coat, plunged through the passage and into the room. His unscholarly brow and rotund jowls were beaded; his agonized eyes saw nothing; he ran to the bar, and vaulted over it, vanishing behind it half a second before the person looking for him appeared in the doorway.

She was a small, rather shabby woman, who held one hand concealed in the folds of her skirt, while with the other she hastily cleared her eyes of some loosened strands of her reddish hair.

"I got you, Chollie!" she said. "You're behind the bar, and I'm a-goin' to make a good job of it, and get George and Limpy, too. I'm goin' to get all three of you!"

With that she darted across the room and ran behind the bar; whereupon Daisy and Elsie were treated to a scene like a conjuror's trick. Until the bald-headed man's arrival, they had supposed themselves to be quite alone in the room, but as the little woman ran behind the counter, not only this fugitive popped up from it, but two other panic-stricken men besides—one with uneven whiskers all over his mottled face, the other a well-dressed person, elderly, but just now supremely agile. The three shot up simultaneously like three Jacks-in-the-box, and, scrambling over the counter, dropped flat on the floor in front of it, leaving the little woman behind.

"Crawl up to the end o' the bar, George," the bald-headed man said hoarsely. "When she comes out from behind it, jump and grab her wrist."

"Think I'm deef?" the little woman inquired raucously. "George's got a fat chance to grab my wrist!"

Then her eyes, somewhat inflamed, fell upon Daisy and Elsie. "Well, what—what—what—" she said.

Daisy stepped toward the counter, for she felt that she had indeed delayed her business long enough.

"We'd like to look at some nice unb'eached muslin," she said, "an' some of your very best orstrich feathers."

The subsequent commotions, as well as the preceding ones, were indistinctly audible to the mystified person who waited upon the sidewalk outside the place. Finding that his eyes revealed nothing of the interior, he had placed his ear against the window, and the muffled reports, mistaken for firecrackers by Daisy and Elsie, were similarly interpreted by Laurence; but he supposed

208

Daisy and Elsie to have a direct connection with the sounds. A thought of the Fourth of July entered his mind, as it had Daisy's, but it solved nothing for him: the Fourth was long past; this was not the sort of store that promised firecrackers; and even if Daisy and Elsie had taken firecrackers with them, how had it happened that they were allowed to explode them indoors? As for an "ottomatick" or a "revolaver," he knew that neither maiden would touch such a thing, for he had heard them express their aversion to the antics of Robert Eliot, on an occasion when Master Eliot had surreptitiously borrowed his father's "good ole six-shooter" to disport himself with in the Threamers' garage.

Nothing could have been more evident than that Daisy and Elsie had definite affairs to transact in this café; the air with which they entered it was a conclusive demonstration of that. But the firecrackers made guessing at the nature of those affairs even more hopeless than when the pair had visited the barber-shop and the harness-shop. Then, as a closer report sounded, Laurence jumped. "Giant firecracker!" he exclaimed huskily, and his eyes still widened; for now vague noises of tumult and altercation could be heard.

"Well, my go-o-o-od-nuss!" he said.

Two pedestrians halted near him.

"Say, listen," one of them said. "What's goin' on in there?"

"Golly!" the other exclaimed, adding: "I happen to know it's a blind tiger."

Laurence's jaw dropped, and he stared at the man incredulously. "Wha-wha'd you say?"

"Listen," the man returned. "How long's all this been goin' on in there?"

"Just since they went in there. It was just a little while ago. Wha'd you say about—"

But he was interrupted. Several other passers-by had paused, and they began to make interested inquiries of the first two.

"What's the trouble in there? What's going on here? What's all the shooting? What's—"

"There's something pretty queer goin' on," said the man who had spoken to Laurence; and he added: "It's a blind tiger."

"Yes, I know that," another said. "I was in there once, and I know from my own eyes it's a blind tiger."

Laurence began to be disconcerted.

" 'A blind tiger'?" he gasped. "A blind tiger?" What caused his emotion was not anxiety for the safety of his friends; the confident importance with which they had entered the place convinced him that if there actually was a blind tiger within, they were perfectly aware of the circumstance and knew what they were doing when they entered the animal's presence. His feeling about them was indefinite and hazy; yet it was certainly a feeling incredulous but awed, such as any one might have about people well known to him, who suddenly appear to be possessed of supernatural powers. "Honest, d'you b'lieve there's a blind tiger in there?" he asked of the man who had confirmed the strange information.

"Sure!"

"Honest, is one in there? Do you honest—"

But no one paid him any further attention. By this time a dozen or more people had gathered; others were arriving; and as the tumult behind the formerly green door increased, hurried discussion became general on the sidewalk. Several men said that somebody ought to go in and see what the matter was; others said that they themselves would be willing to go in, but they didn't like to do it without a warrant; and two or three declared that nobody ought to go in just at that time. One of these was emphatic, especially upon the duty men owe to themselves. "A man owes something to himself," he said. "A man owes it to himself not to git no forty-four in his gizzard by takin' and pushin' into a place where somebody's usin' a forty-four. A man owes it to himself to keep out o' trouble unless he's got some call to take and go bullin' into it; that's what he owes to himself!"

Another seemed to be depressed by the scandal involved. He was an unshaven person of a general appearance naïvely villainous, and, without a hat or coat, he had hurried across the street from an establishment not essentially unlike that under discussion— precisely like it, in fact, in declaring itself (though without the accent) to be a place where coffee in the French manner might be expected. "What worries me is," he said gloomily, and he repeated this over and over, "what worries me is, it gives the neighbourhood kind of a poor name. What worries me, it's gittin' the neighbourhood all talked about and everything, the way you wouldn't want it to, yourself."

Laurence took a fancy to this man, whose dejection had a quality of pathos that seemed to imply a sympathetic nature.

"Is there one—honestly?" Laurence asked him. "Cross your heart there is one?"

The gloomy man continued to address his lament to the one or two acquaintances who were listening to him. "It's just like this— what worries me is—"

But Laurence tugged at his soiled shirt-sleeve. "Is there honest one in there?"

"Is there one what in there?" the man asked with unexpected gruffness.

"A blind tiger!"

The gloomy man instantly became of a terrifying aspect. He roared:

"Git away f'm here!"

Then, as Laurence hastily retreated, the man shook his head, and added to his grown listeners: "Ain't that jest what I says? It gits everybody to talkin'—even a lot of awnry dressed-up little boys! It ain't right, and Chollie and Mabel ought to have some consideration. Other folks has got to live as well as them! Why, I tell you—"

He stopped, and with a woeful exclamation pointed to the street-corner south of them. "Look there! It's that blame sister-in-law o' George's. I reckon she must of run out through the alley. Now they have done it!"

His allusion was to a most blonde young woman, whose toilet, evidently of the hastiest, had called upon one or two garments for the street as an emergency supplement to others eloquent of the intimate boudoir. She came hurrying, her blue crocheted slippers scurrying in and out of variegated draperies; and all the while she talked incessantly, and with agitation, to a patrolman in uniform who hastened beside her. Naturally, they brought behind them an almost magically increasing throng of citizens, aliens and minors.

They hurried to the once green doors; the patrolman swung these open, and he and the blonde young woman went in. So did the crowd, thus headed and protected by the law's very symbol; and Laurence went with them. Carried along, jostled and stepped upon, he could see nothing; and inside the solidly filled room he found himself jammed against a woman who surged in front of him. She was a fat woman, and tall, with a great, bulbous, black cotton cloth back; and just behind Laurence there pressed a short and muscular man who never for an instant relaxed the most passionate efforts to see over the big woman. He stood on tiptoe, stretching himself and pushing hard down on Laurence's shoulders; and he constantly shoved forward, inclosing Laurence's head between himself and the big woman's waist, so that Laurence found breathing difficult and uncomfortable. The black cotton cloth, against which his nose was pushed out of shape, smelled as if it had been in the rain—at least that was the impression obtained by means of his left nostril, which remained partially unobstructed; and he did not like it.

In a somewhat dazed and hazy way he had expected to see Daisy and Elsie and a blind tiger, but naturally, under these circumstances, no such expectation could be realized. Nor did he hear anything said about either the tiger or the little girls; the room was a chaos of voices, though bits of shrill protestation, and gruffer interruptions from the central group, detached themselves.

"I never!" cried the shrillest voice. "I never even pointed it at any of 'em! So help me—"

"Now look here—" Laurence somehow got an idea that this was the policeman's voice. "Now look here—" it said loudly, over and over, but was never able to get any further; for the shrill woman and the plaintive but insistent voices of three men interrupted at that point, and persisted in interrupting as long as Laurence was in the room.

He could bear the black cotton back no longer, and, squirming, he made his elbow uncomfortable to the aggressive man who tortured him.

"Here!" this person said indignantly. "Take your elbow out o' my stomach and stand still. How d'you expect anybody to see what's going on with you making all this fuss? Be quiet!"

"I won't," said Laurence thickly. "You lea' me out o' here!"

"Well, for heaven's sakes!" the oppressive little man exclaimed. "Make some more trouble for people that want to see something! Go on and get out, then! Oh, Lordy!"

This last was a petulant wail as Laurence squirmed round him; then the pressure of the crowd filled the gap by throwing the little man against the fat woman's back. "Dam boy!" he raved, putting all his troubles under one head.

But Laurence heard him not; he was writhing his way to the wall; and, once he reached it, he struggled toward the open doors, using his shoulder as a wedge between spectators and the wall. Thus he won free of the press and presently got himself out to the sidewalk, panting. And then, looking about him, he glanced up the street.

At the next crossing to the north two busy little figures were walking rapidly homeward. They were gesturing importantly; their heads were waggling to confirm these gestures; and they were chattering incessantly.

"Well—dog-gone it!" Laurence whispered.

He followed them; but now his lips moved not at all, and there was no mumbling in his throat. He stared at them amazedly, in a great mental silence.

"What wears me out the most," Daisy said, as they came into their own purlieus again, "it's this shopping, shopping, shopping, and they never have one single thing!"

"No, they don't," Elsie agreed. "Not a thing! It just wears me out!"

"F'instance," Daisy continued, "look at how they acted in that las' place when I wanted to see some orstrich feathers. Just said 'What!' about seven hundred times! An' then that ole pleeceman came in!"

For a moment Elsie dropped her rôle as a tired shopper, and giggled nervously. "I was scared!" she said.

But Daisy tossed her head. "It's no use goin' shopping in a store like that; they never have anything, and I'll never waste my time on 'em again. Crazy things!"

"They did act crazy," Elsie said thoughtfully, as they paused at her gate. "I guess we better not tell about it to our mothers, maybe."

"No," Daisy agreed; and then with an elaborate gesture of fatigue she said: "Well, my dear, I hope you're not as worn out as I am! My nerves are jus' comp'etely gone, my dear!"

"So're mine!" said Elsie; and then, after a quick glance to the south, she giggled. "There's that ole thing, still comin' along;—no, he's stopped, an' lookin' at us!" She went into the yard. "Well, my dear, I must go in an' lay down an' rest myself. We'll go shopping again just as soon as my nerves get better, my dear!"

She skipped into the house, and Daisy, humming to herself, walked to her own gate, went in, and sat in a wicker rocking-chair under the walnut tree. She rocked herself and sang a wordless song, but becoming aware of a presence that lingered upon the sidewalk near the gate, she checked both her song and the motion of the chair and looked that way. Master Coy was staring over the gate at her; and she had never known that he had such large eyes.

He was full of formless questions, but he had no vocabulary; in truth, his whole being was one intensified interrogation.

"What you want?" Daisy called.

"I was there," he announced solemnly. "I was there, too. I was in that place where the pleeceman was."

"I doe' care," Daisy said, and began to sing and to rock the chair again. "I doe' care where you went," she said.

"I was there," said Laurence. "I saw that ole bline tiger. That's nothin'!"

Daisy had no idea of what he meant, but she remained undisturbed. "I doe' care," she sang. "I doe' care, I doe' care, I doe' care what you saw."

"Well, I did!" said Laurence, and he moved away, walking backward and staring at her.

She went on singing, "I doe' care," and rocking, and Laurence continued to walk backward and stare at her. He walked backward, still staring, all the way to the next corner. There, as it was necessary for him to turn toward his own home, he adopted a more customary and convenient manner of walking—but his eyes continued to be of unnatural dimensions.

MARY SMITH

HENRY MILLICK CHESTER, rising early from intermittent slumbers, found himself the first of the crowded Pullman to make a toilet in the men's smoke-and-wash-room, and so had the place to himself—an advantage of high dramatic value to a person of his age and temperament, on account of the mirrors which, set at various angles, afford a fine view of the profile. Henry Millick Chester, scouring cinders and stickiness from his eyes and rouging his ears with honest friction, enriched himself of this too unfamiliar opportunity. He smiled and was warmly interested in the results of his smile in reflection, particularly in some pleasant alterations it effected upon an outline of the cheek usually invisible to the bearer. He smiled graciously, then he smiled sardonically. Other smiles he offered—the tender smile, the forbidding smile, the austere and the seductive, the haughty and the pleading, the mordant and the compassionate, the tolerant but incredulous smile of a man of the world, and the cold, ascetic smile that shows a woman that her shallow soul has been read all too easily—pastimes abandoned only with the purely decorative application of shaving lather to his girlish chin. However, as his unbeetling brow was left unobscured, he was able to pursue his physiognomical researches and to produce for his continued enlightenment a versatile repertory of frowns—the stern, the quizzical, the bitter, the treacherous, the bold, the agonized, the inquisitive, the ducal, and the frown of the husband who says: "I forgive you. Go!" A few minutes later Mr. Chester, abruptly pausing in the operation of fastening his collar, bent a sudden, passionate interest upon his right forearm, without apparent cause and with the air of never having seen it until that moment. He clenched his fingers tightly, producing a slight stringiness above the wrist, then crooked his elbow with intensity, noting this enormous effect in all the mirrors. Regretfully, he let his shirtsleeves fall and veil the rare but private beauties just discovered, rested his left hand negligently upon his hip, extended his right in a gesture of flawlessly aristocratic grace, and, with a slight inclination of his head, uttered aloud these simple but befitting words: "I thank ye, my good people." T' yoong Maister was greeting the loyal tenantry who acclaimed his return to Fielding Manor, a flowered progress thoroughly incomprehensible to the Pullman porter whose transfixed eye—glazed upon an old-gold face intruded through the narrow doorway—Mr. Chester encountered in the glass above the nickeled washbasins. The Libyan withdrew in a cloud of silence, and t' yoong Maister, flushing somewhat, resumed his toilet with annoyed precision and no more embroidery. He had yesterday completed his sophomore year; the brushes he applied to his now adult locks were those of a junior. And with a man's age had come a man's cares and responsibilities. Several long years had rolled away since for the last time he had made himself sick on a train in a club-car orgy of cubebs and sarsaparilla pop.

Zigzagging through shoe-bordered aisles of sleepers in morning dishevelment, he sought the dining car, where the steward escorted him to an end table for two. He would have assumed his seat with that air of negligent hauteur which was his chosen manner for public appearances, had not the train, taking a curve at high speed, heaved him into the undesirable embrace of an elderly man breakfasting across the aisle. "Keep your feet, sonny; keep your feet," said this barbarian, little witting that he addressed a member of the nineteen-something prom. committee. People at the next table laughed genially, and Mr. Chester, muttering a word of hostile apology, catapulted into his assigned place, his cheeks hot with the triple outrage.

He relieved himself a little by the icy repulsion with which he countered the cordial advances of the waiter, who took his order and wished him a good morning, hoped he had slept well, declared the weather delightful and, unanswered, yet preserved his beautiful courtesy unimpaired. When this humble ambassador had departed on his mission to the kitchen Henry Millick Chester, unwarrantably persuaded that all eyes were searching his every inch and angle—an impression not uncharacteristic of his years—gazed out of the window with an indifference which would have been obtrusive if any of the other breakfasters had happened to notice it. The chill exclusiveness of his expression was a rebuke to such prying members of the proletariat as might be striving to read his thoughts, and barred his fellow passengers from every privilege to his consideration. The intensely reserved gentleman was occupied with interests which were the perquisites of only his few existing peers in birth, position, and intelligence, none of whom, patently, was in that car.

He looked freezingly upon the abashed landscape, which fled in shame; nor was that wintry stare relaxed when the steward placed someone opposite him at the little table. Nay, our frosty scholar now intensified the bleakness of his isolation, retiring quite to the pole in reproval of this too close intrusion. He resolutely denied the existence of his vis-à-vis, refused consciousness of its humanity, even of its sex, and then inconsistently began to perspire with the horrible impression that it was glaring at him fixedly. It was a dreadful feeling. He felt himself growing red, and coughed vehemently to afford the public an explanation of his change of colour. At last, his suffering grown unendurable, he desperately turned his eyes full upon the newcomer. She was not looking at him at all, but down at the edge of the white cloth on her own side of the table; and she was the very prettiest girl he had ever seen in his life.

She was about his own age. Her prettiness was definitely extreme, and its fair delicacy was complete and without any imperfection whatever. She was dressed in pleasant shades of tan and brown. A brown veil misted the rim of her hat, tan gloves were folded back from her wrists; and they, and all she wore, were fresh and trim and ungrimed by the dusty journey. She was charming. Henry Millick Chester's first gasping appraisal of her was perfectly accurate, for she was a peach—or a rose, or anything that is dewy and fresh and delectable. She was indeed some smooth. She was the smoothest thing in the world, and the world knows it!

She looked up.

Henry Millick Chester was lost.

At the same instant that the gone feeling came over him she dropped her eyes again to the edge of the table. Who can tell if she knew what she had done?

The conversation began with appalling formalities, which preluded the most convenient placing of a sugar bowl and the replenishing of an exhausted salt cellar. Then the weather, spurned as the placative offering of the gentle waiter, fell from the lips of the princess in words of diamonds and rubies and pearls. Our Henry took up the weather where she left it; he put it to its utmost; he went forward with it, prophesying weather; he went backward with it, recalling weather; he spun it out and out, while she agreed to all he said, until this overworked weather got so stringy that each obscurely felt it to be hideous. The thread broke; fragments wandered in the air for a few moments, but disappeared; a desperate propriety descended, and they fell into silence over their eggs.

Frantically Mr. Chester searched his mind for some means to pursue the celestial encounter. According to the rules, something ought to happen that would reveal her as Patricia Beekman, the sister of his roommate, Schuyler Beekman, and to-night he should be handing the imperturbable Dawkins a wire to send: "My dear Schuyler, I married your sister this afternoon." But it seemed unlikely, because his roommate's name was Jake Schmulze, and Jake lived in Cedar Rapids; and, besides, this train wasn't coming from or going to Palm Beach—it was going to St. Louis eventually, and now hustled earnestly across the placid and largely unbutlered plains of Ohio.

Often—as everyone knows—people have been lost to each other forever through the lack of a word, and few have realized this more poignantly than our Henry, as he helplessly suffered the precious minutes to accumulate vacancy. True, he had thought of something to say, yet he abandoned it. Probably he was wiser to wait, as what he thought of saying was: "Will you be my wife?" It might seem premature, he feared.

The strain was relieved by a heavenly accident which saved the life of a romance near perishing at birth. That charming girl, relaxing slightly in her chair, made some small, indefinite, and entirely ladylike movement of restfulness that reached its gentle culmination upon the two feet of Mr. Chester which, obviously mistaken for structural adjuncts of the table, were thereby glorified and became beautiful on the mountains. He was not the man to criticise the remarkable ignorance of dining car table architecture thus displayed, nor did he in any wise resent being mistaken up to the ankles for metal or wood. No. The light pressure of her small heels hardly indented the stout toes of his brown shoes; the soles of her slippers reposed upon his two insteps, and rapture shook his soul to its foundations, while the ineffable girl gazed lustrously out of the window, the clear serenity of her brilliant eyes making plain her complete unconsciousness of the nature of what added to her new comfort.

A terrific blush sizzled all over him, and to conceal its visible area he bent low to his coffee. She was unaware. He was transported, she—to his eyes—transfigured. Glamour diffused itself about her, sprayed about them both like showers of impalpable gold-dust, and filled the humble dining car—it filled the whole world. Transformed, seraphic waiters passed up and down the aisle in a sort of obscure radiance. A nimbus hovered faintly above the brown veil; a sacred luminosity was exhaled by the very tablecloth, where an angel's pointed fingers drummed absently.

It would be uncharitable to believe that a spirit of retaliation inspired the elderly and now replete man across the aisle, and yet, when he rose, he fell upon the neck of Henry as Henry had fallen upon his, and the shock of it jarred four shoes from the acute neighbourliness of their juxtaposition. The accursed graybeard, giggling in his senility, passed on; but that angel leaped backward in her chair while her beautiful eyes, wide open, stunned, her beautiful mouth, wide open, incredulous, gave proof that horror can look bewitching.

"Murder!" she gasped. "Were those your feet?"

217

And as he could compass no articulate reply, she grew as pink as he, murmured inaudibly, and stared at him in wider and wilder amazement.

"It—it didn't hurt," he finally managed to stammer.

At this she covered her blushes with her two hands and began to gurgle and shake with laughter. She laughed and laughed and laughed. It became a paroxysm. He laughed, too, because she laughed. Other passengers looked at them and laughed. The waiters laughed; they approved—coloured waiters always approve of laughter—and a merry spirit went abroad in the car.

At last she controlled herself long enough to ask:

"But what did you think of me?"

"It—it didn't hurt," he repeated idiotically, to his own mortification, for he passionately aspired to say something airy and winsome; but, as he couldn't think of anything like that, he had to let it go. "Oh, not at all," he added feebly.

However, "though not so deep as a well," it served, 'twas enough, for she began to laugh again, and there loomed no further barrier in the way of acquaintance. Therefore it was pleasantly without constraint, and indeed as a matter of course, that he dropped into a chair beside her half an hour later, in the observation car; and something in the way she let the Illustrated London News slide into the vacant chair on the other side of her might have suggested that she expected him.

"I was still wondering what you must have thought of me."

This gave him an opportunity, because he had thought out a belated reply for the first time she had said it. Hence, quick as a flash, he made the dashing rejoinder:

"It wasn't so much what I thought of you, but what I thought of myself—I thought I was in heaven!"

She must have known what pretty sounds her laughter made. She laughed a great deal. She even had a way of laughing in the middle of some of her words, and it gave them a kind of ripple. There are girls who naturally laugh like that; others learn to; a few won't, and some can't. It isn't fair to the ones that can't.

"But you oughtn't to tell me that," she said.

It was in the middle of "oughtn't" that she rippled. A pen cannot express it, neither can a typewriter, and no one has yet invented a way of writing with a flute; but the effect on Henry shows what a wonderful ripple it was. Henry trembled. From this moment she had only to ripple to make Henry tremble. Henry was more in love than he had been at breakfast. Henry was a Goner.

"Why oughtn't I to?" he demanded with white intensity. "If

218

anything's true it's right to tell it, isn't it? I believe that everybody has a right to tell the truth, don't you?"

"Ye-es—"

"You take the case of a man that's in love," said this rather precipitate gentleman; "isn't it right for him to—"

"But suppose," she interrupted, becoming instantly serious with the introduction of the great topic—"Suppose he isn't really in love. Don't you think there are very few cases of people truly and deeply caring for each other?"

"There are men," he said firmly, "who know how to love truly and deeply, and could never in their lives care for anybody but the one woman they have picked out. I don't say all men feel that way; I don't think they do. But there are a few that are capable of it." The seats in an observation car are usually near neighbours, and it happened that the brown cuff of a tan sleeve, extended reposefully on the arm of her chair, just touched the back of his hand, which rested on the arm of his. This ethereally light contact continued. She had no apparent cognizance of it, but a vibrant thrill passed through him, and possibly quite a hearty little fire might have been built under him without his perceiving good cause for moving. He shook, gulped, and added: "I am!"

"But how could you be sure of that," she said thoughtfully, "until you tried?" And as he seemed about to answer, perhaps too impulsively, she checked him with a smiling, "At your age!"

"You don't know how old I am. I'm older than you!"

"How old are you?"

"Twenty-one next March."

"What day?"

"The seventh."

"That is singular!"

"Why?"

"Because," she began in a low tone and with full recognition of the solemn import of the revelation—"Because my birthday is only one day after yours. I was twenty years old the eighth of last March."

"By George!" The exclamation came from him, husky with awe.

There was a fateful silence.

"Yes, I was born on the eighth," she said slowly.

"And me on the seventh!" At such a time no man is a purist.

"It is strange," she said.

"Strange! I came into the world just one day before you did!"

They looked at each other curiously, deeply stirred. Coincidence could not account for these birthdays of theirs, nor chance for their meeting on a train "like this." Henry Millick Chester was breathless. The mysteries were glimpsed. No doubt was possible—he and the wondrous creature at his side were meant for each other, intended from the beginning of eternity.

She dropped her eyes slowly from his, but he was satisfied that she had felt the marvel precisely as he had felt it.

"Don't you think," she said gently, "that a girl has seen more of the world at twenty than a man?"

Mr. Chester well wished to linger upon the subject of birthdays; however, the line of original research suggested by her question was alluring also. "Yes—and no," he answered with admirable impartiality. "In some ways, yes. In some ways, no. For instance, you take the case of a man that's in love—"

"Well," interrupted the lady, "I think, for instance, that a girl understands men better at twenty than men do women."

"It may be," he admitted, nodding. "I like to think about the deeper things like this sometimes."

"So do I. I think they're interesting," she said with that perfect sympathy of understanding which he believed she was destined to extend to him always and in all things. "Life itself is interesting. Don't you think so?"

"I think it's the most interesting subject there can be. Real life, that is, though—not just on the surface. Now, for instance, you take the case of a man that's in—"

"Do you go in much for reading?" she asked.

"Sure. But as I was saying, you take—"

"I think reading gives us so many ideas, don't you?"

"Yes. I get a lot out of it. I—"

"I do, too. I try to read only the best things," she said. "I don't believe in reading everything, and there's so much to read nowadays that isn't really good."

"Who do you think," he inquired with deference, "is the best author now?"

It was not a question to be settled quite offhand; she delayed her answer slightly, then, with a gravity appropriate to the literary occasion, temporized: "Well, since Victor Hugo is dead, it's hard to say just who is the best."

"Yes, it is," he agreed. "We get that in the English course in college. There aren't any great authors any more. I expect probably Swinburne's the best."

She hesitated. "Perhaps; but more as a poet."

He assented. "Yes, that's so. I expect he would be classed more as a poet. Come to think of it, I believe he's dead, too. I'm not sure, though; maybe it was Beerbohm Tree—somebody like that. I've forgotten; but, anyway, it doesn't matter. I didn't mean poetry; I meant who do you think writes the best books? Mrs. Humphry Ward?"

"Yes, she's good, and so's Henry James."

"I've never read anything by Henry James. I guess I'll read some of his this summer. What's the best one to begin on?"

The exquisite pink of her cheeks extended its area almost imperceptibly. "Oh, any one. They're all pretty good. Do you care for Nature?"

"Sure thing," he returned quickly. "Do you?"

"I love it!"

"So do I. I can't do much for mathematics, though."

"Br-r!" She shivered prettily. "I hate it!"

"So do I. I can't give astronomy a whole lot, either."

She turned a softly reproachful inquiry upon him. "Oh, don't you love to look at the stars?"

In horror lest the entrancing being think him a brute, he responded with breathless haste: "Oh, rath-er-r! To look at 'em, sure thing! I meant astronomy in college; that's mostly math, you know— just figures. But stars to look at—of course that's different. Why, I look up at 'em for hours sometimes!" He believed what he was saying. "I look up at 'em, and think and think and think—"

"So do I." Her voice was low and hushed; there was something almost holy in the sound of it, and a delicate glow suffused her lovely, upraised face—like that picture of Saint Cecilia, he thought. "Oh, I love the stars! And music—and flowers—"

"And birds," he added automatically in a tone that, could it by some miracle have been heard at home, would have laid his nine-year-old brother flat on the floor in a might-be mortal swoon.

A sweet warmth centred in the upper part of his diaphragm and softly filtered throughout him. The delicious future held no doubts or shadows for him. It was assured. He and this perfect woman had absolutely identical tastes; their abhorrences and their enthusiasms marched together; they would never know a difference in all their lives to come. Destiny unrolled before him a shining pathway which they two would walk hand-in-hand through the summer days to a calm and serene autumn, respected and admired by the world, but finding ever their greatest and most sacred joy in the light of each other's eyes—that light none other than the other could evoke.

Could it be possible, he wondered, that he was the same callow boy who but yesterday pranced and exulted in the "pee-rade" of the new juniors! How absurd and purposeless that old life seemed; how far away, how futile, and how childish! Well, it was over, finished. By this time to-morrow he would have begun his business career.

Back in the old life, he had expected to go through a law school after graduating from college, subsequently to enter his father's office. That meant five years before even beginning to practice, an idea merely laughable now. There was a men's furnishing store on a popular corner at home; it was an establishment which had always attracted him, and what pleasanter way to plow the road to success than through acres of variously woven fabrics, richly coloured silks, delicate linens, silver mountings and odorous leathers, in congenial association with neckties, walking-sticks, hosiery, and stickpins? He would be at home a few hours hence, and he would not delay. After lunch he would go boldly to his father and say: "Father, I have reached man's estate and I have put away childish things. I have made up my mind upon a certain matter and you will only waste time by any effort to alter this, my firm determination. Father, I here and now relinquish all legal ambitions, for the reason that a mercantile career is more suited to my inclinations and my abilities. Father, I have met the one and only woman I can ever care for, and I intend to make her my wife. Father, you have always dealt squarely with me; I will deal squarely with you. I ask you the simple question: Will you or will you not advance me the funds to purchase an interest in Paul H. Hoy & Company's Men's Outfitting Establishment? If you will not, then I shall seek help elsewhere."

Waking dreams are as swift, sometimes, as the other kind—which, we hear, thread mazes so labyrinthine "between the opening and the closing of a door"; and a twenty-year-old fancy, fermenting in the inclosure of a six-and-seven-eighth plaid cap, effervesces with a power of sizzling and sparkling and popping.

"I believe I love music best of all," said the girl dreamily.

"Do you play?" he asked, and his tone and look were those of one who watches at the sick-bed of a valued child.

"Yes, a little."

"I love the piano." He was untroubled by any remorse for what he and some of his gang had done only two days since to a previously fine instrument in his dormitory entry. He had forgotten the dead past in his present vision, which was of a luxurious room in a spacious mansion, and a tired man of affairs coming quietly into that room—from a conference at which he had consolidated the haberdashery trade of the world—and sinking noiselessly upon a rich divan, while a beautiful woman in a dress of brown and tan, her hair slightly silvered, played to him through the twilight upon a grand piano, the only other sound in the great house being the softly murmurous voices of perfectly trained children being put to bed in a distant nursery upstairs.

"I like the stage, too," she said. "Don't you?"

"You know! Did you see The Tinkle-Dingle Girl?"

"Yes. I liked it."

"It's a peach show." He spoke with warranted authority. During the university term just finished he had gone eight times to New York, and had enriched his critical perceptions of music and the drama by ten visits to The Tinkle-Dingle Girl, two of his excursions having fallen on matinée days. "Those big birds that played the comedy parts were funny birds, weren't they?"

"The tramp and the brewer? Yes. Awfully funny."

"We'll go lots to the theatre!" He spoke eagerly and with superb simplicity, quite without consciousness that he was skipping much that would usually be thought necessarily intermediate. An enchanting vision engrossed his mind's eye. He saw himself night after night at The Tinkle-Dingle Girl, his lovely wife beside him— growing matronly, perhaps, but slenderly matronly—with a grace of years that only added to her beauty, and always wearing tan gloves and a brown veil.

The bewilderment of her expression was perhaps justified.

"What!"

At this he realized the import of what he had said and what, in a measure, it did assume. He became pinkish, then pink, then more pink; and so did she. Paralyzed, the blushing pair looked at each other throughout this duet in colour, something like a glint of alarm beginning to show through the wide astonishment in her eyes; and with the perception of this he was assailed by an acute perturbation. He had spoken thoughtlessly, even hastily, he feared; he should have given her more time. Would she rise now with chilling dignity and leave him, it might be forever? Was he to lose her just when he had found her? He shuddered at the ghastly abyss of loneliness disclosed by the possibility. But this was only the darkest moment before a radiance that shot heavenward like the flaming javelins of an equatorial sunrise.

Her eyes lowered slowly till the long, brown lashes shadowed the rose-coloured cheek and the fall of her glance came to rest upon the arms of their two chairs, where the edge of her coat sleeve just touched the knuckle of his little finger. Two people were passing in front of them; there was no one who could see; and with a lightning-swift impulse she turned her wrist and for a half second, while his heart stopped beating, touched all his fingers with her own, then as quickly withdrew her hand and turned as far away from him as the position of her chair permitted.

It was a caress of incredible brevity, and so fleeting, so airy, that it was little more than a touch of light itself, like the faint quick light from a flying star one might just glimpse on one's hand as it passed. But in our pleasant world important things have resulted from touches as evanescent as that. Nature has its uses for the ineffable.

Blazing with glory, dumb with rapture, Henry Millick Chester felt his heart rebound to its work, while his withheld breath upheaved in a gulp that half suffocated him. Thus, blinded by the revelation of the stupefying beauty of life, he sat through a heaven-stricken interval, and time was of no moment. Gradually he began to perceive, in the midst of the effulgence which surrounded the next chair like a bright mist, the adorable contour of a shoulder in a tan coat and the ravishing outline of a rosy cheek that belonged to this divine girl who was his.

By and by he became dreamily aware of other objects beyond that cheek and that shoulder, of a fat man and his fat wife on the opposite side of the car near the end. Unmistakably they were man and wife, but it seemed to Henry that they had no reason to be—such people had no right to be married. They had no obvious right to exist at all; certainly they had no right whatever to exist in that car. Their relation to each other had become a sickening commonplace, the bleakness of it as hideously evident as their overfed convexity. It was visible that they looked upon each other as inevitable nuisances which had to be tolerated. They were horrible. Had Love ever known these people? It was unthinkable! For lips such as theirs to have pronounced the name of the god would have been blasphemy; for those fat hands ever to have touched, desecration! Henry hated the despicable pair.

All at once his emotion changed: he did not hate them, he pitied them. From an immense height he looked down with compassion upon their wretched condition. He pitied everybody except himself and the roseate being beside him; they floated together upon a tiny golden cloud, alone in the vast sky at an immeasurable altitude above the squalid universe. A wave of pity for the rest of mankind flooded over him, but most of all he pitied that miserable, sodden, befleshed old married couple.

He was dimly aware of a change that came over these fat people, a strangeness; but he never did realize that at this crisis his eyes, fixed intently upon them and aided by his plastic countenance, had expressed his feelings and sentiments regarding them in the most lively and vivid way. For at the moment when the stout gentleman laid his paper down, preparatory to infuriated inquiry, both he and his wife were expunged from Henry's consciousness forever and were seen of him thenceforth no more than if they had been ether and not solid flesh. The exquisite girl had been pretending to pick a thread out of her left sleeve with her right hand—but now at last she leaned back in her chair and again turned her face partly toward Henry. Her under lip was caught in slightly beneath her upper teeth, as if she had been doing something that possibly she oughtn't to be doing, and though the pause in the conversation had been protracted—it is impossible to calculate how long—her charming features were still becomingly overspread with rose. She looked toward her rapt companion, not at him, and her eyes were preoccupied, tender, and faintly embarrassed.

The pause continued.

He leaned a little closer to her. And he looked at her and looked at her and looked at her. At intervals his lips moved as if he were speaking, and yet he was thinking wordlessly. Leaning thus toward her, his gaze and attitude had all the intensity of one who watches a ninth-inning tie in the deciding game of a championship series. And as he looked and looked and looked, the fat man and his wife, quite unaware of their impalpability, also looked and looked and looked in grateful fascination.

"Did you—" Henry Millick Chester finally spoke these words in a voice he had borrowed, evidently from a stranger, for it did not fit his throat and was so deep that it disappeared—it seemed to fall down a coal-hole and ended in a dusty choke. "Did you—" he began again, two octaves higher, and immediately squeaked out. He said "Did you" five times before he subjugated the other two words.

"Did you—mean that?"

"What?" Her own voice was so low that he divined rather than heard what she said. He leaned even a little closer—and the fat man nudged his wife, who elbowed his thumb out of her side morbidly: she wasn't missing anything.

"Did you—did you mean that?"

"Mean what?"

"That!"

"I don't know what you mean."

"When you—when you—oh, you know!"

"No, I don't."

"When you—when you took my hand."

"I!"

With sudden, complete self-possession she turned quickly to face him, giving him a look of half-shocked, half-amused astonishment.

"When I took your hand?" she repeated incredulously. "What are you saying?"

225

"You—you know," he stammered. "A while ago when—when—you—you—"

"I didn't do anything of the kind!" Impending indignation began to cloud the delicate face ominously. "Why in the world should I?"

"But you—"

"I didn't!" She cut him off sharply. "I couldn't. Why, it wouldn't have been nice! What made you dream I would do a thing like that? How dare you imagine such things!"

At first dumfounded, then appalled, he took the long, swift, sickening descent from his golden cloud with his mouth open, but it snapped tight at the bump with which he struck the earth. He lay prone, dismayed, abject. The lovely witch could have made him believe anything; at least it is the fact that for a moment she made him believe he had imagined that angelic little caress; and perhaps it was the sight of his utter subjection that melted her. For she flashed upon him suddenly with a dazing smile, and then, blushing again but more deeply than before, her whole attitude admitting and yielding, she offered full and amazing confession, her delicious laugh rippling tremulously throughout every word of it.

"It must have been an accident—partly!"

"I love you!" he shouted.

The translucent fat man and his wife groped for each other feverishly, and a coloured porter touched Henry Millick Chester on the shoulder.

"Be in Richmon' less'n fi' minutes now," said the porter. He tapped the youth's shoulder twice more; it is his office to awaken the rapt dreamer. "Richmon,' In'iana, less'n fi' minutes now," he repeated more slowly.

Henry gave him a stunned and dishevelled "What?"

"You get off Richmon', don't you?"

"What of it? We haven't passed Dayton yet."

"Yessuh, long 'go. Pass' Dayton eight-fifty. Be in Richmon' mighty quick now."

The porter appeared to be a malicious liar. Henry appealed pitifully to the girl.

"But we haven't passed Dayton?"

"Yes, just after you sat down by me. We stopped several minutes."

"Yessuh. Train don't stop no minutes in Richmon' though," said the porter with a hard laugh, waving his little broom at some outlying freight cars they were passing. "Gittin' in now. I got you' bag on platfawm."

226

"I don't want to be brushed," Henry said, almost sobbing. "For heaven's sake, get out!"

Porters expect anything. This one went away solemnly without even lifting his eyebrows.

The brakes were going on.

One class of railway tragedies is never recorded, though it is the most numerous of all and fills the longest list of heartbreaks; the statics ignore it, yet no train ever leaves its shed, or moves, that is not party to it. It is time and overtime that the safety-device inventors should turn their best attention to it, so that the happy day may come at last when we shall see our common carriers equipped with something to prevent these lovers' partings.

The train began to slow down.

Henry Millick Chester got waveringly to his feet; she rose at the same time and stood beside him.

"I am no boy," he began, hardly knowing what he said, but automatically quoting a fragment from his forthcoming address to his father. "I have reached man's estate and I have met the only—" He stopped short with an exclamation of horror. "You—you haven't even told me your name!"

"My name?" the girl said, a little startled.

"Yes! And your address!"

"I'm not on my way home now," she said. "I've been visiting in New York and I'm going to St. Louis to make another visit."

"But your name!"

She gave him an odd glance of mockery, a little troubled.

"You mightn't like my name!"

"Oh, please, please!"

"Besides, do you think it's quite proper for me to—"

"Oh, please! To talk of that now! Please!" The train had stopped.

The glint of a sudden decision shone in the lovely eyes. "I'll write it for you so you won't forget."

She went quickly to the writing desk at the end of the compartment, he with her, the eyes of the fat man and his wife following them like two pairs of searchlights swung by the same mechanism.

"And where you live," urged Henry. "I shall write to you every day." He drew a long, deep breath and threw back his head. "Till the day—the day when I come for you."

"Don't look over my shoulder." She laughed shyly, wrote hurriedly upon a loose sheet, placed it in an envelope, sealed the envelope, and then, as he reached to take it, withheld it tantalizingly. "No. It's my name and where I live, but you can't have it. Not till you've promised not to open it until the train is clear out of the station."

Outside the window sounded the twice-repeated "Awl aboh-oh," and far ahead a fatal bell was clanging.

"I promise," he gulped.

"Then take it!"

With a strange, new-born masterfulness he made a sudden impetuous gesture and lifted both the precious envelope and the fingers that inclosed it to his lips. Then he turned and dashed to the forward end of the car where a porter remained untipped as Henry leaped from the already rapidly moving steps of the car to the ground. Instantly the wonderful girl was drawn past him, leaning and waving from the railed rear platform whither she had run for this farewell. And in the swift last look that they exchanged there was in her still-flushing, lovely face a light of tenderness and of laughter, of kindness and of something like a fleeting regret.

The train gained momentum, skimming onward and away, the end of the observation car dwindling and condensing into itself like a magician's disappearing card, while a white handkerchief, waving from the platform, quickly became an infinitesimal shred of white—and then there was nothing. The girl was gone.

Probably Henry Millick Chester owes his life to the fact that there are no gates between the station building and the tracks at Richmond. For gates and a ticket-clipping official might have delayed Henry's father in the barely successful dash he made to drag from the path of a backing local a boy wholly lost to the outward world in a state of helpless puzzlement, which already threatened to become permanent as he stared and stared at a sheet of railway notepaper whereon was written in a charming hand:

Mary Smith
        Chicago
        Ill.

www.ingramcontent.com/pod-product-compliance
Lightning Source LLC
Chambersburg PA
CBHW011521240626
47154CB00009B/2917